WHICH:

THE RIGHT, OR THE LEFT?

Life is *real*—Life is EARNEST,
And the grave is *not* its goal:—
Dust thou art, to dust returnest,
Was not spoken of the SOUL.

LONGFELLOW.

NEW YORK:
GARRETT & CO., PUBLISHERS,
NO. 18 ANN STREET.
1855.

PREFACE.

In every temple dedicated to our Lord—that is to say, in every branch of the One Temple—there are two churches, viz.:

The Church of Christ, which is a church of goodness, is productive of gentleness, humility, and single-heartedness, and leads its people to Happiness;

And,

The Church of Society, which is a church of evil, is productive of pride, arrogance, and selfishness, and leads its people to Misery.

The first is made up of The Few, who walk in the light of their Redeemer's countenance, and regard their Lord as their Patron.

The second is made up of The Many, who walk in the light of Money, and complacently regard themselves as *The Patrons of* The Lord.

The Few worship Him meekly, lovingly, contritely; the Many fashionably, elegantly, superciliously.

Christ's Christians measure all men by the goodness of their hearts, and the gentleness, simplicity, and correctness of their deportment, as prescribed by the Law of God;

Society's Christians measure all men by the fullness of their pockets, the texture of their coats, and the correctness of their deportment, as prescribed by the Law of Society.

The former believe that all things should be done for the glory of their Blessed Lord, who is their all in all;

The latter, that they should do everything for *their own* glory—which is their all in all.

The first believe that Life is a REAL and an EARNEST thing; that it is a season for Action, not Play;

The second believe it to be simply a Great Joke.

The Few believe that Man's first, last, and only business is, To secure his inheritance in the Bright Beyond, whose duration is eternal. "I must work the work of Him that sent me, *while it is Day*—for the Night cometh, wherein no man can work."

The Many believe that Man's first, last, and only business is, To accumulate Money, to make a show, and to be talked about—till he is gone.

The first believe that they should do good unto all men;

The second, that they should look out for Number One, and let others do the same.

CHRIST'S Christians believe that the Business of life consists in

Business truthfulness;

Church Membership; and

The right of every Man and Woman to glide onward to Everlasting Happiness, piously, peacefully, and lovingly.

SOCIETY'S Christians recognize as legitimate—

Business lying;

Church Membership without Religion; and,

The right of every Man and Woman to glide down to Everlasting Perdition, fashionably, gracefully, and respectably.

When, therefore, it is said of a known knave, "He is a member of The Church,"—it ought always to be added, "of Society's—*not* CHRIST'S."

DEDICATION.

TO

The Memory

OF

A RARE FRIEND OF HUMANITY,

THE LATE

ANSON G. PHELPS,

WHO,

AMID ALL THE TEMPTATIONS OF COMMERCE, SOCIETY, AND GREAT WEALTH,

Preserved his Spiritual Trust,

AND DIED, AS HE LIVED,

A MEEK AND HUMBLE CHRISTIAN.

WHICH:

THE RIGHT, OR THE LEFT.

CHAPTER I

The evening of the 5th of April, 184–, was a solemn one throughout the quiet, secluded town of Enfield. Of its seven or eight hundred inhabitants—composed, with three or four exceptions, exclusively of husbandmen who inherited with the broad acres of their fertile farms, the industry, the intelligence, and the strong religious spirit of their Huguenot ancestors—there was scarcely one, whether old or young, who did not feel like weeping. For Samuel—they never spoke of the town's only school-teacher in any other way, nor called him by any other name, although he was now a full-grown man, and hard upon his twenty-fifth year—Samuel, the mark and model of Enfield—Samuel, their beloved pastor's oldest son—Samuel, whom everybody knew and whom everybody loved, was about to leave them, to try his fortunes in the metropolis, and this was his last night at home.

A stranger to Enfield, had one been there on the evening in question, would have found it difficult to understand why so simple an event as the departure of one of their number—an every-day occurrence in most rural districts—should produce so much distress upon the minds of its people. Nor would his surprise have lessened in any perceivable degree until he had become intimately acquainted with the religious character of the inhabitants, observed the tender interest which they took in one another's welfare, and learned the strong hold which moral worth had upon their simple, honest hearts.

To the worthy people of Enfield, the thought of losing one whom they had known and loved from his infancy, as in the school-teacher's case, was a trying one. They could hardly realize it, although they knew it to be true: for the fact of his intended departure had been rumored for a long time, and they had all been to the parsonage that very day, and shaken their favorite tenderly and feelingly by the hand for the last time, and left him, notwithstanding his assumed calmness and his pleasant smiles, which even the children saw through, suffering with emotions equally as deep and mournful as their own.

Those of the inhabitants who had reached life's thoughtful autumn, viewed Samuel's design with mingled solicitude and pain. To them his departure appeared like a dreadful blow to the moral interests of the town. They had known him from his infancy; had observed the singular simplicity and marked uprightness of his character, and had held him up to their children as a pattern of all that was exemplary, and as a model worthy of their love, their study, and their imitation; and with a success which was visible in the minds and deportments of the larger proportion of the young men of the town. And now this mind, whose purity, strength, simplicity, and clearness had become a living marvel—this heart whose natural nobleness, and high courage in all things relating to honor, humanity, and religion, had stamped its owner as a great moral hero—this form, whose deportment was not more remarkable for its gracefulness than for its meek, unpretending dignity—this MAN, whose moral influence was visible in all who associated or came in contact with him—whose example was, in all things, the standard of uprightness and correctness; whose tranquil happiness impressed even the young, inspired them with a tender respect for heavenly things, and prompted them to fly spontaneously to religion, the source of so much permanent joy—whose benevolent spirit, radiating like the sun, spread from heart to heart, in young and old, until nearly all the town had realized the gentle truth that it is more blessed to give than to receive; whose rare magnanimity, while it ever made him the champion of the weak, led him to return loving words for harsh ones, and to repay good for evil, as if evil had only been created to show the greater beauty, strength, and power of goodness—whose general character was gradually influencing all within the circuit of his rural range, and moulding them slowly but not less surely into so many reflexes of his own upright nature: this mind, this heart, this form, this man whom all knew, whom all loved, and in whom all had confidence; this spirit of benevolence, peace, and good-will—this mark and model of the town, of whom young and old had been accustomed to say: "Behold! this is Samuel, the upright!" —was about to remove from their midst, not temporarily, but permanently—forever!

As the aged ones thought of all this, their pious hearts were shaken mournfully. It was true he would leave many glorious natures whom his own example had likened to himself, behind him; but not one—no, not one—whose name was so familiar, so loved, or so significant of goodness, as his own; not one who had been noted from his earliest years for the purity of his thoughts equally with himself—not one who enjoyed so large a measure of public confidence; not one whose patronymic was the synonyme, with young and old, of all that was pure, and good, and noble—in a word, not one SAMUEL.

The good old hearts were sadly moved as they reflected upon this. They had always appreciated the worth of their young friend; but they had never fully comprehended his exceeding richness in those qualities which invest their possessors with absolute moral grandeur, nor dreamed of the deep hold which he had upon their affections, until now—now that they were about to lose him. Once before they had taken leave of him; but it was only for a time, that he might finish at college the education which he had begun under his father, their pastor. Then they knew he would return, and he did return; but it was to take a firmer hold than ever of their hearts, and to prove to them that all the bright promise of the Christian boy was more than fulfilled in the Christian man. But there was no hope of that kind to console them now. His departure on the morrow was to be a final one; and, save perhaps an annual visit or so, the scenes of his youth and the friends of his youth would know him henceforth no more.

All this touched the hearts of the old folks deeply, as only hearts can be touched that feel an abiding interest in the place where they were born, and in the morals of the generation that shall rule its destinies when they themselves shall have passed away.

From these considerations, the old thinking hearts of Enfield passed to the chances of the young man himself in the great city whither he was bound. The good souls themselves had not gone through life's long, crooked lane without gathering pearls of wisdom on the way. They had seen flowers fall, as well as blossom, in the spring; they had seen them fade and wither in the summer, and drop long before the airs of autumn or the chill breath of winter had approached, and the lesson was remembered, and stored away with other memories which had been garnered by experience as well. They had seen brave oaks which had long withstood the tempest, riven and hurled headlong to the earth in unlooked-for hours; while younger trees, that had bent timidly to every storm, escaped, and grew bravely, and boldly, and firmly into strong and stalwart giants, that laughed to scorn the roar and energies of the fiercest hurricane. Would Samuel withstand the pressure of temptation as firmly? Would *their* flower, who had been reared amid the pure airs and free sunshine of the country, bear up as bravely in the withering hot-house atmosphere of city plants?

They knew the city well, these old hearts of Enfield. They understood the operation of its blighting breath upon its own sons and daughters, whom its tiger-nature rarely spared; and they knew, too, while it welcomed with its brightest smiles and its gentlest tones every rural stranger that approached its gates, that its smiles were hollow as its own heart, and its dulcet voice assumed to beguile them to destruction. And they would not have their Samuel—*their* Samuel, at once their fairest flower, and their bravest oak—fall a victim to its wiles.

They remembered how, many years before, Deacon Morley's son, a brave, intelligent, moral-minded youth, had left Enfield for the city; how he grew in time, amid the temptations which surrounded him, to acquire the factitious ways and thoughts of those who lived there, and to forget the pious ways and thoughts of his own people; how he turned, by degrees, from the simple habits of his youth and the high moral aim which the good deacon had labored so many years to impress indelibly upon his heart; how he yielded, slowly, to be sure, but in the end yielded, to the tempting voice of ambition, and became at length a cold, calculating getter of riches, for riches' sake alone; how he fell, step by step, from his original love of truth and fair, manly dealing, into the gulf of falsehood, meanness, and that equivocal honesty which is just inside the law; how, using falsehood, hypocrisy and dishonesty for his ladder, he mounted step by step to power and high fortune—despised by all who knew him, and to the great sorrow of the friends of his youth, most of whom still preserved, sacred and inviolate, the moral purity which had been bequeathed to them by their sires; how his fall from uprightness broke the heart of the good old deacon his father, while it brought to the stricken spirit of her who had borne him the mournful consciousness that her boy's departure from truth, for the sake of worldly gain, had destroyed all hope of their reunion in that better land which none but the just can enter; how he grew rich and cold, and hard, till he became lost in the vortex of his vast wealth—his heart eaten up by pride and pomp and glitter to the last! They would not have their Samuel fall like Deacon Morley's son, for the world.

Then there was neighbor Grantley's son. He, too, had gone to the city, carrying with him, as was generally hoped and believed, the innocence, integrity, and piety of his youth. The law had a charm for him, and he embraced it. His friends were fearful; but he assured them in his letters, that he would be firm, that he would preserve the purity of his heart and the confidence of his Redeemer; and that, come professional failure or success, he would never take up a case that had not the right on its side. His friends hoped, prayed, and trusted. A year flew by—two—three—and report stated that the young advocate was a rising man, and that he had been true to his promise. Who shall depict the joy of all Enfield at this glad tidings? But by-and-bye another rumor came, and their hearts were saddened. Grantley had at length *fallen.* Talent is better paid on the side of wrong than on that of right. Not content with a fair and growing income, he had caught the city fever—ambition. He no longer remembered the bright lessons of his youth—he no longer thought of the glorious crown which awaits the hero who holds out to the end—greed was now his object, the empty praise of a hollow-hearted world his leading aspiration. For these he threw his rare talent to the highest bidder; for these he cast aside his piety, his purity, his moral manhood. For a few years of wealth, and that men might say of him "Behold one of our city's great!" he had sundered all ties that bound him to the lowly few; had sent an arrow to the two mild loving hearts who had never forgotten their own allegiance to their King and Prince; had swept away his chances of becoming one of that noble multitude whose highest ambition is to enjoy the friendship of their Maker throughout eternity. He fell as men fall who give up truth for money. From that hour his peace of heart was gone; in its place came wealth, reputation and position. His tireless energies, his intellectual powers, and the faculty which he had acquired of using truth and falsehood as they suited his purposes, helped him in time to a judgeship. Here he was willing to rest, having achieved the two objects of his ambition—riches and a name. But at what a sacrifice! His integrity to his God—where was that? His once guileless heart—where was that? His simplicity of mind, the connecting link between his conscience and his acts—where was that? His once brave spirit, which dared all things for the right, and quailed only before wrong—where was that? His father's peace, his mother's love, the confidence of his friends, the approving smile of his Prince, his seat around the heavenly throne—where were *they?* What had he in their stead? Riches—a feeble position among men—a reputation for legal craftiness—a broken, bankrupt, worn-out body — and a consciousness that he had betrayed the trust reposed in him by his God.! What wages!

The good old hearts of Enfield would not have their Samuel fall like Grantley.

And yet they knew that their young friend would be tried, as all are tried who set foot in cities and delve in the fields of business in quest of fortune. For he had talent, energy, and intelligence — qualities which command success everywhere, but especially in the metropolis where opportunities are continually turning up to incite them to exertion. But what kind of figure would Samuel, with his simple mind and honest heart, cut in that great crowd of business strugglers where every man has a double mind—one for his fellows, and another for himself; where men smile lovingly upon those whom they are plotting to destroy; where hypocrisy is the study of men's lives; where men mine and countermine for the purpose of rising upon each other's ruin; where men blind one another with false reports to veil the triumphal passage of their own respective movements; where men are *not* what they seem; and where, it would appear, Honesty is laughed sneeringly aside, and Knavery alone marches forward to success? What could be hoped for Samuel, with all his truth, his candor, his simplicity, and his piety, in a cauldron, steaming with all the ingredients of roguery like this? Place his honest mind in collision with that of a sharp city fox—*what then?* Put a lamb in the presence of a wolf for ten minutes, and then look for *what is left* of the lamb!

The good old hearts felt sad at this prospect of their favorite's. They hoped he would succeed, but with their knowledge of the temptations which beleaguer all men in New York, they could perceive but little to encourage that hope. With their view of moral responsibility, it was comparatively impossible for an honest man to pass through the perilous journey of business with profit. Still it might be done; and if so, Samuel, of all men, was the one to test it. His effort, at least, would be a *gallnat* one; for he was young, and had a young man's energies; brave, with a brave man's will; prudent, with a prudent man's carefulness; together with a ripe, well-balanced mind, which would equally preserve him from summary conclusions, hastiness of action, and undue errors in judgment. In any event, they knew he would be faithful to the great aim of the Christian's being—that, come failure or success, he would never lose sight of the great trust which is reposed in every Christian—the purity of his own heart. Meanwhile, they, like true men in the Lord, would pray for him, and invoke the Divine Eye to be ever over him, and the Divine Hand to be ever near him; for *he was a brother in a perilous pass*—A BROTHER IN DISTRESS.

And from many a hearth in Enfield, there ascended, on that and many a night besides, many a touching prayer, of which this was the pith and idea: "Be thou, O Lord! with SAMUEL—with SAMUEL, O Lord!"

CHAPTER II.

THE inmates of the parsonage consisted of the pastor himself, his wife, their two sons, Samuel and little Joe, the latter in his seventh year, and Betsy the housekeeper, who, having occupied that position ever since our hero was an infant, regarded herself as a regular member of the family.

Mr. Leland, the pastor, judging by the silver which intermingled with the short jet hair which covered his fine Roman head, was somewhat turned of fifty. Though only slightly above the medium height, the slenderness of his make gave him a commanding appearance. His features were small, but defined with a boldness and delicacy which made them singularly impressive. The dark eyes were full of depth, and their amber clearness indicated a ripe, well-balanced and richly stored intellect, tempered with fine observation and experience. The tone of the face was that of a man whose mind associated only with high and serious things, and whose heart could only be enlisted by the finer phases of humanity.

Mrs. Leland was a small, fair-haired, blue-eyed, delicately formed lady; and although of nearly the same age as her partner, time had dealt gently by her. Her fair face, straight features, and girl-like form, bating a certain thoughtful, matronly air, were still almost as young, graceful, and winning as on her wedding night, some six-and-twenty years before. A single glance at her mild, seraphic countenance would have satisfied the most inexperienced observer that her mind was a casket of pure thoughts, and her heart a fountain of rare tenderness and feeling, tinctured with an abiding consciousness of moral responsibility.

Samuel was, in height, shape, and general appearance, the counterpart of his father. He had the same earnest air, the same boldness and delicacy of feature, the same resolute lip, the same indications of elevated thought, and the same quiet dignity of manner—mingled, however, with the serenity, tenderness, and depth of feeling which shone so conspicuously in the countenance of his mother.

Little Joe was a slender, fair-haired boy, of seven or eight summers. He had the fine Roman features of his father, with the blue, lustrous eyes, so redolent of angelic sweetness, of his maternal parent. The expression of his face was singularly mild and pleasant; but it only required a glance to tell an observer that the two bright blue orbs whose beauty so much charmed him, were, like two imprisoned souls, shut out forever from the light of the beautiful world around them. Poor little Joe was blind. He had but one companion, but of that one he never tired. It accompanied him all the day; it was his only bed-fellow when he laid him down at night. This companion was a small flageolet, which had been presented him by his brother some three years before. With his flageolet, little Joe was usually as happy as a king. He would talk to it, fondle it, and play with it, as if it were a human thing, and understood and could return it all. When tired of exercising with his instrument thus, he would apply its mouth-piece to his lips, and, as he laughingly expressed it, make it *talk back*, which it did, in its own peculiar way. Then his blue, sightless eyes would fall, with a loving expression, upon the body of his friend, and every sense was swallowed up in listening to its voice. The melody that followed depended altogether upon the state of the player's feelings at the moment. If anything occurred to sadden him—as, however, was rarely the case, for great care was taken by the household, as well as by their visitors, to give a sunny tone to every word uttered in his hearing,—his flageolet took a plaintive strain, which told of the mournful pageant that was passing through his little heart. If gay, the music of the song-bird, when trilling its merits to its coquettish mistress, was not more sweet or inspiriting than the melody of Joe's pipe. It is true, Joe, or rather, his instrument, could play but a single tune, and that it was always the same tune; but then, if it was, it had its variations, like any other tune, and Joe could play them all: for the tune itself, with all the variations, was of Joe's own composing, and though, *as* a tune, it might make a professor of music smile, yet, to Joe himself and all in the parsonage, and, for that matter, everybody in Enfield, too, it was just such a tune as no other composer ever made or could make, let him be ever so great. But it was a tune that Joe loved, and all in the parsonage loved, and all Enfield, too, because it was Joe's own. It might not have been composed—we incline to the opinion it was not—according to the regular rule, but for all that, it *was* a tune, —one which the members of the parsonage prized more than all other tunes in the world, and one which, while it frequently made them smile, often drew tears of anguish to their eyes; for, when the voice of the pipe was sad, they knew that it merely uttered the feelings of the poor blind boy.

Aunt Betsy was a short, stout, active, happy old soul, with the silver of sixty winters under her close-fitting cap. Although "waxin in years," as the good old creature was wont to observe, "she had no notion of givin' in yet. She was of a race who never gave in afore a hundred, and she intended, the Lord willin! to hold out to the reg'lar time. There was her great-gran'father, who fout the Injins ever so far back, when they were thick as bees round Enfield; he got wownded in more'n twenty places, and yet he lived his hundred out *full*, and two years over. Then gran'father John, who fout the British in the Revolution times, and got wownded in the head by a British bullet, which they found afterwards in a tree right behind where he had stood, lived on to his hundred. Then there was her father, John Fargis—everybody had heerd of *him*—he was postmaster in Enfield, once, and therefore a hearable man;—*he* didn't give in nuther till he'd made his hundred, with three years more, besides: and she meant to keep up the number. If her dead and gone man, Frank Disosway, hadn't went and fout the Britishers in the last war, and bin killed, he'd most likely bin alive still; for he was of a long race, too, who always held out till ninety. As for herself, she was young enough yet. She didn't say it to coax for'ard another husband, for she didn't want and wouldn't have another, if she was enticed ever so hard—she knew her feelins as Frank Disosway's widder too well for that—and so there was no use in any one's offering. But she was young enough yet—she knew that—and she meant, the Lord willin! to hold out to the reg'lar time!"

Excepting in her hours of sleep, in which the worthy housekeeper was as regular as night itself, Aunt Betsy's eye and hand were always busy. The most captious fault-finder would have failed to detect a solitary flaw in anything belonging to her department. She was neatness and economy personified. Everything in and about the parsonage bore a thrifty and an inviting look. A speck or stain, either in the house or around it, would have been as difficult to discover as a mine of gold or a bed of pearls. Parlor, bed-rooms and kitchen were always as bright, clean and cheery as the smiling face and trim, modest countenance of the good old soul herself. When everything else was done, Aunt Betsy had her knitting to do, and *that* was *never* finished. Morning and evening, summer and winter, every otherwise unemployed moment was devoted to knitting—her eyes meanwhile wandering all around, above and below her, to see if a speck had previously escaped her, if anything had been left unfinished, if anything required attention, and if everybody around her was perfectly comfortable.

On the evening in question, the members of the household were grouped around the parlor hearth: for old winter's breath lingered yet in the cold airs of spring.

On the right, in her straight, high-backed chair, sat Aunt Betsy, knitting away, for dear life; the master of the parsonage, with his wife and eldest son on either side of him, occupied the centre; on the left, beside the mantel-frame, was little Joe.

It was a tender and a touching scene.

Aunt Betsy was in a high state of excitement, as was evidenced by the extraordinary rapidity with which her needles and fingers chased one another in her knitting; her face was pale, too, and a tear-drop, which *would* not be restrained, fell every now and then from her moist eyelids to her cheeks, from whence it glided to the finger tips as they worried the glittering needles. In very truth, the dear old soul was very sad: why, could easily be guessed from her frequent stolen glances at the young handsome face of him who was to leave the parsonage on the morrow, for a stern, manly struggle with the world.

Samuel himself was the only one in the party whose features wore a happy and contented look. But it was all assumed, as every one around him knew, to veil his heaviness of heart, and to inspire his companions with a cheerfulness which he was conscious, after all, they could not feel.

Mr. Leland, the pastor, was grave, thoughtful, and apparently tranquil. But everybody there knew that his big heart was suffering; and when, as sometimes happened, in the course of the evening, he put on a smiling look, they felt intuitively that he was *then* suffering the most.

Mrs. Leland did her best to appear cheerful; but her attempts were so feeble and transparent, that even little Joe, as his fine, sensitive ear caught the tones of her voice, understood what was passing in her breast.

Of all the group, poor blind Joe deserved sympathy the most. Too young to call the stoicism of philosophy to his aid, he was the victim of a heart which was wholly made up of sensitiveness and feeling. His little head was almost bursting with its big, painful thoughts. He felt that all around the hearth were suffering; and as he loved them all with indescribable fervency, the intense sadness of his spirit may be readily imagined. Of his own individual grief he was scarcely conscious, if indeed he thought of it at all. And yet his great heart was almost breaking with its woe. Seated in his little chair, he spoke to no one but his friend the flageolet, through which he poured out, in the mournfullest of strains, the sad burden of his soul: his blue, sightless orbs turned, with an expression of mingled sorrow and affection, upon the sympathizing pipe, while a small tearful rill glided silently, but steadily, from his either eyelid to the fever-heated cheek below.

The conversation was principally carried on by Mr. Leland and our hero—Mrs. Leland rarely venturing a remark, and Aunt Betsy scarcely uttering a word.

It was a solemn parting hour between two loving parents and an equally loving son. Much was therefore said, and much left unsaid: for each instinctively felt the propriety of uttering nothing which would call up a painful thought, and both desiring to leave a cheerful impress on the other's mind. At length the conversation took a more general turn.

"Samuel, my son," began the pastor, speaking in a livelier tone than his feelings had yet permitted him to assume, "you will carry with you the consolation that your little friends of the school-room are in good hands. Mr. Griswold, your successor, happily combines with the ripeness of the scholar, the refinement of the gentleman, and the earnest piety of the Christian."

"True, father; and when the little ones learn his worth, they will love him as we do."

"He comes of a good stock," continued the worthy pastor. "As far back as we can trace,—and that dates with the first settlement of the town—the Griswolds have borne the good man's name!"

"They're of good blood—always hold out till ninety-five!" observed Aunt Betsy quietly to herself. "They showed the true grit in the Revolution times. One of 'em fout side by side with gran'father, and got a bullet in the left knee. I've heered of it often, in the old winter nights, from gran'father."

"Frank," ventured Mrs. Lindsay, speaking of the new teacher, "is a nephew of Mr. Townsend?"

"Yes, my dear, on his mother's side," answered the clergyman.

"Poor blood!" remarked the simple-minded housekeeper to herself. "Always give out a little this side of seventy. Good-natur'd, and fond of money, but always exact in their dealins."

"Mr. Townsend," said the clergyman, "is one in a thousand. Amid all the temptations of commerce, he, from all I can gather, maintains an unsullied name. Were it otherwise, believe me, my son, I should hesitate long before intrusting your business novitiate to his house. Mr. Grosvenor, our village merchant, who is one of his correspondents, represents him as a fair man in the strictest sense of the term. He is spoken of by all whom I find in connection with him as an honest, truth-telling merchant, and as they speak from a long business acquaintance with him, and are themselves truth-telling men, there is good reason for believing in the correctness of their report. With such a man for an instructor and employer, you will, my son, enjoy advantages which fall to the lot of few in their primary business course."

"I feel grateful for them, father!"

"And I, my son. But," turning his eye towards his youngest born, "poor Joe takes your departure sadly. How mournfully he utters the solemn feelings of his heart! Poor boy!" he added, stifling a sigh, "he is *all* heart! Nay, my dear," to his wife, who was about to catch up the poor blind child to her breast, "do not touch him. Let him finish his plaintive hymn; his heart will sooner be relieved."

"Poor Joe!" murmured Aunt Betsy, running her needles more furiously than ever. "He will never hold out to his people's seventy! Hearts like his were never made for a rough world like this! Poor Joe—my natur's bleedin' for you, dear!"

Samuel was shaken in his resolution at the sight.

"Father," he whispered.

"No, my son—no," returned the pastor, shaking his head as he met and understood the young man's glance. "Resolves, once made, should be firm—if they be founded upon good intents and worthy thoughts! Poor boy!" he added, alluding to Joe, "it is natural to him to weep at small sorrows,—how much more at great ones! A few days, and sunshine will come to him again. Let him," he continued, with a violent effort to recover his own composure, "let him sing out his grief—he will be happier when it is told! To break your own resolution would be wrong—to interrupt the outpouring of that little heart cruel! Let us resume our discourse."

"Proceed, dear father."

"I had hoped, my son, that when I should be summoned from my post, you would be my successor in that sacred office, as I succeeded my father, as my father succeeded his, and as he succeeded his, the original founder of our village church. Nay, do not grieve. Let us rather consider the matter in a calm, philosophic light, and not in that of feeling. My hope was a cherished one, I confess; but it was not to meet with a fulfilment. While it agreed with your own sentiments up to the date of your entrance *into* college, it did not meet with your views after your return *from* it. There your copious draughts from the luminous fount of varied knowledge, and your collision, for the first time, with bold, cultivated, *miscellaneous* minds, while they deepened and enlarged your own conceptions, gave them at the same time another tone as well as a widely different current. Bear in mind, my son, that I do not complain of this; I only repeat it as a fact, or rather as an illustration for your future, to show you how radical are the changes in our views when we associate or come in contact with minds to which we are unaccustomed, and which have penetrated further than our own into the enlightening realms of observation, general learning, and mental criticism."

"I understand you, father."

"Nevertheless, my son, I shall give you an illustration in point. You will, of course, understand it in the candid and affectionate spirit in which it is uttered. When you *entered* college, it was to complete your studies for the ministry: naturally supposing yourself fully qualified, in all other respects, for that sacred calling. *While* at college, you came in contact with minds at least as pure, and, as you thought, richer in promise than your own. These pure minds, so rich in promise, measured the competence of men for the ministry by a standard so high that it drove you to a conscientious examination of yourself. That examination resulted in the conviction that your qualifications for that highest of all human offices were far below the prescribed standard. Sorrowfully, therefore, but bravely—for it requires courage to comply with the mandate of conscience when it bids us give up a long-cherished object—you relinquished your aspirations for the ministry as a profession to which you had not been called by your Creator: since, *had* He called you, He would have endowed you with qualifications which would enable you to follow it with benefit to Him and honor to yourself. This conclusion reached, and having, like a right-thinking man, no disposition to waste your talents in forbidden idleness, you turned your thoughts—shall I say at the suggestion of *another* mind?—in the direction of worldly business. Business—which to the sanguine eye of inexperience, is simply a *mere lake*, whose opposite banks, glittering with gold, are distinctly visible and easily reached; but which graver experience knows to be a deceptive, *seething sea*, whose stormy waters wreck daily thousands of brave men, and hurl them, broken, beggared, unpitying and unpitied, on brankruptcy's bleak, inhospitable shore. I make not these remarks, my son, to discourage you—you know me better—but to open your eyes to the real character of that world which you are about to explore. You will find in it more savages—worse, *civilized* ones!—than ever greeted the eye of Columbus. Creatures with all the outward semblances of men, but with the ravenous appetites and ferocious natures of tigers—human beasts of prey, who live by running down and devouring the vitals of credulous, unsuspecting men."

Samuel looked thoughtfully in the fire.

"You may possibly regard the picture as overdrawn," continued the clergyman, quietly observing him, "but time will evolve its accuracy."

"Are there then no good men there, father?" inquired Samuel, looking up.

"Many," was the reply; "but their number is small, and themselves so scattered, and intermixed with the great mass, that it takes time to find them. My dear," turning to his wife, and calling her attention to little Joe, whose head was bent upon his breast in gentle slumber, "the pipe has played out its mournful song, and the minstrel's spirit is with the angels. Mark the smile which hovers around his little lips!"

Mrs. Lindsay and Aunt Betsy sprang to their feet at the same instant. The tender-hearted mother was, however, the first to reach the little dreamer, and catching him up in her arms, and imprinting a fond kiss upon his pale forehead, she bore him from the room.

It was now nine o'clock, Aunt Betsy's usual retiring hour, and deeming it a good excuse for leaving father and son to a private conference, which, her heart told her, they both desired, she bade them good-night, and hurried after her mistress.

Her departure was followed by a short silence, which was broken by the pastor.

"My son," he began, in a tone which penetrated to the very core of his hearer's heart, "you will appreciate the feelings of a father when he sees his first-born going out for the first time to do battle with the world. However well he may have previously prepared him for the conflict, he cannot help trembling for the result. The painful dread of uncertainty will creep in upon him, and send a shudder through his breast, resist it as he may. He experiences then, that his child's hold upon his heart is stronger than he thought, and that the boy is carrying the dearest part of it away. He feels that his Young Hope is thenceforth a stranger among strangers; that he must now be his own sole friend and counsellor; that he is treading perilous ground, where a single false step is followed by years of anxiety and disaster; that it is youth and inexperience against a subtle horde, who are veterans in guile; that he is now in a field whose stormy din proclaims the ferocity of the conflict; where every man is his own general and soldier, fighting his own individual battle, little heeding and little caring whom he maims or slays, so he

2

come off himself with a victor's bays, and more—a victor's spoil: in a word, that he is, with his youth and inexperience, in the midst of a crafty, merciless throng, whose trade is pillage, and who will destroy him—if they can! What wonder, then, if the sire's heart be shaken in that solemn parting hour?"

The hand of the father fell spontaneously into that of his son as he concluded. The sympathizing touch was electrical. It opened wide the door of human nature's cells, and the sacred streams darted forth like gushing lava, and mingled into one. Their eyes met, and, yielding to their emotions, they bowed their heads upon each other's necks and wept.

A long silence followed, which was at length broken by the entrance of Mrs. Leland. The wife and mother paused a moment to contemplate the picture before her; then approaching the sighing pair, she put an arm around each, and burst into tears.

The clergyman himself was the first to recover his composure.

Then, giving one arm to his wife, and the other to his son, he said, as they paced up and down the apartment:

"Your dear mother and I, Samuel, have to thank you for nearly five-and-twenty years of parental happiness. We thank you for the comforting stream of uninterrupted joys with which you have filled our hearts, from your earliest infancy until now. We thank you for your uniform piety, kindness, and affection; for your uprightness in all things; for the love which you have ever borne our King and Prince, your parents, your companions, and your fellow-men; for the brightness of your example to the mates of your childhood, your youth, and your young manhood; and for the genial spirit of peace and good-will to man which you have inculcated among your little friends in the secular and Sabbath schools. We thank you for preserving the purity and integrity of our own family name. And we thank you," added the pastor, pausing, and placing his hands over the young man's head, "for so comporting yourself all your days until now, that we can turn our eyes to Him, and say: 'Lord of Righteousness, of Goodness, and of Love! we bless Thee for this, Thy tender gift. Ever has he been to us, Thy servants, a thing of beauty and of joy; never has he brought to our eyes a tear—never to our hearts a pang!'"

He paused, and trembling with emotion, made a familiar sign. All knelt reverently in prayer.

"Lord of the Heavenly Kingdom," began the clergyman, "three humble suppliants, who have heard of the greatness of Thy heart, who have faith in the shelter of Thy smile, and who would share in the riches of Thy love, come to Thee. Of the glory of Thy name, of the wondrousness of Thy power, of the goodness of Thy heart, of the grandeur of Thy Kingdom, we have heard, and believe. Turn Thine eye upon us; let us feel the comfort of Thy presence; we are petitioners for Thy grace.

"Lord! the home of Thy servants has long been in the shadow of Thy love—we give Thee the praise.

"Our hearts have tasted of the sweetness of Thy smile—we give Thee the praise.

"We have found peace in knowing and believing that Thy ways are pleasant ways, and Thy people pleasant people—we give Thee the praise.

"Long years of joy, from the dawn to the even, have been granted us—we give Thee the praise.

"Thy name, and that of Thy Son, our Prince, have been to us like the light of the morning—we give Thee the praise.

"Hearken to us, O Lord!

"A shadow darkens the home of Thy servants. A temporal grief is upon us. Give us strength to bear them.

"One whom we love, since he was Thy gift, is about to leave us: give us strength to endure it.

"He goes in the way of Pride, of Temptation: give him strength to resist them.

"For evil will be about him, and upon him, and without Thy smile to protect Him, and Thine arm to uphold him, he will fall.

"Stand Thou between him and evil, O Lord!

"Be Thou his Sun by day, his Star by night.

"Should it be Thy pleasure that he prosper, or Thy pleasure that he fail, we shall bow, in either event, meekly to Thy will.

"But whether he prosper or fail, be Thou, O Lord! with him a perpetual presence: whether prosperity or adversity, let him not falter for a moment in his allegiance to Thee!

"Should it be Thy will to try his devotion with the temptations of success, give him strength, O Lord! to bear up against them; ennerve him, day by day, that his heart may not wander, a moment, from Thee.

"If it be Thy pleasure that he pass through the valley of disaster, that tribulation be the only reward of his efforts, and that envy, malice, calamity and disappointment assail him: Be Thou, O Lord! with him in his hour of trouble; let the light of Thine eye be upon him; preserve the purity of his heart, and give it courage to endure bravely and loyally to the end.

"And when, at last, his day of trial shall reach the shadow of its even, when his spirit shall lay down to await the coming of Thy messenger, let the lamp of his faith shine dazzlingly a little moment in honor of Thy name.

"And when his work shall be done, take him, O Lord! to Thine own glorious kingdom, and let him be one of Thy people evermore.

"Hearken to us, O Lord!"

The prayer was ended. The petitioners bowed their heads upon their clasped hands, for a few moments, and then rose. Their hearts were full, but not with sorrow. Their eyes were bright, but not with sadness. They greeted each other with a genial smile.

As the petition approached its close, the petitioners themselves experienced a sensation: Their perturbed spirits underwent a gradual change. A holy calm entered and tranquillized their souls, which then became heated with a gentle glow, and then illumined with a mild, radiating light.

The joy of the petitioners was unspeakable; for they knew that the SPIRIT OF THE LORD had been with them!

CHAPTER III.

NIGHT glided into morning. With the first gray streaks of dawn, the inmates of the parsonage were up and stirring. Parents and son greeted each other joyfully; for the memory of the Divine Presence was still in their minds, with all its inspiring freshness. The glad tidings were revealed to the worthy housekeeper, whose pious heart was aroused into enthusiasm at the news. From that moment a spirit of tranquil happiness took possession of the household. Little Joe himself shared in the general joy, and his pipe rang through the parsonage in strains as lively and invigorating as a lark's.

Aunt Betsy declared that "the child must have bin communin with naters as innocent as his own, or else he could never have woke up in such good spirits—perticklerly when he had spent such a miserable evenin'!"

Whatever was the cause, Joe's pipe warbled merrily all the morning: so merrily, indeed, as to bring Rover, the guardian of the village store, on the opposite side of the road, over, who put his head in at the kitchen door and looked up in the little minstrel's face, as if desiring to know what it all meant. The morning meal passed over cheerfully; and at its conclusion, everything was got in readiness for Samuel's departure. His well-filled trunk was brought down; the lock examined and the straps drawn an inch tighter than before, and the trunk itself then placed beside the garden gate. Samuel drew on his overcoat, an example that was followed by his father, for the morning was fresh enough to render an extra garment exceedingly welcome to those who contemplated a moderate drive. Mrs. Leland put on her hat and shawl, and taking little Joe, who was also dressed for a journey, by the hand, she quietly sat down, with the others, to await the arrival of the vehicle which was to convey them to the next village, where Samuel was to take the cars.

As the kitchen clock struck seven, there was a rattling of wheels, and immediately after a double-seated spring wagon, driven by one of Samuel's former scholars, drew up at the gate. The lad—a fine, bright, ruddy fellow of seventeen or eighteen years—was dressed as for a holiday. He sprang from the wagon, and was passing through the gate, when his eye fell upon the trunk. He lifted it without ceremony into the vehicle, and then passed to the door of the parsonage, where he found his late teacher quietly awaiting him.

"Good-morning, Samuel!" cried the lad, greeting him with a hearty air of mingled affection and respect. "I see I'm not too early for you. Folks all ready?"

"Thank you, Charles—thank you. All ready. You are not a whit too early, nor too late either. Have you breakfasted?"

"Oh, yes: an hour ago. I might have been here before. But as seven was the appointed hour, I thought it would not please you so well; as you always told me that punctuality, to the letter, was ever to be remembered."

"Right, Charles—right. Never lose sight of that! Come in, my friend—come in!"

After a few minutes of courteous interchange, the parties left the parsonage to take their places in the wagon. As they reached the open air, they beheld a number of friends and neighbors outside the gate, some waiting to take a parting look, and others a parting grasp of the hand of their young friend.

This, however, occasioned but little delay, for all were aware of the importance of time, and Samuel followed his relatives into the vehicle. Upon taking his seat, he raised his hat to his friends, who returned the salutation with a hearty cheer, and then settled himself between his father and Charles, on the front seat, the ladies and little Joe occupying the back.

As the wagon swept down the road, the field-workers and inhabitants of the cottages approached the fences and waved friendly adieux to the general favorite as he passed by, while many wished him a pleasant journey and a prosperous career in tones as loud as they were hearty.

Samuel was touched by these evidences of affection and esteem, and was frequently forced to return them with silent gestures of farewell, as his feelings were too agitated to allow him to answer them in words.

It was a sunny, bracing morning. The air was pure and bright—a little keen, it might be, but not too much so for young, vigorous blood like that of our hero. With his parents and Aunt Betsy, however, the case was different, and they were not sorry to see their young friend Charles whip his pair of grays into a lively, stirring trot.

But few words were exchanged on the journey—the feelings of each being too deep for utterance.

The parents cast frequent glances at their son, but considerately forbore to add to the disturbance which the circumstances of his situation naturally produced in his sensitive and tenderly cultivated mind.

They were now within a mile of the next village; but, thus far, with the exception of Charles, Samuel had not seen a single face of his many little friends. He strained his eyes from one side of the road to the other, in hope that at least one of them would appear and wish him a kind word, but in vain. The heart of the young man was grieved; for he had long fancied that his own respect and affectionate solicitude for his scholars were spontaneously reciprocated. But now that he was leaving home, and perhaps for the last time, not one of them appeared to bid him a cordial good-bye—not one! An expression of sadness passed over Samuel's features at the thought, while a tell-tale moisture at the eyes, of which he was wholly unconscious, told the watchful orbs of his companions that he was suffering in heart. Still no one ventured to remark audibly upon the subject, feeling instinctively that such a course would be both indelicate and impolitic.

A few minutes brought the party to a bend in the road, lead ing to the next village. As they approached the turning-point, Charles glanced archly both at the pastor and the ladies, who, however, as their looks gave him to understand, had not the slightest comprehension of his meaning, while they at the same time desired an explanation. The lad answered them with a shrewd, quiet grin, which was as little understood as the smile, and they to whom it was addressed, had no help for it but to wait patiently until either Charles himself or the cause of his singular behavior should furnish them with a key to his mystery.

Meanwhile they were rapidly approaching the angle of the lower road, into which they turned a few moments later, when the two church spires and the scattered cottages of the adjoining village loomed up pleasantly before them.

As they drew nearer, all eyes were attracted to a gathering

near the railroad depôt, which was situated on the main road, or rather street, as it was more generally termed, and then the parties in the wagon began, as they conceived, to get a glimpse of their young friend's meaning. Ere long they were confirmed in the correctness of their conjecture.

Charles, who was all excitement, whipped up the grays, and springing to his feet, exclaimed, while he waved his cap,

"Hurrah, boys! Here he is!"

A loud shout from the throng around the depôt responded to his cry, and a single glance in that direction told Samuel that he was not forgotten by his little friends, who, headed by their new teacher, and attended by many of their parents, were drawn up in a body at the depôt to bid him a tender adieu.

Touched by this unexpected evidence of his old pupils' affection, and sensible of the injustice which he had done them in his thoughts, a gush of hot tears rushed like a flash of fire to the young man's eyes. He trembled, and would have fallen, but a whisper from his father of "Be firm, my son—be a man!" reënnerved and restored him to a full sense of his situation.

Dashing the tears hastily aside, he raised his hat and returned the greeting of his little friends with a low, grateful bow. The latter comprehended intuitively the state of his feelings, and endeavored to reassure him by three prolonged, spirit-stirring cheers.

Samuel, however, was not one to enjoy an ovation, nor anything else which would have the effect of making him an object of general attention, and he heard with unmixed pleasure the ringing of a locomotive bell which announced the rapid approach of the train.

Charles, however, was perfectly merciless. He drove forward rapidly and drew up beside the depôt, exclaiming, as he halted,

"Here he is, boys. Three cheers for him now, and with a will!"

And they *were* given, Charles himself setting the example, and joining in the roar with a lustiness which was distinguishable from all the rest.

"Now, then," added the youngster, with the air of one who knew perfectly well that he but uttered the sentiments of all around him, and meant to have them complied with, "now, then, Samuel, we want a speech. Come, no backing out. Are we not your own boys—are you not our Samuel?"

Samuel was agitated to a degree. He blushed, trembled, and could hardly stand. He wished himself away; shook, turned pale and red by turns, and then wished himself away again: and yet he felt that he was wrong, that his little friends were right, and that they were yearning to hear a last word from one whom they loved; that they looked for it, as a matter of course, that they would be disappointed very much if they should not hear it, and that under the circumstances they were justly entitled to it. He felt also that he desired himself to speak to them; that his heart would be the better for it, even if he only gave utterance to a single word. But yet he could not, so he thought, speak that one word, if his life depended upon the effort.

He glanced reprovingly at Charles for placing him so rudely, as it were, in a situation of so much embarrassment, and yet he knew that it was dictated by a generous motive, and that there was not one in all the throng who loved him deeper, nor one more anxious to hear the sound of his voice.

He rose to his feet, determined to make at least an effort.

Charles glanced at him, and detecting his weakness, cried out, for the purpose of securing him a moment to call up his courage—

"Now, boys, we are going to have it. But first let's clear the air for him with an honest ring!"

The "ring" that followed was "honest" enough to satisfy even Charles himself, who was at length compelled to bring it, with a wave of his hand, to a close, in order to give Samuel an opportunity to be in time for the train, which was now within forty yards of the depôt.

A deep silence followed Charles's gesture, and Samuel determined to make an effort. His first attempt was a failure; his lips appeared to be glued together, and it seemed impossible for him to part them. Better success followed his second attempt, which was sustained by a violent action of his will.

"My little friends," he said, in a trembling voice, "your kind presence here to bid your old teacher good-bye has taken me by surprise. I did not expect it, but I am grateful—very grateful—to meet you. I am about to leave you, but whether forever, or only for a season, I do not know; I would tell you which, if I could. If you would make me happy while away, write me as often as you can; and always let me hear that you are good, that your new teacher loves you, that your friends love you, that you love your Heavenly King and Prince, and that you hope they love you in return. Should we not be permitted to see one another again here, let me hope that we shall meet There. I would say more; I should be happy to take you all, separately, by the hand, and tell you how happy each and all of you have made me in our day and Sabbath schools—but there is not time. The train is here, and I must go. Dear friends, I love to look upon your faces, but I may not stay. I love to listen to your dear voices, but I cannot now. Therefore, I must say to you, one and all, love me, for I love you; remember me, for I shall remember you. Farewell, dear friends—farewell!"

There was no shouting now. They would have cheered him, if they could—but voices they had none. They raised their hands, they waved their caps, but not a sound went up, save a deep, heart-breaking sob.

CHAPTER IV.

THE train swept on, with its living freight; dropping here, taking up there, and then sweeping on again, like a wild, fearful thing, that had a thousand miles to travel, and with but a breath to do it in,—through the bowels of the hills, high over the valleys, across wildly rushing streams, through the houses of cities, grazing barns and churches, over trembling bridges and dykes, through mountains of rock, across marshes and plains—roaring madly all the way. Halting suddenly—strange men and women gliding in, strange men and women gliding out, and then sweeping on once more—with now and then a screech like that of the tempest in a rage. Then a ringing of a bell; then a stoppage—strange men and women hurrying in, strange men and women hurrying out; then a shock—then a start, and then a long, unbroken roar, as before.

Samuel was on his way to the city.

Beside him, looking now through the small window-pane near him, anon at the faces in the closely packed car, and glancing occasionally down at a soiled, crumpled morning paper, which lay open on his knees, sat a tall, gaunt, broad-shouldered personage, habited in a suit of black, the fineness of whose nap, and the mingled neatness and symmetry of whose cut, stamped their owner as a man of taste, as well as one of means.

The countenance of this gentleman was significant and impressive. A high, full, massive forehead, indicated it as the temple of a bold and fruitful mind. The arched, protruding brows told of keenly observant faculties, which caught meanings at a glance; the eyes were large, clear, and apparently measureless in depth; the nose darted in a long, straight line from the brows, its base marked on either side by a nostril whose bold but delicately chiselled curve was significant of a high spirit, which it might be dangerous to arouse; the upper lip was small, but it spoke of a calm, stern will, which would not be easily shaken in its resolves; its lower neighbor was larger and fuller, and softened the bold and somewhat cynical expression of its mate; the chin was bold, but so softly rounded as to deprive it of every vestige of harshness. The color of the skin was of that peculiar paleness which is native to consumptives with black, glossy hair, although the general aspect of the personage was that of one in sound, if not robust health. The tone of his face was on the whole pleasant, and would have been absolutely winning, were it not for a sarcastic shadow which hovered around the lips. Despite of this deformity, however, which disappeared when its owner spoke, the general air of the stranger was well calculated to impress a looker-on favorably, while it could not fail to command his respect. He was evidently one who both mingled with and understood the world, and knew how to work his way through it, with the shrewdest and bravest.

He paid but little attention to our hero at first; but in the course of a quarter of an hour, he moved around in his seat, and placing his back to the side of the car, he rested his head in the palm of his left hand, and fixed his keen, penetrating eye upon the young man's profile, studying feature after feature, until he had taken a complete inventory of his nature.

"An honest, earnest, simple-minded youth!" he muttered to himself, as he completed his quiet and unnoticed survey. "I'll sound him." Then slightly changing his position, so as to attract the young man's notice, he said: "A pleasant day, neighbor!"

"Yes, sir," replied Samuel, turning a little in his seat, so as to obtain a view of his companion's features, "for riding in a comfortable car, or a climbing jaunt among the hills!"

"Is there much pleasure in the latter?" inquired the other, with a quiet smile which was full of manly sweetness, and which revealed two rows of small glittering pearls.

"Yes, sir, when the heart and blood are young."

"Ah!" observed the stranger. "But if the heart and blood be old?"

"In that case, sir, they would, I fancy, prefer not to climb at all."

"And yet," said the stranger, "that rule would hardly be received in the world. *There*, the old are in most instances the best climbers."

"But not of country hills?"

"Granted. But of hills far more difficult to master, and whose summits are rarely touched by the young."

"Human honors?"

"Yes."

"I had thought them hardly worth the seeking, sir," said Samuel diffidently, "and still less by gray hairs. Give me one of nature's green hills to mount before all the other hills in the world!"

"So young and yet so wise!" thought the stranger. "He has the ring of the pure metal; come, we'll try again. It will never do to confess defeat to a simple heart like this!" Then he said, in a tone which was tinctured slightly with a sneer, "We are sometimes governed in our choice by the consciousness of inability, and therefore prefer doing those things which *are* within our compass."

Samuel reddened at the sarcasm, but did not permit him self to venture a reply until he had recovered his previous equanimity.

"That, I judge, sir," he then said, "would be the most commendable course in all cases."

"The most *prudent*, no doubt!"

"Surely prudence is deserving of respect?"

"That," returned the stranger, with a perceptible sneer, which, however, as the reader will readily comprehend, was entirely assumed, "would depend altogether upon circumstances, and upon the man. For instance, two soldiers, while returning to camp, find themselves attacked by a number double that of their own; in this situation one regards it as most prudent to run, while the other, being made of different stuff, unhesitatingly shows fight. The first loses his honor, while the second—" He paused.

"Loses his head!" said Samuel, naively finishing the sentence.

"Would that naturally follow?"

"I think so, if the four had their wits about them," answered Samuel, with a simplicity of which he was himself unconscious.

"But the 'prudent' man—" suggested the other, for the purpose of drawing him out.

"Would be in a condition to return with a force large enough to capture the assailants without shedding a single drop of blood!" returned Samuel.

"But his desertion of his comrade, independent of its baseness, has resulted in the latter's destruction."

"By remaining he might have met his own! Besides, there is no certainty that both would not have been slain. Had the second followed the same prudent course, the one would have preserved his honor, the other his life. True courage does not consist in foolhardiness, nor real wisdom in attempting impossibilities. As for myself," he added, modestly, "I should hesitate to undertake a task which my judgment whispered to be beyond my capacity."

"'Know thyself,' is an honest maxim," said the stranger, "but one which few remember. You, however," he added, dryly, "appear to have studied it with care!"

"I might retort," said Samuel, with quiet firmness, "that to never *forget* one's self is equally as honest!"

"Good! I like the fellow's spirit. It is as refreshing as his wit!" thought the stranger. "Men," he said aloud, "are sometimes tempted to utter as well as do things which they afterwards regret."

"Surely *they* are not persons to imitate, sir! We owe more to our self-respect than to our blood! Regret palliates, but it does not atone for a fault. A man, in the heat of temper, strikes his friend—maims him, perhaps, but his sorrow for the act, while it may alleviate the anguish, does not do away with the *effects* of the blow. *They* are visible in the wound itself, which, when healed, still leaves a—scar! Worse—in the breast of him who gave it, lives the memory of an hour when he relinquished his self-respect and his claims to the character of a thinking being, to the brutal hands of his riotous blood. How much nobler to have sustained his moral manhood in that trying hour, than to sacrifice it on so low an altar!"

The stranger could not help admiring the moral grandeur of this sentiment, but he was too much of a man of the world to permit his real thoughts to be mirrored by his features; and as his proud spirit revolted at even the shadow of defeat, he replied, in a tone tinged with a certain degree of irony—

"You think, then, sir, that a man should pass over the grave results of his rashness without so much as a regret?"

"No, sir. I would have him avoid them altogether!"

"But if he be hot-blooded?"

"Does it follow that he should be hot-minded as well? Children are sometimes the creatures of impulse; but something better is looked for in full-grown men. Brutes are the subjects of instinct; man, cast in a higher and more glorious mould, the subject of reason."

"Not always," returned the man of the world, dryly. "He is more frequently the fettered vassal of society and its absurd conventionalisms. Society says to him, 'Do as we do, think as we do, comport yourself as we comport ourselves;' and he meekly, or rather servilely, obeys. A 'reasoning being!' Why, sir, he is the bondsman of his tailor, of his hatter, his newspaper, his minister, his party, his 'set.' His opinions are made by the circle that he moves in, and he clings to them according as they humor his own peculiar *whims*, which he innocently flatters himself are genuine THOUGHTS, and as they subserve his various ignoble interests. A 'reasoning' being! He reasons as his 'position' lets him, and not like a free, unbiased mind. If he be a sordid, grasping money-getter, he reasons as the love of money will permit him; if a fashion-follower, as fashion will allow him; if a drawing-room hanger-on, as the drawing-room dictates; if a partisan, as his leaders prescribe; if a soldier, as the department orders; if in any one rank of society, according to the usages of that rank. A 'reasoning being,' indeed! Let him but dare to show himself a being of that exalted order, and society will ostracise him as if he were a felon; it will shower upon him anathemas as numerous and ludicrous as those fulminated by the impious simpleton of St. Peter's chair himself; nay, every man, woman, and child will rise up in virtuous indignation and hunt him like a wild beast—happily for the poor daring wretch, if they do not run him down! True, now and then, a brave spirit rises, who sunders and throws to the winds the fetters that had been imposed upon his youth, and, strong in the consciousness of his genius and his bold, energetic will, startles the world with the grandeur, the brightness, and the dignity of his great manhood. His mighty mind detects and laughs to scorn the paltry fallacies which hold society together; he sifts, riddles, and holds them up to the ridicule of mankind—and then dares the combined efforts of society to do their worst, and to move him if they can. Society surveys him first with astonishment, then with doubt, then fear—for in him it has found its Master. The conflict is brief, for where is the modern David that will grapple with a giant? From that moment society quietly yields to this Intelligence, whose power is greater than its own; it caresses him, flatters him, calls him sweet names; terms him 'queer,' 'original,' 'sagacious,' 'bold,'—quietly biding its time in the meanwhile, for a faltering, careless, or unguarded moment, when it can turn, like an avenging wolf, upon the poor wretch, rend him, and slake its wild thirst in the blood of his downfall! And yet you are pleased to call this monster, Man, a 'reasoning' being! Lord help us!"

"Lord help us, indeed!" answered Samuel, "when a lofty Intelligence like yours, sir, can find food for laughter, for mockery at so sad a picture of humanity as that which you have drawn! Ah! friend,—may I not call you so?—that is not kind, not generous, not noble! There is a higher summit in the human mind than Sarcasm—Magnanimity! The pipe whose songs are all of bitterness dreams not of the joys of the harp whose strings are touched by angels' fingers! Humanity, be it in rags or satin, whether on the side of truth or on that of error, whether noble or ignoble, is still our brother. If he be cast down, what a joy to raise him; if ill, what a joy to nourish him; if struggling in the waters of want, sorrow, calamity, or of error—what a pleasure to rescue him! Say we should see a brother who is crazed in mind, standing unconsciously upon the brink of a precipice; we would not laugh in mockery at his peril, but lead him gently back to safety, soothing him the while!"

The man of the world shook his head.

"All very fine to talk of," he said, "but not to practise. Angel hearts are not often found among men, nor among women either. They prefer breasts of a sterner mould, and spare no efforts to render their own as hard as possible—and hard enough they make them! The market, sir, governs everything; and *that* is governed by the broad universal law of supply and demand. Now the demand is unlimited the world over for that which will freeze the human heart and make it colder, harder, and more capable of resisting the appeals of Pity, Sorrow, Suffering, and Benevolence, than it is already; and the supply, if the truth must be told, is far behind the demand! But there is *no* demand for angel voices, nor angel fingers! The harpist that would melt their icy natures would be smiled at for his simplicity; if he persisted, they would drive him off with ridicule."

"Surely men love not to be thought cruel!"

"Oh, no—not to be *thought* cruel! They would be *regarded* as mild, amiable, benevolent, magnanimous—because such a reputation *pays!* And therefore, as such a name can only be obtained at a cost which they feel by no means inclined to pay, they unite in constructing a general pleasing deception, which answers their purpose equally as well as the original! Under the influence of this pleasing deception, they get along very happily. They have a substantial respect for everything that will pay—a superficial sympathy, like the thin coating of an ice, for things that *don't* pay. Thus, while each professes a tender interest in honesty, they will let honesty itself starve, rot, die, ere they will help it. True, they will give it *advice*—liberally, but not a doit, not a sixpence to save it from starvation. Honesty? Oh, yes—they love it—at arms' length! They will follow it the world over—seemingly! Hear them talk, and pure honesty itself is an arrant, transparent rogue to them! They will not *openly* rob. Oh, no—that would send them to prison. But they will lie—in a *negative* way; they will cheat—little by little—step by step—until their pockets groan with superabundance. Short measure helps a little—adulteration helps a little—a gentle admixture of falsehood with truth helps a little—soft, unvarnished, but excusable conventional lies help a little—all snugly glossed over by a thin gauze of *It pays!* till each is a little Crœsus in wealth, respectability, morality, and—honesty! They honor virtue? Yes, *sir!* From instinct, sir—from very love of it, sir—from admiration of it, sir! Virtue, sir? Virtue is a flower—the fairest that ever bloomed in the garden of the soul, sir. Why, sir, there was my mother, my sister—the very embodiments of virtue, sir. They are gone now—they lie in Greenwood; the green turf over them, and—a tombstone that cost a thousand dollars—I can show you the bill, sir! By-and-bye, Virtue comes along; her rags faintly shield her gentle form from the cutting blast; gaunt want is in her eye, hot famine in her cheeks; her step is feeble, her voice low and timid; while from the arches of her eyes, lustrous with suffering, hunger has pinched a tear. 'A shilling, sir—please—I am sore beset; want is biting at my vitals; the cold is cutting to my bones; my shoe is wearing at the toe, it is worn already at the heel. I'm staggering towards the churchyard, with none to save me in the fall. A shilling, sir—please'. Oh, good woman, go to the alms-house—do. 'They are all full, there.' Go to work, then. 'I am too ill, too far gone, I'm ragged, there is no work to do.' The times are hard, certainly; but do run along—you annoy me—it's astonishing how full of professional beggars the world is—an honest man can't pass twenty rods without encountering the trumpery things at every step—it's really too bad—he'll petition at once to have the wretches kept out of the streets, and have them kept out, he will, or know the reason why! Honor virtue, sir—certainly! What a ridiculous question, sir! Do they honor Religion, too? Oh, yes. 'They have found, they still find, and they hope they shall continue to find, unspeakable consolation in its sacred fount. Yes, they have experienced its solemn joys; they have a grateful knowledge, an abiding sense of gratitude for Him who died that they might live; they adore his holy name, and hope to sing praises to him in a blessed immortality. They are conscious that but for religion society would have fallen to pieces long ago; that it is at once the corner-stone of society and the State; that without its sanctifying influences, public and private morality would disappear, education vanish, business shiver into atoms, property crumble into dust, the bonds which rivet men together be sundered forever, and the human race turned, like the sons of Ishmael, into homeless wanderers. They feel their obligations to a system which has done so much for them and for humanity in general. There's Mr. Smith, their preacher—they pay *him* six thousand dollars a year. Their church cost them eighty thousand dollars; and they think they can safely say it was dirt cheap at that. To be sure, there's Mr. Jones—a good man, who preaches in the little church around the corner—finds it rather tight work, with his large family, to creep through on his nine or ten hundred dollars, but that's *his* look out; and if his little church, with its humble congregation, *is* struggling with two or three thousand dollars of debt, that's none of *their* business. People ought to be careful how they contract debts. If they want churches, and haven't got the money to pay for them, let them do without them. What business *have* people with churches when they can't pay for them? They ought to look out and mind what they're doing. As to expecting help from *them*, they needn't think it. Sink or swim, live or die, let every tub stand on its own bottom! *Do* they honor Religion? Yes, sir! And everything else which they, as good citizens and good Christians *ought* to honor —in a *paying* way!"

"This state of things, sir," said Samuel, "is very sad—too sad for laughter, too sad for mockery! All men are not so bad as you would picture them. But you omit all mention of the *good!* Have you no kindly word for them?"

"*They* have no need of any praise of mine!" returned

man of the world. "The tranquillity of their own hearts is enough. You remember the adage, 'Virtue is its own reward!'"

"Ah! would you but believe in *that!* Then would you cease that icy sarcasm upon the failings of poor weak humanity, and that painful levity when touching on sacred things!"

"Young man," returned the stranger coldly, "when you shall have seen as much of this hollow world as I have—when you shall have seen as much of its hypocrisy as I have—when, like me, you have drunk of the hyssop and the gall which it puts to the lips of every young, confiding mind that falls within its grasp—when you shall have imbibed from its tempting but bitter chalice as deeply as I have, then you will despise it as heartily and honestly as I do!"

"You have suffered?"

"What matters that? All men must suffer. That is the price of association with your 'reasoning' men; with that bright host of intellects who only resemble brutes in their—acts!"

"Dear friend—may I take the privilege of calling you so?—you have started wrong in life, for your own happiness. Pardon me if I am too bold; for you are further advanced than myself, have necessarily seen more of the world, and may therefore regard it as impertinent in me to tender counsel to one so much my own senior in years."

"Let that pass," said the stranger, courteously. "Wisdom comes not always with gray hairs, nor does folly follow ever in the track of youth. Proceed!"

"Many thanks! In man's brief passage over the high-road of life there are two pathways—the Right and the Left: the ne leading to never-ending happiness, the other to never-ending Standing at the head of the first is an agent of the Prince ght; at that of the second, an agent of the Prince of

Darkness. Says he of the Right, 'Come this way, brother; peace and concord are with *us;* the fountains on the wayside are sweet, refreshing, strengthening—drink freely as you go; anguish then will lose its keenness, sorrow then will lose its depth, and bitterness its sting. There may be thorns of trial and temptation on the way, but the thorns do not kill; there may be rocks and ruts, and you may get sore and aweary—but the rocks and the ruts can be borne: for there are soft resting. places on the route, there is *light all the way*, and our Prince awaits your coming at the end. Come, come this way!' Ah, dear friend! happy he who hearkens to this voice, and takes the path so kindly, so earnestly pointed to his eye. For him thenceforth sorrow has no pain, calamity no sting. For him a mild and pleasant heart—for him pure present joy—for him prospective bliss, whose duration is eternal. Says he of the Left, 'Come *this* way; we have pleasure and pride, and tempting things to beguile you into waking and sleeping dreams which shall last while you live. There are thorns on the way, it is true, but we can show you how to blunt their points, so you shall not feel their pain. We have ways of making the rocks softer than couches of eider down; and then the ruts are all covered, so you càn avoid falling in. We have syrens whose voices will woo you to short slumbers, music softer than that of the stars; riches that will crush the voice of conscience and fill you with the vanity of power; rank, influence, and fame shall be yours—come and take them. You shall be strong enough to tread upon your enemies, to grind down the poor, and gratify every whim. Men shall wait upon your beck, slaves shall fly at your bidding, and you shall enjoy thé fruits of pride, of wealth, of worldly fame, of One-man power, to the utmost. We have artificial lights all the way, and—*our* prince awaits your coming, as his prey, at the end!' Ah! there is anxiety among the angels while the poor pilgrim is hesitating which road he will take;

there is joy in their hearts, if he turn to the Right, a song of sadness on their lips if he walk to the Left. In his own heart the spirit of good bows its head in sorrow and in tears, while its foe, the spirit of evil, utters an exultant shout o'er his fall! With him mildew, with him blight, with him canker, yearning, disappointment, bitterness—evermore. For though the world be bright, its brightness is not real; though it have its wisdom, its wisdom is most pitiful; though it have its pleasures, they are fleeting as the wind; though it has its lures, they *are* lures, and no more; there is no substance in its joys, no permanence in its glories, no honesty in its smiles, no stability in its riches. A sense of insecurity, of temporariness, of unreality, floats uppermost in the minds of its votaries, neutralizes their enjoyments, and fills them with doubt and dread of all around them, and of The Beyond whither they are hastening. Ah! my friend, is *this* a life to choose for happiness?"

The stranger made no reply. He dropped his deep, thoughtful eyes, and mused awhile in silence. At length he looked up, and observed—

"I will not say it *is* a life to choose. But it is nobler to be an open worldling, than to add another to the vast army of hypocrites who use religion as a cloak with which to worm themselves into the confidence of men, that they may the more easily betray it!"

"What need of joining either?" asked Samuel, calmly. "Religious hypocrites are simply worldlings of a *subtler* order than the herd! They are *in* the Church, but not *of* it. If they deceive men, they do not deceive themselves, and still less Him whom they profess to serve. In the meanwhile they are marching onward, like other worldlings, to their reward. But why should an earnest heart be governed in its conduct by *them?* Would a man hesitate to enter a gold mine and enrich himself with its dazzling stores, because its entrance was strewed around with fungi? It is the gold he wants, and not the fungi. What is the fungi to him? If the gold be there, and can be reached—*that* is all he needs to know; and then fungi or no fungi, the gold he will have! And are not peace and concord in life's journey, and the certainty of an eternity of bliss at the end of that journey, worth an earnest effort, whether hypocrites be in the Church or no! Say he will not, even for his own salvation, enter the Church, *because* hypocrites are there, but hold on doggedly to the world, will he not also find them *there?*"

"Granted. But there is a satisfaction in *knowing* that you are dealing with a scoundrel; on the other hand, you are never safe—the man whom you most regard, may be simply a rascal in disguise. What satisfaction in that?"

"None, I confess. But what satisfaction there can be in *either* case, I am unable to comprehend. Surely to *know* a man a scoundrel is to know him to be in peril, and therefore to warn him of his danger!"

"For doing which, my friend, nine times in ten, the scoundrel would knock you down!"

"He might, and he might not. In any event, I should have done my duty; and that," he added with his usual simplicity, "would compensate for the fall!"

The stranger was too well bred to indulge his inclination to laugh outright at this naive reply, but he could not wholly subdue a lurking smile. Still the honesty, the earnestness and the simplicity with which it was uttered, made a deep impression upon him; while he could not resist the conviction that the speaker was rising gradually higher and higher in his esteem.

"Come, sir," he said, at length, and with a cordiality of which he was himself unconscious, "you are a good fellow. What you have said is no doubt all very fine, and very true, and to a certain extent I agree with you. But it will not do—I say it as a friend—it will not do to carry these views with you into the world. *They* would be laughed at, and yourself covered with ridicule. Nay, hear me—one word! Men in the gross are arrant knaves, unworthy of a single thought from a mind like yours. They are vile, ignoble, and stubborn as asses. They will listen to you with wonder, marvel at your simplicity, and wind up by hooting you off and making you a target for their small wit. Let them run! No efforts of yours can save them. Their natures are grovelling—let them pass on to the perdition whither they are bound. If you would be popular with them, drop down to their own level. If you would be hated, reviled, persecuted, rent in pieces, attempt to stem the tide of their iniquity, and your wish will be gratified. But if you wish to prosper, like other men, you must drop down to the level of other men, be base and mean like other men—and lie, cheat and steal—*conventionally*, of course, like other men. Swim with the current, drift along with the great human tide, become one of the world, since you are in it, or you will live and die a beggar!'

"I thank you for your counsel," returned Samuel, who was touched by the kindly spirit with which it was tendered, "but I cannot consent to follow it."

"As you like, friend!" returned the stranger, coldly. "The fellow is a simpleton!" he muttered to himself.

"I had a previous counsel," continued Samuel, observing with pain the change in the stranger's manner.

"From one who understood the world?" asked the stranger, in surprise.

"Better than all within it!" The stranger laughed.

"A wonderful fellow, indeed!" he said, with an ill-concealed sneer.

"My PRINCE!" returned Samuel, solemnly.

The sneer disappeared from the stranger's lip. A tear leaped to his eye. He bowed his head to the rebuke. A dreadful paleness swept over his countenance. For a few moments he was like one dead.

He recovered slowly. Then looking up, he extended his hand to the young man, and said, in a voice that was far from tranquil—

"Follow the counsel of your FRIEND, sir! Far be it from me to shake your confidence in it, or Him. Worldling as I am, I bow to the beauty, the grandeur, and the humane spirit which beam in the language of the Cross. Go on in the course which your Redeemer has pointed out. It is the only true one!"

"May I not add, friend, of *our* Redeemer? Surely you—"

"Enough," interrupted the stranger; "I understand you, and will think the matter over. At some future time we may perhaps meet again. But stay—here is my card. Put it in your pocket. One of these days, when you have nothing better to do, give me a call. I shall, believe me, be happy to make your acquaintance. Meanwhile, if I can, in any way, serve you, do not hesitate to inform me of the fact."

"I thank you, sir!" answered Samuel, returning the warm pressure of his hand.

"And now favor me with your name," said the stranger; "I should like to know it, if for no other reason, to remind me of one who has caused me some pleasant railroad hours."

Samuel complied with his wish, and the stranger put the card on which it was written carefully in his pocket-book.

"Thank you," he said. "And now, sir, shake hands. We are approaching Utica, where I get out, and where business will keep me over till to-morrow. I shall be in New York the day after, and will esteem it a favor if you will then drop me, through the city post, your address. I shall observe your course with interest; and believe me, nothing will give me more satisfaction than to learn that you maintain, at every hazard, your devotion to the Right, never wandering, even in thought, towards the Left."

"Many thanks, sir. I shall endeavor, with the kind aid of my Prince, to endure loyally to the end."

"Do so, and be happy. But here we are at the depôt. Good-day, my friend!"

Samuel returned the warm pressure of the stranger's hand. The latter then passed from the car, and disappeared among the outside throng. Samuel reflected a few moments upon the peculiarities of his late companion; and then, with the ease of mercurial youth, turned his thoughts upon his own affairs.

The train swept on with its living freight; dropping here, taking up there, and then sweeping on again, like a wild, fearful thing, that had a thousand miles to travel, and with but a breath to do it in—through the bowels of the hills, high over the valleys, across wildly rushing streams, through the houses of cities, grazing barns and churches, over trembling bridges and dykes, through mountains of rock, across marshes and plains—roaring madly all the way. Halting suddenly; strange men and women gliding in, strange men and women gliding out, and then sweeping on once more—with now and then a screech like that of the tempest in a rage. Then a ringing of a bell; then a stoppage —strange men and women hurrying in, strange men and women hurrying out; then a shock, then a start, and then a long, unbroken roar, as before. Then a ringing of a bell; then a wilderness of houses and of steeples; then a low, sullen roar, as of a thousand steeds and chariots rushing madly over the earth; then the din of varied voices—"Have a carriage, sir? Right off to the Irving House!" "Carriage, sir? Astor!" "Carriage, sir? carriage?"

Samuel was in the city!

CHAPTER V.

Taking a conveyance, Samuel proceeded at once to a hotel. The following morning, he inquired for and found his way to the dry goods house of Mr. John P. Townsend, to whom he had a letter of introduction from his father.

Samuel was somewhat astonished at the magnitude of the establishment. It was a little world in itself. In the elegant language of "down town," it was "a dozen large stores knocked into one." To the eye of our simple-minded hero, it was a wilderness of little low counters, standing every which way, with a thousand little bewildering passages, leading anywhere and everywhere, but nowhere in particular. The little low counters heaped with piles of bright, dazzling calicoes, which threw silks and satins into the shade—sheetings, whiter far than snow—shirtings bleached, shirtings brown, shirtings striped—merinoes of more hues than were ever discovered in a rainbow—de laines of every figure and color that ever glided through the grotesque mind of a draughtsman, or combined under the fanciful pencil of a painter—flannels, broadcloths, cassimeres, tickings, were visible everywhere, and in a profusion that was both stirring and awe-inspiring to behold; in large heaps, and little heaps, with here and there a vacant space, telling of perhaps a great big heap which had just been whipped away by some invisible hand for packing, with lots of other heaps, in some invisible box, and dispatched by order to some invisible customer, living in some invisible corner of the country, whose name is duly registered as that of a "very esteemed" correspondent of the invisible firm of this very visible "house."

Amid this vast waste of counters, calicoes, sheetings, flannels, shirtings, broadcloths, cassimeres, tickings, merinoes, and glittering de laines, might be seen, here and there, in the little, narrow, wandering passages, like bees peeping out from the cells of a great hive, in quest of daylight, a scattered army of young clerks.

One is "laying down the law" of prices to a new customer, who is supposed to believe every word of the young gentleman's statement, that "their house can sell him lower by a *great deal* than any other establishment in town, as he himself can see, by the very low figure which they put upon their goods. They can furnish him with everything in the way of dry goods that he may want, as their immense, he may say, their *unequalled*, assortment easily enables them to do. They can do better by a dealer than any other house in town, as everybody knows, because their enormous capital gives them facilities which smaller concerns cannot of course command. They wouldn't like to have the statement get abroad, but they *know* that there isn't a house in town that can *begin* with them, either in variety, freshness, quality, or quantity of stock. As for the *way* in which they serve their friends, there is one fact that can't be got over, viz.: that no dealer who once opened an account with them was ever known to leave them. They believe in *accommodating* their customers; because they know, from long experience, that *that* is the only *correct* policy; it enables customers to do their own business more promptly, consequently more extensively; and *that*, as the gentleman himself can see, is to the interest of both parties. As for packing they never charge a friend for *that*—he can have *all* of his goods sent in to them, and they will pack them for him freely, indeed gladly. Then, in the way of *time*, they flatter themselves they can tender customers all the satisfaction they can possibly desire. They *believe* in giving a man an opportunity to turn himself around, without squeezing him;—they never *think* of selling their friends on less than *six* months, while they frequently sell them on *eight*, and even nine, if that will serve them better!"

All of which the "new customer" is supposed to drink in with a simplicity and gusto truly rural and refreshing.

In another passage, another spruce young gentleman is regaling a Western buyer with a true and reliable account of his difficulties in "getting through the custom-house" the brilliant French moussellin de laines which the buyer is examining so closely, and which were imported by their house, expressly, all the way from —the State of Massachusetts!

Another young gentleman, who looks as if he had just come out of a band-box, so nicely is he "got up," is assuring another Western buyer that the de laines *he* is looking at are *warranted* not to fade—without washing.

A third is industriously engaged in assuring the country dealer at his side, that "*them* prints have just been opened; that they are the *latest* styles; that they came in for the first time that very morning; that the cases from which they were taken can be seen down stairs in the packing department"—judiciously omitting all mention of the fact that they had been quietly stored away *up* stairs, near the roof, for some three or four years.

A fourth is doing the agreeable to a young, inexperienced rural gent, who desires a "blazing stock of roaring goods, which will enable him to smash up an old-established rival—an old fogy who will shortly find that Young America is too much for him, and who will have to vacate in double quick time with his antediluvian traps, and give place to one who can whip his hide off any day in the way of trade."

A fifth, pale and languid from the last night's spree, is driving away a sick headache in a bold effort to "rope in" a close, shrewd old codger from the interior of the State, who always makes it a point when he "comes down" in the spring and fall, to call in at that very store, run through all the goods, learn all their prices, and to invariably go away without "making a bill."

A sixth is "feeling" a Missouri gentleman, who "has been buying in St. Louis heretofore, and who has now come to New York, to see if the difference between St. Louis and New York prices is great enough to make it an object for him to change. Of the two, he would rather buy in New York—they gouge a fellow so in St. Louis, that a man can scarcely pay his bills and live. What he wants to come at now is, whether New York prices and the freights—freights are positively awful, almost bad enough to compel a man to throw up business altogether! —foot up in the gross so as to fall below the prices of St. Louis, and leave a small margin besides. If so, he is going to change the direction of *his* trade, right quick. He's been gouged by St. Louis long enough; and if he's compelled to submit to its monstrous extortions any longer, it won't be *his* fault!"

A seventh is exercising his own lungs and the patience of a cautious old dealer at his elbow with information to the effect that he is "absolutely buying too little of that print. It is perfectly new; will be all the rage, and if he isn't careful he will be caught napping." Old gentleman shakes his head, and hasn't the least fear of being detected in that way, at all. Young gentleman insinuates that he'd better reconsider the matter; that print will have a desp'rit run, and what will make it very bad is the important fact there is only a small supply of it in the market." Old gentloman will run the risk of all that. Young gentleman "thinks he'd better be careful, now—he'd better take a few more pieces." Old gentleman quietly but firmly declines, and they pass on to other patterns.

An eighth is selling a tremendous bill to an Illinois friend, an old good-natured customer, who always pays, and who always takes whatever is suggested to him by that clerk, in whose judgment he has far more confidence than in his own.

A ninth is earnestly urging a Jersey friend, who buys moderately, and always for cash, that he'd better "go a bigger assortment" and heavier lots of each. Jerseyman is very modest, very cautious, and "thinks not. Besides, he only brought a thousand dollars for his dry goods, and that is now nearly all used up by what he has already laid out." Ninth suggests that Jersey, whom he knows to be "good as wheat," "needn't let that deter him, as he—Ninth—will sell him all he wants, and take his note for the amount at six months." Jersey thinks he has got all he wants now; as to notes, he never gives any. "Don't know what might happen. Suppose he should die, and he had notes out—what then? They would create trouble for his executors, and that wouldn't do. Besides, his family would'nt like it. They never gave notes, because they knew very well there was no telling what might happen. Suppose one of them should die,—suppose he should die himself, and with notes out that the estate couldn't pay—what then?" Ninth was "quite willing to run the risk." Jersey quietly affirmed that "*he* was not," and Ninth smiled like a gentleman suffering with the toothache.

A tenth is telling an eleventh confidentially, how he is looking every moment for "a Buckeye, a particular friend of his, who, whenever he comes to town, never makes a bill of less than five thousand dollars, and always pays cash." Eleventh smiles incredulously; as Tenth has been telling that same story for more than two years, and the Buckeye hasn't made his appearance yet! Tenth grins and colors up, and says, "he's looking for him any how, and means to wait patiently till he comes." Eleventh impressively intimates that he will wait for the Buckeye a long time.

A twelfth is explaining to an old customer, who, as the house has recently discovered, is rather loose in the joints—loose in the joints meaning that his ability is as dubious as his willingness to pay—" how the house is now only selling for cash, its numerous heavy losses of late, by the caving in of many of its oldest and heaviest correspondents, having driven it to that course; how it will sell him very, *very* low, and thus make it an object for him to buy; how it—the house—has closed all its accounts, and is now selling wholly and exclusively for cash." Loose-in-the-joints is somewhat taken aback at this startling intelligence: " thinks it is hardly fair treatment to one who has dealt with the house so many years, and always paid so punctually; and would like to know the meaning of it," although he knows the meaning of it very well already.

A thirteenth, who is noted throughout the establishment for his "sharpness," is "managing" a Michigan gent, and " putting him through" on "scientific principles," which few in his way understand or know how to practise better than himself. He is regarded as a star of the first magnitude in his line. He can handle the oldest, shrewdest, and closest buyers with equal dexterity. He can tell the character of a customer at a glance. He has a trick of " sticking" old shop-worn goods upon the shrewdest, and of making them believe that they are the latest patterns out. He possesses a " knack" for making the most cautious dealers buy at least five times as heavily as they designed when starting away from home. He will convince the oldest buyers, by evidence which is wholly overwhelming, of their utter ignorance of the first rudiments of their own business, although they may have been pretty successful in it for more than thirty years; and he will satisfy the youngest and most inexperienced that *they* are perfectly "posted up," and that they will ere long wholly " use up" their competitors, and whip them clean out of sight: all of which the buyers unhesitatingly believe, although they are somewhat staggered in the end at the enormous bills which Thirteen adroitly led them to insensibly run up, while he was duly impressing them with a "realizing consciousness" of these flattering facts. Indeed, so firmly established is Thirteen's reputation in this respect, it is a common saying in the trade, that "when a dealer passes through *his* hands, he comes out like a squeezed lemon."

Thirteen's present victim is a "very knowing" gentleman from Michigan, who innocently flatters himself it "will take a smart fellow indeed to come it over *him*. He understands himself, *he* does. He aint bin in trade twenty years, right in the face of the tearingest opposition a merchant ever had, for nothing. No, *indeed!* He has bought cloth, he has bought dry goods, and what is more, he allers knew how to get rid of all he bought. Now, although it don't invariably foller that because a man knows how to sell, he knows equally as well how to buy, he kinder reckons *he* does know a little of both. So it's no use in anybody's trying to come city dodges over *him*, because he knows all about 'em. He's bought in New York afore—*he* has; thinks his face is known to a *few* of the houses there, and that many of the biggest on 'em would be mighty glad to get his name on their books and his note in their hand for a few thousands. But he is keerful—*he* is; and when anybody gets *his* note, he is allers a *leetle* curis to know what it's for. As to putting old shop-worn goods on to him, they can't do it, and they might as well know it first as last. As for decoying him into the purchase of goods that he don't want, *that* can't be did, nuther, and they might as well know *it*, too. And then as for stickin' him on big bills, when he only intends to make small uns—let 'em try it, that's all! When he comes to New York, he comes there to buy, like an honest merchint, and he don't mean to be chiselled. If any of the fellers there are smart enough to *lay him out*, let them try it on; he's willin'!"

To all of which Thirteen smilingly accedes, and after two hours of mingled flattery, insinuating smiles, and masterly management, Michigan *is* "laid out," with all the honors; Thirteen deeming it a point of honor to "chisel" him to the fullest extent and in the most scientific manner: with a magnificent array of old shop-worn goods, a moderate proportion of articles really fresh, and all at prices which would fill a tyro with amaze—the whole terminating in a bill which shook poor Michigan for the next six months with all the agony of pecuniary terror.

Samuel, however, was too ignorant of the business details of a New York dry goods jobbing-house to comprehend more of the picture before him than appeared upon its surface. All he saw was what his eye took in, and that told him simply of a vast store, a vast stock, a vast body of clerks, a vast business, and vast wealth: all of which impressed him with a certain sense of awe, which he found it difficult, for a few moments, to subdue. He *did* subdue it, however, and then calmly bent his way to the nearest clerk.

"Is Mr. Townsend in?" he inquired.

"Yes, sir. Walk this way," was the polite reply.

Samuel followed his conductor, who was some years younger than himself, through a long line of sinuous passages, towards the rear, where three steps led to a platform, on which were three small but spacious offices, whose glazed fronts commanded a view of the entire floor. The office on the right, as a showy sign near its door indicated, was that of the book-keeper and his assistants, who could distinctly be seen through the panes; the one in the centre—the largest of the three—as the lettering on its door made evident, was the private sanctum of the head of the establishment himself; the third, on the left, which had no sign at all, was the office of a personage of no little importance, either in his own eyes, or those of the establishment, viz.: Mr. Edward Brigham, the confidential clerk.

His young guide opened the door of the central office, and pointing to a gentleman who was sitting before a showy but massive walnut desk, leisurely running his eye over a morning paper, Samuel found himself in the presence of his future employer.

Mr. Townsend was a tall, portly man, with a fine Grecian head, which was covered with a superb shock of coarse but snow-white hair. He had a blue, pleasant eye, and a pleasant, well-cut lip: both of which told, however, of a calm, resolute will, and a happy temper, which could not be very easily disturbed.

The merchant received his visitor with a genial urbanity, which speedily set the latter at his ease; and ere twenty minutes had flown, the latter was as much at home in his presence as if he had known him for twenty years.

It was to his indomitable resolution, which smiled even at impossibilities—to his constant good-nature, which made him a general favorite, and to his happy talent for placing himself and all around him on a genial footing—a rare faculty, and one which few men know the value of, or it would be more extensively cultivated—that the merchant owed a large share of his prosperity. To these, however, must be added a somewhat elastic conscience, which enabled its owner to "lie upon occasion," *in a business way*, without remorse, and to do as all other people did who were *not* above making money, and *were* above letting the world know to what small meannesses they were capable of descending for the purpose of obtaining it. Still Mr. Townsend, as the world goes, was by no means a bad man. He could lie when it served his pecuniary interest to do so, but then he flattered himself that, as a business man, he was not alone in that little weakness, "and besides, *who knew it*, and what was more, *who wouldn't?*" He paid his employees liberally, because he was sagacious enough to discover that *that* was the truest business policy. "It brings the best talent in the market to your hands," muttered the crafty worldling, "and the best talent brings in the most business, and the most business brings in the most money!" He had a name for liberality in his church, and that name brought him numerous customers; he had also, in his church, a name for fervent piety: "And that," mused the cunning merchant, "is a paying thing, too—for piety implies honesty, honesty begets confidence, confidence brings business, and business brings money!" He had a name also for frankness: "Frankness," thought the wily merchant, "helps one wonderfully as a name. It begets frankness in others, and *that* sometimes helps a man, who has means in his pocket, to golden opportunities. Besides, it preserves one from a suspicion of depth. To say of a man 'He is deep,' is to say 'Look out for him!' and *that* is ruin. Men have an instinctive dread of 'deep' persons—they smell theft, heartlessness, and treachery in them. But frankness inspires confidence, and with it, for a name, one can *be* deep without being suspected; and then he can *play* deep, and that brings money!" Still, *as the world goes*, Mr. Townsend was by no means a bad man. He always kept his word—because it paid; was punctual in all his engagements—because it paid; liberal—because it paid; good-natured—because it paid; frank—because it paid; and what the world calls 'pious'—for the same weighty reason. And yet, Mr. Townsend had his good traits, as well. He was occasionally generous from impulse, and what he agreed to do in such moments, he always honestly fulfilled—so far as the world knew! Thus he had promised, some years before, having no children of his own, to take care of two orphan nieces, both of whom had been left with property; a promise which he honestly fulfilled, as all the world knew—but as all the world did *not* know, he was handsomely rewarded for his benevolence, by leasing their properties at certain fixed rates, and then renting them out on his own account, realizing about one hundred and twenty-five per cent. by the operation. This fact, however, was known only to himself, and as he never presented the young ladies with bills for their board, they, in common with all the world, regarded "guardy" as a "dear good soul, whose great heart would be the ruin of him some day!"

The simple inhabitants of Enfield innocently believed the reports which reached them from time to time from the city, that of all their number who had left their native village for the metropolis, Mr. Townsend alone was the rare exception, who, amid all the temptations of commerce, preserved intact the piety of his youth and the great moral trust reposed in him by his Maker!

"Well, Samuel," said this "good man," in his mild, pleasant way, "let us come to an understanding. My dear friend, your father writes me that you desire to learn the dry goods business, with the view of entering it, at a future day, on your own account. Well, that presupposes a clerkship; and that in our establishment?"

Samuel bowed.

"Very good," continued the merchant, genially. "Now, then, for the consideration. In our business, the salaries of clerks are graduated by the sales which they effect; or, more properly speaking, by the amount of business which they influence. For instance, if you should influence sales to the amount of thirty thousand dollars, you would be worth from eight hundred to a thousand dollars a year. That is the average trade influence of what we call our clever clerks. Others run higher, and their earnings are in proportion. Some, but their number is few, influence business to the amount of one hundred and one hundred and fifty thousand dollars. These are worth from three to three thousand five hundred dollars per year. Rather princely for a mere clerk—eh, Samuel!"

"Very, indeed, sir! Have you many of that description in your establishment?"

Two only—which is just one more than most houses can boast of. One of them is Mr. Brigham, our confidential clerk, and the other a Mr. Stubbs. The first earns from thirty-five hundred to four thousand dollars a year; the second from three thousand to three thousand five hundred, although we have known him, in one or two instances, to run up as high as thirty-seven hundred and fifty. That is the gentleman out there," and he pointed to thirteen, whose features were illumined by a peculiar smile, which his fellow-clerks understood very well to mean that he was "doing his man up brown."

"He looks cheerful!" observed Samuel.

"Yes," returned the merchant, "he is 'getting on' with his customer. A man of talent, Samuel, and understands himself. He will be a merchant yet! You would do well to court his acquaintance, Samuel. He can teach you more of the business in an hour than you could pick up yourself in three years!"

"Indeed, sir? I thank you for the kind suggestion!"

"You are welcome. But to return. It is usual in our business to put new-comers into certain departments: for instance, to give to one the charge of the ginghams, to another the prints, to another the merinoes, to a fourth the bleached muslins, to a fifth the cottons, to a sixth the flannels, to a seventh the cloths and cassimeres,—and so on; changing them from time to time from one department to another, till they become perfectly familiar with the character, qualities, and prices of each and all. This takes from one to two years, during which time we allow them from fifty to a hundred dollars per annum. When they have become posted up in all the details of the business, we then send them off on short drumming tours—sometimes South, sometimes West—to see what they're made of. If they are successful in drumming up customers and influencing business, we then raise their salaries, graduating them, of course, by the amount of business which they influence. In your case, however, being a friend, we shall deviate slightly from the regular course. We will put you, for instance, in the gingham department, and let you remain there till you become familiar with its details, when you can change off to another, and from that to another, until you obtain a complete general knowledge of the business, and then you may stay altogether in the store and attend to the chance customers."

Samuel expressed his acknowledgments for this favor, and the merchant continued—

"For this we will allow you, for the first year, three hundred dollars; your salary for the second will depend considerably upon yourself. If you are smart, and study the interest of the house, we may find it advantageous to raise it to six or seven hundred. Is this satisfactory?"

"Perfectly, sir!" answered Samuel.

"Very good. Then you can enter upon your duties when you please. Let us see. This is Wednesday—half of the week. The other half you might as well employ in becoming acquainted with the city, and brushing the effect of its novelty from your mind. On Monday morning you can commence fresh and lively, and with your wits about you. You will want them all," added the merchant, laughingly, "in the dry goods business!"

"I suppose so, sir!"

"You will be *sure* of it, ere you get to the top of the ladder!" rejoined the merchant, with genial significance. "And now to another matter. Your father desires me, in his letter, to give you, if possible, a home in my own house, where you will enjoy the benefit of the pure society to which you have been accustomed. This is a very natural request on the part of my worthy friend the pastor, but I hardly know what to say. It is so uncommon for a merchant to take his clerks under his own roof, that I must think—yes, I must think the matter over a few minutes! Let me see—let me see!"

And the merchant's pleasant eyes dropped thoughtfully upon his desk.

Samuel was under the impression that this was already decided upon, and a promise given by Mr. Townsend to his "dear friend," the pastor, to that effect; but, as the merchant had apparently forgotten it, our hero, with his usual diffidence, did not deem it either just or delicate to remind him of the fact.

"If I take this young man to my house," mused the "honest" merchant, "I shall make—what? Let me see. There are four of us, and I am the only man. The ladies want society, and this young fellow is young enough, handsome enough, and intelligent enough, to meet that want, and give it zest. The girls, too, need an occasional jaunting companion, and Samuel will meet that want, which will be a great relief all around—and particularly to myself, since he will fill the post, which has been too long expected of 'guardy,' who can then be a little more of his own master. Then, too, the young dog is handsome enough to give some uneasiness to Brigham, who fancies himself perfectly secure in the affections of my eldest niece, and rides of late altogether too high a horse in consequence. He thinks that with her fortune and his own savings, he could make an effort on his own account, and give the house of John P. Townsend a stout tug, posted up as he is in all the details of its business and the qualities of its customers. He *might* prove a troublesome competitor, and, should he wander to any other house, an annoying enemy. To bring him down a peg or two, would do him no harm; while the dread of a rival would lead him quietly to a more proper appreciation of his p's and q's: an important object, since he feels his oats a little too proudly. Thus will this young simpleton pay me handsomely for the pure society which he will find under my roof! There are rooms enough to spare, and his food would be of but little account. It would not do, of course, to charge him anything—it would *sound* bad; while to *give* it to him would sound well. The amount would be too insignificant to make a figure of; while the act itself would be talked of greatly: and that, in the end, would *pay*. I have not to learn, at this late day, that every dollar given, with an *appearance* of liberality, returns four-fold to the giver. Yes, I see—I see. It will pay, in more ways than one, to take this young simpleton home."

Having reached the end of his soliloquy, the merchant flung his pleasant glance upon the young man, and said—

"I have been thinking, Samuel, how we could make room for you, and at length see my way. It appeared rather dubious at first; but one must stretch a point for a friend. Besides, the old village is dear to me, and by having one of its sons near me, when business cares are over, I shall, as it were, be in beloved Enfield again. Ah! the bright memories of youth, how we cherish them in our age! With you at our board, I shall be happy; youth will return, with all the richness of its glittering visions; boyhood will come again, like the fond dream of a long and joyous holiday; the village green, the emerald fields, the verdant hills, the old school beneath the church, and the old church itself, which our sires built long years before, and from whose pulpit our venerable pastor—your grandfather, Samuel!—used to point our little hearts to heaven—these will all return, to rejuvenate this old frame and fill it with childhood's laughing joys. Yes, for old Enfield's sake, your dear father's, and your own, my friend, we will break through custom, and enjoy the same fireside!"

Samuel was touched, to the verge of tears, at this kindness; and he looked the gratitude which he felt, but could not speak.

"As to recompense," pursued the crafty merchant, "we'll say nothing. Study the interest of the house, and that will be enough. I will send a messenger up with a note to Mrs. Townsend to prepare her for your coming, and you can remove your trunks up and take possession of your room any time after two o'clock."

Samuel bowed. His simple heart was full. He could not speak.

"You will find your mate in the gingham department," continued the merchant, whose keen eye divined the nature of the young man before him, " a fellow after your own heart. He is clever, generous, frank and honest; a little given to impulse, but full of talent. His name is Gibbs—Charles Gibbs. He is out at present, I see," he added, glancing through the glazed partition, " or I would call him and introduce you. It will be all the same, however, for I will speak to him on his return, and let him know that you are coming."

"Thank you, sir—thank you!" cried Samuel.

" You can draw your salary every week," continued the merchant, " and thus keep yourself in spending money. By the way," he added, suddenly taking out his pocket-book, with a generous air, " how are you off for your immediate wants? Be frank!"

"I am amply supplied, sir—many, many thanks!"

"I knew that, or I had not asked him!" muttered the merchant to himself as he quietly returned the wallet to his pocket. "Ah!" he said, aloud, " in that case, all is well. But if anything should turn up in future, remember that we are both sons of old Enfield, and command me without reserve! And now, my friend, shake hands. I'll see you at dinner—if not, then at supper!"

Samuel withdrew, and returned to his hotel, with feelings which we shall not attempt to describe.

CHAPTER VI.

Everything moved smoothly with our hero. He was received by Mrs. Townsend and her two nieces with much cordiality, and his time passed away pleasantly. On Monday morning, he made his appearance in the "gingham department," which consisted of six little low tables, heaped with all sorts of patterns two and three feet deep, with occasional spaces to indicate "lots just sold" to somebody whose name and local habitation were matters of deep commercial mystery.

The clerks stared furtively at the handsome new-comer, and whispered together very knowingly, very grinningly, and very mysteriously; and cracked sundry jokes at his expense, all of which were doubtless very full indeed of rich, mirthful meaning, as each invariably elicited a smothered roar, in which it would be difficult to say which predominated, the snicker, the giggle, or the broad guffaw.

One—a young gentleman of twenty, with a very flashy vest, a very flashy coat, very flashy trowsers, very small patent leather boots, a very high collar, which threatened every instant to cut off his very large ears—considerately inquired of the new-comer whether the fields were well cultivated up his way, and if so, whether the cabbages grew very big? A second, equally as witty as the first, curiously inquired whether there were many in his family, and if so, whether their phrenological developments were as well developed as his. A third wanted to know how many hundred thousands of dollars he expected to sell in the course of the coming week, and whether he had any idea of the price of putty? A fourth had a desire to learn how ginghams were—whether up or down, out or in? A fifth wondered whether the circus had ever passed through his village, and if so, whether he had seen the elephant? A sixth asked him, with a serious air, when he designed to drive that fast team out on the avenue? A seventh thought it would be cruel in him to show his handsome face on Broadway, because it might have the effect of breaking up ever so many matches which were now looked upon as regularly settled, as well as tempt a great many women to snatch him up and run off with him. An eighth hoped he would never set the North River on fire, as he—Eighth—had on the Jersey side a whole lot of property, which, not being insured, he wouldn't like to see burnt up. A ninth suggested that in case he should conclude, on the strength of his first year's salary, to run the old house a stiff opposition, he—Ninth—would like a situation at a moderate salary, say of three thousand a year. A tenth hoped he *wouldn't* start an opposition to the old house, because in that case, he—Tenth—would soon be out of a situation. An eleventh had an idea that he wasn't long for this world, and wanted to know if Second Gingham—Gibbs being First Gingham—wouldn't give him some spiritual consolation, as he thought it might help him some in going off. A twelfth hoped that, in case he should sell out all his ginghams before the week was over, that he would come and give him a lift in the de laines, as they wanted to be sold mighty bad, because they disliked very much to remain any longer in the vicinity of a stick. A thirteenth had an idea that flats had an advantage over common people, because, when they had made their piles, they always had a big house to retire to—viz.—the lunatic asylum.

And yet these witty young gentlemen were charitably supposed by their friends to possess an average share of intelligence and self-respect, and to thoroughly understand the laws of good breeding!

There were two exceptions, however, who considerately refrained from joining in the hue-and-cry against "Second Gingham"—viz. First Gingham, and Bill Bradley, the packer.

Charley Gibbs—First Gingham—was a young fellow of twenty-three: moderately good-looking, a little dressy, somewhat simple, thoroughly honest, slightly observant, rather generous, exceedingly impulsive, and running over with ideas, which, if not very brilliant, very deep, or very original, were invariably very harmless. He had three passions: first, "to make old guardy disgorge that money;" secondly, "a silent interest in some big house which would give him a cozy living without requiring his services;" and thirdly, "a cozy cottage, with his dear little Fan, who, poor thing! was dying herself to death for him, all the time."

Bill Bradley, the packer, was a tall, gaunt fellow, of about twenty-five. He had the build and pluck of a gladiator, and "didn't turn his back to *no* man in packin'. He ran with 'forty-four,' and allers stood up for his number. When there's work to do, he's 'around,' *he* is; when the hall bell rings, he's on hand to roll the machine and put the first stream on the fire. He aint much in the schoolin' line, 'cause he had to go to work in them days; but he understands the four rules for all that, and can cipher 'em up with any man. To learnin' generally he don't make the first claim; but he knows what's right, and he aint afraid to do it. He's down on lyin', cheatin', and bullyin'; and any man that's mean enough to do either he can lick. He don't owe no man the fust red; and if any man's got a claim agin him, let him step for'ard with his bill. He allers does his duty, 'cause its his natur, and he'll thank anybody to point out to him wherein he fails to do it. He's down on everybody who's mean enough to take advantage of another's weakness or ignorance, and what's more, he can take their hides off. He only gets fifteen dollars a week, but he reckons he can live on that, and keep square with the world, too. Does he save money? No, sir-ee! He j'es don't. How in reason can he, and pay all the bills as they come along? Tell him that, will you! How many cases of goods can he pack in a day? Fifty, sir—and strap 'em all over, too. If you've got any packers down your way, who *think* they are 'some' in that line, send 'em along, and he'll give 'em a few lessons that'll make up modest! What does he do with his fifteen dollars? Do you want to know very pertickler? He puts it in his pocket! Who was that old lady that Tom Bates saw him taking to church last Sunday night? That's the blessedest old creeter of her age in the country, sir—yes, sir, in the country. She's a dear old soul, and likes to go to meetin', 'cause it makes her happy. She aint got her ekewil for goodness, bless her dear old heart! in the world—no, sir, not in the world! Do I allers go to church with her? Yes, sir; and glad to do it. too! Why, sir, that dear old lady brought me up, from the time when I was a little toddler not half so high as that case; and why shouldn't I be glad to take her to meetin' so long as it makes her happy? Is she my mother? No, sir, not by natur. We adopted each other when I was one-and-twenty, and so it's all the same, sir. Have I got any father? No, sir; he died when I was a little babee, sir—he was a fireman and a widderer, and got killed one night at a fire. He used to board with the old lady, and when he got killed the old lady took me under her own protection. A noble act? Yes, sir-ee! It wasn't nothin' shorter. She was a poor woman; and two years after, she got burnt out, and that made her poorer still. She then took in washin', and brought me up like a gen'leman till I was ten years old, when she got the pallysis—paralysis—in her left shoulder, and then I went to work to help both ends along. Four years after that, the poor soul was taken down to the hip, and then I had a chance of showin' her what I could do in return for all her kindness. From that day to this, we have got along first rate. The old soul is a good manager—very economical, and the way she can make her one hand fly through a new pair of pants, or a new fire shirt, which she makes up for me very often, sir, would put life into a whole hospital! Cant't anything be done for the old lady's pallysis? Well, we've been tryin' everything for more'n ten years; but they haven't done much for the old soul yet. But there's no knowin'—some'n *may* turn up. There's an ingeneis feller—a watch-spring maker—up our way, who's makin' a merchine which he thinks 'll cure it. But he aint got it done yet; says he will, though, one of these days, and then we'll give it a trial. How long has he been at it? About three years. He's goin' to get a patent out, when it's done, and if it's the thing he says it is, it'll make his fortune. Does the old lady suffer much? Guess you'd think so, sometimes. But the dear old soul says she's so accustomed to it, she don't mind it: but that's all put on, you know, j'es to keep me from grievin'! What do I think of religion? I think it's a good thing, 'cause it makes my old lady happy: anything that'll do that, in a sufferin' case like hern, must be good. Least ways, I think so, and I'll stand up for it, no matter who's agin it. I aint much of a religionist myself, but I respect it, 'cause I've seen the blessedness of its fruits. One of these days, pr'aps, I'll go in for it, the whole figur; in the meantime, I'll respect it, 'cause there's no tellin' when the hall bell may ring a poor fellow's last turn-out!"

Neither Charley Gibbs nor Bill Bradley countenanced the pop-gun volleys which were discharged so mercilessly at the new-comer; while the latter put an effectual stop to it, in his department, at least, by giving his assistants notice that if they "didn't know no better than to guy a fellow because he was a little green, *he'd* take 'em in hand and learn 'em beans, in short order. They were green themselves—yes, softer than mush—once; and they oughter remember it. If they didn't, he had some'n would bring it back to 'em—some'n he could *use!*"

As his listeners understood very well that Bill Bradley never talked this way only when he was in earnest, and as they had a wholesome respect for the "some'n" to which he so impressively alluded, they were careful thenceforth how they spoke of Second Gingham in his hearing.

Up stairs, however, there being no Bill Bradley to put a stop to it, poor Samuel endured for a time all the humiliating mortifications which little minds know so well how to inflict upon new-comers, especially when the latter are from rural districts whose inhabitants are comparatively ignorant of life and the world. There are bounds, however, to manly patience; there are limits when human fortitude yields to human infirmity; there is a point when the "old Adam" of every heart bids its owner to stand up manfully and strike a brave blow for the dignity of poor human nature. That hour came around at length to our hero.

He had been in his new situation about six weeks, during all of which time he had patiently submitted to the gibes and sneers of his fellow-clerks, all of whom, with the exception of Charley Gibbs and Bill Bradley, as we have already mentioned, vied with each other in the number, variety, and coarseness of their jokes upon Rural Piety, as Thirteen had facetiously styled the new-comer.

Samuel bore with them all good-naturedly, innocently supposing that the witlings would get tired of their sport by-and-bye, and relinquish it of their own accord. He was averse, both from principle and education, to checking it by physical force; and yet he had fears that he would eventually be driven to that course: still he hoped not, and he endeavored, by refraining from replying to their attacks, to escape the humiliation of a quarrel, which might eventuate in an exchange of blows.

But his hopes were destined to disappointment. The gibes, and sneers, and jokes, and tricks continued with undiminished vigor. Nay, finding no resistance on the part of their victim, whose simple, truthful nature became day by day more and more developed, the witlings concluded to "rake him," as First De Laine expressed it, without mercy.

Ever an early riser, Samuel was generally the first at his post. His seventh Monday came around. On reaching the store at his usual hour, he was somewhat surprised to find his fellow-clerks assembled in full force. They received him with a politeness which was as grateful as it was novel, since it appeared to imply that they had, either from remorse or some other cause, concluded to give over their attacks, and allow him to attend to his affairs in peace. He remembered, too, that on the preceding Saturday they had annoyed him less than usual; that, in fact, the storm had settled down into a comparatively quiet calm; and he innocently flattered himself that their hearts had at length suggested to them the wrongfulness of their course.

Samuel's dream of peace, however, was destined to be speedily and rudely swept away. A new mortification was in store for him. While on his way through the narrow passage leading to his own department, his elbow struck against a protruding "piece" forming one of a pile of de laines, which had been previously so arranged that the slightest touch would precipitate the whole to the floor. Samuel saw through the trick in an instant. His cheek flushed indignantly; but restraining his feelings from an outburst, he meekly and sorrowfully picked up the fallen pieces, placed them in a neat, compact heap, and then, with a sigh, passed on to his post.

The clerks looked at one another with a knowing smirk, which seemed to say—"Won't there be fun by-and-bye? Oh, no!"

A half hour passed by, during which time the clerks, forming themselves into little knots of twos and threes, conversed in low tones, throwing their eyes every now and then in the direction of Rural Piety, who was leaning against one of his tables in an attitude of deep thought. It was evident from their manner that they were enjoying something which their active imaginations told them was overflowing with rare richness.

While the innocent young witlings were amusing themselves thus, another of their number—First De Laine himself—entered the store.

"Hurrah, boys—here he is!" cried Second Broadcloth to his companions. "Now for fun!"

"Take care, Tom," said another, "don't get mad now. Rural Piety couldn't help it!"

"Couldn't help what?" demanded First De Laine, with affected astonishment.

"Oh, nothing," was the reply.

"You're a fifer!" observed First De Laine, contemptuously as he passed on to his department.

The clerks laughed, and looked towards Samuel with an air which said—

"Won't you catch it, now? Oh, no! Of course not!"

First De Laine was a showy fellow of about twenty-three, and was made up in the tawdry style of the "fast" youth of the metropolis, who make up in show for what they lack in principle. First De Laine was regarded as a fine salesman, and could spin out a good round lie, in all its delicate details, with a dexterity truly marvellous. His earnings were large enough to enable him to "drive a 'fast' horse," but too small to allow him to pay his landlady, and hence he was continually changing his boarding-house, and "doing" credulous washwomen. First De Laine was familiar with billiard-rooms, theatres, and sparring-cribs, and was regarded by his fellow-clerks as high authority in everything pertaining to sporting matters, whisky punches, and fancy things generally. He was a regular attendant at boxing exhibitions, and considered himself as 'some' in that line himself. Finally, First De Laine had a reputation among his fellows of being a "high boy," and "considerable of a bruiser."

This individual, on reaching his department, discovered that some one had been "mixing up his patterns," and with a loud oath demanded who had been near his tables, accompanying the inquiry with a look which implied that he would do something very terrible indeed to the offender.

On hearing the inquiry, Samuel at once replied—

"I think, sir, I am the unfortunate party. While—"

"You?" thundered the other, interrupting him with a fierce scowl, which was of course entirely assumed, "you, you double-headed squash!—you, was it? If you take such a liberty again, I'll mash your soft pate into buttermilk!"

"I had no intention, sir," returned Samuel, coloring to his temples, "of—"

At this instant his voice was drowned amid a loud, simultaneous roar, in which "Go it, Tom," "Pitch in to the country lout," "Let him have it," "Show him beans, Tom," "Drop the smooth-faced hypocrite," "Give him a sweetener in the gills," mingled with deafening hoots, and yells, and cat-calls, went up from all parts of the store.

The simultaneousness of the tumult took our hero somewhat by surprise. He saw in an instant that the calm of Saturday was a mere blind, that the incident of the falling of the de laines was a planned thing, that the anger of First De Laine himself was altogether put on, and that his fellow-clerks had no disposition to let him up. The coarse language, too, of the "fast" young man was in itself of so provoking a character, that it is no wonder if he to whom it was addressed felt for a few moments that there are seasons when the gentleness of the Christian can only be sustained by the firmness of the man.

"Sir," he said, grasping the fast gentleman firmly by the collar, and looking him boldly in the eye, "you owe it to yourself and to me to take back every word that you have uttered. Do you hear me, sir—every word!"

"Take your hand from off my collar, fool!" cried the fast gentleman, rolling up his cuffs like one who intended to make an example of somebody, "take your hand from off my collar, or I'll drop you!"

Samuel's grasp tightened; his eye was slowly kindling, and an expression of resentment was gathering around his firm lips. An indignant glow suffused his countenance from the chin to the temples.

"You have forced me to this, sir," he said, "and you shall abide the consequences. Come, sir," he added, dragging the struggling fast gentleman down the passage towards the large space between the counters and the doors leading to the street, "your desire shall be gratified. Come, sir—come with me to a spot where we can turn around!"

"Let me go! Take off your hand, or I'll mash you into mince-meat!" cried First De Laine, struggling, but vainly, to release himself. "Let me go, I tell you!"

"Come, sir—come!" said the aroused Samuel, firmly, and dragging him along as if he were a mere infant.

"Let me go, will you? Let me go, I say!" continued the fast young man, striking at him blindly, but without making any more impression upon his nerve-strung opponent than if his blows had been turned against a rock. "Let me go!"

"Come, sir—come!"

"Let me go, will you? Let me go, I say!"

They had now reached the end of the passage, and were, so to speak, in an open field.

Samuel instantly grasped the fast gentleman by the shoulder, and looking at him sternly, said—

"Now, sir, one word before we proceed further. You have made use of language which may be natural to men of your stamp, but it is not of a kind to which I am accustomed, or to which I will submit. Take it back, sir—take it back—every word, or I will treat you as I would a mad dog!"

"I'll see you—"

Before he could complete the sentence, before he could lift a finger, Samuel caught him by the body—between the breast and the hips—lifted him up as if he were a feather, shook him like a quivering aspen, and then set him down, pale, helpless, and exhausted, upon the floor.

"There, sir! sit there, till you are favored with manlier thoughts and a cleaner tongue!"

With these words, he turned from the spot, and, with a calm, dignified step, retraced his way back to his department.

Bill Bradley, who had been a silent spectator of the scene, now approached First De Laine, whose head was bowed upon his breast with an air of abject humiliation, and looked down upon him for a few moments as upon something equally amusing and offensive.

Then bending his tall form, he caught the defeated individual by the collar, and raised him to his feet, saying—

"Well, ole boy, you *are* a pretty one, aint you, now? Ah! go 'long—you make me sick! Come, propel!"

And to expedite the worthy fast youth's progress, he favored him with a gentle tap behind, as a father might spank an unruly child, and then turned from him in contempt.

First De Laine glared at him for an instant, as if he meant to resent the indignity; but a single glance at the manly proportions of the packer brought him to another conclusion, and he returned to his tables, his cheek white with mingled shame, bitterness, and rage.

The effect of Samuel's conduct in the affair was electrical. From the moment when he first laid his firm hand upon the collar of the fast young gentleman to that when he had closed his account with that individual, his fellow-clerks—who beheld his resistance with as much interest as surprise—preserved, as if with common consent, a deep silence, for the double purpose of catching and enjoying every word of the combatants, as well as of witnessing their movements without interruption. The result of the contest was so different from that which had been looked for—they having regarded Samuel as a "milk-and-water genius," and First De Laine as a "sporting gent," and therefore a "dangerous customer"—that their sympathies turned with the change; and as the victor returned to his ginghams, they testified their admiration of his course, or rather of his spirit, by three hearty, generous cheers.

Not content with this, they crowded around him with their congratulations, and vied with each other for the pleasure of taking him by the hand. "Bravo, Greeny"—cried one, "you are a trump, after all!" "Give us your hand, old boy," said another, "I like your pluck." "Good, Gingham," said a third, "you've got the right stuff in you—*you* have, and blame my buttons, if you didn't serve him just about right." "Hurrah!" exclaimed a fourth, "tip us your maulers—you are one of 'em, and no mistake. If you didn't give it to him pooty, I wouldn't say so." "Hey, Gingham," joined in a fifth, "you're the boy for my money. I'll bet high on you. You're game up to the hub. Lay it there, ole feller!" he added, as he extended his open palm to the victor.

Samuel submitted passively to their felicitations; and as they returned to their respective departments, he bowed his head in thought.

"You appear disturbed," remarked a voice near him.

Samuel looked up, and beheld the mild, pleasant face of Charley Gibbs.

"I feel ashamed of myself," returned Samuel. "I have done

that for which I should weep: I have disobeyed the Divine injunction: 'When ye are reviled, revile not again.'"

"O come, come, Samuel, don't give way to that notion. It won t do in this every-day world."

"For what world *will* it do?"

"For heaven, I suppose," said Charley Gibbs, who was rather taken aback at the question.

"For heaven? There are no revilers there."

"I presume," said Charley Gibbs, "it is meant for us, but I don't see how a man can carry it out, unless he is willing to be kicked from world's end to world's end. I know one thing, however, and that is, very few attempt to comply with it."

"That should not govern me, Charley."

"Very true. But in that case, men will say you have no spirit—and they will treat you with contempt."

"I have no desire to be regarded as a person of spirit."

"I know that, Samuel; but you mustn't be too mild, either. It won't do. Men, who are naturally bullies, will take advantage of it, and serve you like a dog, just to show their own spirit. My parents brought me up just so, too; but when I mingled with the world, I soon found that it wouldn't answer. Now, just look at your own case. So long as the clerks thought you a non-resistant—one who would patiently endure everything, they put it to you strong; but the moment they find you will resist, then they fawn upon you, and tell you you are a good fellow. That is the world, Samuel. It don't relish meekness, because it savors of goodness; but it *does* relish pluck, because it savors of its own brutal nature. And this gives me an idea."

"Ah?"

"Yes. If you want to be respected, you must get into an occasional fight, to let the world know you are a man of spirit;

then you will be admired: otherwise it will regard you as a spooney, and treat you accordingly."

"But I do not wish to be thought a man of spirit."

"That makes no difference at all," said Charley Gibbs. "Even in a career of gentleness, you cannot succeed without a previous reputation for pluck. For instance: Two men of equal piety set out in doing good. The one is uniformly meek, gentle, and dove-like, and we'll say, timorous as well. He goes among his friends and makes an earnest effort to relieve their temporal wants, and to lead them spiritually aright. They listen to his counsels, they partake of his benevolence, but they pay no heed to either. Why? Because they know him to be a weakling! Let him go out among strangers, where his lack of physical courage is unknown, and moral force will follow his benevolence and his preaching *until* his timidity is discovered. Then his influence vanishes like magic; the moral force which accompanied his labors dies out, and the man himself is a nullity from that hour. Why? Because there is, in the minds of men, no moral force in timidity. The other goes on a similar errand; and there is a double power, a doubly moral force in his benevolence and in his pious teachings. When he puts on the garments of meekness, the effect is deep, stirring, and wholesome. Why? Because the man himself is bold, brave, intrepid, and—they know it. He is meek from principle, not necessity, and they respect both the man and the principle. 'He *could* be brave,' they say to themselves, 'but voluntarily is meek.' *That* settles them; and admiration of the man leads them to an honest admiration of his principle. *That* is why he is successful. The *man* first, the *principle* afterwards!"

"The Bible teaches no such doctrine as that."

"No. It is the doctrine of human nature. I discovered it some time ago," said Charley Gibbs, "and it suggested to me an idea."

"Indeed!"

"Yes. You see I am myself naturally of a timid, retiring nature. I detest violence, and have no sympathy with brutality. I like to see everything harmonious, and everybody gentle. The sight of two men quarrelling or hitting each other makes me nervous, and I feel like running away, lest I should myself get mixed up in it, and somebody should hit me. This constitutional weakness came to the knowledge of my guardian, who imputed it to cowardice, and he flattered himself he could easily do me out of my property, as I would be too timid to fight for my rights. This reached my ears, and it gave me an idea."

"Ah! You appear to have a great many ideas, Charley!"

"I think," said Charley Gibbs modestly, "I can flatter myself a little in that way. You see, Samuel," he continued, with an air of innocent simplicity, which would have elicited a smile from any other than the ingenuous mind before him, "I have been favored with large intellectual faculties. The phrenologists tell me they are a great deal larger than common. My ideality, for instance, is higher than seven."

"Indeed?"

"Yes. And that accounts for the rapid flow of my ideas. I write poems occasionally for the newspapers and magazines; and every line has an idea."

"And do they accept them?" asked Samuel, innocently.

"Oh—yes, in some instances."

"And publish them?"

Charley Gibbs hesitated. He didn't like the question. He looked Samuel steadily in the eye, as if he suspected some hidden meaning, or some satirical thought. But he was soon satisfied that his interlocutor had put the interrogatory in perfect simplicity and good faith, and he said, not, however, without a slight blush—

"I cannot say that they *have* published any of them yet; but they evidently mean to, or they would return them. They are keeping them, I presume, in reserve, to be used at the first opportunity. You see editors are perfectly flooded, every day, with communications from all parts of the continent, and it is impossible to get them all in at once. Every accepted article is placed on file, and has to wait its turn for insertion, so the editors tell me: and that is the reason why none of mine have yet appeared. But I have copies of them at home, and I'll lend you a manuscript volume of them with pleasure."

"I shall be most happy to read them," said Samuel, naively.

"Thank you. I'll bring the volume to you to-night," said the delighted Charley, who now felt sure of at least one reader.

"It will be too much trouble—"

"Oh, no—no trouble at all," said Charley Gibbs. "I'll take advantage of the opportunity to spend the evening with you."

Samuel was very grateful, and told him so.

Charley Gibbs bowed, and then Samuel wanted to know what his idea was.

"I'll tell you," said Charley. "The moment I learned guardy's notion, I concluded to show him that he was laboring under a mistake in regard to his man. So I went to a boxing-master, who gave me some lessons, and then I picked a quarrel with the old fellow's son, who deserved a thrashing for trying to cut me out with a certain young lady who is devoted to me, and to whom I am engaged, and I gave him the finest flogging he ever had in his life. The fellow told his father, of course—I knew he would—and it rather startled the old gentleman's calculations. He found I could fight when occasion called for it, and it made him a little more civil."

"Did he give up the property?" asked Samuel, with his usual simplicity.

"No; but it made him respectful towards me, and that was something. Finding that it worked so well, I made it a point for a year or two afterwards, to get up a quarrel with his son every time I met him; and as I invariably flogged him, and as it invariably reached the old gentleman's ears, the consequences were as happy as could be expected."

"The old gentleman relinquished you the property?"

"*No;* but it made him excessively respectful, whenever I called upon him for money, which he forked over without grumbling: a thing he never did before."

"What kind of a man is he?"

"Crafty as a lynx, and avaricious as a Jew. But I'll make him disgorge the whole of it yet, keen as he is; and then I mean to marry my Fan, who, dear little thing, is crying herself to death for me all the time, and buy a silent interest in some big dry goods house, which will allow me a cozy living without requiring my services."

"Have you taken any active steps in the matter?" asked Samuel.

"Yes. I've put it into the hands of my lawyer, who says he will recover every cent of it for me. The old gentleman is a sharp old fox, and gives him a great deal of trouble; but my lawyer tells me he will settle him to his satisfaction, and mine, too. Every time I see him—"

"Who?"

"My lawyer, of course—he tells me things are going swimmingly; and as he has been saying the same thing for nearly a year, the matter must be rapidly drawing to a head, and old guardy will have to disgorge. Hey! won't that be fine?"

"Capital!" returned Samuel.

"And then," said Charley Gibbs, his sanguine eye lighting up with his prospective happiness, "hurrah for a cozy cottage with my Fan, and a silent interest in some big house, like that which Mr. Crittenden has in this. Won't I have jolly times, then? Oh, no—not at all!"

"You mentioned a Mr. Crittenden," said Samuel. "Who is he?"

"He is the silent partner in our house."

"In this—in Mr. Townsend's?"

"Yes. Didn't you know it?"

"No. What sort of a man is he?" asked Samuel.

"What do you mean—in his business abilities, or in his appearance?"

"In his appearance."

"Tall, well made, Roman head, dark hair, black eyes, consumptive complexion, very intellectual, sarcastic lips, small, pearly teeth, and keen as a hawk; dresses in black, very gentlemanly in his manner, aged about forty, and is a bachelor; knows business and human nature like a book, and can whittle common men down into little less than nothing any time within two seconds and a half. Hates everything in the shape of drudgery or confinement, and spends, therefore, the most of his time in travelling, which suits him to a T, as it enables him to combine business with pleasure. Rarely home oftener than four times a year, and then seldom more than a week at a time. Was here yesterday—didn't you see him?"

"No; at what hour?"

"Two."

"Just when I was out! How long did he stay?"

"An hour or so."

"Then he left without my seeing him!"

"And no wonder. It is his way. He glides in and out without making noise enough to disturb a cat—a habit of his. But, now I remember, you were engaged with a customer at the time he was leaving, or you would probably have seen him."

"What is his first name?"

"Robert."

Samuel opened his pocket-book, and taking out a card, handed it to his companion.

"Why, where did you get this?" asked the latter, in surprise.

"From himself, I judge," returned Samuel. "While on my way to New York, I met, in the cars, a gentleman answering to his description. He left the train at Utica, and just before taking his departure, he gave me his card."

"It was Mr. Crittenden, indeed," remarked Charley Gibbs "for this is his signature, and he always has his sign-manual printed on his cards. But here comes one of my customers, and I must attend to him. Excuse me!"

Charley Gibbs hurried off, and Samuel returned the card to his pocket-book, with a sigh.

"What will Mr. Crittenden think of me," he murmured, "when he hears of my conduct in this affair—particularly when he remembers our conversation in the cars? Lord help me! for once I have forgotten the Right, for once strayed away to the Left. Lord help, pity and forgive me!"

Charley Gibbs was right. Before the world will allow a man to be meek and gentle, it first exacts an unmistakable evidence that he can be a brute upon occasion. When it is satisfied upon that point, it will let him be as meek as he pleases, and, if called upon, it will gladly testify to the sincerity of his humility, and favor him with all the encouragement he may desire.

Samuel's inoffensive gentleness *before* his quarrel was as nothing. Its only effect was to call forth persecution and ridicule; but his inoffensive gentleness *after* the quarrel was altogether another affair. *That* stamped it with legitimacy, gave it a moral force which no one felt an inclination to dispute, and furnished Samuel himself with a *carté blanche* to be as gentle, pious, and simple as he liked, without let or hindrance.

From the moment of his victory, the clerks abandoned their annoyances against him at once and forever. From being their butt, he was thenceforth their favorite; and all were glad to own him for their friend.

So much for a "becoming spirit" on occasion. But it was an unfortunate hour for that self-important individual, First De Laine. With his defeat departed all of his little greatness. In proportion as Samuel's popularity went up, that of the fast youth went down. In his own chaste phraseology, from being "some," he was "no whar;" and ere two months passed away, he found it convenient—to use his own choice language again—to "propel" to another city, where his talents would enable him to "blaze" again in all his ancient splendor.

Samuel beheld him depart more in sorrow than in anger.

"Would he but make up and stay," he thought, "how much better it would be for himself, for me, and for us all!"

But no; the fast gentleman was "none of *that* sort. He would neither forgive nor forget." With this sentiment on his lips, he turned his footsteps towards Boston, where his business talents being of a positive order, he was not long in finding a respectable situation, at a respectable salary. His ambition to be considered a "blood" was in due time fully gratified. He shone, for a season, to his heart's content. His face was a familiar one at sporting clubs, theatres, gambling-houses, brothels, and bar-rooms. He dressed flashier than ever, and "sported" a fast horse, a flashy breastpin, a knowing hat, a dashing imperial, which was carefully dyed every morning, an extensive variety of rings, and a very long, very heavy, and very showy watch-chain. His "liberal" habits, his jaunty air, and his reputation as a "perfect blood," made him as popular with the sporting gentry of that city as he could wish, and he was rising rapidly in the estimation of blacklegs, rum-sellers, fighting-men, brothel-keepers, and fancy characters generally, when he was thrown from his sulky, while racing with another "perfect blood" out on the road. When taken up by the passers-by, it was discovered that his neck was broken, and that the fast spirit which, but a few seconds before, had tenanted his body, was gone to its account.

Samuel was by no means pleased with his own share in the quarrel. It cost him many a burning tear, many a bitter pang. Men's opinions in the matter had but little influence upon him. He weighed the whole transaction over, from beginning to end, with a calm, conscientious eye, and found everything but comfort in the result. "When ye are reviled, revile not again," loomed up, as in burning letters, continually before his mental vision, and he knew that he had broken a part, at least, of the command. He knelt down in his chamber, and poured out the burden of his contrite heart, but when he arose it was not with his usually joyous smile: for his prayer had not been answered. Again and again—in the fresh hours of the early morning, and in the silent watches of the night—he petitioned, like a little child, for mercy; and in the end, after a week of mental suffering, the smile of joy returned to his lip and to his eye—for he had received an assurance of forgiveness from his Heavenly Father. His prayer had been answered!

Thenceforth, Samuel's prospects brightened. He passed from the ginghams to the de laines, from these to the cottons, and from these to the prints, with fair rapidity, gaining a thorough business knowledge of each, and gleaning much valuable general information, as well, on the way; giving back, in return, to the clerks in these departments some few well-timed suggestions on a topic which was of far more importance, but which is rarely brought up in dry goods, or other houses, unless for ridicule, or for—a paying impression. Thus he glided, like a spirit of light, from department to department, dropping better thoughts in each than prevailed before his coming, and leaving an influence for good all along his path.

Now, with him all things wore a smiling aspect. His letters to Enfield breathed a happy, tranquil spirit, while those he received in return filled him with gratitude and joy; for they told him that his friends were all well, that they still loved him, that their interest in his welfare was unabated, and that their confidence in his loyalty to his moral trust was unshaken; that his father, and mother, and Aunt Betsy, and little Joe—who still played his old solitary tune, and always in a lively strain—were all happy as ever; that his old scholars, one and all, sent him their regards, and hoped they had still a share in his thoughts; that their new teacher was equally successful in guiding their little minds aright, and in winning their confidence, their friendship, and their love.

For all these Samuel was grateful; for these he poured out his gushing heart to the Ever Kind.

"THOU hast stood by me!" he murmured. "Thou hast been with me all the way. To Thee be all the praise!"

He was happy; and to the query of the scrutinizing monitor within him—

"Well, watchman—what of the night?"

He could lay his hand upon his heart, and answer—

"ALL IS WELL!"

CHAPTER VII.

On a pleasant evening in October, Mrs. Townsend and her two nieces were assembled in the drawing-room. It was one of the off-nights, as they were called in the family; which meant that it was one of the two evenings in the week when the gentlemen—Mr. Townsend and Samuel—were rarely at home, and when, as Mrs. Townsend herself expressed it, the ladies had the house all alone to themselves.

Mrs. Townsend, whose large, clear, dark, penetrating eye and straight features pronounced her a woman of talent, contrived to give to her four-and-fifty years the appearance of thirty-three or five. Thus, for her superb hair, whose glorious profusion was only equalled by its rich ebon gloss, she was indebted to a skilful wig-maker, who had taken his degrees in Paris; her brilliant complexion to certain mysterious cosmetics, which were made up by her own hand, from recipes which had been left her as a precious legacy, some thirty years before, by her mother—herself a magnificent lady of forty, even in her sixty-seventh year; her superb eyebrows to one of the same mysterious recipes; her fine, pearly teeth, to the genius of an eminent Philadelphia dentist; her fine bust to a certain French corset-maker; her noble figure, in part to her dressmaker, and in part to her own native tact; her mingled ease and dignity to lessons which had been given her by her parent; her active brain, partly to nature, partly to education, and partly to herself; her smooth air and benignant manner, to years of careful study; and her apparently happy, but really miserable heart, to a long apprenticeship to the studied formalities and solemn hypocrisies of the world. She was an actress of rare genius on the stage of the little sphere in which she moved. She knew how to smile and sigh in the proper places. With the serious, she was serious; with the gay, gay; while with the sorrowing, she could drop tears as mournful as their own. Her masterly acting, in all situations, deceived all but her husband. The latter was himself too cunning a player to be imposed upon by one of his own profession; but he could not help every now and then, when his wife had acquitted herself a little better than common, exclaiming, when they were alone, "Ah! Jane—you are a rare girl!" And if the "rare girl" sometimes returned the compliment, "Ah, John! you are a rare boy!" it was not perhaps to be wondered at, seeing that the precious pair understood one another so well.

And yet this couple were on the *down*-hill side of life; were drawing nearer and closer, day by day, to the bottom; were wholly unprepared for the dark valley which lay at the foot of the hill; were within reach of safety, and yet put forth no effort to preserve themselves; were still as worldly, still as calculating, still as hollow, formal, and affected as ever;—were still adding, day by day, to the catalogue of moral frauds and delinquencies already scored against them. *And they knew it all!* They were duly sensible, also, that their benevolence was simply a matter of worldly calculation; that their piety was a solemn mockery; that they had voluntarily thrown aside their great moral trusts; and that in their own eyes, as in that of Him whom they *professed* to serve, they were hopeless bankrupts. WHY they continued in this perilous course, they never cared to inquire. Meanwhile they went on with their several parts, satisfied if they performed them to the world's satisfaction, and their own.

Isabella Langdon was the daughter of Mr. Townsend's widowed sister, who died when Isabella was in her fourteenth year, leaving her some seventy or eighty thousand dollars in real estate, which was quite sufficient to secure her a "brilliant position in society," and to "render her independent for life"—the only points which the fair widow, either when living or dying, regarded as of any serious importance. A brilliant position for so small a thing as the soul, and an independence for eternity, never entered into that lady's head at all. Her dying injunction was in keeping with her life: "Money and position, my dear—never forget them. *I* never forgot them, and I hope *you* will not. Without them, one is a nobody. Adieu, dear. In a few moments I shall be in heaven!"

And with these words, her spirit entered upon its solemn journey.

Isabella herself was what a stranger would term a glorious creature. She had a fine, graceful, showy head; small, aristocratic features, a dazzling complexion, a commanding figure, small, delicate hands, and a princess-like air, which was partly natural, and partly the result of study. She had been educated according to the approved principles of her aunt, and was therefore at twenty-three as formal as her naturally cold, selfish, and frivolous nature would permit. Still her native self-possession, coupled with her rare dissimulating talent, enabled her to assume a genial frankness and warm-heartedness which, with those who only saw her abroad, might easily pass for genuine. At home, where she was less guarded, she was, of course, better understood; but not by all, even there. As she presented a brilliant show in a drawing-room, her society was courted by the ball, party, and *converzatione* givers of her "set," while her fortune rendered her an "object" to hosts of managing mothers and young gentlemen, whose "kind attentions" were as well understood by the young lady herself as by those who so freely tendered them!

As religion was the *mode*, Isabella was of course a member of the Church; and, when abroad, she lived up to its formalities with a carefulness which led to the general supposition that she was as "good" as she was beautiful. Her "goodness," however, did not deceive the experienced eye of her pastor, who sighed over the hollowness of her piety, although, for reasons best known to himself, he did not deem it advisable to make it a matter of comment.

To Isabella, religion was simply one of the conventionalisms of society—nothing more. She regarded it as she did music, dress, education—a sort of matter-of-course, which every person of consequence should know all about, support, and become identified with, because *it was expected*, and because *it was the fashion.* Beyond this, religion was to her a dead blank. Of its superior richness, of its tender sweetness, of its solemn joys, of its enduring delights, of the stirring happiness which it pours into the soul, of the *genuine* pleasure which reigns perpetually in the hearts of the believing, and of the bright future which they realize in part even on earth, she knew nothing, cared nothing. It is true she *heard* of them, every Sabbath; but they fell on her ear like so many pretty sentiments, which were all very well to hear of, and to talk about, but as of no more absolute importance than pretty sentiments of any other character. A sermon was to her as a lecture, a play, or a concert—something that worked up the feelings a little, and extorted a certain degree of admiration. Thus, after listening to an able discourse, she would observe—"What an admirable preacher Mr. Engold is! It really does one good to hear him! His figures are so beautiful, and his eloquence so overpowering!" And this was *all* of our fair friend's view of religion! What an "admirable preacher" Mr. Engold was, indeed!

Miriam Selden was Mrs. Townsend's only brother's only child. Although orphaned at an early age, she had never forgotten the religious lessons which had been taught her by her mother. Her fortune was only about a third as large as that of her cousin, but her income more than satisfied the wants of her gentle, retiring nature. In person, Miriam was small; in appearance, *spirituelle*. Her small Grecian features were boldly yet modestly defined, and fully expressed the mild earnestness and beauty of her character. Her movements were light, easy, and graceful—the rustling of her garments conveying the only sound of her coming or departure. Her voice, which was low and musical, was rarely heard. She had a thoughtful air, and a pair of dark, thoughtful eyes, whose clear depths were not purer than her own sinless spirit.

On the evening in question, the cousins were reading at the centre-table: Isabella running through the still damp pages of a new novel—Miriam perusing the memoirs of a missionary. Mrs. Townsend, from her seat on a lounge, was quietly observing them both.

Isabella at length put aside her book, observing, at the same time—

"Really, aunt, reading is a great bore!"

"I presume that depends very much upon *what* you are reading, my dear!" answered Mrs. Townsend. "How do you find *your* book, Mirry?"

"Very entertaining, dear aunt!" said Miriam, who understood the query in the light in which it was intended, and laid down the volume accordingly; "but not so overpowering that I cannot relinquish it for a while."

"Thank you, my dear! And now, girls, if you have nothing to urge against it, let us have a little cozy chat!"

"Excellent!" cried Isabella. "Chat is one of our sex's privileges; and as I am a firm believer in woman's rights, I vote for it with both hands!"

"And you, Mirry?"

"I presume I must not be found in the minority, aunt!"

"Very good. Then the proposition is carried without a dissenting voice."

Mrs. Townsend seated herself at the centre-table in such a position that she could command a full view of the features of her companions.

"Talking of woman's rights, 'Bel," she said, "I have some news for you. Mr. Jones, the grocer, failed on Monday, and ran away yesterday, leaving his wife without a dollar!"

"Shocking!" exclaimed Isabella. "Why, it was her money that set him up in business!"

"Exactly! And this is the result of her folly in letting him have the control of her property, which she should have settled upon herself! I hope, my dears," she added, "you will remember the lesson when you conclude to enter upon matrimony."

But, aunt," said Miriam, whose gentle nature led her to look hopefully upon everything, "perhaps the poor gentleman could not help failing, and has only fled, for a time, to avoid the first outbursts of his creditors!"

"I think not, Mirry. His failure, Mr. Townsend tells me, is a very bad one. It bears, in fact, the evidence of premeditation."

Miriam cast her eyes down, sorrowfully, for she remembered that the fraudulent bankrupt was a member of her own church, and that she had always looked upon him as a faithful follower of the Prince of Righteousness.

"How much did he fail for?" inquired Isabella.

"Two hundred and twenty thousand, Mr. Townsend tells me."

"Shocking! It's enough to give one a sensation!"

"It *did*, my dear, to several; but particularly to his creditors, three of whom are ruined by it. But it serves them right. They should have known better than to risk their business positions upon the honesty of a single man."

"Who are the principal sufferers?"

"Mr. Weston, our next-door neighbor, Mr. Judson, the sugar-dealer, and Mr. Lent, the tea-importer: all of whom, Mr. Townsend tells me, will have to 'go by the board,' as it is termed, before the week is out."

"Shocking! Why, these gentlemen all have pews in our church! What a time it will create, when it becomes known!"

"What will become of their families, dear aunt?" inquired Miriam, looking up, with an expression of deep sympathy.

"They will return to their original poverty, for all I can see, my dear!" returned Mrs. Townsend, who was struck with the marked contrast in the sentiments of the two cousins.

"That, however, will be no *very* great hardship," remarked Isabella. "It will only be going back to an old acquaintance."

"I fear," said the gentle Miriam, "they will find it very painful. Had they never known affluence, poverty could be met without a shudder; but to leave it once and then be driven back to it, through no fault of their own, must be very hard, as well as humiliating!"

"I'm sure, cousin," said Isabella, with a slight air of virtuous indignation, "there is nothing humiliating in honest poverty!"

"To the already poor, no; but they who have known wealth cannot help looking at it in that light."

"I am sure I should not look upon it so!" returned her cousin.

"I hope you may never be tried, dear cousin. Poverty is a sore tempter!" replied Miriam, generously. "But can we not do something for these worthy people, aunt?"

"That has already been thought of, Mirry. It is perhaps a delicate matter to mention, but Mr. Townsend and myself have inclosed a few hundreds to each of them to help them in their strait."

An expression of mingled joy and relief swept over Miriam's sweet countenance at this reply.

"Dear aunt!" she exclaimed, taking her hand and pressing it in her own with all the warmth of her generous nature, "that is so like you and dear guardy! Ah! you know not how happy you have made me!"

If poor Miriam had but known that the "few hundreds" were given for the sole purpose of reaching the public ear, and thereby adding to the giver's business popularity, she might not have been so lavish of her thanks. But the simple-hearted girl, in common with all the world, never dreamed of the crafty spirit of her guardian.

"Pray, don't mention it, Mirry!" returned Mrs. Townsend. "There is as much pleasure in giving as in receiving; and I am sure we ought to take all the pleasure we can. Let me see: it is Shakspeare, is it not, 'Bel, who says:

> "The quality of mercy is not strained.
> It is twice blessed: it blesseth him that gives,
> And him by whom it is received,"

or something to that effect!"

"But what has that quotation to do with it, aunt?" inquired her eldest niece. "The one alludes to benevolence, and the other to mercy. They are not identical, I believe?"

"Not always, my dear, I grant. But in the present instance, they are somewhat allied. For with our few hundreds, Mr. Townsend dispatched, at the same time, some notes of Mr. Jones's, which had come into his hands in the course of business, and which bore the endorsements of some of the ruined creditors!"

"Oh, aunt!" said Miriam, "that was generous in guardy—it was noble!"

"What think *you*, 'Bel?"

"I agree with Mirry," was the reply. "It was both noble and generous!"

"You confess, then, the appositeness of the quotation?"

"How can I do otherwise? The act is enough to give one a sensation. It is really delightful!"

"When I think," said her aunt, "how Mr. Townsend might have pressed the payment of those notes, and thereby secured himself from loss—which, of course, he had a perfect right to do—and when I think that he has sacrificed his private interest to that of humanity, I confess it makes me love him, if that were possible, ten times deeper than ever!"

"I am sure he will be rewarded for it!" cried Miriam, with pious enthusiasm. "If not here, certainly hereafter!"

"Too much benevolence, aunt," said her more worldly cousin, "is as hurtful as too much selfishness, and it oftener leads to misery. As for me, I have no faith in it. His liberality will be the ruin of guardy some day!"

"Fear it not," returned her aunt: "Mr. Townsend knows how to temper benevolence with judgment!"

The exceeding truthfulness of this observation was known only to the speaker herself. Notwithstanding its utterance, however, her auditors still adhered to the idea which Isabella had so naively expressed.

"Aunt," said Miriam, "you have not yet given us the particulars of Mr. Jones's failure."

"I have purposely refrained from doing so, because the details are too revolting for young minds. It is enough that they display unmistakable evidences of a long-designed and successfully sustained fraud, not only against his creditors, but against his wife, whom he has left in a position which makes my heart bleed to think of."

"Dear aunt," cried Isabella, "do give us the particulars. You cannot fancy how I am pining for a sensation!"

Miriam was also anxious to hear the particulars, but from a very different motive.

"I can do that in a few words," said Mrs. Townsend, calmly enjoying her mental perusal of the two natures before her. "It appears that Mr. Jones had determined to make the most of his wicked scheme, and with this view he converted all his business availables into money. Not content with this, he, under a plea of necessity, persuaded his wife, some few weeks before his failure, to sell their house, and also to give a mortgage upon their furniture. The notes obtained for the house, he turned into cash; the mortgage went the same way; and now, besides the desertion of her husband, the unfortunate woman has to bewail the loss of her very house and furniture. She is literally stripped of everything, and is without a shilling in the world!"

"Mercy on me!" cried Isabella. "What a thrilling subject for the newspapers! How the world will stare when it hears the harrowing details! Ugh! it has given me *such* a sensation! I shall not get over it for a month!"

"Does the unhappy lady still live in Bleecker street, aunt?" asked Miriam.

"No, my dear," answered Mrs. Townsend, whose perfect knowledge of the questioner's tender nature enabled her to comprehend the motive of the inquiry, "she disappeared this morning with her child."

An expression of mingled sadness and disappointment passed over Miriam's features, and she dropped her eyes, with a low sigh.

"Of course, the woman will not think of showing herself at *our* church again!" remarked Isabella.

"Why not, cousin?" timidly inquired Miriam. "Mr. Jones has a pew there!"

"What an absurd question!" returned Isabella, gazing at her in astonishment. "Aunt, did you ever hear of anything so stupid?"

"I presume Mrs. Jones will avoid the ridicule which would naturally follow such a step!" replied Mrs. Townsend.

"There, Mirry!" cried Isabella, glancing at her cousin with an air of triumph.

"I do not see why it should," replied Miriam, with modest earnestness. "Her claim to a seat in her own pew is perfectly legal; and surely her husband's error ought not to be laid upon her shoulders. Besides, in God's house—"

"What nonsense, coz! You know very well, that whether it be God's house or not, our church, and every other church that is built by rich people's money, is not a place for poor people. For whom do we build them, but ourselves? Let mechanics and laborers, and people of their rank, associate with their own class. We don't want them in *our* way. I never heard of anything so shabby in all my life. It's enough to give one a sensation!"

Miriam made no reply.

"I think," observed Mrs. Townsend, in her calm, impressive way, "there is no danger of Mrs. Jones's incurring the risk of general remark by showing herself at our church in future. Her own good sense will tell her that!" Then turning to her youngest niece, who was evidently suffering with some painful thought, she added, "You know, Mirry, that the mingling of rich and poor in God's house is a very pretty sentiment to read of, to talk of, and all that; but as society is at present constituted, it would not do to practise: at all events, it is *not* practised, and that, as you will of course admit, is equally to the point."

"Fancy, for instance," said Isabella, in a tone of triumphant mockery, "a greasy mechanic, and his vulgar calicoed wife, stalking, in all the consequence of their Sunday-go-to-meetings, along the carpeted isles of *our* church, seating themselves upon our velveted cushions, and looking coolly around at our satins, jewels, and irreproachable broadcloths! What a sensation it would make! I do not believe our dear minister himself could realize that he was in his own church. I'm sure I shouldn't!"

"I have too good an opinion of our minister to believe any such thought would enter his mind!" returned Miriam, gently.

"It does not follow because he is the pastor of an aristocratic congregation, that he shares in the aristocratic sentiments of his people!"

"What sublime simplicity! Why, coz, it is positively amusing to hear you!"

Miriam neither quailed nor blushed at this impudent outburst. Still, her features showed how deeply she was pained at the remark.

"'Bel!" said Mrs. Townsend, "you are too harsh, and Mirry too gentle. You must both permit me to explain the consistency of our 'exclusiveness.' Aristocracy reigns in everything; that is to say, everything is graduated, in the natural as in the artificial world. This aristocracy is governed wholly by the universal law of Inferiority and Superiority; which means that the superior is better than the inferior—all of which is true, whatever may be said to the contrary. For instance, Honesty is an aristocrat, because it is the superior of Dishonesty; and however charitable and kindly may be his sentiments, Honesty would revolt at placing himself on an equal footing, morally or socially, with Dishonesty. Hence, from every point of view, Honesty is a better man than Dishonesty. The artist who paints a *perfect* picture is the superior of him who paints an imperfect one, and he would shrink instinctively from associating or placing himself on a level with one so far inferior to himself; and very justly, too, because *positive* merit is the natural superior of negative or questionable merit. A gentleman is, for the same reason, the superior of the commoner, because his position in the world is higher; and he could not consent to place himself on a level with that commoner, because society has lifted him above him. *To* associate with the commoner, would be as revolting to his tastes and habits, as to his feelings. There is nothing in common between them; and consequently, to put them upon a level, would be to perpetrate an outrage upon the broad law which governs nature and society. Gold is better than copper, than iron, than brass. Refinement is better than coarseness; Intellect better than Ignorance; Strength better than Weakness; Modesty better than Brazenness; Elegance better than Roughness; Wealth better than Poverty. This law is universal; and since it governs the world, it is idle to pronounce it unjust."

This was delivered with so oracular an air, and it was so subtly interlarded with speciousness and truth, that it was no wonder that poor gentle Miriam bowed her head in utter bewilderment.

"And for that reason," continued her aunt, "it would be utterly impossible for our pastor, who is himself a gentleman, a scholar, and an 'exclusive,' to entertain any sympathy for parties whom nature and society have united in placing below him. Of course, we do not parade these views before the world; they would have a tendency to render us unpopular. But they are perfectly understood by all intelligent minds."

"There, coz!" cried Isabella, triumphantly. "What have you got to say for the greasy wretches now!"

"This, 'Bel!" returned Miriam, with an expression of winning sweetness—"that the point at issue, so far as I can see, is untouched."

"My dear coz, you are entitled to the laurels of a Columbus! The ground has been wholly gone over—penetrated to its very depths—and yet it is reserved for your brilliant ladyship to discover that it has not been touched at all! Really, it is as good as a play!"

"We must not be too severe on our dear Mirry, 'Bel!" observed her aunt. "The saying, 'strike, but hear me,' is a noble one. We must give Mirry an opportunity to explain!"

"Certainly, aunt. We should be generous. It is our duty to be so. There is a text for it: 'He that giveth to the poor lendeth to the Lord!'"

Miriam looked at her cousin with mournful surprise. Then changing the expression into one of entreaty, she said—

"Please, 'Bel! don't speak of sacred things in that way. It pains me. Please don't!"

"Well, then, coz! do talk reason. It is perfectly shocking to hear how you go on with your simple nonsense. So long as we are in the world, we should think as the world thinks, and do as the world does. Else what is the use of living in it at all, I'd like to know!"

"You were saying, Mirry, that the point is left untouched," said Mrs. Townsend. "Why?"

"I fear you will think me over-bold, dear aunt, when you hear my reasons," replied Miriam, timidly; "and yet," she added, with an air of modest confusion, "it would make me unhappy to give up my confidence in their truth!"

"Go on, coz. Do let us hear what you have to advance! Who knows but *you* may yet favor us with a sensation?" observed Isabella, with a slight sneer.

"Go on, Mirry," said Mrs. Townsend, with protecting kindness. "You may be sure we shall receive your views with all the respect to which they may be entitled."

"I was simply thinking," said Miriam, with a smile which mirrored the sweetness of her nature, "that society cannot control the Church; for *that* exists wherever a single heart bends in pious reverence to God. At least, I have ever found great comfort in the thought, and I would not willingly relinquish it."

"And is that all, Mirry?"

"Yes, aunt. I cannot think of any more; although I feel that I ought to say a great deal more for Him who gave His life for me: but," she added, with an artlessness which well-nigh provoked her auditors into a broad, vulgar laugh, "I am not capable of saying much. If our friend Samuel were here, I think he could explain my meaning better. He is braver than I am, and—"

"I presume, coz," said Isabella, interrupting her with a sneer, "that you would be very glad indeed to have Samuel *explain* your meaning. I have no doubt he *understands* it!"

Miriam glanced at her reproachfully for an instant; then, as a deep hot blush shot up to her temples, she covered her face with her handkerchief, and murmuring, "Cousin—this is cruel!" she burst into tears.

"'Bel!" said Mrs. Townsend, in a reproving tone.

"Oh! let her put on her airs, aunt! Who cares? I'm sure," she added, in a tone which Mrs. Townsend's practised ear recognized as one of burning jealousy, "any one can see how she throws herself in his way, and tries to make Sam—Mr. Leland, I mean—understand her!"

"Oh, cousin—cousin!" cried Miriam, her blushes burning her like fire. "I—I—"

"Out with it, do!" cried Isabella, tauntingly.

"'Bel!" said Mrs. Townsend, impressively, "no more of this. It is unfair. These are matters that should never be alluded to."

"That depends upon circumstances, aunt. Cousin knows very well that Mr. Leland and I—"

She paused, suddenly—blushed—and then added—

"If Mr. Leland sees fit to favor me with his attentions, I am not aware that any one has a right to call him to an account for it but myself."

"Who presumes to call him to an account for it, 'Bel?" inquired her aunt.

"Mirry!"

"I, cousin?" cried Miriam, looking up in astonishment.

"You!" returned Isabella, with energy. "By your interference, if in nothing else!"

"Cousin—"

"Oh, put on your airs, and call up your blushes—do!"

"'Bel!" said Mrs. Townsend, "this will not do, my dear. You forget yourself!"

"Aunt! permit me to understand my own affairs best!"

"Certainly, my dear!" returned Mrs. Townsend, with her usual suavity. "I have no desire to interfere with them. But," she added, partly for the purpose of rescuing Miriam from the imperial beauty's rage, and partly for the purpose of drawing her impetuous niece into a more lucid explanation of a matter which had hitherto escaped her own penetrating eye, "I had no idea that you and Mr. Leland had had any understanding of this nature. It is perfectly new to me."

And the lady uttered what was unqualifiedly true.

"Who spoke of any understanding, aunt?" returned Isabella, detecting her motive. "I simply referred to Mr. Leland's attentions. No harm in that, I presume?"

"No harm, certainly. A mere misapprehension on my part; that is all."

"Am I to blame for that?" demanded Isabella, who was now rapidly recovering her self-possession.

"By no means, 'Bel. But it led me into an error, notwithstanding; especially," she continued, with a meaning smile, "when I had, all along, been under the impression that your sentiments were running in a very different quarter!"

"I do not understand you, aunt!" said Isabella, with a blush which was a flat contradiction of her words.

"Mr. Brigham—" suggested Mrs. Townsend, quietly.

"Mr. Brigham!" returned her niece, with a haughty curl of her proud lip. "Mr. Brigham, indeed!"

"I had supposed, my dear, that he was an accepted admirer," said her aunt.

"Mr. Brigham has, I doubt not, a strong admiration for my—*fortune!*" said Isabella; "but I am not aware that his chances of obtaining it are any better now than they were before he *honored* its owner with his acquaintance!"

"'Bel, you amaze me! Surely, you will not deny that Mr. Brigham entertains directly opposite views?"

Mr. Brigham is privileged to entertain whatever views he pleases, but he will find it difficult to impose them upon me!"

"Hark!" said her aunt, raising her finger, warningly. "Some one comes!"

"Mr. Brigham!" said a servant.

A moment later, and that worthy made his appearance.

Mr. Brigham was a gentleman of some three or five-and-thirty years. He was tall, slender, and well-built. His hair, of a jet black, contrasted strongly with his naturally pale complexion, and gave it a somewhat consumptive tinge. His forehead was flat, and of moderate height; the brows protruded heavily over a pair of large, dark eyes, which were generally half closed, with a keen but thoughtful air. His nose was hooked; the nostrils lapped, like those of a wild beast when in repose. His lips were small and thin, and might have been pronounced handsome, but for a crafty expression which lurked, like a shadow, around their corners. His retreating chin was covered by a short, black beard, which always looked as if it had just been shortened by a barber's shears. He wore a buff vest, with yellow buttons, and a coat and pantaloons of fine blue cloth. His small hands were covered with buff kids; his feet with boots of patent leather. His movements were easy and smooth, without being graceful. His general air was that of one who understood himself and others also.

"Good-evening, ladies!" he said, with a bow which was not devoid of refinement. "I am fortunate in finding you at home."

The ladies returned his salute, and Mrs. Townsend, with her usual urbanity, motioned him to a chair.

"You are very good!" he said, seating himself. "Mr. Townsend is off to prayer-meeting, I suppose?" Mrs. Townsend replied in the affirmative, and Mr. Brigham added: "So I imagined. He neglects nothing; and yet he has cares and duties enough, of one kind and another, to kill a dozen ordinary men. It has always been a mystery to me how he gets through them all; and yet they appear to make no impression upon him. He is a wonderful man!"

This dose of flattery was meant for the domestic partner of the "wonderful man." That lady smiled, and answered—

"Mr. Townsend has an excellent constitution, I believe."

"And an excellent heart, as well," added Mr. Brigham, with a smile which answered its design, viz.: to show two rows of teeth, which, if not as small as a woman's, were at least as white and glistening.

"That is a charge which I fear will never be laid at Mr. Brigham's door!" observed Isabella.

"Ah! you are very good!" returned that gentleman, with the tranquil air of one who was accustomed to jokes of that nature, and he added, with another display of his fine teeth, "When a poor fellow's heart is rudely torn from him by an enchantress, he cannot expect to be flattered for the vacuum!"

"Mr. Leland!" said a servant.

And Samuel entered the drawing-room.

There was no mistaking the warmth with which our hero was received by Mrs. Townsend and Isabella. There was a heartiness in it which contrasted strongly with that which greeted the entrance of the confidential clerk. The latter quietly bit his lip as he remarked it; but he was too shrewd to permit its effect upon him to appear.

Miriam was somewhat reserved; a fact which the confidential clerk noticed also, and with surprise; for he had long imagined that the timid Miriam had a secret predilection for Mr. Leland.

"Something has happened!" he thought. "They have had a

rupture, perhaps. But what does Isabella mean by her conduct towards the religious simpleton? I must look into this; and if I find the fellow poaching upon my manor, let him look to himself!"

'Ah! Mr. Brigham!" said Samuel, saluting him, "I am happy to see you!"

"You are very good!" returned the confidential clerk, with a gracious bow, and showing all his teeth at the same moment. "From prayer-meeting?"

"No," answered Samuel, who had lost none of his simplicity; "from a journey in quest of an unhappy lady, whom perhaps you may know—Mrs. Jones?"

The ladies pricked up their ears.

"I have not the honor!" said Mr. Brigham, laughingly. "Some friend of yours, I presume?"

"Yes, and a very worthy lady."

"Do you mean the grocer's wife, Samuel?" inquired Mrs. Townsend.

"The same."

"Poor thing!" exclaimed Isabella, in a tone of assumed sympathy. "Her husband failed a few days ago."

"Unhappily—" returned Samuel.

"And fled, I think!" observed Mr. Brigham. "It appears to me I heard something of it. Disappeared suddenly?"

"Yes, sir—leaving his unhappy wife and child without means of support. Can't we do something for her?"

Mr. Brigham was silent.

"Have you her address?" asked Mrs. Townsend.

"No. —— Laurence street," returned Samuel.

Mrs. Townsend bowed, and taking out her tablets, wrote down the address.

"What sort of a place is it?" asked Isabella.

"Up an alley, rear building, second floor. You would scarcely believe it," added Samuel, "but her husband's failure has deprived the poor lady even of her friends!"

"Shameful!" cried Isabella, in virtuous indignation.

"We must look into this!" observed Mrs. Townsend, who never lost an opportunity for creating an effect.

"Has the poor woman no relatives?" inquired Mr. Brigham.

"Several," replied Samuel; "but none of them have been to see her."

"Why don't she drop them a note?" asked the confidential clerk.

"She has done so; but they paid no attention to her letters. And yet," he added, with an expression of uneasiness, "they *must* have received them!"

Mr. Brigham showed his teeth, and observed—

"And yet they will all shine, in their silks and satins, next Sabbath, and be highly edified at their pastor's discourse!"

"For shame, Mr. Brigham!" said Isabella, with an air of playful reproach.

"Nay, the shame will be with *them*, Miss Landon!" said Mr. Brigham. "And, now I think of it," he added, with his noiseless smile, "I'll make a memorandum with anybody here, that they will be the most devout of all the congregation!"

"Let us not judge them too harshly," observed Samuel, gently. "Human nature is not so bad, after all!"

The teeth of the confidential clerk fairly danced with laughter at this remark, although no sound came from their owner's lips.

"I called on two of them, on my way home," continued Samuel, "and left a note for each, with a brief statement of the lady's distress, and where she might be found. So, there is hope yet!"

"What makes you think so, Samuel?" inquired Mrs. Townsend.

"Because they cannot now plead ignorance of the poor lady's situation or whereabouts."

"Let us hope for the best!" said Mrs. Townsend, benignantly. "In the meanwhile, Mrs. Jones must not be left to chance."

"From my heart I thank you!" said Samuel, taking her hand and pressing it warmly. "Ah! you do not know how happy you have made me!"

A peculiar smile passed over Mrs. Townsend's face, and her eyes dropped with a thoughtful air.

The confidential clerk was a quiet observer of this little incident, and his teeth glistened.

"I see—I see!" he said mentally. "This religious simpleton is sweeping all before him!"

"Samuel!" said Isabella.

"Well, Miss Landon!" said Samuel, approaching her.

"Ah ha!" mused the confidential clerk. "There is fun ahead. Isabella is growing jealous of her very aunt. A certain individual of my acquaintance is in peril. Who knows but he may yet find it necessary to take this rural youth in hand!"

"Can you keep a secret, Samuel?" asked Isabella, looking him laughingly in the eye.

"I think so. Try me!"

"Then read this," she said, putting a card into his hand, "and let me see a specimen of your abilities in that way!"

"I'm very much afraid I shall have to take this youth in hand!" thought Mr. Brigham.

"And yet I dare not say a word to him!" murmured Miriam. "What—what will he think of me! and cousin, too—forcing herself upon him before our very eyes!"

An expression of unutterable anguish was visible in her simple features.

"Miriam is in torture!" muttered the confidential clerk,

quietly observing her. "Well, it is a pleasure to find that one is not alone in his misery!"

Samuel read as follows:

"It is early enough yet to pay poor dear Mrs. Jones a visit. Help, to-night, may be of service to her. Assistance is doubly valuable when it is timely. Will you go with me? If so, put this in your pocket, and I will get ready at once. My heart is always easier, and my dreams pleasanter, after a good action!"

Samuel was silent for a moment or two.

Isabella looked at him as if she would read his very soul.

The confidential clerk observed them both—his eyes half closed, and his teeth smiling and glistening like the glittering light produced by the squirming of a serpent.

Miriam was regarding the carpet with a mournful air.

Mrs. Townsend, from her seat at the further end of the sofa, surveyed, with her keen orbs, every movement and expression of each actor in the group before her. Her cheek was paler than usual, and an occasional spasmodic movement of her lips betrayed the agitation of her heart, or mind—it would have been difficult to say which.

"And not a word from Miriam!" thought Samuel. "I always thought her kind, and good, and generous; and yet in this solemn hour, when suffering sends up its cry for help, her voice alone is silent! I fancied she would have been the first to extend the hand of charity. How I have misapprehended her! And Miss Landon, too, whom I had thought the last to hearken to distress! How I have misjudged *her!*"

Then turning to Isabella, he said—

"Do you really wish this to be kept secret, Miss Landon?"

"Really and truly!" answered that young lady, lifting her finger with an archness which was truly fascinating.

The teeth of the confidential clerk fairly writhed.

"Hang her!" he muttered. "How I could tear her now!"

"So be it, then!" returned Samuel. "You have a noble heart!"

"No conspiracy against the peace and welfare of the country, I hope?" laughed Mr. Brigham, showing his teeth.

"Oh, yes—a very dreadful one!" answered Isabella. "And that it may be successful, no time shall be lost in putting it into execution!" she added, sweeping past him.

"Is our princess about to deprive her poor subjects of the light of her countenance?" inquired the man of teeth.

"For a time!" returned the proud beauty, with flattering condescension. "I shall be ready in a few moments, Samuel," she added, gliding from the drawing-room. "The jealous fool can scarcely restrain himself! This will give him food for pleasant dreams!" she muttered to herself, as she ascended to her chamber.

"I shall wait for you!" said Samuel. Then turning his eyes upon Miriam, who was still looking thoughtfully upon the carpet, he murmured: "And *she* is silent!"

"You will wait for *me* one of these days!" mused the confidential clerk.

"How did you learn of Mrs. Jones's trouble, Samuel?" asked Mrs. Townsend, as that gentleman seated himself on the sofa.

"Through Charley Gibbs," returned Samuel, "who got it from a lady friend of his, who lives next door to the poor lady's late residence.

"Fanny Adriance, I suppose?"

"Yes," answered our hero. "And a dear good soul she is!"

"You must not let Charley Gibbs hear you say that!" laughed Mr. Brigham.

"I have told him so frequently; and he fully agrees with me!" returned Samuel, with his usual simplicity.

The teeth of the confidential clerk glittered with silent irony.

"They are engaged, I believe?" said Mrs. Townsend.

"Yes," answered Samuel: "and as they love each other dearly, they will of course be happy!"

"Does happiness always follow love?" inquired Mrs. Townsend.

"If it be mutual and abiding—yes."

"Ah—*if!*" exclaimed the man of teeth, with a sardonic grin.

"I have had no experience—or if any, but little—in such matters," said Samuel; "but I should think—"

"Should *think!*" said the teeth, as plainly as any words.

"Should think," continued Samuel, modestly, "that love, if it exist at all between two hearts, must naturally be as enduring as the hearts themselves. For love is generous, caring more for its mate than for itself, and therefore spares naught that will bring happiness *to* its mate. And thus the perpetual interchange of tender kindnesses and considerations keeps up the flame, and the mutual fire burns, uninterruptedly, on!"

"Samuel, I am ready!" said Isabella, now appearing at the door, with her hat, and shawl, and gloves on.

Miriam looked up, and the eyes of the cousins met. Triumph, pride, and gratification in those of the one—gentle reproach and soulful suffering in those of the other.

"I am ready," said Samuel, rising. "Good-bye for a time!" he added.

And he passed from the drawing-room.

Miriam sighed.

The confidential clerk's teeth withdrew behind their guardians, the small, thin lips: an indication that their owner was in a fume. His lapped nostrils rose from their repose, and shook themselves like the wings of a great owl preparing for a flight, and then returned to their rest: a sign that their owner had had what Miss Landon was wont to term a "sensation."

"There's a devil in that man that will do mischief, if it be not caged!" mused Mrs. Townsend, who had quietly observed him. And as it was a part of her husband's policy to keep on good terms with his confidential clerk, for the present, at least, Mrs. Townsend concluded to soothe that individual's wounded vanity, and soften him down to harmlessness. While she was thinking how to commence her proposed task, Mr. Townsend himself entered the room.

"Ah! Brigham!" he exclaimed, throwing his pleasant eyes upon that worthy, and shaking him by the hand with as much heartiness as if he had not seen him before for many years, "I'm glad to see you. What's new?"

"Nothing, that I know of. From prayer-meeting?"

"Yes, this moment. And a pleasant time we had of it, I assure you. Brigham, my boy—you ought to join!"

"What—the prayer-meeting?" asked the teeth, which now remade their appearance, bright, saucy, and expressive as ever.

"No—the church. The prayer-meeting is a luxury which you will enjoy afterwards!"

"I've always had an impression that the church rather discountenanced luxuries!"

"All wrong, Brigham, my boy—all wrong. It only sets its face against the luxuries of the world—that is," he added, as if correcting himself, "those which are unnecessary. But the church has its own luxuries, compared with which those of the world are perfectly flat and insipid."

"Such, for instance—" said the teeth, querulously.

"As our lectures, hymns, prayer-meetings, and private devotions," said the merchant, with rare unctuousness. "Get religion, my boy, and you will experience the richness of its delights!"

And the happy merchant rubbed his sleek hands with pious fervor.

The teeth curled into a very pretty bijou of wreathed smoke, and their owner said—

"Ah! you are very good. But there are so many kinds of the article, I should be puzzled for a choice."

"All a mistake, Brigham, my boy—all a mistake, I assure you. There is but one religion—"

"And that is—" inquired the teeth.

"To love God, and serve him with our whole hearts!" answered the merchant, with solemn fervor.

The teeth roared, in their silent way, with jolly laughter.

"If that be the only kind," said their owner, "the genuine article is rarer than I had supposed!"

"What makes you think so?" asked the merchant, throwing his pleasant eyes upon the other with an air which seemed to say—"Look! a specimen of a believer in the *real thing* is before you. Isn't he a rouser? And can you entertain the shadow of a doubt after seeing *him?*"

"For many reasons," answered the confidential clerk, "the principal of which is, that I have never yet seen a man courageous enough to act up to it!"

"My dear Brigham!" exclaimed the merchant, with tender reproach.

"I have a pair of eyes—"

"And sharp ones, too, Brigham, as all Liberty street will testify!"

"You are very good!" answered the confidential clerk, with a low bow. "But, as I was saying, I have a pair of eyes, and, being a member of no particular church, I am privileged to wander, without scandal, among them all."

"And you see the same happy unity of purpose *in* them all—

the same one idea: the worship of the Most High God!" said the merchant, with pious enthusiasm.

"As you say—"

"I thought so, my dear Brigham—I thought so!" cried the other, rubbing his fat hands in delight. "Do you hear that, Jane, dear? Mr. Brigham finds everywhere—among all churches and all sects—the same beautiful oneness of purpose, the same singleness of idea: the worship of our common God!"

"Mr. Brigham's testimony is dearly prized, my dear, if that *be* his testimony. But," she added, with her usual benignity, "I fear we are too premature in the conclusion. I shall be happy to hear Mr. Brigham's evidence, however, be it what it may!"

"You are very good!" said that worthy, with a low bow.

"But, my dear Brigham," said the merchant, "you certainly admitted that the same oneness of devotion was visible in all churches?"

"Yes," returned the confidential clerk, his teeth glittering like the folds of an anaconda, "the same oneness of devotion, to—*various* gods!"

"Dear Mr. Brigham!" exclaimed Mrs. Townsend, in sorrowful astonishment.

"My dear Brigham!" cried her husband, with an air of pious horror, "how *can* you say so!"

"Very easily indeed!" returned the teeth.

"But, my dear Brigham," said the merchant, "that would imply a *variety* of RELIGIONS!"

"Exactly," returned the confidential clerk. "For instance, the religion of dress, with which I find no fault, since it is the chief support of *our* trade; the religion of pride, which leads Satin to look down upon poor Calico with the most insulting scorn; the religion of envy, which persuades Calico to regard Satin with feelings of solemn hatred; the religion of Arrogance, which bids its votaries to say, 'Come not near me—I am holier and better than thou!' the religion of Insolence, which inspires its worshippers to exclaim—'Away, I am more benevolent, I give more than thou;' the religion of Support, which leads the hypocritical poor—for there are of them as of the hypocritical rich—to affect piety for the sake of assistance from the Church; the religion of Humbug, which makes the open, unscrupulous, and audacious rascal of the week, a sleek, smooth, gentle, and sanctified rascal on the Sabbath; and over all, and around all, the religion of the Almighty Dollar! But the religion of GOD—where is *it?*"

And the teeth absolutely danced with wild scorn, frenzy, and satanic rapture.

Miriam shuddered as she listened. She surveyed the satirical speaker with instinctive dread; and when he had brought his remarks to a close, she dropped her eyes mournfully to the floor. A sense of uneasiness—why, she could not explain—crept over her gentle heart, and filled it with an undefinable terror. She moved her chair back, unconsciously, or rather instinctively, not a great way, to be sure, but still far enough to render her a little easier—as if for relief. Her pure, timid nature could not endure a nearer contact with that malignant spirit, which seemed to gloat, with fiendish pleasure, over the weaknesses of humanity.

Of the correctness of Mr. Brigham's remarks, Miriam knew not. She herself had never observed them. Nor, although a constant attendant at God's house, was that a matter of wonder. Poor Miriam went there to worship—not to see; to praise her Redeemer—not to mock his people, not to ridicule the errors of poor human nature!

"Oh, my dear Brigham!" said Mr. Townsend, shaking his head with pious sadness. "My dear boy—how *can* you talk in that way? You make me shudder. You do, indeed! I wouldn't think that way, nor speak so, for the world—no, not for *all* the world!"

The teeth laughed immoderately in their peculiar way, and said, as plainly as teeth could be expected to say: "That's all very pretty; but you *act* it for a VERY SMALL *fraction* of what is *in* it!"

The conversation was by no means to the merchant's taste, and he concluded to change it.

"Ah! Brigham, my boy," he said, with an arch grin, "you are a sad dog!"

"You are very good!" returned the man of teeth, with a low bow.

"You are a queer fellow," continued Mr. Townsend, with a knowing look; "always cracking hard jokes. Ah!" he added, with a dubious sigh, "that's just like you young blades. Dealing in sarcasms and home thrusts all the while, sparing nothing and caring for nobody, so long as you get your own fun. Well, well, there's one consolation: we think better of heavenly things as we grow older!"

The teeth laughed uproariously at this observation, and their owner's eyes met those of the merchant's in a sly, meaning way; and the merchant's met his in a way equally as full of meaning and equally as sly; and they glanced at each other for about ten seconds, with a look which seemed to say—"We understand one another, tip top—eh? You can't gammon me, any more than I can gammon you—eh? Rare humbugs both—eh? Sly boys, we are—very sly—eh?" and then both eyes turned a somerset, as it were, and each went his own way, like two little truant boys who were having lots of fun on a bright sunshiny day.

"But how is this, Jane?" said the merchant. "I don't see Isabella!"

"She went out with Samuel a few minutes before you came in."

"Dear me! How very like her! So full of spirits, too! With Samuel, you say?"

"Yes. Some crink got into her head, and she invited him to accompany her!"

"That is very singular. Why, Brigham, my boy—why didn't you stand up for your rights? Bless your soul! my boy, this will never do. What—let another cut you out? I'm astonished at you!"

"Am I Miss Landon's keeper?" asked the confidential clerk, whose teeth intimated that he felt somewhat sore somewhere.

"If you are not now, you will be one of these days, my boy, and then, I fancy that the house of John P. Townsend will have another new partner. Shall he be a silent or a known one—eh, my boy?" said the old gentleman, giving "my boy" a sly touch of his finger in the ribs.

This was hitting the confidential clerk in the right spot. His reserve melted at once into a pleasant smile, in which every tooth joined with right good-will.

"That will be as *you* please, sir!" he said, very graciously.

"No, sir, as *you* please!" returned the merchant, in his jocular way; "for you will then be the youngest and most active member of the firm, and, of course, it will be a pleasure, on our parts, to yield to your wishes in that, as in every other particular!"

"You are very good, sir!" said Mr. Brigham, with a very low bow.

"The silly fool believes every word of this guy!" thought the *pious* merchant. "And he has heard it, off and on, these six years. The simpleton! It is singular how a man will assist another in making a fool of him on his own cherished hobby!"

Mr. Brigham now rose, and commenced buttoning up his coat.

"What, Brigham, my boy!" cried Mr. Townsend, "you are not off?"

"I have an engagement at nine, and it only lacks a few minutes of that time. I should be most happy to remain a while longer, but—you know my weakness—punctuality!"

"Say, rather, your strength, my boy! Nothing like it—nothing like it. It will make you a bank president yet!"

"You are very good! Be kind enough," he added, turning to Mrs. Townsend, "to give my respects to Miss Landon, and say Good-Night for me to Mr. Leland."

"I shall take great pleasure in doing both, Mr. Brigham."

"You are very good! Good-night!"

And after a gentle bow to each of the occupants of the drawing-room, the confidential clerk took his departure: a smile on his lip, and bitterness in his heart.

As he disappeared, Mr. and Mrs. Townsend exchanged glances, which said as plainly as glances could—

"A crafty fish; rather shy of the hook: but *we* know how to make him bite—eh?"

A few minutes later, Samuel and Isabella returned; the former serene and happy, as usual; the latter radiant with triumph.

"Ah, 'Bel!" said her guardian, playfully, "your knight is off, you see, and the chair that once knew him knows him no more!"

"Indeed, uncle! You amaze me! Pray, to whom do you refer?"

"A pretty question! To whom but your Knight of the Rueful Countenance—the dear, delightful Mr. Brigham!"

"Mr. Brigham, indeed! *My* knight? Dear guardy, what put that silly notion into your head?"

"Silly, 'Bel!"

"Very silly, indeed, guardy! What is Mr. Brigham to *me?* Oh, Samuel—will you join me in a sacred melody? I do so *love* sacred music!"

Samuel signified his willingness, and in another moment Isabella was seated at the piano, her rich voice and Samuel's uniting in an inspiring anthem.

Mr. Townsend glanced at his wife. Their eyes met, and they exchanged a meaning smile.

"A rare, bold girl!" muttered the former, in a low whisper. "She is bent upon a conquest!"

"In which, with all her art, she will not succeed!"

"Umph! I don't know! In the battle of life, the boldest oftenest take the prizes. Hark, how she plays—the cunning baggage! With what vigorous confidence she strikes the keys! Observe her melting glance up at her victim, as if her very soul were in her eyes. And *he*—poor, inexperienced simpleton!—takes it for the inspiration of devotion! Well, I don't know that I should laugh at him. Such a pair of eyes might well capture an older heart and a wiser head!"

"Nay, she has not won him yet!" said Mrs. Townsend in a dry, husky voice, and raising her left hand to her breast, which was throbbing with singular violence and rapidity.

"But she *will*—depend upon it. She is playing upon his sympathies!"

"What then?" said Mrs. Townsend, withdrawing her gaze from the piano, and turning it upon Miriam.

"What then, Jane? How dull you are! Why, 'Bel is a master-spirit in that line; and *he* a simple, impressible, inexperienced youth!"

"True!" observed his wife, passively, with her eye still fixed upon Miriam.

"As I live," continued the merchant, "she *feels* her triumph. Note how she struggles to catch his eye. She is evidently proud of her conquest!"

Mrs. Townsend made no response to this remark.

"Well," added her husband, "he is a magnificent fellow, to be sure. But then, that isn't much, after all, in a man. Money is the main thing, and Samuel is troubled but little with that. 'Bel, however, thinks, I presume, she can afford to indulge her own wishes in this case, since she has enough for both. Well, perhaps she is right. Samuel, with or without money, is, after all, an object. Young, handsome, noble—really, I cannot help admiring 'Bel's taste. The young fellow is well worth the winning!"

Mrs. Townsend made no answer.

Her husband looked at her, as if for an explanation of her silence. As his glance fell upon her, his features became grave with surprise.

And no wonder. Mrs. Townsend was at that moment a sub ject for an artist.

A round, pale spot, of a snowy whiteness, was visible in the hollow of her cheek. Both hands were pressed tightly upon her left breast, as if to stifle the loud beatings of her heart. Her dark eye, which was riveted upon the fascinating Isabella, appeared to be shooting at the latter balls of malignant fire.

"Jane, my dear," said her husband, touching her softly on the shoulder, "what is the matter?"

A blush—a slight start—an air of confusion—a quick, brave struggle, and Mrs. Townsend was herself again, and in the full possession of her intellectual powers.

"Look there!" she said, in the low tone in which they had been conversing, as she pointed towards the window.

Her husband turned his eyes in that direction, and started. He was about to speak aloud, but Mrs. Townsend's hand was over his lips in an instant, and the half-uttered word was drowned by the swelling voices which accompanied the stirring music of the piano.

Prostrate, and apparently lifeless, her face downward, upon a lounge, lay their mutual favorite—Miriam.

"Not a word!" whispered Mrs. Townsend.

"She has fainted—"

"Hush!" said his wife, as they passed softly towards the body. "She loves him—"

Samuel?"

"Yes, and this has been too much for her."

"Poor thing!"

"Hush! Raise her head gently while I apply my salts. So—not a word. *They* must know nothing of it, for the world!"

A few seconds passed away, and the couple were rewarded for their solicitude by a low sigh. This was followed by a gentle quivering of the muscles; that by a second and deeper sigh, and Miriam looked up. Her face was pale, her eyes dry, her hands cold, and her frame trembling with a cold shiver.

The music was still pealing—the two voices still ascending.

A glance—and Miriam comprehended all. In an instant, her face was crimsoned with a burning blush. The poor girl uttered a low moan, and hid her face on the bosom of her aunt, who was sitting on her left—her uncle, holding and rubbing her small trembling hand, on her right.

"Hush, Mirry, darling!" said Mrs. Townsend, in a low whisper; "not a word. Compose yourself. Inhale my salts. Be calm. *They* know nothing of it!"

"Art sure, aunt?"

"Quite sure, darling. There—wipe your eyes, and look bright and cheerful, as if nothing had happened. There—that's a love!"

"Call up your courage, Mirry!" said her uncle, encouragingly. "They are bringing their anthem to a close."

"Put on a smile, Mirry, love. There—that's it. Now you are our own darling once more!"

"Dear aunt, stay by me. I am feeble still!"

"Summon all your nerve, dear. I'll keep near you."

"They are finishing," observed Mr. Townsend. "Are you composed, my dear?"

"Quite, dear uncle. How shall I thank you?"

"Hush! Don't mention it. They are done. I must rise and keep them away!"

"Bravo, 'Bel! bravo, Samuel!" he continued, approaching them, and taking a hand of each. "Admirable! I really must thank you for the pleasure which you have given us. You cannot conceive how deeply you have touched our feelings!"

"Say, rather, the music," returned Isabella; "it is so solemn, so inspiring. Don't you agree with me, dear aunt?"

"Something should be said for the singers, 'Bel! You are really too modest!"

"What think you, Mirry, dear?" continued Isabella.

"Matchless hypocrite!" murmured Mrs. Townsend, mentally.

"The music is certainly very inspiring, cousin."

"And solemn, too—eh, coz?" persisted Isabella.

"There can be no doubt of the solemnity of sacred themes, in whatever shape, I think!" answered Miriam, modestly.

"True, Miss Selden!" observed Samuel. "Sacred themes are ever solemn, because they are higher than all of earth; because they purify, ennoble, and elevate the soul; and because they lift the heart, as it were, to heaven, and bring it into a joyful communion, if only for a little time, with God!"

"This man, at least, has courage," mused Mr. Townsend, remembering Mr. Brigham's observation; "for he is in EARNEST!"

"But, dear friends," continued Samuel, with a serene smile, "there is a something higher and more inspiring than even music—a something which takes us nearer and quicker to our Prince—PRAYER! To him who knoweth not its use, it is as nothing; to him whose heart approaches it in feebleness or in doubt, it returns no joy; but to him who goes to it in faith—a little thing, but ah! how full of price!—it is as the refreshing breath of the morning, when cleansed and gilded by the sun!"

"I always feel happier after prayer!" exclaimed Isabella, with affected feeling. "Don't you, Mirry, dear?"

"Precious hypocrite! you play your game boldly and well! I'll preserve Miriam from your malevolence, however," mused the merchant.

Then speaking aloud, he said—

"Yes, there is an unction in prayer. Let us partake of it now!"

All dropped upon their knees: two, at least, in reverence.

Mrs. Townsend and Miriam by the lounge, near the window; Mr. Townsend by the sofa, his face towards the wall; Samuel on the floor, midway between the centre-table and the folding-doors; Isabella, in a studied attitude, her face towards the object of her new attachment, her forehead bowed upon her clasped hands, and her eyes turned stealthily upon him, whom she was now exerting all the fascination of her woman's powers to win.

"Samuel," asked the merchant, "will you kindly lead the way?"

There was a momentary pause—a solemn silence, and then the pure soul of Samuel was communing, in artless, earnest simplicity, with our Common Friend.

CHAPTER VIII.

Between nine and ten o'clock of the following morning, Miriam ascended to her chamber, and quietly dressed herself for a visit to Mrs. Jones. Her dress was in keeping with her modest, retiring nature: simple, neat, and plain. On her way to the hall door she was met by her aunt.

"Going to take the air, Mirry?" inquired the latter, who had a shrewd conception of her real object.

"Partly, aunt. Good-bye for an hour!"

And she passed from the house. Fifteen minutes later, Miriam was threading her way up a short arched alley leading to a small yard which faced a dingy two-story brick building, with a door at either end, which communicated with the first and second floors; a flight of stone steps in the centre led to an area, which branched off, right and left, to as many doors, each leading to a small, narrow, dirty den, termed by courtesy a basement, which was partially lighted by a small window-sash, whose "panes" were variously made up of castaway hats, protruding bunches of discarded frocks, tacked and ragged newspapers, "cut to fit," and here and there a genuine sheet of glass, miscellaneously spotted with greasy finger-marks and serried ridges of congregated dust. A hod leaning against the area before one door, and an unwashed, uncombed urchin peeling potatoes at the other, indicated the character and nationality of the basement tenants.

The yard, or rather the narrow space which was dignified by that name, was paved with medium-sized cobble-stones, between the spaces of which a mess of discarded suds, of a bluish tinge, was struggling to find its way into the absorbing earth. Three or four scattered poles upheld two sagging clothes-lines, which threatened every instant to give way beneath their drying burdens of shirts, and caps, and frocks, and flannels, and kerchiefs, of every size and color, and let them shift for themselves. Midway in the yard, as if to indicate the equal right of the tenants of both sides of the house to its use, was an open cistern, from which an Irish woman was drawing water, and equally interesting herself in filling a large tub, and in regarding our heroine with a prolonged stare.

In a corner, on the left, before a tub which was supported by a small bench, stood a short, stout female, whose lively, intelligent eye, and clean, pleasant features, bespoke her the possessor of a happy, cheerful, and contented spirit.

Mrs. Farley was a poor widow, who gained a subsistence for herself and little Bob—a short, timid, simple-minded boy of ten years, with a broken back, a misfortune which, instead of exciting the pity, evoked the derision of his schoolmates, who always called him "Humpy"—by washing, and, as her sign at the corner of the alley stated, going out to day's work.

Naturally tidy, prudent, and industrious, Mrs. Farley, as the good creature herself expressed it, "had always enough to do, enough to eat, enough to wear, and enough to be thankful for; and if the boys would only let her Bob alone, and not call him names, and not hit him, she would be the happiest woman in the world."

Mrs. Farley was a devout Christian, a good neighbor, and a faithful friend. She understood religion as they understand it who know it by its realities, and not alone by its forms; and she enjoyed it as they enjoy it who are sometimes favored with visits from its Founder. Every Sabbath Mrs. Farley went up to the house of the Lord to thank Him for His loving-kindness to herself and boy during the week; and to renew her grateful praises to her Redeemer for securing her and hers a home in His house of many mansions. So humble, gentle, and consistent was her deportment, both as a Christian, a neighbor, and a friend, that even the Irish Catholics, by whom she was surrounded, were reluctantly compelled to admit that "Misses Farley, the little Methodist woman," or, as they sometimes varied it, "the little Prodisint craycher," was, after all, a "nice body," and stood almost as good a chance of reaching heaven as themselves.

Mrs. Farley was one of the few who are wise enough to make a pleasure of business. It was really delightful to see her work. She went at it with the same joyful alacrity which most women display when preparing for a ball; and she took hold of it with a spirit which seemed to say—"Here's fun; now for it." As she worked, she sung; and as she sung, she worked; and thus it was with her the livelong day, from Monday morning to Saturday night, and from January to December. Her songs were those of the Christian—hymns: hymns of joy, and prayer, and praise.

Sneer not at them, reader. Try them, rather; and when, happily for thee, thou canst sing them with the same zest and the same heart-gushing fervor as did our humble laundress, thy spirit will have realized the truth that there is a *higher* state of mind than a scoffer's.

As Miriam passed up the alley, she heard the voice of the happy laundress singing—

"And let this feeble body fail,
  And let it faint or die,
My soul shall quit the mournful vale,
  And soar to worlds on high;
Shall join the disembodied saints,
  And find its long-sought rest—
That only bliss for which it pants,
  In the Redeemer's breast."

The words were accompanied by a sound like that of a rippy dippy, dip, dip, dip, which Miriam's delicate ear recognized as that made by wet linen when rubbed and shaken by an energetic set of knuckles.

As our heroine entered the yard, her eye followed the sound, and it rested upon the cheerful countenance of the laundress, who was working and singing away like one who thoroughly enjoyed both—

"'In hope of that immortal crown,
—A-rippy dippy, dip, dip, dip—
I now the cross sustain,
—A-rippy dippy, dip, dip, dip—
And gladly wander up and down,
—A-rippy dippy, dip, dip, dip—
And smile at toil and pain—'"

"How do you do, madam?" said Miriam, as she approached the singer.

Mrs. Farley looked around at the inquirer, but without relinquishing her work, and politely returned the salute, which was followed up by the perpetual a-rippy dippy, dip, dip, dip.

"A pleasant morning, miss!" a-rippy dippy, dip, dip, dip. "Can I do anything for you?" a-rippy dippy, dip, dip, dip.

"I'm looking for a lady by the name of Jones," continued Miriam. "Can you direct me to her?"

"Yes, miss!" returned the laundress. "One moment, and I will lead you to her with pleasure." A-rippy dippy, dip, dip, dip—dip—dip—*dip*—DIP!

And the shirt was plunged into the clean white suds, then wrung till it fairly squealed, and then folded up and laid carefully upon a small pyramid of similar articles which rested upon the bench.

"Now, miss," said the laundress, as she raised her apron and wiped her arms and hands, "I am at your service. This way, if you please."

She entered the house and ascended the narrow, naked staircase—every step of which was scoured as clean and bright as the top of a new table—which led to the second floor.

"Your name, if you please?" asked the laundress, as they reached the landing.

Miriam gave it, and Mrs. Farley tapped gently at the back door.

"Come in," answered a voice, which was recognized by the visitor.

Mrs. Farley turned the knob, and they entered.

A lady, with a child in her lap, sat near the solitary window which lighted the small square apartment, which was divided from the front room by a thin partition. The lady was dressed in a bright, showy silk dress, which contrasted strongly with her present humble home. Her hair was of a light color; her eyes of a rich blue; her features straight; her lip proud and haughty; her complexion fair.

This was Mrs. Jones.

"Miss Selden," said the laundress, with an air of deep respect.

And, having announced the visitor to her guest, Mrs. Farley quietly withdrew, and returned to her work, over which she might have been heard, a few moments later, singing—

"'Oh, what are all my sufferings here,
—A-rippy dippy, dip, dip, dip—
If, Lord, thou count me meet
—A-rippy dippy, dip, dip, dip—
With that enraptured host t' appear,
—A-rippy dippy, dip, dip, dip—
And worship at thy feet?
—A-rippy dippy, dip, dip, dip.

Give joy or grief, give ease or pain,
  Take life or friends away,
But let me find them all again
  In that eternal day.'
    —A-rippy dippy, dip, dip, dip,
      Rippy dippy, dip, dip, dip."

"Mir—I beg your pardon—Miss Selden!" said Mrs. Jones, motioning her visitor to a chair. "To what am I indebted for the honor of this visit?"

It was evident from her manner that the speaker was a creature of pride, and that her change in circumstances had had no effect in subduing the haughtiness of her spirit.

"To a sincere wish to serve you," returned Miriam, gently.

"I thank you," returned the proud woman, in a cold, sarcastic tone. "But, as I am not in a position to require your aid, you need not give yourself any trouble."

Miriam felt hurt at this reply, but she stifled the indignant feeling, and replied—

"I do not wish to be considered obtrusive, but on learning that you were in affliction, I thought that—"

"You might follow in your impertinent cousin's wake," interrupted the other; "that you might, like her, *condescendingly* step down from your pride, and insult with your condescending alms one whom fortune has exerted herself to crush! You are very kind, miss; but I am not yet a beggar!"

"Oh! dear Mrs. Jones, you misapprehend me; you do, indeed! I had no such thought. Nor was I aware that my cousin had called upon you."

"Know it now, then," said Mrs. Jones, rising and taking a roll of bills from the mantel. "She came here last night, with her smooth-faced lover, Mr. Leland, and, with an air of ostentatious generosity, threw this into my lap. 'There,' she said, with impertinent condescension, 'there's a hundred dollars for you. I would give you more, but that is all I have with me. Keep up your spirits, trust in the Lord, and you shall not want. Come, Samuel!' And, before I could recover from the shock of the insult, she was gone!"

"I fear you misunderstood cousin's motive," said Miriam. "I do not think she—"

"Her motive was perfectly transparent!" interrupted the other. "It was to dazzle her lover; it was to impress him with the melting kindness of her heart—the humane richness of her nature. *That* was the motive; and he—simpleton that he is!—rewarded her generosity with a smile. If it were not that I am not yet satisfied of his real character—whether he be absolutely what he appears, or the reverse—I would have hurled the money at his retreating head!"

Miriam's heart throbbed violently.

"I think," she said, with some confusion, "that Mr. Leland is all that he seems; and I am quite sure he would not knowingly wound any one's feelings, for the world. I could tell you more of him, but—"

She paused a moment, and then added, with an effort, as a deep blush overspread her artless countenance—

"I meant to say that I esteem Mr. Leland very highly, and have seen so much of the purity of his nature, that I do not believe him capable of an ungenerous action. If you had seen how happy he was last evening when my aunt promised to step in between you and want, you would understand him better!"

"Perhaps so!" returned Mrs. Jones, who read the secret of that little, artless heart. "I am willing," she added, with a slight abatement of her hauteur, "to confess that I have not entirely lost my confidence in the gentleman. But why did he bring that brazen creature here to mock me in my misery?"

"I am not prepared to say. But it was with a kindly motive—I feel assured of that!"

"Well, let it pass," said Mrs. Jones. "And now for yourself."

"I understood from Mr. Leland that you were in distress, and—"

"Enough," interrupted the haughty woman. "I am not in want of sympathy; nor do I ask your assistance. When I stand in need of either, I know where to look for it!"

"I had no thought of wounding you," said Miriam, dropping her eyes in confusion. "I really had not; and if you will only forgive my boldness in coming, I will—"

Mrs. Jones regarded her while she spoke with a steady eye; but as she paused, her features softened. The tone and manner of the speaker touched her.

"Keep your seat," she said, as Miriam attempted to rise, "and give me your hand."

Miriam complied with her request, and the proud woman looked at her for a few moments with a cold, dry eye, as if to detect a spirit of lurking pride, of curiosity—of condescension, or of affected humility; but she could discover naught in that sweet, artless face, nor in that clear, frank eye, but tender sympathy, and real Christian feeling.

As this conviction impressed itself upon her mind, her haughty nature melted, and with a convulsive pressure of her visitor's small hand, she burst into tears.

Miriam considerately dropped her eyes, which lighted upon the unhappy woman's little one, who was looking up at her with mingled curiosity and dislike.

"Do you love poor me?" asked Miriam, holding out her hands invitingly to the child.

The latter drew back, and said—

No. Go away. You make my mamma cry!"

Miriam turned aside her head to hide an uprising tear.

"Hush, Ada—hush, you saucy little thing! Miriam is your mamma's friend. You must love her!"

"Do *you* love her, mamma?"

"Yes, darling."

The child was silent; but the expression of her eyes indicated that she had some misgivings upon that point.

"You must kiss Miriam, darling, and make up friends."

The child looked doubtfully at the visitor; but a sweet smile from the latter conquered her, and putting her little arms around Miriam, she pressed her ruby lip to hers with an earnestness which showed how completely every doubt was banished from her mind.

"Forgive my rudeness, Miriam," said Mrs. Jones, as her child sunk back in her lap. "My recent experiences of the world's pride and faithlessness have shaken my confidence in humanity."

"But not in me, I hope, dear friend!"

"No, Mirry—no!" answered the other, wringing her hand. "But"—she paused—emotion choked her utterance.

Miriam was silent from sympathy.

The child's doubts of Miriam were beginning to return.

"I have had so much to try me, of late!" added the woman, recurring to the same idea. "My husband's failure, and sudden absence—the abandonment of my dearest friends—my abject poverty—!"

"Take comfort," observed Miriam. "Better times will come. It is good for us to taste, once in a while, of adversity—we can the better appreciate prosperity. It teaches us also who is our Best Friend."

"Oh, Miriam—I cannot endure it! My heart will break!"

"Trust in Him!" said Miriam, with an impressive gesture. "He is good and kind. Trust in Him!"

The woman shook her head. Her heart was still in the world; Miriam's religious suggestion had fallen upon an icy ear.

"Think of it, Miriam!" she said, impetuously. "To be left without a dollar; to be abandoned by one's most valued friends; to be avoided by one's very relatives; to be shunned in one's adversity by those who have thriven on one's prosperity. By one's very sisters, too!"

Miriam looked down. She knew not how to answer. She was puzzled what to make of her companion, upon whose ear spiritual comfort fell as on a block of stone.

"And yet," murmured Miriam, "she has always professed to be one of God's people!"

Poor Miriam little guessed that it was a mere worldly profession; a conventional matter: nothing more.

"You do not answer me, Miriam!"

"It is very sad," said Miriam.

"Sad!" exclaimed the other, with energetic scorn. "It is terrible! Fancy it, in little. I—richly born, and tenderly cared for—I, who till now have enjoyed all that fortune could give or heart desire—I, the daughter of an opulent merchant, and the wife of an opulent merchant—I, a favored child, a caressed wife—I, who have ever revelled in the lap of luxury, and who have known poverty only by its name—I, the nursling of wealth, of pride and fashion—I. *I am a dependent on the bounty of my laundress!*"

Miriam was silent.

"While," added the impassioned speaker, "those whom I have befriended, and those who are allied to me by blood, are living in their accustomed luxury, perfectly regardless of my position! Is it not exasperating?"

Miriam could not speak, if she would. It affected her to learn that her companion was an utter stranger to that beautiful spiritual system which enables the human heart to greet prosperity and adversity, want and plenty, joy and sorrow, happiness and affliction, with an equal welcome, and an even tranquility. She had not looked for this, and the discovery brought tears to her eyes

Mrs. Jones observed them, and continued—

"I see you feel for me!"

"I do, indeed!" murmured Miriam.

"But they shall pay for it!" added the other. "For every tear they have made me shed, they shall return a groan. If they have forgotten their pride, I have not mine! I'll shame them —shame them to the very dust!"

Miriam looked up at her in astonishment.

"Ah! you may well stare at me, girl. But I have said it—they shall drain the cup of humiliation to the dregs!"

Miriam regarded her inquiringly.

"I will tell you what I mean," said the vindictive woman. "Think you I was *forced* to hide my head in this vile hole? Know me better!"

Miriam shuddered; but her companion was too absorbed in her own energetic thoughts to observe it.

"When," said the latter, "I received notice to abandon my house, I sent copies of it, without remark, to my sisters—you know them, Miriam,—they are our 'first families,'" she added, mockingly, "fully expecting they would at once hurry to my rescue, and tender me a home and support for myself and child. But—would you believe it?—they returned the copies without comment, without a word! Do you hear me, girl? My very sisters did this—my *very sisters!*" she repeated, with a vehemence which caused her timid auditor to tremble like a fluttering leaf. "I could scarcely credit my eyes," continued Mrs. Jones. "My heart sunk, my brain reeled. But *I did not fall*—no, I did not fall!" she cried, exultingly. "They did not drive me to *that!* It would have been too glorious a satisfaction for them. My pride sustained me, and I determined to punish them. There was but one way to do that—one only way: through *their family* PRIDE! I dispatched a note at once to my laundress; told her of my embarrassment, of my husband's failure and flight, of the faithlessness of my friends, of my poverty, and of my want of a roof to shelter me. She replied as I wished, and—my proud relatives have the satisfaction of knowing that their sister is a beggar, and herself and child dependents upon the bounty of a common washwoman! Ha! ha! is not that a Roland for their Oliver?"

Miriam was visibly uneasy.

"What means have you?" she asked.

"Not a dollar! Not a jewel—not a ring—not a second dress. *Their* humiliation would have been incomplete if I had reserved a solitary shilling!"

Miriam shuddered. She drew out her purse, and said—

"Will you not allow me—"

"No!" interrupted the haughty woman, with a proud wave of her hand. "Put up your money, girl. You mean well, and I am grateful for your kindness; but I would not touch a dollar of it for the world!"

Poor Miriam was troubled. She had that on her mind which she felt it a duty to give utterance to; but her gentle nature shrunk from arousing the animosity of the fierce spirit beside her. Still it *was* a duty, and she concluded to perform it, be the consequences to herself what they might.

"You are thoughtful, Miss Selden!" observed Mrs. Jones, who was quietly regarding her. "Speak out, girl. Am I the subject of your reflections?"

"Yes," answered Miriam, frankly. "I have been wondering why—but I fear you will think me over bold!"

"No, girl! I possess myself too much spirit to censure it in others. Speak out! You say you have been wondering—at what?"

"Yes," said Miriam, with a heroic effort, "that in your hour of affliction you never thought of calling upon the Lord for help."

Her companion laughed.

"Why should I?" she asked, half scornfully.

"He is so good, so generous, and so reliable a helper," said Miriam, simply. "And it is so sweet to turn to one who we know will understand our troubles, and joyfully remove them."

"I have not the honor of His acquaintance; and certainly not the faith in Him, which you appear to have, miss, or perhaps I might have done so!"

"But if you only *would* get acquainted with Him, dear Mrs. Jones," said Miriam, not heeding her sarcasm, "you would like Him, and believe in Him, and have faith in Him, too. I have known Him ever since I was a little girl, and I can testify—very humbly and very simply, to be sure, but still joyfully—that He has been *very* good to me. In sorrow I have turned to Him, and He has wiped away my tears; in affliction I have appealed to Him, and He has sent peace unto my heart. Oh, do try Him, Mrs. Jones—try Him once, and see if He be not the rarest and best friend you ever knew. He is so good, so kind; so full of truth and love; so willing to hear, and to be found by all who wish to tell Him of their troubles, and to find peace and rest. Do try Him once, dear Mrs. Jones; and you will find peace, and comfort, too, and strength to bear up with your afflictions, which must, I know, be very hard to sustain all alone. Try Him once—what He has so often done for me, He will, so full is He of goodness, as gladly do for you!"

"Would you have me play the hypocrite?" demanded her companion.

"Oh no, Mrs. Jones. I would not, indeed. But it would not be wrong to ask the Lord for help? *He* would not regard it so, I know. He would be very glad to hear what you might have to tell, and to assist you, too, Mrs. Jones, as no one else could. He tells us so, Himself. 'Call upon Me,' He says, 'in your day of trouble, and I will deliver you!' Open your heart to Him, Mrs. Jones, and only see how He will answer you!"

"Why should I?" asked the other, calmly. "He knows it well enough already! Why should I?"

"Because He asks it, Mrs. Jones. '*Give* me thine heart!'"

"It would not be worth His acceptance," returned the woman, in a voice that indicated how much she was disturbed.

"Oh, don't delude yourself with any thought like that, dear Mrs. Jones. The Lord is very full of graciousness and goodness, and He will take it with as much joy as if it were the best heart in the world!"

"I fear not," said the woman, with a shudder. "I am looking in upon it now, and I see things which make me tremble!"

"Dear Mrs. Jones," cried Miriam, with an air of simple joy, "that is a *good* sign: it is the first dawn of repentance. The Lord is looking in upon you; and the mild radiance of His eye is lighting up your heart, so you and He can see it together—so you can know what you are giving, so He can know what He is taking. Do let us kneel down and pray, Mrs. Jones—it is not fitting that we should sit or stand in *His* presence!"

"You are in error, miss!" returned the other, coldly. "I see no light there—all is darkness!"

"Dear Mrs. Jones—"

"Hear me, girl. I look in upon my heart, and see three-and-thirty years of life—but such a life! Shall I tell you of what it is made up?"

"Oh, not to me, Mrs. Jones—but the Lord; and, then, no matter of *what* it is made up, He will take it, thank you for the gift, and bless you as no one else can, for the balance of your days."

"Well, to the Lord, then, if you will have it so. Of this my life is made:—Of an infancy which was sinless, because it was pure and thoughtless. Of a childhood which was made up, in the main, of a world of studies and preparations *for* the world, but not a single solemn one for aught beyond it. It is true, I was sent, in a formal way, to Sabbath-school; but the lessons were formal, they were formally read, formally hurried through, and formally forgotten. I was sent to church, but everything and everybody was formal there, as in the Sabbath-school. The prayers were formally uttered, the sermons formally read, the hymns of praise formally sung; the congregation entered formally, joined in the services formally, and when they departed, departed formally. No one appeared to be in earnest, neither old nor young; neither preacher, nor hearer, nor singer: all were alike formal, cold, undisturbed. And yet it was called God's house; its preacher was called God's preacher; its attendants were called God's people. I could not understand it. At home, we had prayers morning, evening, and at meal-times. But it was there as at church: mere formality. My father said grace —it was short, cold, formal: without earnestness, without feeling. He opened family prayer in the morning, in the evening: but it was ever the same: formality—nothing more. Formality without feeling, formality without earnestness. My parents, my sisters, my acquaintance, my friends—all were alike. They prayed, and after prayer, the theatre; they prayed, and after prayer, a ball; they prayed, and after prayer, a jest, which was not always either pure or refined; they prayed, and after prayer, the opera; they prayed, and after prayer, slander, slang, and ribaldry, in which each deemed it a glorious feat to outdo his or her neighbor. And thus, amid formalities and informalities, beneath the pressure of solemn preparations for the world, but not a single solemn preparation for aught beyond it, my childhood passed away—stamping upon my young mind the indelible impression that life was a joke, religion a conventionalism, and everything *unreal.*

"I glided into maidenhood. I had looked forward to it long, with yearning and impatience, as the Christian looks forward to the celestial kingdom. It was to my young heart the one great season of woman's life—her golden era of love, of dress, of balls, of music, of fond hopes, of bright thoughts and happy dreams; and I found all these, enjoyed all these, mingled, however, with other things for which I had never looked. If maidenhood has its sweets, it has its bitternesses as well. It is the era of observation: for the eye then is young, fresh, sensitive, and brought for the first time in absolute contact with the *realities* of the world. I will now tell you what I observed:

"That men and women were educated systematically and thoroughly *for* the world, and only formally for the eternity beyond it.

"That while society affected to venerate religion, it set him down for a simpleton who really did venerate it.

"That the church was simply a temple where all the world assembled on a stated day in the week to witness the last triumphs of fashion.

"That it was an institution where a slight moral tone was given to the young mind—just enough to enable it to walk respectably through the world.

"A kind of market, to which managing mothers brought their marriageable daughters weekly to exhibit, and incite buyers.

"A place of resort for young men, to stare at women, and display their own mental imbecility, impertinence, and bad breeding.

"A show-room, where young women went every Sabbath to exhibit their youthful charms, to smilingly encourage the impertinence of young men, and to add to their own acquaintance.

"A forum, from which the preacher made weekly exhibitions of his intellectual acumen and oratorical powers; from which he displayed his dexterity in depriving religion of its body, and holding up its naked skeleton to view; from which he preached the Gospel to accommodate his patrons, and keep up an appearance of morality.

"An institution, which appeared to owe its construction to the mind of man, and not to that of God; which seemed to have been built to serve the interests of men, and not those of God; which appeared to have been made to endorse and legitimate the hollowness, the hypocrisies, the frivolities, and flimsy formalities of society.

"This is what I observed in the Church: Reality nowhere, Formality everywhere! What wonder, then, if, on seeing all around me formal, I grew insensibly into a firm belief that everything in life was formal and unreal, and that I grew formal too!"

Miriam could not say. She had herself never looked at religion, or the Church either, in that way; but she thought if Mrs. Jones had at that time only asked the Lord if she saw them in their true light, that He would have answered "No," and that He would then have given her other and trustier eyes, which would have enabled her to take of them a very different view. She said that humanity was naturally frail and weak, and that our Heavenly Father, in His great compassion, had given them religion to make them firm and strong; that they were liable to err, and that religion pointed out the only path of right; that they were prone to guile, but that religion made them pure; that they were proud, and hard, and bold, but that religion made them meek, and kind, and gentle; that they were cold and selfish, but that religion made them mild and open as the day to melting charity; that the Church good and gentle walked on their road to heaven; that the minister was one of Jehovah's angels to point out to them the way; and that if they heeded not His teachings, His warnings, or His pleadings, and walked a wholly different path, that the fault would be with *them*, and not at all with *Him*, in the great judgment-day.

"'I am the way and the life,'" quoted Miriam. "Ah, would you but believe in *that*, Mrs. Jones—I'm sure you'd find a comfort in it which *may* not be found in the world. The heart that is in sorrow, it relieves; the head that is bowed down, it lifts up; the mind that is in darkness, it illumines; and the spirit that is weak, it makes strong."

The proud woman shook her head.

"Too late—too late!" she observed. "My heart is too hardened and embittered by the world!"

"Oh, say not so, dear Mrs. Jones. Were it more obdurate than steel, or iron, or rock, or anything that is hard, it would break up and melt, and overflow with sweetness at HIS word! Dear friend, let us ask Him, like little children, on our knees, to be gracious, and His goodness will descend, in a stream, to your soul!"

"No," said the other, coldly, and in doubt. "The training of my life was *not for heaven*, but THE WORLD."

"But faith—ever so small a grain—will undo it all, Mrs. Jones, and put you in the heavenly way!"

"Faith?" repeated the woman, her eyes flashing with mingled terror and derision. "Faith! I *have* none. The little that I possessed when a child, society robbed me of long ago; not all at once—Oh no, society is subtler than that!—but slowly, imperceptibly, now a little and then a little, until it had filched it all, by degrees. Faith? Society allows its victims *no* faith, except in—itself! Faith in coldness, in frivolities, in appearances, in permissible frauds, in excusable falsehoods, in conventional deceits, in utter belief in unbelief, in confidence in non-confidence, in hollow pomps, in veneered piety, in *skeletons* only! Faith! Society taught me to have faith in family pride, in a brilliant position, in a fair outside, in the all-importance of wealth and an imposing appearance. It taught me how to sigh becomingly, how to smile becomingly, how to weep, walk, dance, sing, pray, flirt and laugh, becomingly; how to go to church, to the opera, and to the theatre, becomingly; how to dress, and eat, and drink, becomingly; how to enter a church, a drawing-room, a ball-room, and a thousand other places, *with an air*. How to listen to known liars, and affect implicit belief in every word they uttered. How to receive professional libertines and *retired* fraudulent bankrupts—as if the first were gentlemen, and the second honest men. How to veil anguish beneath a cheerful smile; indifference, with an aspect of intense interest. How, in fine, to become a thorough-bred hypocrite, like the world; to follow it in its habits and deceits; to join in its solemn mockeries and hollow pomps; to crown successful Knavery with honors, simple Honesty with sneers; to worship the gilded Seeming, mock at the homely Real; and," she added, with a sarcastic laugh,, "*to glide down the broad road to everlasting perdition*, FASHIONABLY, GRACEFULLY, AND RESPECTABLY!"

Miriam shuddered. Her companion observed it, and remarked, in a hollow voice—

"There is, therefore, as you see, girl, but little hope for one like me!"

"Nay, I think not so," returned Miriam, rising, however, with an uneasiness which she made no effort to conceal. "The Lord is very full of goodness; and He will gladly help you, if you will only let Him. 'Ask, and you shall receive,' He says. Why will you *not* ask Him, dear Mrs. Jones? He will listen like a father, and His Son, the Prince, will come and bring you comfort like a friend. Do ask Him, now—won't you?"

"I'll think of it," returned the other, musingly. "Yes, I'll think of it!"

"Ah, thank you—thank you!" cried Miriam, embracing her. "You will be so happy, then—so very, *very* happy!"

"You are a good girl, Miriam!" said the unhappy woman, hoarsely, as she pressed her to her bosom. "And one of these days, when my husband returns, and we are all settled again once more, you and I, Mirry, will see what we can do towards leading little Ada here in the right path! She, at least," added the woman, with a shudder, "shall not worship skeletons!"

"So we will—so we will!" cried Miriam, joyfully. "And now, dear Mrs. Jones, I must go. I promised aunt to return in an hour, and I fear she will be uneasy. But before I go, I want you to grant me two favors!"

"A thousand, Miriam. I can deny you nothing. Name them."

"You must let me lend you some money. You can return it to me again, you know, when Mr. Jones comes back. Ah! now, don't look cold again on your poor Mirry—don't. It will make me so happy. There is no indignity in *borrowing*, is there? Do take it, now, and I'll promise to borrow some of you when Mr. Jones returns—*do*, now, won't you? I shall be miserable if you refuse!"

"Well, then—" said the proud woman, reluctantly, "I will break my resolution: what is the amount?"

"Fifty dollars!" said Miriam. "It is not much; but you can borrow another fifty when this is gone, you know: and nobody will be aware of it but ourselves. Dear, dear—won't that be nice!"

Mrs. Jones surveyed the artless being before her for a few moments with an unsteady eye, a quivering lip, and a heaving breast. Then murmuring—"And but for the skeleton usages of society, I might have been like *her*!" she burst into tears.

"Dear Mrs. Jones!" exclaimed Miriam, throwing her arms

around her neck and kissing her affectionately, "don't cry—don't! Forgive me. I didn't mean to offend you by offering you the money—I really didn't. You can return it whenever you like, after Mr. Jones comes back, you know. Now don't cry—there's a good soul. You will make me so happy, if you only won't!"

"You musn't make my mamma cry!" cried little Ada, tugging with energy at Miriam's frock. "Go away, do, and let my mamma be!"

"Dear Ada," said Miriam, releasing herself from Mrs. Jones, and catching up the child, "I wouldn't make mamma cry for the world. Would I, mamma?"

"Miriam *loves* your mamma, Ada!" said the mother, with an effort. "She don't make mamma cry; mamma cries for herself."

"Mamma *musn't* cry!" said the child. "It makes Ada feel bad—*here!* Baby don't like to feel bad, mamma; makes her cry!"

"Mamma won't, then, darling!" said the mother, smiling through her tears.

Baby looked as if she had her doubts, and said no more, but was very watchful, for all that.

"I was not crying about the money, Miriam," said Mrs. Jones, yielding to the caresses of baby; "but at a thought which struck me at the moment. And now for your second wish?"

"That you will kindly permit me to call again to-night, with Aunt Townsend, and perhaps Mr. Leland," said Miriam, with a slight glow. "I am not quite so sure of *him:* although I would very much like to have him come," she said, hesitatingly. "He is so good, and—you would like him so!"

"Granted, Miriam. Call, both of you—all of you—as often as you will!"

A ray of joy animated Miriam's handsome countenance.

"Oh, dear Mrs. Jones—you make me so happy with your kindness!" she cried. "I shall always remember it. Good-bye!" she continued, embracing her and baby both at once. "Good-bye—good-bye, Ada!"

And Miriam tore herself away—hastily wiping her eyes as she fled from the apartment.

She paused a moment on the landing to recover her self-possession, and then slowly descended the stairs.

Upon reaching the yard, she found the ever-cheerful laundress working away with right good-will, and singing gayly as before:

"'My God, I know, I feel thee mine,
—A-rippy dippy, dip, dip, dip—
And will not quit my claim,
—A-rippy dippy, dip, dip, dip—
Till all I have is lost in thine,
—A-rippy dippy, dip, dip, dip—
And all renewed I am.'"

Miriam waited till the stanza was concluded, and then laid her hand gently on the singer's shoulder.

Mrs. Farley looked around.

"Oh, is it you, miss? How d'ye do again? Are you going?"

"Yes," said Miriam, with a smile. "But I want to know your name?"

"Oh, dear—is that all?" said the good creature, laughing. "Farley."

"Thank you," said Miriam. "Mine is Miriam. You and I must get acquainted, Mrs. Farley. I see you are one of our Prince's people!"

Mrs. Farley looked at her for a moment in surprise. Suddenly, however, her mild features became radiant with delight.

It was with an intuitive perception of Miriam's meaning.

The eyes of the pair met, and sparkled with mutual gladness. For each recognized in the other an humble, sincere sister in Christ; and the cordial bond of Christian sympathy united them in heart.

A smile of singular sweetness passed between them; and a brief silence followed, as if their joy was too great for utterance.

It was as an unexpected meeting of two pilgrims bound for the same pleasant goal.

Their joy at length found vent in a mutual sigh.

"Oh, dear!" cried Mrs. Farley, "you make me very happy."

"And you make me happy, too," said Miriam. "I shall come and see you very often, Mrs. Farley."

"Do—do!" cried the laundress. "I shall be so glad to see you!"

"Thank you—thank you; I shall be here to-night with a friend or two, and then we'll have a happy time."

"Dear, dear,—so we will!"

"Then good-bye for the present!"

"Good-bye—good-bye!"

And these two simple hearts, of only a moment's acquaintance, kissed each other as cordially as if they had been friends for many years.

As Miriam turned into the alley, the cheerful voice of the pious laundress fell on her ear—

"I hold thee with a trembling hand,
—A-rippy dippy, dip, dip, dip—
And will not let thee go;
—A-rippy dippy, dip, dip, dip—
Till steadfastly by faith I stand,
—A-rippy dippy, dip, dip, dip—
And all thy goodness know."

CHAPTER IX

Miriam returned home with an air of mingled thought and sadness. On her way through the hall to her chamber, her aunt observed her from the drawing-room.

"Poor girl!" murmured the latter. "Something has disturbed her."

Mrs. Townsend waited a while for Miriam to come down; but as the latter did not make her appearance, her aunt ascended anxiously to her chamber.

She found Miriam upon her knees in silent prayer.

"What is it, Mirry?" asked Mrs. Townsend.

"Dear aunt," said Miriam, rising, "our old acquaintance, Mrs. Jones, is in deep trouble, and I have been appealing to Our Friend for her."

"You have been to see her?"

"Yes, aunt."

And Miriam narrated all the details of her interview with the unhappy woman.

"You see, therefore, dear aunt," said Miriam in conclusion, "that we must do something for the poor lady, in addition to securing her from want. We must pray for her."

Mrs. Townsend made no reply, and Miriam added—

"The world has dealt hardly with her. It has cruelly prepared her for life's sunshine only; when want and affliction come, she has nothing to lean on. While fortune remains true, she is strong; when it fails, *she* fails too. The ground glides away from under her; she looks about her for something—a rope, a tree-branch, or a creeping vine, for safety; but in vain—all is ruin, chaos: and she feels herself going down, amid sinking earth and crumbling, toppling rocks, into a dark gulf of unknown depths, whose loud roar and deafening din drown her despairing cries. O, aunt, why *will* the world go on thus—why will it school its people thus? Are souls nothing?"

"My dear," said her aunt, "the world is very bad; but it is its people who make it so. If parents did their duty better, their children would be better, the world better. But neither parents nor the world are alone to blame. Individuals are equally accountable. Every man can distinguish right from wrong, and every woman, too; and if they persist in the wrong, they must abide the consequences. There are too many who, like Mrs. Jones, having no other excuse for their moral delinquencies, are only too glad to attribute them to the world. The world is bad enough, I admit; but it is the Mrs. Joneses who make it so; and when they get pushed into a corner, instead of crying over their own follies, they exclaim, 'The world! the world!' All this is very low, very vulgar, and very silly. Let individuals do their individual duties, and the world will get along well enough."

"But, dear aunt, if individuals do *not* do their duty, is it not *our* duty to do something for them?"

"There are persons employed by the 'world,' as Mrs. Jones calls it, for that very purpose. Ministers and colporteurs, for instance. Then we have extensive moral organizations, whose numerous agents are continually penetrating all classes of society; presses, too, sending forth their Gospel messengers, daily, to all parts of the earth, to open the eyes of the Mrs. Joneses, and prevent them from going astray. If, in spite of all these, they *will* go headlong to destruction, who is to blame? The world? Certainly not. The world, with all its skeletons, all its veneered piety, and all its solemn mockeries, does all it can to prevent it."

"*All*, aunt?"

"All it can reasonably be expected to—yes."

Miriam hung down her head sorrowfully, like one who was far from convinced.

Mrs. Townsend observed her, and said—

"Do you not agree with me, Mirry?"

"I have a thought which will not let me, dear aunt," said Miriam.

"What is it?"

Miriam hesitated.

"You will think me over bold, dear aunt!" she said, timidly.

"Nay, my dear, out with it," said Mrs. Townsend, in a kindlier tone than she had yet used. "It will give me great pleasure to hear your objections, if they are well founded; and I am sure you will be equally gratified to have them swept away, if they emanate from a wrong conception. Say on, Mirry!"

"I was thinking," ventured Miriam, "that the world, for all its charities, is still in serious error. Of what avail its generous support of preachers and presses, if it fail to *second* their efforts? Precept is but of little moment, if example be not hand in hand with it. The preacher struggles in vain, and the presses send forth but dead messengers, if society follow them not up with its own example."

"What would you have society do, Mirry?"

"For its own sake, this:—When it says: We support the Gospel with our money, let it support it also with its deportment. When it says: We hear the Gospel every Sabbath, and believe it, let it act up to its belief, as if it really *did* believe it. What kind of righteousness is that which plans a great fraud on Saturday, goes to church on Sunday, and executes it—the fraud—on Monday? Or that which says, I believe in the Lord Jesus Christ, and yet does the very things which the Saviour bids him not do? Or that which says, I believe not in wicked ness, and yet associates with, and thereby countenances, wickedness? Dear aunt, where will all this end?"

"Mirry, dear, I fear you have been imbibing some of the poisonous opinions of Mrs. Jones!"

"Dear aunt, do not say so. I was afraid you would think me very bold; but I could not help it. The thought *would* come. Poor Mrs. Jones herself made me think of it. It was this kind of righteousness which encouraged her in her own wrong views, which she now so mournfully deplores. Say society had set a better example to her husband, would he now be fleeing with the money that belongs to his creditors, would his poor lady be suffering for his error, would society be holding up its hands in horror at his conduct? Oh, dear aunt, we must do something more than we *are* doing. I almost feel as if it were my duty to go out into the highway and plead the cause of Christ!"

"And be laughed at for your enthusiasm, Mirry!"

"I could endure that, if I could only rescue a single soul from misery. When I think of poor Mrs. Jones, dear aunt, I am filled with terror. Say she should not repent—*what then?* And yet society is preparing millions every year for an existence equally as sad and hopeless as hers! And should *they* never repent—WHAT *then?* Oh, aunt—*you* are good and wise—you have position, means, and influence. The world knows *your* piety, goodness, and earnestness—and it will listen to you. Speak to it in some way. Tell it how it is wandering away itself, and how it is leading astray millions of other hearts who are governed solely by *its* example. And I, dear aunt—I will stand behind you, beside you, or before you, as you may think best, to second you, in my poor humble way."

And as she spoke, Miriam threw her arms around her aunt's neck, and sobbed like a little child.

Mrs. Townsend was moved. She looked down upon the

simple girl, who was nestling, in all the confidence of innocence, upon her breast, with a troubled eye.

"And but for a proud, frivolous mother, and a proud, frivolous world, I too might have been as pure and sinless as this young, artless heart!" she murmured. "Oh, mother! if thy spirit be around me, hear me. Thou might'st have devoted thy daughter to something higher than society; thou might'st have imbued her young mind with nobler aspirations than those which centre upon a hollow world! But, Miriam! thou, at least shalt not be sacrificed. Worldling as I am, I'll stand faithfully by thee!"

Then clearing her throat, which was husky with emotion, she said aloud—

"My darling, we'll think more of this. I agree with you, that something should and might be done to stir up society from its worship of skeletons. We will think it over. In the meanwhile, let us turn our attention to this affair of Mrs. Jones. If we can rescue her from temporal want, that will be a good point gained. Let us see. Her present necessities must be our first care. Suppose we can get ten persons to subscribe one dollar per week each for the next three months—that will be ten dollars per week—enough, in all conscience, to give her a fair support, and to enable her to look around for herself. Before the three months shall have expired, she will either have been joined by her husband, in which case she will be in no further need of assistance, or she will have settled upon some plan for the future."

"All this is very good, dear aunt, only we forget one thing."

"What is that?"

"The poor lady's pride. How shall we get her to accept of the money?"

"O, we'll easily manage that, my dear," returned Mrs. Townsend, with a smile.

Miriam looked at her inquiringly.

"There are two ways," said her aunt. "Through Samuel, who has a winning method of subduing pride; should *he* fail, then through Mrs. Farley, the laundress, who will readily join our little conspiracy, since it has for its object the doing of good to one who might otherwise be a burden upon herself. And we must go about this matter at once, too, Mirry, as I judge, from what you have told me of the unhappy woman's opinion of Isabella, that her proud spirit will not let her touch a fraction of the hundred dollars which your cousin left her: and Mrs. Jones must therefore be in immediate want."

"No," said Miriam, with a slight glow, "I think not in *immediate* want—that is, I believe she can get along for a few days, at least!"

Miriam, in narrating the particulars of her interview with the fraudulent bankrupt's wife, had modestly omitted to mention, or even to hint, of her own benevolent act.

Her aunt smiled. She understood the artless being before her, and read the secrets of her simple heart as plainly as her own.

"In that case, my dear," she said, delicately avoiding any allusion to the point which the instinctive modesty of her niece shrunk from mentioning, "we shall have ample time to arrange our plan and carry it into effect. The next consideration is our business of to-night. Samuel must, of course, accompany us. But how can we manage it, with Isabella in the way?"

Miriam's face crimsoned. Her aunt, however, affected not to notice it, and continued—

"Let me think—let me think. Ah! I have it. I'll fix it all at tea, and in a manner which will prevent Isabella from entertaining any hard thoughts of you. Yes; I have it. So, set your mind at rest, Mirry, and hold yourself in readiness to accompany us. We will start at seven o'clock."

"Dear, dear aunt—you are *so* good!"

CHAPTER X.

At a little later period in the day, that is to say, about two hours after Miriam had taken her departure, a proud, flaringly attired female sailed up the alley leading to the humble apartments of the laundress. She swept into the yard, and looked around her with an air of mingled hauteur and disgust. Every feature was alive with uneasiness, every movement with overbearing insolence.

Her wandering eye fell at length upon a little humpbacked boy, who was sitting in a doorway on the left. He was poorly but cleanly clad. The complexion of his oval face was of a faint brown. His mild, brown eyes were large, and full of thought. His head was supported in his left hand, the elbow resting on his knee. He regarded the stranger with an abstracted air, which told that his thoughts were elsewhere.

"Frightful!" exclaimed the female, as she turned her eyes upon the boy. "The nastiest, dismallest hole I ever saw in my life. Breeds nothing but dirt, filth, and humpbacked children. What a shocking place! It's enough to make one sick. Ugh! It sets me all in a shiver!"

The voice of the speaker was sharp and shrill. It was lost, however, upon the boy, whose mind was still roaming.

"The thing is a fool!" said the stranger, in her high-keyed tones. Then drawing nearer to the lad, she added, sharply, "Don't you hear? A lady is speaking to you!"

Thus appealed to, the boy looked up at the "lady" with his mild, thoughtful eyes, and said, in a voice which was as soft and gentle as a girl's—

"Did you speak, ma'am?"

"*Did* I? you ugly, impertinent, brazen little hunchback! Was there ever such assurance! Is that the way your mother brings you up? But it's so with all low people. They have no more idea of decency or politeness than wild beasts!"

The mild, thoughtful eyes of the boy flashed with indignation at the unfeeling insult. The resentment was but momentary, however. It fell back, timidly, as it were, to the unhappy soul from which it had escaped, as if it had not nerve enough to maintain itself in the presence of another. An instant later, there appeared, swimming about in those clear, brown, molten orbs, two wandering spirits: one of solemn sadness, another of mournful reproach; and both would have told any other than the cold, frivolous creature before him, that the soul of the poor timid boy was weeping.

"Why don't you answer me, you saucy imp?" demanded the woman, in her highest key.

"What shall I say, ma'am?" asked the boy, shrinking back, as if in dread of a blow from some quarter.

"Where can I find a Mrs. Jones? She lives here somewhere in this horrid place, don't she?"

"Mrs. Jones lives up stairs, with my mother," said the boy, timidly.

"Then why didn't you say so before, you little wretch! and not keep a lady in this nasty dirty mud all day?" cried the woman, brushing past him and darting up the staircase.

The boy drew back, in alarm, against the wall, as she swept by; when she had disappeared above, he resumed his seat on the door-step, bowed his head upon his small, slender knees, and wept silently. As he sat thus, a gentle hand was laid softly on his shoulder. He looked up, and beheld his mother, the laundress, before him.

She had been out for a few minutes, to take home some work.

"What is the matter, Bobby, darling?" said the laundress, in a troubled voice.

"Oh, mother!" cried the boy, springing to his feet, catching hold of her frock, as if for protection, and looking up imploringly in her face, "I want to die. Ask the Lord to let me die, mother. They hurt me so here!"

"Who hurts you, dear?" said the laundress, stooping down and impressing a kiss upon his soft cheek. "Who hurts you, dear?"

"Everybody," sobbed the boy. "They hit me and call me names. I cannot bear it. My heart is breaking. Feel," he said, taking her hand and laying it upon his throbbing breast, "how it pains. I want to die and go away from here. Mother, ask the Lord to let me die!"

"Poor dear, poor dear!" said Mrs. Farley, soothingly. "Was it some wicked boy?"

"No, ma'; a lady—she's gone up stairs—to—see—Mrs. Jones," cried the child.

"A lady, darling? A lady wouldn't do so!"

"She called me — names!" gulped the boy. "She said I was an—ugly hunchback, and—and—a little wretch. She *did*, mother!"

"Poor dear—poor dear! She didn't mean it. She didn't mean it, surely!" said the laundress, struggling with her feelings.

"I cannot help being an ugly little hunchback—can, I mother? The Lord made me what I am—didn't He, mother?"

"Well, darling?"

"Then why do they call me names and hit me, mother? I don't hit *them*—I don't call *them* names!"

The unhappy laundress could not answer. Her heart was bleeding for her poor timid boy.

"I can't fight, mother. I can't even bear to hurt a fly. I haven't the heart. It makes me cry to see another in pain. Then what does everybody make fun of *me*, and hit *me*, for? Didn't the Lord make me as well as them?"

"Yes, Bobby, dear."

"But I can't fight, mother, and that is why they hit me and call me names. They don't hit boys who *can* fight. There's Georgy Thompson, *he* can fight when he's a mind to, and they don't hit *him!*"

"Does Georgy Thompson hit you, dear?"

"No, ma'; Georgy's a good boy, and the other boys don't hit me either when he is by. They dassent. Georgy won't let 'em!"

"Georgy *is* a good boy—aint he, Bobby?"

"I guess he is! But then, ma', Georgy can't be near me all the time. I wish he could, and then I wouldn't be afraid."

"And why are you afraid, dear? Why don't you get brave, like Georgy Thompson, and then nobody would dare to hit you?"

"I can't help it, ma'. My heart won't let me. I always *am* afraid. The Lord made me so. I can't help it. And they all know it, and that's the reason why they hit me, and call me names."

"Poor dear—poor dear!" cried his mother, with an unsuccessful effort to stifle her own sobs.

"And therefore, ma," said the poor boy, imploringly, "I want to go away from here. I want to go and live among the angels, mother; away up there—in heaven. Ask the Lord if He won't let me, mother—ask Him to let me die!"

"My child—my child! you'll break my heart!"

"Oh, don't say so, mother. I don't want to do *that.*"

"But if you go away, Bobby, what will become of me?"

"Let us go together, ma'. The Lord will let us both in. Won't He?"

"Yes, darling. But we must wait till He *calls* us."

"But He'll call us now, mother, if you ask Him. Won't He?"

The wretched mother could not answer. She pressed her simple boy to her breast, with indescribable anguish.

"Tell him little Bobby wants to go," whispered the child, as he twined his small, thin arms around her neck, "tell Him little Bobby wants to go among the angels, because everybody hurts him down here, and calls him cruel names. And tell Him you want to go, too, and then He will let us both in together. And then we'll see father, mother, and then we'll all be happy once more!"

The unhappy mother groaned.

"Why do you cry, mother? Wouldn't it make you happy to see father? He was a good man, wasn't he? Don't you remember how he always used to kiss us when he came home from work, and how he used to take us out a-walking every summer night, and tell us such pretty things on the way? Oh, I remember it all, mother—don't you?"

The poor laundress sat down upon the door-step, and taking the boy in her lap, pressed him, in silence, to her bosom; for the poor thing could not speak.

"Don't squeeze Bobby so, ma'! It hurts," said the child. "How the sun is shining down upon us, now—how very nice and warm! It would be a bright world to live in," added the little prattler, "if the boys were only good, and wouldn't hurt me, nor call me names. I like to feel the sun upon my breast; it makes me warm and happy. I like to see it shining on the grass, and on the flowers, and on the water, and on everything, mother, because it seems to make them cheerful; and, then, it makes me cheerful too. Do you remember what father used to call the sun, mother?"

The poor laundress shook her head. Perhaps she had not heard him.

"He called it God's Eye, mother. He used to say that it saw

everywhere, and that we ought always to be very careful, because it was upon us all the time. And I guess it's true, too. It *is* upon us all the time; but the boys don't mind it much, do they? They make fun of me and hit me, all the same as if the Eye was not looking on at all!"

"Cheer up, darling—don't be afraid, even if they do hurt you. One day we shall all be Up There, where no one will hurt us and where the boys will not hit you nor call you names any more."

"Oh, that will be nice, won't it, mother? But will I have to have the cough before I go?"

"The cough, darling? What cough?"

"The cough that father had, before they took him away, and laid him in the ground? Don't you remember?"

"Oh, Bobby, dear—Bobby!" groaned the unhappy mother.

"*I* do," said the boy, knowingly. "You thought I didn't notice it, but I did. He had it such a long time! It hung to him so, I couldn t help it. I used to sit on my low stool in the corner and watch him.

"I couldn't help him—I was so small then; but I could cry, and so I used to sit in the corner and cry all alone to myself, as he coughed. How he *did* cough, though! Oh, dear! When you were away, out washing, he coughed dreadfully. Sometimes it would almost bend him double. But when God's Eye was on him, he never coughed so much; and that is why he liked to see the sun shining through the window. He was always easier then.

"But he grew thinner and thinner every day; and when you were out to work, he'd lay with his hands clasped, his eyes turned up to the ceiling, and his lips moving; telling God how much he thanked Him for being so good to him, for permitting him to pray to Him, for making him strong in faith, for blessing him with His rich mercies, for giving him a good companion in life's burden, for crowning him with happiness far beyond his deserts, and hoping He would be equally good to those he left behind, when he should be called himself away. I didn't understand all he said, but I heard all the words, and they became fixed upon my mind.

"One time—don't you remember, mother?—God's Eye hadn't looked out for many days. The sky was cold and gray; and the air was cold and gray, and it seemed as if the sun would never shine again. Father lay upon the bed, with his eyes looking for the sun; but there was no sun upon the roofs, no sun in the air; no sun in all the sky. And then how father coughed, and shook! I fancied I could hear his bones rattle every time he coughed.

"Oh, how afraid I was then!

"You were sitting by the bedside, your eye on father's—and both of you were whiter than the snow which lay then upon the ground.

"Father was breathing faintly, with his eyes turned anxiously up at the sky, looking for the sun.

"By-and-bye a white cloud, very small at first, but growing larger by degrees, gathered high up in the air; the air grew lighter, too, and milder, and then the gray crept silently away; then the white cloud broke, and the bright sun came stealing through: and then I looked on father's face. It was lit up with a smile, but he himself was *gone*, and God's Eye was on him as he went!

"He thought that he wouldn't cough so hard if the sun would only shine; and when it shone, he died!

"And this is why I ask you, mother, if I must have the cough before God will let *me* die?"

"Dear Bobby, dear—poor mother's heart is breaking! Don't talk so, darling!"

"Ah! mother, dear, how white you are—just like the clothes

there on the lines! And you are shaking, too. Mamma, why *do* you shake so? It's so like me, when I'm afraid."

"My dear, dear boy! come, we'll go up stairs!"

"No, don't mamma! *She* is up there—that fine lady who called me names!"

"Never mind her, darling. We'll go in the other room. Mamma isn't strong; she wants to lie down, a little while, on the bed."

And with her poor timid boy in her arms, the agitated mother staggered up to her litle room, and dropped, weary, and sad, and faint, upon her humble cot.

Ah! who shall measure the thoughts called up, the anguish or the sadness, by a single unkind word!

CHAPTER XI.

UPON reaching the landing, the visitor tapped nervously at the back-room door.

"Come in," said a well-known voice, and in another moment Mrs. Jones was measuring glances with her eldest sister.

"To what am I indebted for the *honor* of *your* presence?" said the fraudulent bankrupt's wife, waving, with a haughty gesture, her visitor to a chair.

"Heyday, Henrietta!" answered the latter, as she threw herself upon the proffered seat; "how very humble we are in our gorgeous palace!"

"You are pleased to be facetious, Mrs. De Witt!"

"Oh—no, madam. I am simply wondering at the magnificence of this more than royal palace," returned her sister, looking around the humble apartment with a contemptuous sneer. "Dear me, what gorgeous furniture! How these superb chairs would set off my drawing-room! They must have cost a fortune, each. And this Holland carpet—it flings the most dazzling Wiltons into the shade—nay, the finest Brussels is but rags to it. And this imperial parlor—how sumptuous in its magnificence, how awe-inspiring in its capacity! The President's reception-room is a very den to it! But what most extorts my admiration is the meekness of its imperial mistress!"

"She cannot but admire the lady-like accomplishments of her guest, whose amiable qualities she has never been able to appreciate so well as now!"

"Ah! you are *so* condescending!" said the visitor. "If there is anything which delights me more than another, it is to see a queen, or a princess, or any great lady, put herself upon a level with her inferiors. It tells so favorably for the ripeness of her judgment and the simplicity of her heart!"

"They who have the honor of a familiar acquaintance with Mrs. De Witt, cannot do otherwise than esteem her!" sneered Mrs. Jones. "They who know her best, admire her most. At her own fireside, who so loved? Her husband sighs for her perpetual presence, as his only source of happiness. Her children look up to her with an affection which no human tongue can express. Her servants—it may be said without irreverence—fairly worship her. In society, who so admired? At her voice, scandal hides its envenomed head; at her voice, discord, malice, hatred, change into harmony, guilelessness, and love. At church, who so devout? who so humble? who so simple in her guise? In the circle in which she moves, who so loved? Among her own sex, who so popular? Among gentlemen, who so esteemed? Whose lips are so full of sweetness, whose presence is felt so sensibly, whose absence more deplored? So wide is her fame among men, that they say of her all the way from New York to Paris—'She is an angel!'"

The eyes of the visitor glittered.

"You flatter my poor qualities, madam!" she hissed, rather than said.

"Nay, that would be impossible! The sweetness of your nature is too evident. It shines in every feature, in every movement—in your very voice, which is so low and musical. So well established is your reputation, your acquaintance would regard the report of an unkind word from your lips as a calumny!"

"Dear Mrs. Jones, you overwhelm me! I shall sink beneath your praises. It is so kind in you, who are so *great* a lady—you, who revel in opulence and splendor—you, who occupy so high a position in the world, to condescend to notice one so humble as myself! I shall never forget it—never!"

"I am aware, dear Mrs. De Witt, of the strength and depth of your memory! When misfortune fell upon her who was simply related to you by a mere sisterly tie, you remembered instantly that she once imbibed from the same breast from which you had yourself, when a babe, drawn nourishment, and with your usual noble impulses, you opened wide your door and asked her in, to shield her and her little one from distress; you wiped away her tears, bade her forget her misery, and said: 'Dear one, fear not; thy sister will screen thee from distress; her purse shall be thy purse, and her home thy home, until better days come again; strangers shall not know of thy troubles; and least of all, shalt thou be left to the cold hand of charity!' Ah! this was so kind in you—so humane, so sisterly, so like your own noble heart! How the world will love you, when it hears of it!"

"Really, madam, I fear you are making game of me!"

"Oh, impossible! You must not think so. Your extreme modesty does both yourself and me a great wrong. The very rarity of virtues like *yours* makes our praise of them at once a duty and a pleasure!"

"I have no doubt of the *pleasure* you take in it, dear madam—none at all!"

"You but do me justice, dear Mrs. De Witt!"

"Ah! you great ones of the earth—ye who dwell in palaces—ye who control the treasures of the earth—can afford to be so condescending to us, who are so poor—to us, the lowly!"

"We like to encourage modest worth; and when it is so modest as yours, we like to encourage it very much indeed! It might pine else, and die unknown: and what a loss *that* would be to the world!"

"Ah!" said her elder sister, with a smile, "that reminds me—"

"Indeed! You have a mind, then! *You!* Are people of your humble nature troubled in *that* way? What a burden! How it must annoy you!"

"We have so many burdens—we, the lowly!"

"I had supposed you to be mere gatherers and venders of rags. And you are really burdened with minds, too! My good woman, what do you do with them?"

"We *think*, sometimes."

"Really! You amaze me! Yourself, for instance—do *you* think?"

"At times!"

"Poor thing! And you look so innocent, too! Who would dream, from your appearance, that you possessed a mind? Poor creature! I pity you!"

"I have a heart, too!"

"No! What—*you!* You have eyes, I will admit; for they are glaring now like a wolf's; and teeth, too—*large* ones, like the tusks of a wild boar. Pray, good woman, do they regard you as *human* in the sphere in which you move?"

"If I have the tusks of a boar, fool!" cried her sister, breaking out, "beware of them!"

"Ah! poor thing! it threatens; its shrill yell reminds me of something very amusing!"

"Ah! amusing?"

"Yes, a cracked pipe!"

"Beware—beware!"

"Oh, dear! The bristles on its upper lip are becoming erect; and the poor thing itself is losing its temper. One may look in the next moment to hear it yelp like a hungry hound. And it came here, poor thing, to make us angry; but it has only succeeded in making us smile! Poor thing! it should learn that to lose its temper is to acknowledge defeat. Pray, good woman, if you *are* a woman, don't make such wild faces—you will frighten my child out of her sleep!"

"Ah! your child?" said her sister, with a sinistrous smile. "A pity it has no father!"

"Oh, its father is safe enough, and near enough. Take your your eyes from off her, serpent! *She* is human."

"Dear me, what a pity!" returned the other, in a silken voice which disturbed the mother. "Were she *not* human, she might feel it less!"

"This is a mere trick to alarm me!" murmured Mrs. Jones, whose heart throbbed with fearful violence. "Yes, a mere trick. But I'll be on my guard!"

"Poor babe!" continued her sister, as if apostrophizing the child. "You little dream of what is in store for you. And a smile is on your face, too. Ah! if you only knew how *near* you are to—*misery!*"

"Croaker!" cried the agitated mother, "take your basilisk eyes from off my child. If you have more venom in your heart than you can bear, spit it out boldly upon ME!"

"Dear me!" simpered the other, silkenly. "How *very* imperious! Pride is so admirable a quality, too! Pity it should have a fall!"

"What mean you?" cried her sister, her lip trembling in spite of all her efforts. "You mean something. Spit it out!"

"Very proud, indeed! And so your husband is quite safe, and *very* near? Dear me! Faith is so very touching, and then so beautiful—yes, *very* beautiful!" continued the brutal woman, enjoying her triumph with satanic delight. "And he will come back, too, of course? Oh yes, he will come back, with all his money, which he obtained so honestly—so *very* honestly! Yes; he *will* come back. He *means* to do so. How good it will be in him *to* come back! And you know *all* about it, too! Dear me—dear me!"

Mrs. Jones surveyed her as if she meditated a spring.

"You will shine, doubtless, *when* he comes back," continued the pitiless woman. "Ride over us all, like some great queen who understands both the whip and the reins. And you will ride with *him*, too. Dear me! what will become of poor me, *then?* I shall be compelled to get down on my knees, and beg for mercy to my *high* sister. Ah! that will be a sad time for me! I think I had better conciliate you now—now, *before* he comes back!"

Mrs. Jones was paler than a sheet. She tried to speak, but could not. It seemed to her as if her lips were riveted together. A dread of some great calamity crept from her heart, and seated itself in her eyes.

"If you are a woman," it said, "have the pity of one woman for another woman!"

But the lips spoke not at all.

"Ah!" said the woman who was not a woman, "you are not so very certain he *will* come back; you are not so certain he *is* safe or near. Dear me! How very condescending an admission, for the imperial mistress of this imperial palace! By-and-bye, you will perhaps make *another* condescension—who knows? If you would come *down*, now, to my poor level—what might happen *then*?"

The eyes grew softer by degrees; and the dread looked more and more imploring.

A cold smile, full of triumph and malignity, lit up the simpering lips of the pitiless woman.

"But I am a detested thing—I," she said, in her chilling, silken key; "hated by all, and—*told* so; a fright, a shrew, a vixen, a scandal-monger; have eyes like a wolf's, teeth like the tusks of a boar, and my smile is enough to frighten infants from their slumbers! How *very* flattering!"

The dread looked out from its blue windows, and said, "I take back every word—every one!"

And the lips broke, with a fierce struggle, their rivets, gurgled out one word, and then broke off suddenly, as if they had said their last, and would never speak more—

"Mercy—"

There was a trembling in the body; the hands met, clasped, and stretched out imploringly.

And then the entire body sank, as if forced down by some powerful but invisible will.

Mrs. Jones was upon her knees!

"Dear me, how interesting!" said her sister, with a silken 'hem! "Our great lady makes *another* condescension. She asks a *favor* of poor humble me—of the fright, of the wolf's eyes—of the wild boar's tusks. Who would have thought it? And she looks *penitent*, too—*very* penitent! Dear me! I'll warrant, now, she thinks me *almost* human—almost a member of the human species!"

The dread repeated its appeal.

The lips strove to second it; but could not. They were riveted again.

But the outstretched arms trembled, and the body shook as if laboring with a chill.

The cold woman enjoyed her triumph like a wild beast at a banquet of bleeding flesh.

Then, concentrating all her venom into as few words as she could, she said, in the same icy key—

"Does my lady want *advice?* She shall have it. Let her change her name; let her put her child out to board, since it is too young to be put out to work; then let her go to some Southern city, and set up a school, or, what might perhaps be better, turn governess. That is my advice.

"Does my lady want *money?* She shall have it. Here are five dollars. When they are gone, let her write or send for more to the 'fright,' and she shall have it.

"Does she want *news?* She shall have it. Her husband will *not* come back. He has fled to Europe. He took the steamer at Boston, where he was met by a paramour—the wife of Mr. Clarke, the hardware dealer—a member of his own church—an old acquaintance of my lady, I believe. He has eloped with Mrs. Clarke—they are now on their way to England—and the Rhine. He will NOT come back!"

The cold woman turned upon her heel—the door behind her opened and closed—and the cold woman was gone.

But she left another cold woman behind her—senseless on the floor.

CHAPTER XII

Dusk came. The family of the dry goods jobber were assembled at tea, which was nearly over.

"My dear," said Mrs. Townsend, as she filled her husband's third cup of steaming souchong, "I have a call to make this evening. How do you feel?"

"Very lazy and very tired," returned her husband, laughing. "Do let me off, and I remain yours most devoted and in debt, for a new dress, or anything else you may think a fair equivalent, John P. Townsend!"

"How very gallant!" returned his wife, with a charming pout. Then glancing at Samuel, she said, "How do *you* feel, Samuel? For I am determined to have a beau!"

"Very like gallanting a fair lady," answered Samuel, "providing she will accept of my company."

"Which she will do with great pleasure and many thanks," said Mrs. Townsend. "And now I think of it," she added, "it will not do for me, a married woman, to be seen walking out alone with a young man. Due regard must be had for appearances. I must positively have a lady companion!"

"Oh, by all means, aunt! Appearances are everything in such cases," cried Isabella, who hoped to be the favored one.

"I agree with Isabella," said Mr. Townsend, "particularly in the present case. Who knows? I might wake up in the morning wifeless. And now I think of it, the steamer for Europe sails in the morning. I decline to run the risk. I insist, Mrs. Townsend, that you take one of my nieces with you. We business men have a weakness—we like securities."

"Barbarous man!" exclaimed Mrs. Townsend. "Have you no pity?"

"Security, madam—security. When I lend my money, I like to know what I shall have to fall upon in case it fail to reappear, in due season. And when I intrust my wife to another, who is of far more value to me than all my money, should I be less cautious? Security, madam—security!"

"Cruel man!" pouted his wife. "Who will be my security? Will you, Mirry?"

"If guardy will consider me sufficient!" replied Miriam, timidly.

"What say you, barbarous man? Is Miss Selden 'good' enough in your judgment?"

"Abundantly so," returned the merchant. "Miss Selden is perfectly 'good.' What say you, miss? I prefer direct replies not intermediate ones. Will you be answerable for Mrs. Townsend's safety with this young gentleman? Will you be responsible to me, her liege lord and master, that she shall not follow in the footsteps of her illustrious predecessors, by taking the first steamer for Europe with this gentleman, and thereby subject me to irreparable loss? Answer; and let your answer be in conformity with the provisions of the Revised Statutes of the State of New York, and all other enactments made and provided for the better security of John P. Townsend, himself, his heirs, administrators, and assigns."

"I will," said Miriam.

"Enough. All right. Go ahead, and Isabella and I will stay at home and make ourselves as miserable as possible."

Isabella smiled, and—quietly bit her lip.

"Will you be gone long, aunt?" she inquired.

"Ah! my dear, do not ask me! Look at my eyes, and tell

me if you ever saw me look more miserable. To think that my own dear, cruel husband would not trust me on my own responsiblity with so respectable a gentleman as our dear friend here. I shall never get over the humiliation!"

"Take comfort, madam," said Isabella. "You are not alone in misery!"

"Good!" thought her uncle. "That last sentence was designed for Samuel! She dies hard!"

"Ah!" said Mrs. Townsend, rising, and shaking her small plump fore-finger at her husband, "you are a naughty, cruel, hard-hearted man. I shall never forgive you—never!"

"Don't say *that*, my dear. You will kill me. The bare thought of the extraordinary risk which I am running makes me tremble, and even now I have a great notion to demand a second security."

"Ah! Then it is high time I look to myself. Come, Mirry—Samuel—aid me. Let us fly. I am in danger!"

Ten minutes later, the trio were on their way to Mrs. Farley's.

Isabella saw them depart with a troubled eye.

"Shall we talk, my dear, or read?" asked her uncle.

"Oh, just as you please, guardy. I am not particular," said Isabella, throwing herself on the sofa.

"Then I will read," said Mr. Townsend. "To tell the truth, I am absolutely worn out. I have had a hard day of it, and a little reading will do me good." Then he added to himself—"Fire and fury are in her heart, if the pattering of her little foot means anything!"

And he picked up an evening paper, and appeared in a few moments to be perfectly absorbed in its leader. An occasional sly glance at his niece, however, indicated that his thoughts were not *wholly* taken up by the article, and that under his grave exterior he was quietly enjoying a very amusing comedy.

Isabella was evidently ill at ease. She looked like one sitting upon thorns. Her eyes were turned towards the opposite side of the drawing-room with an expression of intense thought. An occasional spasmodic twitching of her ruby lip, the perpetual pattering of her foot upon the carpet, and the high color in her cheeks, represented the condition of her feelings.

"Her blood is up. There will be fun presently!" mused her uncle.

In a few minutes, Isabella rose, and approaching the centre-table, she caught up a magazine, and ran her eyes through its pages.

"Bravo!" thought the merchant, silently regarding her. "She runs from the prose to the poetry, and from the poetry to the prose, as if they were one continuous subject. It is better than a play!"

The magazine was soon dropped, and a book picked up.

Her uncle glanced at her slily.

"Well, I shall burst!" he muttered. "She is reading with her whole mind, and with the page upside down!"

The book was not long in following the fate of the magazine.

"What next?" mused the merchant. "The magazine again, as I live!"

It was true; but the young lady was now examining the plates.

A few moments, and the magazine was lying beside the book.

The young lady now took out her watch, glanced at it impatiently, and then put it back, accompanying the movement with a long-drawn sigh.

She looked at her uncle, who was apparently very deeply engaged upon the money article of his newspaper.

Isabella took up the book again, opened it, and laying it upon the table, made a furious attack upon the middle of a chapter. She maintained her share of the combat bravely for nearly twenty minutes; but owing to some inexplicable cause, she did not get beyond the third line, at which she hung with a tenacity which spoke volumes for her will. In the end, however, she drew off from the contest, and returned to the magazine, which she also abandoned a few minutes later.

"Jealousy wakes up a woman wonderfully," mused the merchant. "Here is a living example of its efficacy. Never before have I seen my fair friend so thoroughly aroused. She is always wanting a sensation; and now her wish is gratified. I shall be lucky if I escape a broken head—for she begins to look dangerous. If Samuel could but see her now, and read her as I do!"

Miss Landon was leaning back in her chair, and regarding the obstinate book, and equally obstinate magazine, with a fierce eye.

"She is meditating vengeance against somebody!" thought her uncle. "And Jane tells me that she left Mrs. Jones a hundred dollars, too. Money thrown away, for Samuel, with all his simplicity, is certainly not fool enough to let himself be caught by this tartar!"

Isabella drew off from the book and magazine, and approaching the piano, ran her fingers over the keys. The sounds which followed appeared to rouse her partially from her abstraction. She selected a sheet of music, and then seated herself before the instrument, as if bent upon driving away the nervous impatience of her mind.

Her uncle watched her attentively and in silence.

Isabella struck the keys to a soft, plaintive melody, but broke down ere she reached the second stanza.

"I thought so!" mused the merchant. "Her spirit is up, and has no sympathy with a tranquillizing air like that. Now what is she doing?"

A very simple thing—throwing the music sheet upon the floor!

"Bravo! There's seventy-five cents treated with indignity,

without saying anything of the insult to the unfortunate com poser! I shall burst directly!"

Isabella again struck the keys. This time it was with a bold yet delicate finger. Her air, manner, eye—everything, indicated that her mind was under the influence of an inspiration.

Her uncle regarded her with mingled amusement and surprise. "Her genius is speaking," he observed mentally. "Her mettle is up, and now for a whole opera, extempore. Oh, for some one to take it down!"

He guessed correctly. The composition which followed was Isabella's own. It was the conception of a mind in its highest state of feeling.

The merchant listened: it was to a romance.

—A mild, pleasant strain rose softly in the air.

A shepherd youth, a perfect Apollo in beauty, is sitting on a hill and charming his flock with the melody of his pipe. It is a bright, sunny day, and far away before the player stretches a landscape of surpassing beauty.

A young, noble, and high-born lady, accompanied by a single attendant, appears at the top of the hill. The lady is dressed as becomes her rank. She carries in her right hand a bow, at her back a quiver containing a few arrows. Of all her companions in the chase, her favorite attendant—who is one or two years younger than herself—alone remains; the rest are scattered, lost, and the lady and her companion are seeking their way back to the castle.

They see the shepherd, and approach him: partly out of curiosity, and partly for information of the nearest and best route to the castle.

As they draw near him, they are surprised at the touching pathos of the melody which issues from his pipe. The tenderness of the air, and the skilfulness with which it is performed, tell the listeners that the player, notwithstanding his rustic garb and the humbleness of his occupation, is a youth of deep feeling and rare talent.

The lady, of a bolder nature than her attendant, is the first to face the shepherd, who regards her with surprise.

The suddenness of her appearance, the richness of her dress, and the magnificence of her beauty, amaze him, bewilder him, stupefy him.

On her side, the lady is startled at the noble beauty of the shepherd, at the commanding grandeur of his air, at the pleasing tone of his strikingly handsome features, at the faultless symmetry of his form.

She speaks to him, and when he replies, the lady discovers that the music of his voice is richer than the melting melody of his pipe.

The lady's heart is lost. It is in the keeping of the handsome shepherd youth, whose simple mind never dreams of the rich conquest he has made.

At this moment the humble attendant draws nigh. As the rich brown eye of the youth falls upon her, his countenance lights up with a smile, which the lady mistakenly imputes to derision at the contrast between her own dazzling loveliness and the simpler beauty of her attendant.

The lady endeavors to acquaint the shepherd with the happy impression which his beauty has stamped upon her heart; but the simplicity of his nature prevents him from understanding her.

The lady is in distress, in torture, because she cannot tell him bluntly that she loves him, without overstepping the bounds of delicacy, without sacrificing the modesty of a proud and virtuous maiden.

She leaves him, and returns, with her attendant, to the castle, where she is besieged daily by hosts of high and noble suitors, who vie with each other for the honor of her love and her hand. But she turns a deaf ear to their entreaties, because her affections are fixed upon the humble shepherd of the hill.

She visits him again and again—always accompanied by her attendant—and invariably leaves him with a breaking heart, because his simple mind *will* not understand that the rich, high-born lady loves him, and wishes to make him her liege lord.

One day the lady desires to go and see her shepherd love, as usual, and sends a summons to her favorite attendant; but the latter is not in her apartment, nor yet in the castle. The lady is surprised, indignant, and waits awhile for her return. An hour passes; the girl is still absent; and, with a sigh, the lady sets out alone.

As she reaches the foot of the hill, a sight greets her which palsies her very soul.

Her attendant—the recreant runaway—the great absent!—is seated on a stone, looking tenderly down upon the handsome shepherd, who is kneeling at her feet!

The faithless jade!

The artful creature! to have the temerity to enter the lists for the shepherd's love with her own mistress! Her own mistress, who had heaped upon her so many millions of favors! Who had given her money, old clothes, and one or two of her own embroidered handkerchiefs!

The deceitful, ungrateful thing!—

The tempest around the piano, at this moment, was perfectly dreadful.

Mr. Townsend was looking every moment for a thunderbolt—a loud crash—and a general wreck, which would carry off Isabella, himself, the house, and all, to some dark, unknown waste, where the eye could see nothing, and where the ear could hear naught but a deafening roar of black pitching waters, which were swallowing up and burying everything and everybody in their stern, unfathomable depths.

But, happily for Mr. Townsend, his niece, his furniture, and his house, this catastrophe did not come to pass.

The drawing-room stood firm, notwithstanding the stormy threatenings of the piano. The sofa maintained its usual gravity; the centre-table, its tranquillity; the chairs, their stolidity; the portraits on the walls, their usual serenity. Even the three little statuettes on the mantel did not appear to be afraid, the least bit.

The merchant's pleasant face was streaming with tears—of suppressed laughter. To say that he enjoyed the romance of Isabella, or rather of the piano, would but faintly convey the fact—he *revelled* in it. If he did not shake himself to pieces with merriment, it was because his constitution was more than equal to the demands made upon it by his risibilities.

The tempest, which indicated the wild rage of the high-born lady upon discovering the "shocking treachery" of her attendant, at length lulled, and the romance continued.

—The lady could scarcely believe her eyes; but finding that what they told her was only too true, viz.—that her artful attendant had, somehow, won the affections of the handsome shepherd, who was now entreating her to make him happy by becoming his wife—the rage of the great lady could scarcely be restrained. She looked around her for a weapon with which to smite the faithless thing, who had dared to step in between herself and the object of her affections. She could find nothing, however, which would answer her purpose, and, burning with wrath, she hurried back to the castle, and procured a stout whip, with which she returned to the hill—just in time to witness the lovers sealing their matrimonial pledge with a rapturous kiss.

The high-born lady boiled with jealous madness. She advanced upon the pair with her uplifted whip, the lash of which descended in another instant upon the faithless attendant's back.

The lovers started; the attendant caught her indignant lady's eye, screamed, and, with a blush at her own treachery, turned and fled—hotly pursued by the whip, which, guided by the hand of the high-born lady, fell, every instant, upon her shoulders. Up and over the hill, into a valley—from the valley to a wood—from the wood to a hill—up the hill to a mountain—down the mountain to a vale—through the vale to the sea, into which the maiden plunged, with a despairing moan—the indignant whip lashing her, and marking her, and tearing her, all the way.—

The racket of the piano during the chase was perfectly terrifying. Mr. Townsend bore it with all the resignation of a martyr, flattering himself that the wildest hurricane, like everything else, must come, in time, to an end.

Nor was he wrong.

The chase once over, the deceitful attendant once in the sea, the tumultuous roar changed instantly into a new version of "See, the Conquering Hero Comes!" amid the stirring strains of which, the high-born lady returned to the handsome shepherd, to whom she exposed the shameless perfidy of the artful attendant, breathed out to him her own legitimate love, and then marched him off in triumph to the castle, where they were immediately made one, and where they spent the remainder of their days in uninterrupted happiness.

"A marvellous composition!" muttered the merchant, with a derisive smile. "It is worthy the frivolous intellect of its frivolous composer. Her glorious *genius* has labored, and this silly rubbish is the result. The mountain is safely delivered of—a mouse. Samuel is right—mere worldlings *can*not produce aught worthy the attention of a noble mind. Great thoughts spring only from earnest spirits, intent upon great moral aims. Really, I am ashamed of my handsome but frivolous niece. Her mental capacity enables her to shine in—*puerilities*. But let us look at her romance. Samuel is, of course, the handsome shepherd; Miriam the attendant; herself the high-born lady; her own fortune the castle; Brigham and her other admirers the host of knightly suitors; and the whip simply an expression of her determination to maintain her own claims to the handsome shepherd, at all hazards. Umph! we'll see about that. And now for a small morsel of fun, *mi lady!*"

With these thoughts, the merchant rose from his easy-chair and approached the piano.

"Bravo, 'Bel—bravo!" he cried, clapping his hands. "A magnificent composition—more brilliant than 'Norma,' more inspiring than 'I Puritani.' I haven't enjoyed myself so much in—I don't know how long. I had no idea you had such a genius for—this sort of thing. Dear me! if Mr. Brigham had only been here—or Samuel—how they would have been amused!"

"Mr. Brigham, indeed!" returned Isabella, in disdain.

"Oh, I see!" said her uncle, with a sly leer. "It isn't Mr. Brigham any more—eh? It's another gentleman—eh? It's a certain handsome youth, whose given name begins with an S, and ends with an L. Oh, you little flirt! Poor Brigham will hang himself, and the coroner's inquest will be—'Died of—Miss Landon!'"

"Mr. Brigham is at full liberty to die whenever it shall please him!" returned Isabella, petulantly. "As for myself, I am rich enough to like and dislike whom I please, and I feel strong enough to insist upon my rights."

"Very true, my dear—you *are* both rich and strong; and, as I rejoice to discover, full of spirit, too—*very* full. And that is what puzzles me."

"I do not understand you, uncle!"

"Oh, you little vixen! How innocent we are! How very innocent!"

"What *do* you mean, uncle?"

"Oh, of course. That's it. What do we mean? Oh, yes. Certainly. Of course. We don't mean anything. Oh, no—nothing. Certainly not. Nothing at all. O, you flirt!"

"Really, uncle, I don't see anything so very amusing. What *are* you laughing at?"

"Laughing, my dear? *Are* we laughing? *We?* It cannot be. It is all a mistake. We are only rejoicing."

"But what at, uncle?"

"Because we have got a new B. E. A. U.—beau,—and we are rejoicing because we are so sure of him, that we dare to trust him, for a little while, with another!"

"Now, guardy," said Isabella, "you are certainly telling tales out of school! I shall be very angry with you, if you go on so. I don't *like* it!" she added, meaningly.

"Ah! well, then, we won't say any more about it. But I had thought that a girl of our spirit wouldn't stand any such nonsense. What! sit at home, while our beau goes out with another! Who ever heard of such a thing! Did *you* ever? No, *I* never. And when he comes back, *won't* we teach him who *he* is, who *we* are, and what we *don't* mean to be? Oh, no. Of course not. We haven't got any spirit—not the least mite—none at all. And, as for *her*—the saucy minx!—we *won't* pull her ears, nor tear her clothes, nor scratch her eyes out, and a few other amiable things, just to show her who *she* is. Oh, no; not by any means. We are very humble, we are; and we yield to our rivals, without lifting even a finger in self-defence! Yes, we sit at home very humbly, and see our beau taken away before our very eyes. And when they go away, we take it very coolly. We read books and magazines very carefully and very tranquilly. We play the piano and improvise whole operas. We never dream at all of giving the false one an ice-cream on his return, nor our rival brimstone for the coming week. Not at all. We are so humble!"

"Now, guardy," said Isabella, who blushed at finding her very thoughts so well understood, "do give over this nonsense, and I'll sing you anything you please."

"A bargain, 'Bel. And now, let me see. What shall it be?"

"Your favorite—'My Native Land?'" suggested Isabella.

"No, that's too patriotic for the present occasion."

"'Love not'?"

"Too sentimental!"

"'The Physician and the Dancing-Master?'"

"Entirely too humorous. No, give us something grand, something solemn, something inspiring. Ah! I have it. Let it be that anthem which you sung last night with Samuel!"

Isabella sprang to her feet like a lioness. Her cheeks were crimsoned; her lips trembled; her eyes flashed.

"Uncle—"

"Well, mi lady?"

"You—you are a brute!"

"Oh, my precious darling—"

But the young lady was gone before he could complete the sentence.

The merchant smiled.

"She is off to her room; and now look out for broken chairs and smashed crockery!" he muttered, laughing till his sides ached. "Well," he added, as he returned to his easy-chair, "I've taught her a quiet lesson—one she will remember. In future, she will let poor Miriam alone, or I am wide of my reckoning! Now that she knows she is understood, she will not show her hand *quite* so openly. There is nothing like a little tact in these matters—nothing like a little tact!"

And the merchant resumed his paper, and examined its contents attentively for the first time.

In the meanwhile, Isabella, hot with passion, hurried to her chamber. She lit the gas-burner and taking up a book, threw herself into a chair and made a serious effort to read herself into tranquillity. But the attempt proved abortive, and the book was thrown aside. Her temples were hot, and throbbing as if they would burst. She rose, and approached the wash-stand, to cool her burning brow. Her movements were quick, energetic, and full of passion. She snatched up the water-pitcher; but the suddenness, or rather the violence of the motion, caused the vessel to strike against the basin with a force which shattered it in pieces. Isabella, with a passionate cry, threw the handle upon the floor; then ringing, or rather jerking the bell, she paced the room in a state of irritation bordering upon madness.

A few minutes, and her maid appeared.

"Water—and take these things away. Quick, and no remarks!" said Isabella, in a tone which caused the girl to comprehend the propriety of dispatch.

"Marry, come up!" said the maid, as she descended to the kitchen. "I guess somebody is in her tantrums to-night!"

The fit, however, did not apparently last long. For when the maid returned with a fresh pitcher, she found her mistress somewhat more composed. And the next morning, and indeed for nearly a week afterwards, the domestics observed significantly to each other, that Miss Isabella was as "nice as pie!"

CHAPTER XIII.

But we must not forget our three friends, whom we left on their way to Lawrence street.

"Where are we going?" asked Samuel, as they turned into Broadway.

"To Mrs. Jones's," said Mrs. Townsend, who had possession of his left arm. "Miriam was down to see her this morning, and found her in so very distressing a state, that she promised to bring me to her this evening."

"Oh, I am very happy to hear that!" said the young man.

"To hear what, Samuel?" asked Mrs. Townsend, looking up at him in surprise. "That Mrs. Jones is in distress?"

"No—you could not think *that*. But to learn that Miss Selden has been to see the poor lady."

"Why, Samuel, is there anything strange in that?"

"No; of course not. But still it is a very great relief to me to learn it. I had done Miss Selden serious injustice, which I take this occasion to confess, and to entreat her pardon!"

Miriam attempted to speak, but her agitation prevented her.

"What have you reference to?" asked Mrs. Townsend.

"I had the impression," answered Samuel, "that Miss Selden listened with a cold ear to my statement of the unhappy condition of Mrs. Jones; and the idea gave me great pain. And then, too, her apparent indifference to a fellow-creature's misery contrasted so strongly with Miss Landon's noble readiness and generosity, that I could scarcely credit it. For a time it shook my faith in one whom I had learned to love like a sister. I cannot express the grief which it gave me through the night. It disturbed me even in my dreams. You will understand this better," he continued, turning to Miriam, "when I mention that, when thinking of you, I have often said to myself: 'Had I been blessed with a sister, she would be like Miriam, good as Miriam, gentle as Miriam, pure, benevolent and kind as Miriam.' But I see now how wrongfully I misjudged you; and I sincerely entreat your pardon!"

Miriam bowed the forgiveness which she could not speak. Her heart, to use a vulgar but forcible expression, was in her throat. She was very pale; but fortunately for her feelings, it was not observed by him upon whose arm she now leaned so heavily for support.

Her aunt, who intuitively comprehended the condition of her feelings, stepped forward at once to her relief.

"Oh, Samuel," she said, "you don't know Miriam. She makes no parade of her sympathies or of her benevolence. She is one of the few who go about doing good in silence."

"Dear aunt—" interrupted Miriam, imploringly.

"Nay, my dear," interrupted Mrs. Townsend, "I do not wish to invade your delicacy, nor can I suffer Samuel to labor under a misapprehension concerning one I love. I must add, Samuel, that your first impression of Miriam was correct; your second one, wrong."

"Ah, madam," replied Samuel, "you cannot conceive how happy it makes me to hear you say so. For, indeed, my second impression made me very sad!"

"I do believe the handsome fellow loves her without suspecting it!" muttered Mrs. Townsend to herself. "But, dear me! his simplicity and frankness are making sad havac with poor Mirry's feelings. Poor thing!" she continued, stealing a glance at her niece, "she is as pale as death. I must change the topic, and right speedily. How very stupid in me not to have ordered the carriage!"

"I am glad to hear you confess your error so ingenuously, Samuel," she said, aloud.

"I could not do less," returned the young man, "even to an enemy, let alone to one whom, since my residence under your roof, I have held in so much esteem."

"Poor Miriam!" mutterd Mrs. Townsend to herself. "There's balm for you! *Your* dreams to-night will be pleasanter than your last, or I know nothing of your young heart!"

Then changing the topic, she said aloud—

"We want your attention this evening, Samuel, to Mrs. Jones's case. The poor lady," she added, with a sigh, "is in distress concerning her soul."

"Ah!" cried Samuel, in a tone of delight, "that is glorious news. It makes me very happy!"

"Happy, Samuel?" said Mrs. Townsend, in surprise.

"Dear madam—can *you* ask—*you*, one of *us?* What sound more joyful to the Christian's ear than the sinner's cry for mercy—unless, indeed, it be the transporting burst which announces the consciousness of forgiveness? Oh, *that* is glorious indeed!"

Mrs. Townsend was silent for a few moments. Wild thoughts were in her brain—a deep pang in her heart. The noble simplicity, the Christian grandeur of the being upon whose arm she leant, the purity of his spirit, the moral sublimity of his sentiments, which were so common and so false in *her* and all with whom she associated, and so *true* and natural in *him*, touched the better part of her nature, and filled her breast with sensations and her mind with thoughts which were new to her. Ah! little dreamed the two pure hearts with whom she was walking of the agony of that soul which was now suffering with its *first* spiritual remorse!

"But how did this good thing come about?" asked Samuel. "I saw Mrs. Jones last evening, but there were no indications of that nature then. I made an effort to lead her thoughts to the subject, but it was attended with no perceptible success. In fact, the lady frowned upon the attempt, and seemed to regard it in the light of an insult. And now you tell me that she is, after all, in contrition before our King and Prince. O, what joy—what glory! How very good the Lord is!"

"Pure, innocent heart!" murmured Mrs. Townsend. "And to this simplicity, this unalloyed pleasure, this serenity of soul, *Faith* brings its followers! What a world of happiness I have lost!—and *for what?* Lord, help me—Lord, help me!"

This veteran in the littlenesss, the deceitfulness, the emptiness of the world, was experiencing the solid joy which glides slowly, gradually, and almost imperceptibly, into the heart of the worldling, when in the company of the pure. She was conscious of the moral atmosphere which the presence of her two guileless companions threw around her. The sensation was a novel one; it touched the better part of her nature, leaving the baser to undisturbed repose. It was to her like the discovery of a new happiness, a new delight—a holy joy. And yet, she was at the same time conscious that it was a feeling which could not last; she felt that she had no *legitimate* claim to it. It was a happiness which only belonged of right to the legitimate children of God, of which *she* WAS NOT ONE. With them it was permanent; with them, a perpetual presence. With her, a pleasure that would depart when they departed; a joy that would disappear with their "good-night," for it belonged only to themselves and those of their kind, and she could only participate in it when in the atmosphere which their presence hallowed.

As she thought of all this, the worldly woman felt as feels a poor ragged child when looking through the open halls of a rich mansion filled with happy children—only the rich mansion *she* was looking in upon was heaven, and the happy children the Redeemed.

Mrs. Townsend was recalled from her reflections by Samuel, who repeated his interrogatory—

"Are you aware how this good thing came about?"

"I think," said Mrs. Townsend, "that Miriam knows something about it. She spoke to the lady this morning on the subject, in her own peculiar way."

"Ah! good!" cried Samuel. "It makes me very happy to hear this—happy to hear that the lady is in tribulation, and happy to hear that our dear friend has been the favored instrument of leading her to repentance."

Miriam trembled, but it was with joy. Her eyes, which were modestly cast down, gleamed with indescribable pleasure.

"It is well we are not heard by the passers-by," observed Mrs. Townsend, with assumed playfulness. "They would deem it strange to hear you, Samuel, rejoicing over another's tribulation."

"Ah! dear madam, the tribulation of the SOUL? A joyful thing! Because it tells of another pilgrim on the threshold of of *His* mansion! But, Miss Selden, what is your 'peculiar' way of touching the heart, that our dear friend speaks of? It must be worth knowing, since it has proven so successful. I ask because I sometimes find it very difficult to convince minds of the ease with which they can find joy, if they will!"

"I suspect, Samuel," said Mrs. Townsend, coming up generously to the rescue of her niece, whom this question somewhat disconcerted, "that it was owing in part to the fact that she first nobly put the lady's mind at ease concerning temporal want—"

"O, dear aunt!" interrupted Miriam, "how can you—"

"Why, my dear," continued Mrs. Townsend, "I see no harm in telling the truth. And I am sure Samuel would rather hear that, than labor under a wrong impression."

"You but do me justice, dear madam," said Samuel. "I suspected that Miss Selden's visit was not confined to spiritual good alone. There is something noble in that piety which walks hand in hand with benevolence. Ah! that is *true* piety! Happy they who have the heart to feel and the hand to give in the same moment. *They* are the *real* rich."

"And do *you* never sigh for wealth, Samuel?" asked Mrs. Townsend.

"Yes," answered Samuel, in a tone which warmed up the heart of the questioner; "yes, when I go among my poor friends—when I see them suffering, and many of them *do* suffer, my dear madam!—and myself without means to relieve them. *Then*, my heart is sometimes set on money in a strange way! Then I yearn for some of the riches of the earth. Then I am sometimes tempted to murmur at my poverty!

"There is a wondrous joy in wealth. It will relieve so much want, banish so much affliction, dry so many tears

"Ah! could you but go with me to the haunts of the poor and lowly, and see how much happiness a solitary dollar will create in hearts that *have* no dollars!

"Could you but go with me to the cell-like room which serves at once for parlor, kitchen, and bed-chamber for a family of four or five—its head lying down on a thin couch of straw, in a corner, helpless with suffering, and only able to assist his family with his sighs, his tears, and his prayers—helpless with consumption, with rheumatism, or some other pitiless disease—his pale wife wasting away over the needle or the wash-tub—wasting away with penury, which all her energies can scarce keep from the door; wasting away with grief for the sufferings of her beloved, the stricken one, in the corner; wasting away with anguish at the sight of the lean, wan little ones, whose sole dependence is in her alone for bread; wasting away with iron toil which has already worn her thinner than the stricken one on the straw; wasting away with that consuming fire which enters the heart of every mother when she sees her little ones pale and feeble with hunger, and mutely imploring her for bread, which she has not to give them; wasting away with that corroding anguish which enters the heart of every woman when she sees the manly form on which her eye rested brightest in the summer hours of her youth, now prostrate in a corner, held down by want and disease, with scarce enough left of courage to reward her devotedness with a smile—to see that eye which beamed once upon her in all its pure affection, all its loving pride, bright now only with the intensity of bodily suffering and of mental anguish—to see the lip that once spoke to her young heart of a golden voyage over life's broad ocean, now thinned with want and quivering with pain—to see him who was once the one-thought of her girlish heart—him the first, the only winner of her young love, lying there before her, helpless, broken in spirit and in body—and she the faithful, the fond, the patient, the industrious, the devoted, with but little to help, to save him—dreading every day the coming morrow, lest she herself should wear out, and her love and her loved ones be left all alone:—could you but see, with me, the joy of that stricken man, the delight of his patient, and equally suffering mate, the hope which lights up the faces of the little ones at sight of a solitary dollar kindly given—you would yearn, as I do, were you in my place, for a little of that wealth which can make so many poor hearts glad!

"Could you but go with me to the lone chambers of the stricken poor, and listen to their plaintive sighs, to their touching tales of bodily suffering, you would sink with grief and sympathy. For the poor things have each their little story, and they are all of the same sad burden—want and misery. They have their little bills at the grocer's to pay, before they can get trusted for any more; and rheumatism—that eternal worrier of the poor—has them in its fangs. 'Could they but pay up those little bills of the grocer's and of the apothecary's, they would get along well enough.' Yes, 'then they would feel more encouraged, then they could get a little more credit, and a little more medicine, and then they would feel braver, and, in time, they would get well enough to rise up and go to work, and so glide out of debt altogether.' If you could only see what a single dollar will do among hearts like these; how it will make the wan woman smile, and the feeble man strong; how it will put fresh courage into breasts whom want and suffering have cowed down; how it will make a faint, despairing eye brighten up with hope, and an unnerved lip exclaim, 'Yes, I am better, now—I feel that I can bear my torments easier, now; yes, I am much cheerfuller now; yes, the Lord is very good to me, now'—you would not marvel that I sometimes pine for a little of that wealth which will send joy to so many suffering hearts!"

"I had no idea of the existence of such poverty," remarked Mrs. Townsend, as Samuel concluded. "Did you, Mirry?"

"I have witnessed some of it, aunt," returned Miriam, timidly.

"And you never mentioned it to me? And you have selfishly monopolized the relieving of it? Why," she added, a moment later, "what a flood of light is bursting upon me—what new world is this which you are opening to me? Miriam—"

"Dear aunt—"

"Why have you concealed your secret pleasure so long from me? I am almost vexed with you!"

"Oh, dear aunt—"

"Well, well, my dear, say no more about it. But remember, in future, I must share in this pleasure. And you, too, Samuel—to keep your sources of happiness all alone to yourself, and to deprive your worthy friends of assistance when you knew my purse was overflowing! What have you to say for yourself, sir?"

"That I did wrong, dear madam. In future, however—

"In future, sir, you must bear in mind that you will find an inclosure every Monday evening on the parlor mantel, directed to a Mr. Samuel Leland, who will scatter it according to his best judgment among his stricken friends!"

"Dear madam!" cried Samuel, his voice trembling with emotion, "you make me very happy. I know so many hearts—deserving ones!—who will be made glad by this! Ah! it takes so little, so very little, to light up wan faces, and ease couches of pain. I thank you, madam—I thank you!"

Let us add here, that the merchant's wife kept her word.

A few minutes later brought the party to the laundress's.

CHAPTER XIV.

MRS. FARLEY received the visitors with a sort of subdued cordiality, which impressed them with the conviction that something unusual had happened.

Samuel spoke up at once, with his usual frankness.

"You have something to tell us, Mrs. Farley?"

The laundress pointed to the door of the front room.

"The poor lady is in there," she said, in a low tone, "and I fear all is not well with her here," she added, touching her forehead with her finger.

"What do you mean?" asked Mrs. Townsend. "Not out of her mind?"

"She appeared quite well this morning, Mrs. Farley," said Miriam.

"Some one has been here since then, and brought bad news," suggested Samuel.

"That's it," whispered the laundress. "One of her sisters—a Mrs. De Witt."

"A malignant creature!" remarked Mrs. Townsend; "cold, selfish, and unfeeling; a woman whose presence is acknowledged with a shiver, and whose departure is followed by a sense of relief; a sower of dissension, mischief, anxiety, and slander; whose track is ever marked with misery and tears; an utterer of bitter things; a spirit of evil!"

Samuel shuddered at this portrait. He glanced unconsciously on his left, as if he expected to see its original at his elbow.

Miriam trembled uneasily.

Mrs. Farley sighed. She remembered the cruel words which the evil woman had thrown at her own poor timid boy, and the misery which they had produced.

"What did this woman do or say to Mrs. Jones?" inquired Mrs. Townsend, who alone, of all the party, retained her self-possession.

"She brought her bad news," said the laundress.

"Bad news it must have been, or none at all. Mrs. De Witt could be the bearer of none other. What was its tenor?" said Mrs. Townsend.

"That Mr. Jones had failed intentionally; that he had purposely abandoned his wife, and forever; that he had eloped with a married woman—a Mrs. Clarke—who joined him at Boston; and that, when last heard from, they were bound for Europe and the Rhine."

"And they were both members of our church!" said Mrs. Townsend.

"And this Mrs. De Witt—she too is a member of our church, is she not?" asked Samuel, uneasily.

"Yes," returned Mrs. Townsend. "But why do you ask?"

"What can the *preaching* be that brings forth such fruits?" returned Samuel, sorrowfully. "And yet there may be others there, who meditate the same dreadful course. *They* must be saved, ere it is too late. One word might do it—one little word. Lord, help them and me!"

"The preaching!" repeated Mrs. Townsend. "Why, what can that have to do with it?"

The young Christian surveyed the questioner with an air of mingled sorrow and surprise.

"Have to do with it!" he said. "Everything. What is the duty of a shepherd, but to look to the welfare of his flock? And do these—the Clarkes, the Joneses, and the De Witts—give evidence that *they* have been looked after?"

"They do not. But, what then? A pastor can only *tell* his people what to do; if they fail to follow his direction, the fault is not with him, but themselves."

"True," returned Samuel. "But there is *a kind* of preaching which persuades its auditors to rouse up from their dream of sin, and walk in the way of righteousness like MEN! The preaching that lulls its hearers into silken indifference is not blessed, because it is not of Christ. The business of a spiritual shepherd is to stir up the hearts of his charge *incessantly* to an EARNEST sense of their danger, until he knows that all are within the ark of safety. This kind of preaching is approved of God and men, because it is *of* God. But the preaching that brings forth such fruits as the Clarkes, the Joneses, and the De Witts, is not of God, because the fruits are evil!"

"Samuel!" said Mrs. Townsend, looking at the young man strangely.

"Nay, do not fear for me, dear friend," returned Samuel, with a serene smile. "I understand you. But have no misgivings. I am in *His* keeping!"

Mrs. Townsend was somewhat awed by the majestic gesture

which accompanied his words, while she was at the same time somewhat disturbed by the young man's energy. She turned an inquiring glance at Miriam; but the latter reassured her by a smile which was angelic in its confidence.

This silent but expressive response was certainly encouraging; but it was not wholly satisfactory.

In fact, the mind of the merchant's wife, although partially illumined, was yet too worldly in its conceptions to comprehend the simple earnestness, the childlike simplicity, and the trusting confidence of the heart that walks solely in the light of the Divine Eye.

"'Preaching that brings forth such fruits'—'save the rest ere it is too late,'" she repeated, mentally. "Surely he cannot expect to revolutionize the pulpit! I tremble for his wits!"

"Will you be kind enough to inform Mrs. Jones that we are here?" said Samuel to the laundress, in a tone which did little towards favoring Mrs. Townsend's suspicion. "Perhaps if you were to add that Miss Selden, who visited her this morning, is present, it might have a favorable influence upon her decision. I can readily understand why she desires to avoid visitors—and her feelings are very natural, and under ordinary circumstances should be respected. But you are one of *us*, and you doubtless see that this is one of those peculiar occasions when a temporary feeling must be gently sacrificed for the sake of that which is eternal. Do go, there's a good soul!"

"I will, cheerfully," said Mrs. Farley, whose pure mind intuitively comprehended the noble thought which shone, like a celestial light, in the young Christian's eye: a light which gave Mrs. Townsend serious concern.

The laundress passed through the narrow door on her errand and disappeared.

Samuel cast his mild, dark eye upon the floor. An air of

mournful thought darkened his brow, which was usually so serene.

Mrs. Townsend observed him, silently.

Samuel was, in fact, materially disturbed. He had till within a few moments labored under the impression that Mrs. Townsend's assumed piety was real—that she was, in fine, what she professed to be—one of the Redeemed. But this impression the lady had herself swept away by her ill-timed remark, by her implied doubt of his sanity when he called on the Lord for help, and by her mingled skepticism and alarm when he proclaimed himself in the keeping of his Maker.

His trusting confidence in God, his childlike simplicity, the beatific expression of his eye—those unerring signs which enable a Christian to recognize a brother or sister in Christ, as in lesser organizations brethren recognize each other by certain motions known only to the affiliated—the lady had mistaken for the premonitory symptoms of madness!

Samuel was grieved at this mournful discovery. It added to his gentle heart another anxiety. To his already overburdened back it was an additional burden. At his never-ceasing hands it called out for "More work—more work." It was a soul in peril, which he had all along imagined to be out of danger. And more and more he realized the importance of another kind of preaching than that which lulled its hearers into a silken confidence in surface-piety—a piety which is, and which is known to be, a mere pretence.

But Samuel had not alone made this startling discovery. Miriam had perceived it as well, and by the same unerring signs. It fell upon her tender heart like an unexpected blow. It drove the joy from her eye, the glow from her cheek. While to Samuel it was another anxiety, to her it was an additional sorrow, and a new incitement for private prayer.

And yet both of these fine, delicate natures were ignorant of the fact that the object of their mutual solicitude had, that evening, experienced a certain degree of genuine spiritual contrition; and that that contrition promised to uproot the crust of more than half a century of pride, littleness, and solemn hypocrisy, and let in rays of heavenly light upon her guilt-imprisoned soul, for the first time.

The lady herself was perfectly conscious of the change which had taken place in her heart. She hoped it would penetrate deep enough to thoroughly purify her spirit, and imbue it with the same guileless tone which marked the thoughts and utterances of her two young friends. She *hoped* this; but she felt no disposition to make any *personal* effort to secure it. She hoped it would place her in a state of beatitude of its own power and accord. But she was neither willing nor unwilling to assist it, or resist it. It occurred to her that to second the Silent Power which was working within her, it would be necessary to ennerve herself; to call up every energy; to concentrate all her thoughts into one, and to throw herself, as it were, like a heroine, into the breach, and battle for a time bravely, heroically, almost superhumanly, with all that was evil in her nature—invoking, in the meanwhile, with all the strength and confidence of an earnest mind, the Prince of Righteousness to aid her in the fight. But to do this, it would be necessary, first, to summon up all the forces of her WILL, and to bring them and it under her control. But this required *courage*, or rather *effort*, and *that* she felt herself unequal to. *Not* that she *was* unequal to it; but she *thought* she was—that is to say, she *wished* to think so. She then flattered herself that there was no *absolute* necessity for *immediate* action; that any other time would do as well; that the world did not disturb itself about the matter, and that if *it* didn't, why should *she;* but that, so far as she was herself concerned, she *would* bring her mind to the proper point, *some* time or other; but not *now*—no, not NOW; and thus the blessed moment passed by, but without blessing *her* on the way.

Mrs. Farley was successful. She returned to the visitors in a few minutes, accompanied by Mrs. Jones.

Miriam was startled at the change which had come over the latter since the morning. A few hours had done upon her the work of twenty years. She was pale, haggard, and wan. Her brow was of a cadaverous hue. Her eyes were sunken, while a dark tinge beneath their lower lids intensified their hollowness. Her proud, handsome lip, had lost its spirit. Her haughty air was gone. Her firm step was succeeded by an undecided shuffling. She was the picture of a broken woman—of helpless humility—of timid despair.

She greeted her visitors with an air which seemed to imply an instinctive consciousness of her own inferiority. All present, save the laundress, observed this marked change in the poor woman's manner with mingled grief and amazement.

Mrs. Townsend glanced at Samuel; but his eye was fixed thoughtfully upon the broken spirit who was sitting beside the laundress. She glanced at Miriam; but *her* gaze was settled upon the same touching ruin. She glanced at Mrs. Farley; but her orbs were also upon the poor timid wreck of what was so proud, and strong, and brave in the morning.

Mrs. Townsend was embarrassed—uneasy. She could scarcely retain her seat. She felt strongly inclined, or rather tempted, to spring from her chair and fly. She had but one thought—one conviction: that the poor, meek woman who looked so humble, so helpless, so timid, and so void of all hope, was stark, staring MAD!

Far different were the thoughts of her companion. Their simple minds never dreamt of deserting a fellow-being in distress.

"We have called," said Samuel, in his frank, unaffected way, "to see if we can help you."

"You are very kind," returned the helpless woman, casting her eyes down timidly, "and I thank you very much, I am sure."

"Mad!—crushed down to a *willing* dependence upon charity!" mused Mrs. Townsend. "I never could have believed this in one of her haughty blood!"

"We will secure you from want," dear friend, continued Samuel, whose heart bled at the poor creature's misery; "you and your child."

"My child!" cried the woman, with a slight start, and her eyes lit up for a moment with an energetic flash. But the light subsided again, and then she looked down with the same blank, spiritless expression as before.

"Yourself and child," repeated Samuel, "will be provided for. Be comforted, dear lady, and do not look so sad."

"I thank you very much," said the woman, meekly. "You are very good, and I am very much obliged to you, I am sure."

Samuel observed her attentively for a few moments. An idea struck him.

"Where is baby now?" he asked.

The poor creature looked at him suspiciously.

"Baby?" she said.

"Baby," repeated Samuel. "Where is she now?"

"You want to take her away?" said the woman, fixing her eyes upon him.

"Oh, no," returned Samuel. "That would be cruel. Baby would cry, baby would scream, baby would pine and die."

The woman eyed him still, as if her suspicion was strengthened rather than weakened by his reply.

Samuel understood the character of her thoughts.

"We do not want to *take* baby," he said.

"You think I will give her to you?" returned the woman, with a quivering lip.

"*Will* you give her to us? We can take better care of her than yourself. Besides, you may come once in a while to see her!"

The poor woman regarded him steadily, but made no answer.

"Ada," said Samuel.

The woman started.

"That is her name, is it not? Come, now, do give her to us. We are better off than you, and can of course take better care of her. She is a pretty child, and ought to be looked after. Give her to us!"

The woman looked at him silently, and with an air of touching reproach, while he spoke. A light glow ascended slowly to her chin, from that to her cheeks, and from that to her brow. Her eyes sparkled with returning intelligence. The quivering of her lips quickened. Her chair trembled beneath her agitated frame. Sanity was coming back—urged on by her maternal love and fears, which were now thoroughly aroused. She put out her hand to the laundress, as if invoking her protection, darted at the young man a mournfully reproachful glance, and then, with a loud sob, bowed her head upon the shoulder of her friend, and burst into tears.

Intelligence reigned again in the poor woman's mind.

Samuel had worked out his idea!

No one had understood it, however.

Miriam sprang to her feet to console the unhappy lady. But Samuel arrested the movement.

"Keep your seat, Miss Selden," he said, gently. "Let her weep!"

Miriam looked at him in astonishment.

Mrs. Townsend surveyed him with an expression which said, "You are cruel!"

"Her mind was in a state of stupefaction—tears alone would relieve it," said Samuel. "She will be better now. I thought you would have comprehended it."

This explanation was perfectly satisfactory. Miriam uttered a sigh of relief, and returned to her chair.

Samuel waited until the sobbing had ceased, and then approached the unhappy lady.

"You will forgive me, will you not?" he said, laying his hand tenderly upon her arm.

The woman looked up at him. Her eye was brighter, clearer; and though her features still retained their haggardness, their former air of helpless stupidity was gone. She was sane again; for how long, was yet to be determined.

"Ah! Mr. Leland!" she exclaimed, "I am glad to see you. What! Mrs. Townsend—and you, too, Miss Selden? I thank you for your kindness. I had almost begun to think myself deserted. How is Mr. Townsend?"

"Quite well," returned the lady to whom this question was addressed.

"I have been ill, have I not?" continued the woman, turning to Mrs. Farley.

"A fainting-fit only," said Mrs. Townsend, on observing the hesitation of the latter. "But you are now quite recovered."

"And you came in while it was on me? Really, a sorry welcome!" Then turning to Miriam, and taking her hand, which she pressed tenderly, "Do you know, my dear, that I haven't been able to give a single thought to what we were talking of this morning?"

"You have had other matters to occupy you?"

"Yes, and trying ones, too, my dear. Nevertheless, I am very glad to see you. By-the-way, Mr. Leland—"

"Yes, madam—"

"I have a message for the lady whom you brought here last evening. Will you take it?"

"Cheerfully," returned Samuel.

"Thank you. Give her this," said the woman, taking a letter from the mantel, "and my respects."

"I will do so," said Samuel, putting the letter into his breast pocket. "And now, will you do me a favor in return?"

"*I* am scarcely in a position to grant favors, sir," replied the lady, with a smile of touching sadness; "still I think I can safely promise any favor *you* may ask!"

"Which implies—"

"That I have the highest confidence in you, sir," said the lady.

"Dear madam, you make me very happy. I shall endeavor to retain your good-will. But a thought strikes me. Pray, pardon my impoliteness—I would speak a word in private with our dear friend here."

"It is granted," said Mrs. Jones, turning to Miriam, while Samuel approached the laundress, and whispered—

"Dear Mrs. Farley, we have not a moment to lose. We must take advantage of the present unclouded condition of her mind, and save her, if it be possible. In an hour her insanity may return, and then her case will be hopeless. We must lead her to Our Prince while there is yet time. You understand me, do you not?"

"Oh, yes. You have a good heart. Do let us save her. I had the doctor here a little before dusk."

"Well?"

"He did not tell me so, in so many plain words, but I inferred from his manner that the poor lady had not long to live. Her heart is broken!"

"Not three days," said Samuel. "It is written in her face

In three days she will be at the bar of judgment; and if unrepentant—"

"We must save her," cried the laundress.

"With His help, and ere an hour. Lord, help her! I will send Miss Selden to you. Prepare her to assist us!"

He pressed Mrs. Farley's hand, and returned to the object of his anxiety.

"Ah! you are a pretty fellow," said the latter, archly "Making love to Mrs. Farley before our very faces!"

Samuel smiled, serenely, as he replied—

"And now I am going to add to my enormity by asking Miss Selden to speak a good word for me. Will you do so?" he added, turning to Miriam.

"With pleasure," returned the latter, rising.

"You cannot deceive me, Mr. Leland!" said Mrs. Jones, shaking her finger at him. "You have some plot afoot?"

"I have," said Samuel, with his accustomed frankness. "Shall I tell you what it is?"

And taking her hand, he pressed it, and looked her tenderly in the eye.

"You are one of my favorites," said the lady, "and I can take anything from you."

"Anything?"

"Anything, sir."

"Have a care, dear friend. I shall put you to the proof!"

"Do so. You have my confidence."

"Fully?"

"Fully."

"Then, dear lady, come with me—"

"Whither?"

"To our Prince—the Redeemer!" said Samuel.

"This, then, is your plot?" said Mrs. Jones.

"Yes. You will join us in it, will you not—for His sake, and your own?"

His interlocutor surveyed him steadily for a few moments, and then, her hand still remaining in his, turned her eyes downward, thoughtfully.

All present observed her with affectionate interest.

It was a solemn moment to every one in the apartment.

At least three hearts fluttered as if their own salvation hung upon that one woman's will. It was as if three angels, breathless with anxiety, were mutely asking her to consent to her own salvation.

At length the woman raised her head. The lashes of her eyes were moist. The muscles of her lip quivered. Her cheeks were of the color of snow. Her breast was agitated.

"I am a poor, weak, helpless thing," she said, pressing the young Christian's hand. "If you *can* save me, do so!"

"Not I, dear madam," returned Samuel, "but Our Prince. He is good and gracious, kinder than men think. Open your heart to Him. He will look on you with a smile, listen to you with tenderness. Speak to Him freely, unreservedly, contritely—*believingly*. Nay, be not afraid—He will *welcome* your approach. Reflect: Heaven is *worth* an effort. Cheer up, stand firm, be brave—a little while. One effort—one brave effort. Heaven is in sight—cherubim and seraphim looking down."

"Nay, do not ask me," said the woman. "I thought I could, but I cannot. I have neither faith nor belief. My heart is hardened. I believe, and I don't believe. I have faith, and I have no faith. I know I am in danger, but I do not see my way to safety. All my life, I have heard of sin, of punishment—of repentance, of mercy; but I have never put faith in them, because those around me did not. Example influenced my heart, and hardened it. It is still influenced, still hardened by it. If I could believe, I would—but I cannot; my heart will not let me.

I might *say* I believed, but it would be untrue. I *do* not believe—nor would I deceive you or myself by a pretence. I *cannot* believe; I have heard either too much or too little, to permit me *to* believe. And yet—"

She paused—hesitated.

"And yet——" said Samuel, encouragingly.

"And yet," faltered the impenitent, "if I could see these things more clearly, perhaps—"

She hesitated, and paused again.

"One word," said Samuel. "Aptly is The Disposer called of men The JUST. His decrees are stern, rigorous, unchangeable. Whoso breaks them, must pay the penalty. HE has said it—HE, THE KING, who goes not back a hair's breadth in His word."

"Is he, then, so stern, so relentless?"

"Even so stern, so relentless; Himself hath said it: 'By the deeds of the law shall no man be justified.' '*I* change not.' Spiritual indifference is then no laughing matter, violation of His decrees no jest. Let who will mock, let who will revile, let who will sneer at or pass them heedless by, they must answer for it all, one day, to The August—The Just."

"Lost—lost!" cried the other, in despair.

"Not yet," rejoined Samuel. "'Twixt the sinner *and* The Just stands one whose influence *with* The Just is all-potent—whose eye is mild and gentle, whose heart is full of pity, tenderness, and love—JESUS, *the Prince;*

"Who, knowing the terror—the pitiless rigor—of the Law, framed a compact with His Father, which would enable all who *would* be saved, *to* be saved, and still preserve intact the justice and solemnity of the law;

"Who came down from heaven,

"Assumed the form, and all the tenderest susceptibilities to pain, of man,

"Endured a life of calumny, of persecution, of intense suffering,

"And died a death of excruciating agony,

"That the voluntary sufferings of the *Son* of God might meet the rigorous requirements of the *Law* of God, and render it possible for ALL to come to God, through *Him*, the Prince;

"And that even the vilest might escape the stern penalty of sin, by simply repenting and believing in *Him*, the *Saviour*.

"For He is good, gentle, kind—Our Prince;

"Loving, and beloved of His Father, The King,

"Who will grant mercy to all who will ask it through His Son, The Prince,

"Who can obtain salvation for all who will repent and believe, and ask it of Him *in faith*."

Mrs. Jones looked down, again.

"You see it all clearly now, do you not?" asked Samuel, tenderly.

"Clearly—yes!" faltered the other.

"You see, then, how easy a thing it is to approach Our Prince; and how gladly He will hear and receive you?"

The poor woman was pale, trembling, and undecided.

"I am weak and broken," she said. "Speak to Him for me. I would do it for myself, but I have no heart, no FAITH, no HOPE. The world has led me astray, and I have been a half-consenting party to the wrong. Had the world set me a better example, I would have followed it; it *did* not, and I am—*what* I am. Look at me. I am crushed, worthless—with no hope here, none for The Beyond. The world schooled me for perdition, and I allowed it to do so without even a show of resistance. The world is now done with me; it has finished its work upon me, and cast me off. I am a Miserable, an Unworthy, a Nothing. The world knows it, and says it; I know it, and confess it. If, in the face of all this, you think I dare offer myself to Him, I will do so; if, in the face of all this, you believe He will accept me—me, who am so unworthy; me, whom the world rejects—

then lead me to Him; use your influence with Him for me. Lead me to Him," she added, with a wild, startling sob, "*for the sake of a poor, crushed, helpless soul, that is without faith and without hope!*"

"Dear madam," said the young Christian, with emotion, "faith is a little thing, but it is everything with our Prince. With it, repentance is everything; without it, nothing."

Mrs. Jones trembled, and said huskily—

"You talk of faith *and* repentance, while I do not, cannot, even repent!"

"Do you not grieve for your sins, dear madam?"

"I do, and I do not. I *desire* to; but the world has hardened my heart so, it will not let me. I—I—cannot take hold of repentance *earnestly*. Everything seems hollow to me. I have dwelt so long amid things that are unreal—among minds that entertain only those thoughts which flatter their own silken hollowness, hypocrisy, and convenience—driving away those which do not favor their own wishes, that I have no faith in anything that is real. I know that this is all wrong—that is, I have a presentiment, a sort of shadowy idea—that it is so. But what can I do? Repent? But how *shall* I repent, when I have only a heart which is no heart, a faith which is no faith, a conviction which is no conviction, a certainty which is not a certainty?"

Samuel trembled, as if laboring with a chill.

"No faith?" he said.

"Not a grain. Why should I deceive you or myself?"

The young Christian reflected a moment. His countenance was sad—his heart torn with emotion. He silently invoked the Holy Spirit for counsel. At length a new thought came to him.

"One word, dear madam," he said. "The imminency of your danger is great; still, all is not lost. Will you *hope?* Hope is not far from faith,—it will lead you to it. Our Prince *is* kind, gentle, good—O, believe it. Hope for faith—for pardon—for safety, and He will come to your aid. Say you will hope—*say* it, to *Him!*"

"Alas! I *cannot*—I *have* no hope!"

A shade of agony swept over the features of the young Christian.

"But, *do* hope. Rouse up—be brave. *Ask* Him for it, *in* hope, and He will send it to you. *Do* hope. It is indispensable. Try, I beseech you!"

The impenitent shook her head. She was paler than marble.

"I cannot," she answered. "I wish for it, but it comes not!"

"O, dear madam, *ask* for it—*do*, I implore you. Ask for it. Courage. One effort, now; but one—hopefully. Not all I can do, not all the world can do, will help you, without an earnest struggle of your own. Hope!"

"I cannot. My heart is cold, hard. The evil spirit of formality, which has governed my whole life, sits upon it now, and keeps all that is good and earnest in it—if any there be—down."

"He is good—HE! He will remove it, and send you faith, will you but ask it *in* hope. Come, be brave one moment—one little moment."

Thus adjured, the impenitent resolved upon an effort.

She raised her eyes, as if to heaven, imploringly; anguish was in their glance, and supplication, and sorrow—but not one ray of confidence. It was an appeal from helpless, abject, hopeless despair. A moment, and her orbs fell again—despondent to the last!

A nervous shudder darted through the young Christian's frame. Tears sprang to his eyes.

The laundress and Miriam were already sobbing.

Mrs. Townsend was moved. Scenes like this were new to her. It had therefore all the charm of novelty; but it was only the novelty of a touching play. It absorbed her mind, agitated her feelings, called forth a sympathizing tear—but nothing more. The spirit of vitalizing grace, which had visited her own heart, a little while before, having met with no encouragement, had passed away, leaving her as it had found her—an every-day woman: moderately superior, moderately good, moderately cold, moderately impressible, moderately worldly, moderately honest, moderately pious, moderately deceitful, and moderately respectable; equally ready to laugh at anything that was amusing, as to give a tear to anything which appealed to her sympathies; as ready to listen to the music of an opera as to a chaunt of praise to Jehovah; as ready to criticise a sermon upon the plan of salvation as a disquisition upon dress; as ready to join in the tattle of a *converzatione*, as in a discourse upon sacred things; and as ready to "attend" the House of the Lord on Sunday, as "Burton's," or the *ballet* on Monday evening. She was Mrs. Townsend again: that is to say, Mrs. Townsend moved, but not aroused.

"Mrs. Farley—Miss Selden," said Samuel, in an agitated voice, "a soul is trembling; and the house which it inhabits is trembling, too. Support the latter with your hands, the former with your prayers."

He spoke in time; the feeble frame of the unhappy woman was giving way, and would have fallen, a moment later, but for assistance.

"Let us kneel," said the young Christian.

"Pray for me!" said the forlorn woman, in a weak, imploring voice. "Pray for me. I *want* to hope, but I *cannot*. Pray for me. I am suffering!"

Samuel bowed his head upon his hands, through which trickled tears of molten agony.

"Hope, madam—hope!" he cried. "Hope, I beseech you!"

"I cannot—I cannot!"

"Oh, madam—"

"I *dare* not!" said the woman, with a cold shudder. "It would be mockery. I *have* no hope. But save me—Oh, save me, *you!* I am in despair!"

"One word will do it!" whispered Miriam, through her sobs.

"One word!" cried the humble laundress.

"One word!" added Samuel. "Say it—for your soul's sake!"

"I cannot—I dare not!" cried the agitated woman. "But do not let me go. I feel that my hours are numbered, and—I—I—oh!" she cried, with a loud burst, "hold me—hold me; a gulf, black, cold, and dismal, is yawning before me. Pray for me—pray for me. If you have hearts, pray for me—hold me—save me!"

There was no resisting the tone of this appeal.

The next instant, the voice of the young Christian was ascending to the Holy One.

"Heavenly Father! We are suppliants for Thy bounty.

"Look down in pity on this poor soul, who sits shivering at Thy door.

"The world and her own heart have dealt hardly by her; and she had neither strength nor will to resist their cruel mandates, their bewildering temptations.

"She is sore and aweary, feeble and sad; she is bowed down with afflictions, which press upon her hard.

"Sorrow is in her heart, wretchedness upon her brow; gloom upon her soul. Have mercy upon her!

"Illumine the darkness of her mind with the light of Thy Divine Eye; whisper comfort to her desponding heart; shed hope, in all its rich effulgence, upon her shrinking soul. Have mercy upon her!

"Let her see the brightness of Thy countenance; let her feel the gentle kindness of Thy hand; let her hear the sweet sound of Thy voice. Have mercy upon her!

"Say to her, in the richness of Thy mercy, 'Daughter, thy sins are forgiven thee!' Have mercy upon her!

"She is in peril; and she implores Thee to stretch out Thy hand and save her. Have mercy upon her!

"She has come to Thy gates, hearing of Thy great goodness and loving-kindness, and beseecheth Thee to turn her not away. Have mercy upon her!

"She is helpless, and in want; friendless, and in sorrow; and imploreth Thee to take her in. Have mercy upon her!

"She asketh Thee for succor, shelter, and a little of Thy bread, which is life and health, and strength and raiment, to all who partake of it. Have mercy upon her!

"Smile upon her, Father, for the sake of Thy dear Son. Open Thy gate unto her, and let her in.

"Let her sing the song of gladness, and not that of woe.

"Let her feel the kindness of Thy hand, and not its wrath.

"Let her in, for the sake of Thy dear Son, who died that she might live.

"Let her within Thy Kingdom—save her from that of the Evil One, who is Thine enemy and hers. Let her in!

"She will be grateful to Thee for Thy loving-kindness. Let her in!

"She will make one of Thy servants; she will walk in Thy ways; she will be one of Thy daughters and Thy people. Let her in!

"She will join the Holy Throng in singing grateful Hosannas to Thee, for Thy kindness, Thy mercy, and Thy love.

"Have mercy upon her, for Thy Son's sake! Let her in!

"Hear us, we beseech Thee, for the sake of Thy beloved Son, our Prince, our Redeemer; and to Thee and to Thy name shall be the glory and the praise, evermore!"

"Amen!" said Miriam and Mrs. Farley.

"Break off!" said Mrs. Townsend, gently. "The poor thing has fainted!"

It was even as she said. The nerves of the agitated impenitent were totally unstrung, and she had sunk down in weakness and insensibility.

Mrs. Farley brought some water and bathed her temples. Mrs. Townsend drew forth her salts, and applied the vial to the poor woman's nostrils; Miriam and Samuel rubbed her hands.

Success, at length, crowned their efforts. The impenitent uttered a faint sigh and slowly opened her eyes, but without evincing any consciousness of the presence of those around her.

"She had better lie down," observed Mrs. Townsend. "She is unfit to be here."

Mrs. Farley and Miriam acted upon the suggestion. They raised the poor woman, and bore her tenderly to a bed in the front room.

She sunk upon the pillow like one in the last stage of exhaustion.

"How do you feel now, dear?" asked Miriam, bending over her gently.

The woman looked up at her with a cold, blank eye, and muttered, feebly—

"He will not come back—on the Rhine—with Mrs. Clarke—pretty Christians—pretty people!"

Her auditors looked at each other, sorrowfully.

The poor creature was in mental darkness once more!

Samuel turned away, and wept.

Mrs. Townsend sighed.

Miriam bowed her head upon Mrs. Farley's breast, and sobbed.

The maniac surveyed them with a cold, idiotic, and partially malignant stare.

"Fine clothes you wear!" she muttered, addressing Mrs. Townsend. "Is your heart fine, too? Oh, I know you. You are a *worthy* woman," she added, satirically: "you are one of the Mrs. Clarkes! Who are *you* going to run away with? Some other lady's husband? It is the fashion, you know, in *our* church!"

Mrs. Townsend shuddered, but made no reply.

"You are mistaken, dear," said Mrs. Farley, soothingly. "This lady is good—very good. She is your friend, too. You ought not to speak to her in that way."

The demented woman laughed.

"I know her," she said, with a cunning leer. "I know her! She is another Mrs. Clarke; and you will know her, too, if you have a husband. Look out for her!"

"I cannot bear this!" exclaimed Mrs. Townsend, quitting the room.

"There, dear. Now see what you have done!" said Mrs. Farley.

"Don't let her take my child!" said the demented creature, in alarm. "Don't let that bad woman take my child, too!"

"No one will take your child, dear!" said Mrs. Farley, humoring her.

"I see them!" cried the poor woman, her mind wandering off in another direction.

"See them, dear? Whom?" asked the laundress.

"My husband and Mrs. Clarke—sailing in a steamboat—on the Rhine. But I don't see my baby!"

"Baby is here—baby is safe!" cried a little voice near her It was that of her child, who had been aroused from its slumbers, as it lay on the bed, and who was now creeping to its mother's side, through the blanket and quilt which it had thrown off.

The poor woman uttered a loud shriek, and catching up the child, she pressed it frantically to her breast, covering it with kisses, and giving vent to her maternal joy in successive bursts of laughter.

"I tremble for her!" observed Mrs. Farley to Miriam. "She is too feeble to bear up against so many shocks."

"I will stay with you to-night," whispered Miriam, whose mind had been disturbed by similar thoughts, "and watch her while you sleep. You will have your work to do to-morrow, and to do it you must have rest; while I, you know, can sleep."

The laundress thanked her with a grateful glance and a gentle pressure of the hand.

These two simple, innocent natures understood each other. They were drawn together by that invisible yet positive influence which links the pure with the pure—an influence which only they who have passed from spiritual death unto spiritual life can appreciate or comprehend. Each intuitively recognized in the other a future companion in the bright Beyond.

Their fears were not unfounded. Ere long, the maniacal laugh was over; the lips ceased their kisses; the fire in the eyes went out, the eyes themselves closed, the arms dropped from around the child, which still lay upon its feeble parent's breast, and the poor creature succumbed again to her exhausting weakness, with a low, faint sigh.

Mrs. Farley took off the child, and laid it, with a few soothing words, beside the mother, in which position it fell, after a little while, into a quiet slumber.

Samuel approached the bedside, and observed the distended woman silently. Her breathings were low and faint; her face sharp, thin, and pale, and throwing out with greater boldness than ever the dark shadow underneath the eyes.

The young Christian was moved.

Miriam and Mrs. Farley looked at him as if soliciting his opinion.

"She will be gone ere the morning," said Samuel, in reply,

"and with all her sins upon her. Oh, had she but hoped, for a moment—for a single moment!"

"Let us pray for her!" suggested Mrs. Farley, sobbingly.

"Yes," said Miriam, "with our hearts!"

They dropped upon their knees, and bowing their heads on their clasped hands, silently beseeched for mercy for the victim of flippant society and skeleton religion.

Mrs. Townsend returned while they were thus engaged. A single glance, and she comprehended all. Without being seriously touched, she dropped involuntarily into an attitude of prayer, as much for appearance' sake as from a sense of propriety.

Half an hour passed away thus, and then Mrs. Townsend arose, purposely rustling her dress in the movement, to attract the attention of the others. In this, however, she was not successful; and finding that her companions still remained upon their knees, she quietly returned to the back room, seated herself on a chair near the window, and amused herself by contemplating the stars.

Ten minutes later, the petitioners were disturbed by a low sigh from the lips of the object of their supplications. They rose up and bent over her. Her eyes were open, and dazzling with a light which made those near her shudder.

"Do you know us?" said Samuel.

"My child!" returned the woman, faintly.

"It is here beside you," said Mrs. Farley.

"Let me see it," murmured the dying woman.

The laundress held it up before her. The wretched woman gazed at its slumbering face a few moments, in silence, and then said, in a whispering voice, which was replete with agony—

"Bring her near me. I am going!"

The unconscious child was brought close to her, and its little brow received its mother's last kiss.

"Lay her down again," said the dying woman, with a sigh.

Her wish was complied with, and then her eyes wandered from one to another of the group, till they fell on Samuel.

"You would have saved me," she said, feebly, and with difficulty, "and I thank you. But it was not to be. I had no hope, no confidence, no faith. The world had crushed out all my faith long before. And now I am going," she added, with a painful smile, "to my reward! Nay—don't speak. Every moment is precious. My child—"

"I understand you, dear madam," said Samuel. "I will take care of her, and bring her up in the ways of the Lord!"

"See to *that!*" said the woman, with expiring energy; "see to *that!* All else is as nothing. You will?"

And she bent her dying gaze upon him, imploringly.

"I will," said Samuel.

The woman's eye shone with gratitude.

"Thank you—God bless you!" she murmured, with a last effort. "Your hand upon it!" She tried to press it to her lips, but failed. Her frame was exhausted. The vital spark was struggling to escape. "Hold me—hold me!" she said, in a voice which was reduced to a faint whisper. "I—I am—going. Perdition—I see it! Save me—save me! All—is—dark——ness!"

The lamp was out—the light was gone.

The victim of society's mummeries, of society's frivolities, and of society's skeleton religion, was—WHERE?

CHAPTER XV.

No time was lost in notifying the relatives of the departed of the sad event. They responded by sending an undertaker to take charge of the remains. A costly coffin was brought, and the funeral appointed to take place at one o'clock. At that hour, Samuel, Mrs. Townsend, Miriam, and Mrs. Farley alone were present.

Samuel was surprised.

"Have none of the poor lady's friends been here?" he inquired of the laundress.

The latter replied in the negative.

Samuel could not tell what to make of it.

Miriam was grave.

Mrs. Townsend indignant, but silent. She understood the world.

Steps were heard ascending the stairs.

"Ah! here they are at last!" observed the young Christian, with his usual simplicity.

The door opened, and three men appeared. They were the undertaker and his assistants!

Samuel looked grieved.

"I am just in time," said the undertaker, taking out his watch. "Screw down the lid," he added, addressing his assistants.

"Perhaps we had better wait a little," interrupted Samuel. "The lady's relatives—"

"Will meet the hearse at the corner!" said the undertaker with a supercilious smile, which had a world of meaning in it.

Samuel blushed to his very temples.

Five minutes later, the coffin was in the hearse, behind which stood a solitary carriage—Mrs. Townsend's.

Mrs. Farley remained at home, to attend to little Bob and the tender orphan, who could not comprehend why "mamma was so white and still, why they put her in the mahogany box with the silver nails, nor what they meant by carrying her away."

Mrs. Townsend entered her carriage, followed by Miriam and Samuel. The latter was pale. His companions observed him.

"What are you thinking of, Samuel?" asked Mrs. Townsend.

"Of the littleness of that pride which declines to draw up its livery before an alley, and awaits the corse of a sister at the corner!" said Samuel. "Tell me," he added, turning to the inquirer, "of what avail is the preaching which brings forth such fruits?"

"The fault is not in the preaching," said Mrs. Townsend, "but in the people, who hear, but do not heed."

"But if the preacher did his duty like one who felt the responsibility of his position—"

"He would very soon *lose* his position!" interrupted Mrs. Townsend, impatiently. "Come, come, Samuel, you must get rid of these notions, and learn to take the world as you find it!"

The young Christian regarded her for an instant or two with painful surprise. Then bowing his head, as if in astonishment at the rebuke, he bent his eyes thoughtfully upon the floor of the carriage.

Mrs. Townsend bit her lip. She felt mortified, not at her remark, but at herself, for making it to one whom she so highly esteemed.

The embarrassing silence which followed was happily brought to an end by the temporary stoppage of their vehicle, which had now reached the corner. Mrs. Townsend took advantage of the incident to re-establish herself in the young man's confidence.

"Samuel," she said, in a genial tone, which no one knew better than herself how to employ, "do look out and see what the matter is—there's a good soul!"

The young man cheerfully complied.

"Three carriages are moving up between us and the hearse," he said, after a few moments' examination.

"The friends of Mrs. Jones—her *afflicted* sisters!" remarked Mrs. Townsend, with a smile of deep significance. "Their relations to the deceased entitle them to precedence!"

She moved a little on her seat, to observe the vehicles; as she did so, she caught a view of Mrs. De Witt, who was sitting in the front carriage. The latter held a handkerchief to her eyes, and was in deep mourning.

Mrs. Townsend smiled, in her peculiar way, and leaned back to avoid recognition.

A moment later, her own conveyance was following in the train.

An hour and a half brought the party to Three Hundred and Sixty Acres of Human Vanity—Greenwood. The tower-bell tolled solemnly as the body entered the gate, as if to welcome the lost worldling to that magnificent inclosure of worms, flowers, riding-paths, and—artistical effects.

They passed along the main avenue and turned into a winding path leading to a knoll which overlooked the cemetery and the bay. On the brow of this knoll rose the façade of a gorgeous tomb, resembling in its exterior an Ionic temple. The door stood open, as the hearse drew up—the vault was awaiting its first tenant. Over the entrance, fancifully sculptured, appeared the name of the owner of this show-house of the dead—THEODORE AUGUSTUS JONES—*Fraudulent Bankrupt* might have been added with marked propriety, but it was only impressed upon the minds of those who followed his consort's corse.

The interior of the vault, which was of an oblong shape, was built of dry, solid, compact masonry. The sides and lower end were lined with firm stone shelves, with air-tight lids, for the reception of the dead.

The remains of the first tenant were placed upon the lower shelf, by the cemetery's attendants, in a business-like way; the relatives looked on in a business-like way; they walked out in a business-like way; the vault was closed in a business-like way, and all was over.

Having attended to the last rites of the dear departed, the relatives now gave themselves up for a few moments to enjoyment.

Mr., Mrs., and Miss De Witt examined the Ionic temple with mixed feelings of complacency and satisfaction.

Mr. and Mrs. Jenkins flung their eyes over the cemetery generally, and appeared to survey its numerous mazy, intersecting paths, its countless hillocks, its sylvan slopes, its tiny glens, its gentle declivities, its abrupt knolls, and its artificial valleys, variously dotted with horizontal slabs, marble shafts, granite obelisks, and other fanciful monuments, with mingled curiosity and delight.

Mr. and Mrs. Smith—the latter the third sister of the dear departed—and their two daughters amused themselves by examining the numerous monumental beauties around them. This, they found "very pretty;" that, "so *very* romantic;" a third, "a perfect love;" a fourth, "really exquisite;" a fifth, "so very simple," which was very true; a sixth, "so like a doll;" a seventh, "very touching;" an eighth, "perfectly beautiful;" a ninth, "a real gem;" and a tenth, "bewilderingly magnificent."

The Smiths were in their element. Everything around them spoke of money, taste, talent, extravagance, and absurdity. The Smiths enjoyed themselves. Their senses were appealed to. Each object said to them, "Look at me—I'm a curiosity!" and the Smiths looked; their eyes were fed. The desired chord was touched, and the Smiths were all admiration.

All of these parties were immediately allied, by blood or marriage, to the inmate of the vault, and had therefore a perfect right to be considered in affliction.

"Samuel," said Mrs. Townsend, "this is hardly an occasion for adding to our worldly knowledge, but if you have any disposition to learn how *refined* 'blood' may become, how capable it is of ascending *above* human weakness, allow me to take you to the exhibition."

"What exhibition, madam?"

"The exhibition of nonsense. Keep Mr. Leland's arm, Mirry."

And she led the way to a fine showy vault on the left of the Ionic temple, which was sufficiently attractive and imposing to serve as a pretext for the object with which they approached it.

"Now," said Mrs. Townsend, in a low voice, "listen, and be edified. Nay, don't regard it as either vulgar or impertinent, but as a lesson in the great drama of worldly humbug. Look at this," she added, touching the vault, "and listen to *them!*"

Samuel complied, though not without a feeling of shame.

"A very pretty design!" observed Mrs. De Witt, surveying the Ionic temple. "It reflects credit upon the taste of Mr. Jones. Pity he isn't inside of it! And then the situation—how very elegant! It commands such a magnificent view, and *can be* SEEN from every direction."

"It cost five thousand dollars," said Mr. De Witt, who, being a stock broker, was a gentleman of large practical ideas. "Almost as much as mine—"

"*Ours*, you mean!" suggested his lady, significantly.

"Ye—yes; you are quite correct. Almost as much as ours, the bill of which, if I remember right, was in the neighborhood of six thousand seven hundred and fifty."

This was said with the air of a man who knew what was what, and could afford to lay down the cash for it, too.

"Do you know, my dear," inquired his lady, "whether Mr.

Jones ever paid for the *whole* of it? If he did, it was a wonder. It was a habit of his, I think, to leave a small unsettled balance at the foot of every bill!"

"As you say," replied the stock-broker, "Mr. Jones *had* a weakness that way. And that reminds me—"

"That he owes *you* a small balance?" interrupted his amiable spouse, sharply "Wretch! And you *knew* him, too. I'm ashamed of you, sir—perfectly ashamed. O, if I had only been blessed with a MAN for a husband!"

"But, my dear—"

"Silence, sir! Remember where you are!"

The crest-fallen stock-broker was silent.

A few passers-by approached at this moment, and Mrs. De Witt raised her handkerchief to her eyes to veil her sorrow.

Mr. and Mrs. Jenkins were, meanwhile, getting on as well as could be expected. Mrs. Jenkins being a sister to the new tenant of the Ionic temple, was, of course, fully entitled to a liberal indulgence in Greenwood affliction.

"Dear me, what a delightful situation!" exclaimed the grief-stricken lady. "It"—the Ionic temple—"commands such a magnificent view! Why, one can see everything from here. Really, Mr. Jenkins, we *must* have one like it!"

From her words and manner, it would appear that the speaker anticipated a great deal of enjoyment in the way of magnificent views, when she should, in her turn, take up her residence in Three Hundred and Sixty Acres of Human Vanity. This was perhaps the reason why she manifested so strong a desire for a fine showy abode and a delightful situation.

"We'll think of it, my dear," observed the prudent Mr. Jenkins.

"How *can* you make such a reply to *me*, Mr. Jenkins?" demanded his better half, "when you know very well, sir, that *I* know that you only employ it as a subterfuge to get rid of unpleasant subjects, and that you never mean to think of it again?"

"Excuse me, my dear," said Mr. Jenkins, "it escaped me unawares. I—I—have no intention of evading your wishes in any particular, I assure you."

"I presume not, sir!" said Mrs. Jenkins, significantly.

"You may rely upon it, my dear. But do you know that vaults of this description are somewhat expensive?"

"And what is that to *me*, Mr. Jenkins?"

"Very true, my dear—very true!" said her lesser half, in a tone which implied that it was something to *him*, and something very serious, too. Then, as if anxious to completely reinstate himself in his lady's good graces, he added, "As you say, my dear, the situation of Mr. Jones's vault is very fine, and the vault itself quite imposing. If you think we had better have one like it, I'll give it my attention."

"No, sir, not *like* it," said Mrs. Jenkins, "that would be too akin to imitation. Something in a different style, but equally as grand and impressive. Something—something—new, original, and elegant. Something worthy of a JENKINS, sir!"

"I—I understand you, my dear. I'll think of it—"

"Sir!"

"That is, I mean, I'll think it over, and see what sort of a design it shall be!"

"I believe, Mr. Jenkins," said his better half, severely, "that that is the business of an architect, or persons of that sort!"

"Very true, my dear—very true," said Mr. Jenkins, surrendering. "I'll see one, and give him an order for a design."

"Immediately, Mr. Jenkins?"

"Immediately, my dear. Within a week."

"Very good, Mr. Jenkins. Then we'll take Friday for looking up the proper situation."

"Yes, my dear," said Mr. Jenkins, in a tone which evinced a

solemn consciousness that he was in for it beyond redemption.

"Greenwood," said Mrs. Jenkins, with the tender air of one who, having conquered, could afford to be magnanimous, "is so delightful a spot in which to take the Long Repose! Ah! Mr. Jenkins, when, after life's journey is ended, we come and lie together here—free from the cares, the sorrows, and the din of time; our long home perched upon some charming hill, like this; around us brilliant vaults, showy, inviting, and imposing as our own; the tower-bell tolling, every hour, its subduing requiem; the green knolls, and slopes, and acclivities glittering in the morning with their silver dew, waving gently to and fro beneath the zephyrs, through the day, and joining the silent shades and the pale monuments in the hush of the calm, starry night; the quiet broken only by the low, soothing murmurs of the bay, as its blue waters, gilded by the moon, roll, with playful violence, upon the dark, sullen shore:—what can be more delightful, Mr. Jenkins?"

"Nothing, my dear—nothing!" returned that gentleman, with a glance of admiration at the lady who was doing him so amiably.

Mrs. Townsend, who could scarcely restrain an explosion of laughter, now pressed Samuel's arm, and the trio moved away from the spot, followed slowly by their carriage.

"Well, Samuel, what do you think of the exhibition?" asked the lady, archly.

"That there is no foe so deadly to the human heart as that gilded thing, the world!" returned the young man, promptly.

"Ah!" said Mrs. Townsend, shaking her finger in playful rebuke, "on your old strain again. Why rail out so incessantly against the world?"

"Because it is rushing pell-mell to insanity, madam, and because every true man *should* do something for its rescue."

"Insanity?"

"Insanity, madam! Look at what it has done for Mrs. Jones; see what it is doing for those whom we left but now."

"You do not regard the De Witts and the Jenkinses as insane, surely?"

"Are they any wiser than her whom they escorted to her last earthly resting-place to-day? Are not their thoughts gross, petty, ludicrous, ignoble? Fell a single sentiment from their lips worthy the attention of an earnest or intelligent mind?"

"I confess it."

"And yet their utterances had in them, as they thought, much of life's daily wisdom! *While* they spoke, their intellects were in full play—*what* they spoke, were the fruits of their intellectual culture. Could Bedlam produce mental results *less* worthy?"

"I admit it."

"And yet, not theirs alone the blame. The world has led their poor, frivolous minds to this ignoble pass. The world, which employs all its enginery to drive out, from everywhere, every vestige of aught which has a tendency to inspire the human heart with a single solemn thought. The world, which, with the tenacious malignity of a demon, haunts man at every step, from the cradle to the shroud, and so bewilders him with novelties and vanities, that he cannot find a single earnest moment in which to talk to God; which so engrosses him with earth, that he has no room for thoughts of heaven; so possesses him with cares for his brief dream here, that he has no time to prepare for the long *reality* of eternity!"

"Have you, then, no regard for art, for genius—taste?" asked Mrs. Townsend.

"The highest—*in their places!* They adorn and beautify the world—*with* the world let them stay. But bring them not between me and life's One Purpose—between me and the Solemn—between me and God."

"But they appear to me appropriate in all public places. What more touching and impressive, for instance, than this?"

And she pointed to a sculptured monument of a mother weeping for her child.

"Very touching and impressive it would be *anywhere but here!* In a hall set apart for statuary, it would be eloquent with beauty and with thought. Here its beauty, force, and suggestiveness, are lost!"

Mrs. Townsend regarded him with amazement.

"Because," said Samuel, "the Real is more significant and impressive than the Ideal; because it is placed here, not to illustrate a beautiful thought, but *to be seen;* because it is not *here* a picture of a touching conception, but a flaunting sign of desire, on the part of her who erected it, to be *considered* tender, gentle, and interestingly melancholy.

"Observe the words—

"'MARY, ONLY CHILD OF MRS. EDITH WARREN—AGED FOUR YEARS. *My child, thy widowed mother mourns for thee.*'

"What more significant—a widow, with a tender heart, pines in singleness, and yearns to be comforted! Making even of the grave of her little one a medium through which to communicate her marketableness to the public! Does *genuine* affection expose its sorrows to a gaping world? Grief is solemn, grief is sacred; it is for privacy, not show: it unveils itself, in silence, and to HIM, *alone!*

"But would you see *real* eloquence? Look there!"

And he pointed to a row of five green graves, without mark or stone.

"There is death, in all its solemn sternness, all its impressive silence, all its shrinking *modesty;* with no intervening thing to intercept its stirring suggestiveness, or its eloquent lesson. Compare its touching homily with that of the young widow who flaunts her sorrows in your face, and bids you think of *her,* and not of the wholesome moral lesson which is taught by the mouldering forms that lie beneath the sod!

"It is well for the heart that dwells amid the temptations of the world, to look, now and then, upon the silent habitations of the dead. It weans him from the concentration of his mind upon perishable things; it reminds him *whither he is hastening*, and bids him *think of it;* warning him, in the same moment, that he, too, shall, ere long, make another of the grave-yard host who are dissolving into nothingness, and returning to their original dust.

"But gorgeous Greenwood tells us nothing of all this. Greenwood—to which society brings its dead, not for burial, but for show. Greenwood—which feeds the eye, which ministers to pride, but not to the soul. Greenwood—which takes away our homage from God, turns it insensibly into simple curiosity, and imbues us with an untimely respect for art, and taste, and wealth, and pomp, and pride.

"Gorgeous Greenwood teaches us that which the cemetery should never teach—respect for human vanity. These bewildering paths, these artificial dells, these pretty glens, these gentle slopes, these charming acclivities, these sylvan mounts, and shades, and lakes, with all their royal garniture of granite, iron, stone, and marble, cut into a thousand forms, beginning with the simple, continuing with the noble, the lovely, the sublime, and terminating with the grotesque—step in between us and the solemn, turn our thoughts from the immortal to the mortal, inspire us with conceptions not of human impotence, but of human grandeur, lead us from the contemplation of the Great Beyond to that of the decaying Present, and point us, as it were, back to the world that we have temporarily left, as the great aim and eternal abiding-place of man!

"I find no fault with Art. It is good. It has its uses, its meanings, and its hallowing influences. But let it remain in its place. Let it not step in between me and the Solemn. Keep it in its place. We can appreciate it there! But keep it away from the habitations of the dead. Let it not deprive the grave of its high and stirring moral!"

"Lo! in the world, what is the one lesson taught to all who will lend an ear? PRIDE. What the sermon preached at church before the pastor has said a single word? Pride--pomp, glitter, fashion! What the incentive in man to climb to riches by falsehood, knavery, and craft? Pride. Pride—which drives from him, step by step, all the solemn, all the nobler qualities, retaining only the baser. Is this wise, is it generous, is it noble? Owe we not something to the better part of us—should we pay eternal tribute only to the viler?

"But *as* the world while *in* the world, is not enough. We must still be showy, still vaunt our folly and our weakness, when no longer of it. We must perforce exhibit it *in the* GRAVE!

"Look around—at this myriad of wild fantastic monuments and vaults, each struggling madly with the other for precedence in—what?

"The eyes of the few gay idlers who come here to toy away an hour!

"Of what do they tell us? Of the wholesome moral lesson of the slumbering dead?

"No.

"But of the frivolousness, the mental imbecility, and the overpowering pride of the *yet living*!

"Is it not enough that we parade our brazen egotism before the world—must we make a show of it even in the tomb?

"What! plant in the skeleton hands of our dead a flaunting banner of our own shame!

"And yet for more than eighteen hundred years man has heard the Christian precept of Humility!

"And yet they who thus invite the eye of the moralist to their effrontery, walk, doubtless, every Sabbath, up to the House of God, and listen with complacency to the Word which teaches us meekness—not arrogance; modesty—not brazenness; earnestness—not frivolity!

"Lo! here, as in the world, bloated Wealth and insolent Pride mock Poverty and Meekness. The Ionic temple looks down with haughty eye upon the humble grave whose green sod is its only ornament. The marble obelisk lifts its proud head in solemn mockery beside the plain, unassuming slab, which, perchance, covers a better and nobler heart. While the pretentious, cloud-piercing shaft, with its broad base and brazen cap, stands memorial of one who, most like, with all his riches, never dropped a tear to misery, nor gave a shilling to rescue a brother from hunger or distress!

"The aristocracy of the world?—Revolting! But the aristocracy of the grave? Humiliating!

"Lo, around us millions of dollars, in fancy monuments! and vaults, and dells, and glens, and shades, and paths, and mounts, and lakes, and effects—all appealing to the eye, filling the mind with wonderment, curiosity, and admiration; depriving death of its solemnity; surrounding it with a mingled air of romance and business, converting it into a matter of little or no moment, and making the place of the sepulchre a place of resort for the sauntering idler to smoke his cigar, the rider to try the bottom of his horse, the lover to whisper fond words to his mistress, the stranger to gratify his curiosity, the amateur to take sketches, the world to look at its monumental curosities and delightful situations, and the moralist to mourn over the littleness of Pride and its sickening display.

"Lo! the time when an humble grave-yard—guileless of mazy paths, and romantic shades, and sylvan dells, and gorgeous vaults, and flaring monuments—subdued the heart to awe, and inspired it, when looking upon the modest habitations of the dead, to commune, in holy reverence, with God!

"Then pride was content to display its tinsel, its presumption, and its shame, in the world's domain, alone. Death's dominions were sacred, ever, to the impious and profane; whoso approached its precincts bowed in pious lowliness to its hallowing and impressive lesson.

"Then, as pride looked on the green, half-sunken grave, and listened to the eloquence of its silent teachings, it lost all memory of its gilt, its rouge, its dollars, its vanity, and its arrogance, and imbibed honest thoughts and stirring memories of good things forgotten long ago!"

CHAPTER XVI.

IN the evening, Samuel called again upon the laundress, with whom he concluded a temporary arrangement for the support of his *elève*, the little orphan.

This done, he returned home, and wrote a letter to his parents. He described, clearly and minutely, the circumstances which had eventuated in constituting him the child's protector; expressed his appreciation of the responsibility of his trust; and tenderly solicited for her, at his own expense, a place in the affections and tranquillity of the parsonage, where she would be surrounded by a pure moral atmosphere, until he should himself be in a position to take her under his own immediate care and supervision.

In a few days, Samuel received, as he expected, a warm,

affectionate, and favorable reply; and in forty-eight hours after its receipt, the little orphan was taking tea at the parsonage.

"The dear creeter!" exclaimed Aunt Betsy, after the little ones had been put to rest for the night. "She will make a nice sister for dear little Joe. We must be good to her, for Samuel's sake!"

"And for her own," said Mrs. Leland. "She is an orphan."

"And for HIS!" said the pastor, reverently.

Three excellent reasons, which soon had their effect upon little Ada, who learned, ere long, to forget everything but the happy family of which she was now a member.

Little Joe welcomed her with a burst of rejoicing from his pipe; and for a week, his solitary tune went off into all sorts of variations, invariably returning to the starting-point, and then gliding off into the old tune itself, and from that into another variation, and from that back again, till the old tune had taken journeys enough to fairly entitle it to the reputation of a fine old traveller that had seen all the world, and more too, and was now going to sit down, take it easy, and rest upon its laurels, respectably, like a gentleman.

The De Witts, the Smiths, and the Jenkinses were by no means grieved to learn that their orphan niece, "the little Jones," had found a protector, who would take upon himself the responsibility of her education and support. Their only feeling in the matter was, that that protector was simply, as Mrs. De Witt expressed it, "a poor dry goods clerk, whose prospects were no better than his pocket, and who, if all that people said of him was true, was so stupid as to spend his earnings—which were little enough—upon wretches who ought to be either in the hospital or the alms-house!"

In his private affairs, all went well with Samuel. At home, abroad, in the drawing-rooms of the rich, or the homely apartments of the poor, he was alike exerting an influence for good.

In his business matters, he was advancing calmly, but steadily. Naturally clear-headed and methodical, whatever he undertook to do, he desired to do *understandingly* and *well*. Hence, while his progress was not so *apparently* rapid as that of many of his fellow-clerks, it was, in reality, greater, because it was *thorough*, while that of the others was, in the main, simply *superficial*. Thus, when removed from one department to another, he was a complete master of the one which he had left. He knew all its duties and all its articles, in all their details—*understandingly*. He had a thorough knowledge of all the nice distinctions, not only in each variety of staple and fancy goods, but also of each individual article in that variety. He could tell, at a glance, the graduating character of its threads, and its finish; the relative depth, strength, and durableness of its color; the comparison it would bear to other fabrics of a corresponding character; the *causes* of its strength or weakness, of its superiority or inferiority, and all the *gradations* of such causes; of the gradations in their respective merits, of the various varieties of staple goods, their prices, and the peculiar districts where each was most in demand; of the character of the changes which were constantly going on in the several varieties, and the peculiarities of those which never changed; of the comparative value of absolutely old, moderately recent, and positively new goods; of the various shades in colors, and the gradations in those shades; of the gradations in positively genuine and only imitation fabrics, as well as in those which were so skilfully wrought as to partake of either, to suit the necessity of the dealer; of their asking prices, and the abatements which they would suffer and still leave profit; of the variations and distinctive character in thread, color, and make, between foreign and native goods; of the comparative standing, popularity, and saleableness of each; which stood and sold upon their own merits, and which required "pushing;" which paid the most, and which the least, profit;

which were kept as baited hooks with which to fish for "other trade," and which "thrown in," to show the liberality of the house; and the names, localities, and comparative honesty—positive, medium, or negative—of their several manufacturers, as evidenced in the distinctive qualities of their respective goods.

In "selling," Samuel gave at first but little promise. For a few months, he was rather below than up to the average of new clerks; and it was sneeringly remarked that he would never reach the dignity nor the salary of a "crack" salesman. The reason, according to Mr. Brigham, the confidential clerk, who, for some cause or other, did not regard our hero with a favorable eye, was plain: "He was not made for the business." The trouble appeared to be that he would not lie. As First Broadcloth expressed it, "he was too honest—*altogether.*" He had "conscientious scruples," which would not permit him to represent an article a hair's breadth above its merits, for the sake of "working it off." When asked by a dealer if a certain fabric was "imported," when he knew that it was only imported from one of the four States of Massachusetts, Rhode Island, Connecticut, or New Jersey, he was *very* apt to tell the truth, sale or no sale, and very much to the disgust of First Broadcloth, who "could not understand how he could be such a ninny." When asked if such and such articles were French or English, when he knew that they were *neither*, but simply domestic products, he had a habit of telling the truth, which sometimes choked off their sale, but did not choke *him.* When requested to give the lowest net prices of any particular kind of goods, he did so by going down to the lowest mark at once,—a proceeding which sometimes resulted in a sale, and sometimes did *not,* but one which generally won the confidence of the dealer, and induced him, when he called again, to look up "the young gentleman who was so particular"—rather choosing to buy of one who preferred the truth to a bill, than of one who preferred a bill to the truth.

In this way, Samuel created many friends, and few or no foes. City and country dealers who made a purchase of him once, favored him, most generally, with a second trial; and, as they invariably found that his statements bore the tests of time and examination, in every particular, they "stood by him" in trade It was not, therefore, necessary for him to "watch the arrivals" and "nab" his customers, when they came again to town. They returned to him of their own accord, in spite of the "flattering inducements" of salesmen of other houses, who "laid for them" with all the cunning of foxes, and "hung to 'em" with the tenacity of bloodhounds. But in vain. The dealers "knew their men" and their *man*. Samuel was "safe"—who bought of him once, bought of him twice; "once a customer, always a customer."

In business parlance, all this "told," *in time*—slowly it may be, but steadily; and not more steadily than surely. One drop shows but little in a bucket; but a regular succession of drops fill it by-and-bye to the brim. Calmly, then, steadily, then, and without noise, ostentation, or parade, Samuel passed tranquilly on; gaining knowledge, experience, and a friend or two, at each step; laying a broad, substantial foundation for future operations; and manfully maintaining his probity and his spiritual trust, bravely and faithfully, on the way.

His fellow-clerks were somewhat slow, at first, to comprehend the chances of his success. "He is a good fellow," they would say, with a knowing wink; "but not made for the dry goods business. He is pious, amiable, and good-natured—a first-rate fellow in heart and manner, but rather tender in the upper story. Thinks money can be made in our business without oil (*anglice*, lying), soft soap, and gimleting (*anglice*, gouging). Green, sir—green as the verdure of his native hills!"

But somehow or other, these remarks, which were very common for a year or so, fell gradually into disuse, and ceased, by-

and-bye, altogether. In fact, it was noticed that Samuel was not so *very* unsuccessful, after all. He *did* make *some* sales; and it was also observed, that city dealers who bought of him once, came again, and again, and always bought of *him*—every time.

The clerks pricked up their ears.

And some one else—Charley Gibbs—noticed, that the country dealers within short distances of the city, who made a bill of Samuel once, did precisely like the city dealers—they called again, and again, and always bought of *him*—Samuel. And as Charley Gibbs was very friendly to Samuel, he took care to impart the result of his observation to the rest, and—

The clerks turned their eyes, askant, at each other.

By-and-bye, First Broadcloth made the interesting discovery that eighteen New York, nine New Jersey, seven Pennsylvania, three Vermont, six Canada, twelve Ohio, eight Missouri, eleven Indiana, three Kentucky, six Illinois, nine Wisconsin, four Iowa, seven Georgia, and four South Carolina dealers had not only repeated their calls and orders on Samuel, but had also each introduced a brother dealer to him, all of whom bought, and all of whom promised to do what they could in bringing him *other* customers. He (First Broadcloth) knew it to be so, "because he had seen, heard, and counted 'em."

The clerks looked down—thoughtfully.

And then they began to think that perhaps Samuel's system was not so very stupid, after all. They didn't know; but they thought so. They *might* be wrong; there was no saying; but of one thing they were certain—*their* customers didn't stick by *them* so steadily, nor take a *great deal* of trouble to make others for them. They had an idea that they could say that—*safely.*

And yet they didn't know. Samuel's way wasn't the regular way of doing things. They had been in the business a good many years, and *they* had never done it in that fashion, nor seen others do it in that way either. And yet, *somehow*, it—WORKED. There was no mistake in that. It *did* APPEAR to *work*. And Samuel *did* seem to get along, and make fair bills, too. There was that bill which he made up yesterday with that Ellicottville fellow: it figured up over a thousand dollars—the second bill which Ellicottville had made with him. And yet Samuel didn't seem to think much of it, either: as if he was used to it.

The clerks were bothered.

At what, they didn't exactly know. The system of telling the truth *did* work; they saw that; anybody could see it; and yet they couldn't understand it. The idea of "doing things *on the square*" in—DRY GOODS! It was so amusing. Of course they always *pretended* to "do things up *right*" with customers; it was expected of them; but then not exactly in *Samuel's* way. Who ever heard of a clerk not "putting a dealer through" in the *right* way—all he could? How could he make anything, if he didn't? Men don't do business for nothing. If a dealer is soft enough to let a man "stick" him, he *ought* to be stuck. Every clerk will admit *that*. And why not? What are dealers made for? Besides, how is a fellow to live, if he don't use a little oil and gimlet occasionally? Where's the profit going to come from, if you don't *make* it? And how *can* you make it, if you are *squeamish?* Bah! It can't be done. Do you suppose a country buyer would pay such prices for Lowell prints, if you didn't make him believe that they had come all the way from France, and that you were three weeks in getting them through the custom-house? No, sir—he'd make you knock off a discount that would give you the yellow jaunders for a week. Bah! It's all humbug. Money isn't made in *that* way!

And yet Samuel's system *does* work; and *he* don't use oil, soft soap, or gimlets.

Ye—yes. That's it. He *does* make sales and customers, too. And yet—well, there's no saying what *won't* turn up next!

When a man can do business on the square in *dry goods*, then look out for *any* thing, and don't be surprised.

But Samuel—Samuel! How about *him?* He's in dry goods —isn't he? He sells, and on the square, too—don't he?

There it is! But *how* does he do it? That's the question. *I* couldn't do it—you couldn't do it. And *he* can. There it is!

But why not? It is simply to tell the truth instead of a lie —which even the dealer *knows* to be a lie. That is common sense, isn't it? If *Samuel* can make trade that way, why can't *we?*

There's the *trouble.* Samuel can stick to the truth, because it's natural to him. Everybody knows that, and expects it of him. But we—*we* are not accustomed to it—it wouldn't answer.

Why?

A pretty question! How would it sound to a dealer, to tell him that our French shawls are *not* imported; that they are made *here?* What would he say? And suppose we should let him know that our French de laines, which we have been selling him all along *for* French, came all the way from Connecticut, what would he say to *that?* He wouldn't swear any—oh, no! Nor take away his trade altogether—oh no, not at all! He'd say we were first-rate fellows—perfect trumps, and make *tremendous* bills of us. O yes—certainly—over the left!

This was a clincher. The clerks couldn't get over it, and they concluded to "continue in the good old way;" that is, to serve their country friends "right"—*wrong!*

In the meanwhile, Samuel went on in *his* way, and the system worked to a charm. It was something so new and rare to dealers to find a salesman who carried his Christianity into his business, that they couldn't help speaking of it. Men *will* talk of novelties! Speaking of it led to letters of introduction, the letters of introduction led to Samuel, the two led to trade, and the trade led to bills. This was Mr. Townsend's method of reasoning the matter, and *he* was not *very* far out of the way, in his commercial logic—generally.

Charley Gibbs reasoned the point over, too, and as he was a fellow of some moral spirit, and never much given to extravagance in anything—not even in business lying—he privately concluded to give Samuel's system a trial, on his own account. The result was slow, but not less sure: and ere long, he detected First Broadcloth at the same game. Shortly after, First Cotton fell into it—sneakingly like, as if he felt ashamed of it; but after a while, a little more openly, and then boldly, like a man who knew what was right, and wasn't afraid to do it, or say it either.

The other clerks opened their eyes, and reflected. In time, they began to regard each other suspiciously; and then to—think; and then to venture upon the system carefully, as they thought, and—privately, and then by degrees not *quite* so privately, and then they found that the plan *worked*—SOMEHOW.

But still they noticed at the same time that Samuel's customers *continued to increase;* that, in fact, although their own business improved under the new system, *his* went ahead the fastest. Not that he had *more* customers than they, but that he made more *new* ones than *they* did; that *his* men appeared to have more confidence in *him*, than *theirs* did in *them;* and that *his* "friends" rolled up bigger bills than *theirs* did. They did not understand this *at first;* but the reason was comprehensible in time: Samuel was the *great* ORIGINAL. His name had "got up" first. *They* were only imitators.

But that made no difference. *The imitation* PAID, and far better, too, than the old plan. *This* was with *them* the MAIN point.

At length, however, the system began to bear its *legitimate* fruits. Many of the clerks who had at first taken hold of the truth as a mere matter of *policy*, found it in time so pleasant, that they adopted it, one after another, from *principle*. Upon reaching *this* point, they made a *discovery*, viz.: that *truth as a principle* elevated their thoughts, strengthened their self-confidence, and inspired them with a feeling to which they had previously been strangers—MORAL STAMINA. The delightfulness of this high feeling made MEN of them;—imbued them with a solemn consciousness of their individual duties *as* men to their *fellow*-men, to themselves, to that great principle which has so *few* friends—Truth, and to that principle's creator—The August.

By-and-bye this portion of the clerks and Samuel became, by degrees, very friendly. They appeared to *understand* each other, to entertain an *excellent feeling* for one another, to *counsel* with each other, and to hold little meetings together, nights, down stairs, in the packing-room—Bill Bradley's department, and where that worthy was as much of a monarch as any President or King; and, like a good-natured potentate, he graciously accorded his permission to the "up-stairers" to hold their evening meetings in his royal hall as often as they liked, also authorizing them to use his empty packing-boxes for seats, and his packing-table to sit around; himself joining them, sometimes, and wondering in his silent, meditative way, at the great change which had come over "the spirit of their dreams."

"There's Tom Rickets," mused the wondering packer, "who used to dress so loud (*anglice*, flashily), with his knowin' hat, his green coat, his plaid vest, his great long guard-chain, his blue pants and his pattern (patent) leathers—Lord, how he's altered! Nice suit of plain black, now—just like a gen'leman. And Bill Rider, too, *without* his loud choker. Well, I wouldn't have believed it, if I'd only heered tell on't. And Frank Tisdale, *without* his cigar! And Joe Thompson, *without* his eternal string of oaths, and his talk about the women, and brandy punches, and races, and fast teams, and sparrin' matches, and bluff! And Tom Davenport, *without* his cigar stump, and his gas about that little actress! And Charley Gibbs, *without* his Miss Nancy airs! And then the other up-stairers—tellin' the truth for the first time in their lives, and stickin' to it, too! Well—it's *high!* Dry goods have turned round. It takes me right down!"

But this was not all. The Samuel boys, as they were called, were off other nights, sometimes solitarily, and sometimes in couples—not, as of yore, at balls, theatres, rum saloons, gambling hells, brothels, or sporting-places, but threading narrow alleys, diving into damp cellars, climbing narrow staircases, and penetrating garrets—the homes of the friendless and the stricken; easing the wants of the poor, making glad the hearts of the sorrowing, pouring oil upon the wounds of the sick and feeble, whispering courage to the despondent, clothing the naked, and leading hearts that had long forgotten Him, back again to God—and finding such pleasure in their voluntary good work as they had never received from ball, or spree, or theatre, or gambling hell, or brothel, and such excitement as they had never experienced in all their lives from whisky-punches, egg-nogs, brandy-smashes, mint-juleps, or gin-slings, and an inward satisfaction and delight which they would not have exchanged for empires.

The other "boys" had not reached this point; they rarely disturbed the meetings in the packing-room by their presence, although they sometimes professed an interest in them. They continued to adhere to the truth, however, in "selling," because it—paid.

The "correctness" of the salesmen in the house of John P. Townsend became known. Ere long it was a common topic in the trade. Rival houses spoke of it as they would of a good joke. They were rash enough, for a time, to mention it to their own customers, as "the last best thing out," and afterwards discovered that their friends had "strayed off" to that very house to give its "correct" young gentlemen a trial. Then they laughed—the other way! Country dealers spoke of it among themselves as the greatest wonder in New York; and the report scattered—in every direction; the jealousy of rival houses helping its diffusion more than any other cause, and, as a "runner" expressed it, "the thing took." Old customers, who had not made a bill at the house for years, returned; and new ones at their heels. The clerks were busy as bees, from morn till dusk, many of them till late at night. But as they were as much interested as their employer in the sales, they bore the press of business *patiently*. During the fall and spring, while trade "dragged" at other establishments, dealers remarked that "the house with the correct clerks" was comparatively overburdened with business—nay, absolutely "run down." And when one of its salesmen appeared in the street, the runners of rival houses would point him out, sometimes to a customer, and sometimes to one another, saying, with mixed envy and interest—"There goes one of John P. Townsend's 'correct' boys!"

The "correct boys" became famous—Samuel particularly. The clerks of rival houses regarded them with jealousy—the *heads* of rival houses with marked affability and manifest interest. Indeed, the latter were only *too* happy to meet and treat them with uncommon urbanity. But the "correct boys" understood the meaning of their condescending attentions. "They were not to be caught." "They did very well at Mr. Townsend's—*very* well—as well as they desired to." On discovering which fact, the heads of the rival houses ceased their condescending importunities, and returned to their usual dignity.

The "correct boys" were not to be seduced from their allegiance to John P. Townsend. He *paid well*—it was his policy; and as he was a far-seeing man, he knew it to be a policy which would secure the *best talent* in the market, and enable him to *keep it.* His golden motto was visible in all his transactions: "Who pays well, is served well." He could afford to laugh at the tempting inducements of his rivals to beguile away his clerks —and he *did*.

Mr. Townsend was in raptures.

"The old house stands firm," he would say to himself—"firm as a rock. Everything works in its favor; but truth and honesty most of all!" And he would laugh in his dry, pleasant way. "Samuel is a jewel—his piety *pays!*" and he would rub his sleek, fat hands, and look pleasantly, through the panes of the partition, at his small army of "correct boys," who were busy as bees with their numerous customers, who were also as busy as bees in rolling up their bills. "Ah!" cried the merchant, surveying the scene with a proud, half-laughing eye, "there's a sight to make a jobber shout. A rare sight—a great sight—a *paying* sight! Dear! —dear! what a blessed thing religion is, and—money!"

There was one gentleman in the house, however, who did not relish the turn which its affairs were taking—Mr. Brigham, the confidential clerk. That worthy viewed the new movement with uneasiness. It not only boded him no good—it threatened him with ruin.

For years Mr. Brigham had been to the house of John P. Townsend what the Premier is to the British crown—what the Secretary of State is to the American Cabinet—*the* man, that is to say, the confidential clerk. He was—or rather he innocently flattered himself so—the confidential clerk, John P. Townsend, the silent partner, the stock, the business, the everything. *He* was THE HOUSE; that is to say, he *thought* so, and a great many others thought so, too—the book-keepers, clerks, packers, and porters, for instance—in fact, everybody *in* the house, except—Mr. John P. Townsend himself, and the silent partner. *They*—DIDN'T; but they did not publish their opinion. It was therefore no great wonder if Mr. Brigham entertained that thought, and that he grew in time to believe it as he would any other thing which everybody affirmed to be true, and which it was so very gratifying to his own feelings *to* believe. Nor was this all. The confidential clerk knew himself to be a man of rare talent, which was very true; that he had, in a measure, built up the house of John P. Townsend—that is to say, that it was largely owing to *his* talent, *his* energies, *his* knowledge of the business, and *his* influence with city and country dealers, that the house of John P. Townsend had reached its present high standing and position —which was equally true; that he was, in fact, although only a mere confidential clerk, a perfect business giant—which was also true; that he was known *as* such to all the great houses in the dry goods trade, and that either or all of them would be only too glad to give him even more than he was receiving in the house of John P. Townsend, for the sake of getting him away from that house, and into their own employ—which was no less true; that he was a thorough master of his business, and of the business of John P. Townsend's business also, and that he could, if so disposed, leave the house of John P. Townsend, and carry with him to any other house a very large proportion of that business—that is to say, the custom patronage, which was, perhaps, no less true than the rest; that if he was so largely instrumental in *building up* the house of John P. Townsend, he could doubtless, if urged either by passion, self-interest, or any other motive, to do so, be equally instrumental in *breaking it down*—that he had, in any event, the ability, if so disposed, to do it a serious amount of harm: all of which was doubtless partially true, but not perhaps *quite* so true or correct as the confidential clerk fancied it to be.

He was not, however, *very* far wrong in his estimate of his own talents, nor in his opinion of the estimate which was placed upon them by the house. Both Mr. Townsend and the silent partner did him full justice in this and several other respects—that is to say, they equally understood and appreciated his *talents* and—*himself*. To keep him in good-humor, they paid him well; to flatter his vanity and retain their hold upon him, they gave to him a certain degree of confidence, a certain degree of power, and a certain degree of influence—just enough of each to flatter his self-love, and lead him to believe that he was all-important, and all-powerful; while to keep their grip upon him until they should feel themselves sufficiently strong to either send him adrift, or make him *understand* his place, they pampered him with the hope that they would, at no distant day, give him an interest in the house—that is, when the house should, through his energies, reach a satisfactory point in its yearly business—at which point, they *privately* designed to wake him from his fond, delusive dream, and let him—*run*, and do his worst. In the meanwhile, they trusted to a judicious application of flattery to keep him in the traces, and hold him with a firm, but easy, hand.

But all this was under the *old* system—the old system, in which the confidential clerk was so able a master. The new movement was bringing about *another* state of things—altogether. It was popularizing the house in city and country, all over the Union, in fact, as well as in British America—strengthening the house—augmenting its reputation, its business, and consequently its profits—and rapidly rendering it entirely *independent* of HIM—the confidential clerk, of *him*—the all-powerful!

The gentleman turned pale at the thought; his lips parted, and his teeth absolutely cowered in terror. And this new system, which was doing such wonders for the house, and threatening *him*—the till of late all-important—with disaster—who was it that produced it, wrought it out, set it going?

Who but one who had already given Mr. Brigham some trouble in *another* quarter, and threatened him with more still!

Who but the reigning favorite—whose name was in everybody's mouth—whose acquaintance was courted by all in the house and in the trade—whom city and country dealers sought out, as they would some great man who could confer lasting favors upon them—who had accomplished more in his first eighteen months than most clerks perform in five years—whom the head of the house, John P. Townsend, appeared to take particular delight in honoring with long familiar interviews in his office, and who alone, of all the clerks, had the privilege of entering the office at pleasure, of reading the morning papers there, of sitting there, and of making himself perfectly at home there, whether John P. Townsend was in or no. Who but—Samuel!

The name came hissingly through Mr. Brigham's large glistening teeth, which seemed to writhe at it.

Samuel!

The lips all but blistered at its sound.

"If I should take him in hand, now!" continued Mr. Brigham, musingly. "What then? Let me see. I have read of a man who was in power and in peril, as I am. A courtier wasp came in his way, and was near to unseating, near to destroying, him What did the man do? He put out his hand, while yet it was strong with the iron panoply of power, and when he drew it back, the wasp was—CRUSHED!"

The teeth wriggled and danced, and appeared to be intoxicated with wild joy, at the result.

"And I—I," mused Mr. Brigham, "might put out *my* hand, and do the like. There are two interests at stake to incite me. SHALL I?"

"Oh! do—do!" laughed and danced the teeth. "It would be glorious fun. Do—do!"

Mr. Brigham was for a long time—ten minutes—a long time for *him!*—undecided. But at the end of that period his will was settled.

The teeth sent up a shout in their own way, at the character of his decision. They hooted, and yelled, and leaped, and rolled, and jumped, and screamed, like cannibals round a roasting fire, with a prisoner, who was timid, and chained, and helpless, burning at the stake.

The man's cold, gray, cat-like eyes, ever all but closed, from habit, peered through their half-pent lashes like the sharp, dread orb-glitter of a basilisk.

The demon of his bold, serpent nature was in that glance. It boded mischief, wrath, triumph—all in one.

CHAPTER XVII.

"OH, dear—I shall die!" cried Isabella, laughingly, one afternoon, on her return from a walk.

"Why, my dear—what now?" asked her aunt, looking up from an evening paper.

"Oh! dear—*such* a good thing!" returned Isabella, throwing off her things, and sinking back upon a lounge. "You wouldn't believe it!"

"Believe what, my dear?"

"Samuel—" began Isabella, clapping her hands in the exuberance of her mirth.

"What of *him?*" asked her aunt, with an air of interest.

"Is on a new tack," cried Isabella, with screaming laughter. "Oh dear—Oh dear!"

"Indeed? I should have thought that with his poor, and his packing-room society, he had business enough!"

"I should think so, too, aunt. But his new movement is one of the wildest, strangest—"

"But what *is* it?" demanded her aunt. "What is he doing now?"

"Trying to convert the *ministers!*" answered her niece, clapping her hands. "Oh, dear!" placing her hand upon her sides, "I shall die. I know I shall!"

"I fear," said Mrs. Townsend, after a few moments' reflection, "that Samuel will have his labor for his pains."

"I think so, too!" laughed Isabella.

"Clergymen," continued her aunt, "who *need* converting—and the number is by no means small—are the last persons in the world to *be* converted. They get so accustomed to *professional* piety, that they become, in time, perfectly coated with it, as a leaden plate is coated by a surface of copper or silver, through which nothing can penetrate."

"I think," ventured Miriam, with her usual modest deference, "that we misjudge the members of that noblest of all professions."

"Only hear our credulous Mirry, aunt!" cried Isabella.

"On what do you base that impression, my dear?" asked Mrs. Townsend, mildly.

"Yes; do let us hear!" laughed Isabella.

"Upon my conviction of its truthfulness," replied Miriam. "The world is so fond of taking ungenerous views of God's people, that when it discovers a single sign of weakness, it exults over it with a loud shout of rejoicing—never pausing to inquire whether there may not be some fair excuse for that weakness. And when it descries a single unfaithful member, it rails out against the entire body! Is this fair?"

"No, my dear. But when it finds that the '*un*faithful' ones are more numerous than the faithful, it has good reason for its outcry."

"That is too sweeping a charge, dear aunt!" said Miriam, with gentle reproach. "If you would only examine the subject in a spirit of generous candor, you would find the number of the really unfaithful to be very small indeed!"

"What a dear delightful little innocent!" cried Isabella, jeeringly.

"I do not think so," said Mrs. Townsend. "If the number of the faithful ones is so much greater than that of the unfaithful, why are not more converts made?"

"Because," answered Miriam, "a pastor can do but little unless his efforts are seconded by his people. They expect him to do the *whole* of the work, and will not, except in rare instances, even lend him the influence of their example. When a stranger to religion goes to church, and finds himself touched by the holy utterances of the preacher, he looks around, and finds perhaps a face or two with which he is familiar. These faces belong to men or women whom he knows, either in a social or business way, to be everything *but* Christians, and he gets the impression that religion is a mere farce, since those who *profess* to be governed by it, are scarcely deserving of respect. Thus the heavenly drop which fell from the lips of the preacher, dries up and disappears; and thus the good resulting from the labors of the pastor is neutralized by the unfaithfulness of his people. The pastor knows this, and yet he bravely struggles on. But this, although a great, is yet only one of many obstacles with which he has to contend—all of them arising from his own people; and yet, in the face of them all, he nobly works on, yearning to be the instrument of good to many, and yet thankful if he can be the means of grace to one."

"If that be true," demanded Isabella, "why has Samuel entered upon his crusade against the pulpit infidels?"

"I think," returned Miriam, "you misapprehend the real character of his movement!"

"Indeed! You think *that?* How very *modest* and *knowing!*" jeered her cousin.

"What *is* he doing, then, my dear?" asked Mrs. Townsend, kindly.

"Encouraging the *discouraged*," replied Miriam, with a sweet, glad smile; "waking up those, who, from any cause, have lost their enthusiasm, or fallen, insensibly and by degrees, into unfruitful mannerism."

"A hopeless task!" observed Isabella.

"And yet," ventured Miriam, "he has not wholly failed."

"How, my dear?" said her aunt, in surprise. "You were aware of this before, and yet withheld the information from us!"

Isabella was at once mortified and indignant. She had flattered herself that she alone had been the first to discover the young Christian's new movement; and now—

"The secret was not mine, aunt," returned Miriam. "It was imparted to me in confidence."

"But," said her cousin, "now that it is known, I presume, you are at liberty to give us the name of your informant?"

"Aunt," said Miriam, "would it be proper in me to do so?"

"Why do you ask it, 'Bel?" inquired Mrs. Townsend.

"I should like to know," returned the latter, "who is more in the way of learning Samuel's movements than ourselves?"

"In that case, Mirry, I can see no harm in your mentioning the name of your friend."

I had the information from Fanny Adriance," said Miriam.

"Who got it, of course, from Charley Gibbs," observed Isabella. "I see it all, now!"

"But you were saying, Mirry, that Samuel had had some success in his new idea?"

"Yes, aunt. He has won the love and confidence of seven worthy clergymen, who are very grateful to him for his kind encouragement and assistance."

"Is that all?" asked Isabella, contemptuously.

"No, coz. They have woke up, taken hold of their work with fresh vigor, enthusiasm, and earnestness; and—"

"With what result?" interrupted her impatient cousin.

"The happiest," replied Miriam, joyfully. "To the agreeable surprise of the majority of the members of their congregations, who, at the gentle but stirring solicitation of Samuel, who has seen them separately, as well as jointly, have also started from their lethargy, and come up to the support of their pastors, who, finding themselves encouraged by their people, have risen up, in all the strength and power of their pious might, and are now dealing, every Sabbath, brave and successful blows for our Lord and Redeemer."

"'Brave blows!'" repeated Isabella, with a dry, cutting smile. "One of *Samuel's* phrases!"

"It is a striking one, 'Bel!" said her aunt, for the purpose of giving Miriam an opportunity to recover from the blushing confusion into which she had been thrown by her cousin's satirical remark.

"Oh, aunt," laughed Isabella, "I have no fault to find with anything of Samuel's. But now that he has taken the subject up, I should be glad to have him give Mr. Engold—our own pastor—a little stirring up. It would improve *him!*"

"In what respect?" asked her aunt, with a lurking smile.

"In many," answered Isabella.

"Come—come, 'Bel, specify!"

"I think," said Isabella, with a mischievous glance at her cousin, whom she knew to be exceedingly sensitive at the slightest disrespectful reference to her pastor, "he needs arousing! I always fancy, when listening to him, that he is more mindful of the euphony of his periods than he is of the salvation of his hearers!"

"Is there any harm in a preacher's showing himself a scholar?" asked Miriam.

"Very great harm indeed, cousin, when, as in Mr. Engold's case, he makes that his principal business!"

"That is a grave charge, 'Bel, to make against one's own minister!" observed her aunt.

"Oh, it isn't mine alone!" returned Isabella. "Everybody says so—that is," she added, with an arch smile at her cousin, "everybody who does not stand in awe of him because he *is* their pastor! I have heard uncle, for instance, say it a hundred times; and Mr. Crittenden, also; and *they* are pretty good authorities, I imagine!"

"I esteem guardy and Mr. Crittenden very much," said Miriam, gently; "but I think they are wrong in this."

"And I think they are right!" rejoined Isabella.

"Frankly, cousin?" asked Miriam.

"Frankly!"

Miriam's brow became saddened.

"More than that," continued her cousin. "I have never fancied that Mr. Engold was even a converted man!"

"Oh, cousin—cousin! You are cruel!"

"In what? For speaking what I think?"

"No!" answered Miriam; "but for speaking so unkindly of one of God's agents!"

"*His own* agent, rather!" retorted Isabella.

Miriam looked at her imploringly.

"Now don't, don't, coz!" she said. "I will take it as a favor if you won't talk so!"

"Pshaw! Nonsense!" exclaimed Isabella, impetuously. "I'll say what I think! I am my own mistress, I presume!"

"True, dear cousin! But there are subjects which, it appears to me, we should never touch, even so lightly—that is, I mean, with a single disrespectful breath. And this is one of them!"

"Are clergymen any better than other people?" demanded Isabella, impatiently.

"Yes, dear cousin," replied Miriam, gently, "because they are the ambassadors of Our Prince!"

"Not when they do their own work, instead of their Master's!"

"Oh, cousin—dear cousin! don't talk so, don't. You hurt me!—I will give you anything, do anything for you, if you only won't!"

"Miriam—" said Isabella, surveying her sternly

"Well, cousin?"

"You are wrong!"

"Oh, no—cousin. Oh, no—don't say so. I wouldn't hurt *your* feelings for the world!"

"You are wrong, I tell you, to permit your prejudices or your feelings to blind your judgment! If you want to pass for a thinking, reasoning being, you must give your mind free, untrammelled play, and believe in the evidence of your eyes!"

"I see well enough already, dear cousin," replied Miriam; "and what I see makes me very happy. I am content with that."

"Your prejudices blind you, coz!"

"Don't say so, dear 'Bel—don't!"

"I will say so, when I think it!"

"Then you may, dear cousin—you may. Say what you will *of* me, and *to* me, but don't speak slightingly of the workmen of our Prince!"

"I am doing nothing of the kind, Mirry. I am speaking of one whom I, in common with many others, regard as *his own* workman. If I thought for a single moment that Mr. Engold was one of GOD's ministers, I would cut off my right hand sooner than breathe one word against him!"

"If he be not one of GOD's preachers," asked Miriam, with a bewildered air, "whose, then, *is* he?"

"SOCIETY's!" returned Isabella, with a freezing smile. "*That* is *his* only God and Master!"

"Oh, cousin—cousin!"

"I see him with a stranger's eye, and not his dupe's!" said Isabella, coldly. "He uses the pulpit, *not* to serve his Maker's interests, but—*his own!* His discourses exhibit, *not* the burning earnestness of an ambassador of Christ, but *the scholarly accomplishments of Henry Engold!* Mark, with what an air of studied dignity he rises before the sacred desk; with what studied rhetoric he invokes Divine Grace; with what studied elegance and grandeur he commences his discourse, which he has polished to the silvery smoothness of a graceful, but soulless poem; with what studied mellifluousness he reads, not his sermon, but his *masterly literary composition;* how studiedly he meanders through this soft, gurgling rill of—dry emptiness; how gracefully he *ges*ticulates, how gracefully he *ar*ticulates—the graceful cadences of his oily voice falling on the silken ears of his complacent hearers like strains of lulling music, to the close; when, the doxology over, he, with a mingled air of studied gracefulness, benignity, and honeyed sweetness, sends his auditors home to—*ponder upon their good fortune in possessing so charming a rhetorician, so polished a scholar, and so accomplished a gentleman for their preacher!*"

Mrs. Townsend smiled; Miriam was full of sadness.

"You are unkind, cousin!" she said.

"I have no doubt you think so," returned Isabella, "still I am satisfied, and so is aunt, and uncle, and Mr. Crittenden, and everybody else, who have ever heard Mr. Engold, and are independent enough to speak what they think and know, that I have not overdrawn his Sunday portrait."

"Do *you* think so, aunt?" asked Miraim.

"Well, my dear," said Mrs. Townsend, "I incline to the opinion that, Bel is nearer right than wrong."

"There, coz!" cried Isabella, triumphantly.

Miriam looked at them alternately for a few moments, like one bewildered, and then shaking her head, observed, with modest diffidence—

"I have experienced great comfort from Mr. Engold's preaching, and have ever found it full of sweetness and of goodness!"

"I doubt it not, my dear," said her aunt, kindly. "To an organization like yours, *auy* discourse that had in it a single grain of piety, would seem full of Christian beauty. 'Bel and I can comprehend that. But *we* are sterner, and more rigorous in our demands. We require a sermon to possess, not a *single* grain, but to be wholly made up of, and imbued with, the spirit of Divine Truth!"

"There, coz! What have you got to say now?"

"I have a great respect for aunt's superior knowledge, observation, and experience," answered Miriam, "and for yours too dear cousin; but I still think that Mr. Engold is a loyal servant to his Prince. If I thought otherwise, I should be unhappy!"

"But only look at it once," said Isabella. "Whom has Mr. Engold been instrumental in saving? He has been our pastor for five years, and where are the fruits of his labors? He preaches his flowery homilies year in and year out, to the same number of exclusives—that is, if they don't run away, like Mr. Jones or Mrs. Clarke!—and without accomplishing anything. Point, if you can, to a single soul that he has startled from its dream of sin, or to a single heart that he has turned from its evil ways to God?"

"Surely," cried Miriam, "Mr. Engold has brought some members to the church. Don't you remember how many vacant pews we used to have before he became our pastor? And they are all filled now, and have been for a long time. *That* is some evidence in his favor—is it not?"

"Yes," answered Isabella, "to his *talent!* But you forget that these pews have all been rented by new arrivals among our fashionables, who have taken them, in part because ours is a fashionable church, and because Mr. Engold is a fashionable preacher, and in part because they like to have it known and said that they belong to the 'Church of the Exclusives!'"

"I still think," persisted Miriam, with generous confidence in her pastor, "that you do Mr. Engold great injustice!"

"I am astonished at your blind infatuation, coz!" said Isabella. "You put me out of all patience!"

"I don't mean to hurt your feelings, dear 'Bel. I really don't! But I cannot help thinking that our pastor is a good man. Haven't you ever noticed how tenderly solicitous he is for his parishioners?"

"Doubtless, coz," mocked Isabella; "for *without* his parishioners, where would *himself* be!"

"That is unfair!" returned Miriam, with a gentle smile of mingled sweetness and reproach. "Because Mr. Engold's great talent alone would secure him as good, if not a better, position, anywhere!"

"His *talent* would, doubtless!" sneered her cousin.

"It was only a few months ago," continued Miriam, "when a church in Boston offered him a thousand dollars more per year than we were paying him, if he would only resign his post with us, and become their pastor. But he nobly resisted the temptation—"

"*And showed the letter to our trustees,*" interrupted Isabella, mockingly, "who agreed to add *fifteen* hundred to his salary, *if he would stay!* A noble resistance against temptation, truly!"

Miriam dropped her eyes in mingled anguish and bewilderment.

"And it is even suspected," continued the pitiless Isabella, "that Mr. Engold got a friend in that city to manage the Boston church into the offer, so that he could use it as a weapon with which to beguile us into an increase of his salary! Guardy and the other trustees smilingly term it a 'smart financial operation.'"

"Aunt," said Miriam imploringly, "What do *you* think?"

"I agree with the general sentiment upon the subject," returned Mrs. Townsend, with a smile which she could not wholly repress.

"That this ungenerous suspicion is true?" asked Miriam.

"No, my dear; that the operation was *pretty* shrewd!" returned her aunt, slily. "As to the correctness of the suspicion, I have nothing to say!"

"Still you have an opinion?" asked Isabella.

"Yes," returned Mrs. Townsend, slowly.

"And it concurs with that of guardy?"

"We should always respect the opinions of an experienced mind—particularly when it is that of one's husband!" was the laughing but dubious reply.

Miriam shook her head.

"You are still skeptical?" demanded Isabella, with a cold, pitiless sneer.

"No, cousin," returned Miriam, with an expresssion of rare sweetness: "I have still the same trusting confidence in my pastor! He has come to me in my Redeemer's name; he has said words of comfort to my soul; he has suggested to me many a pleasant thought; he has often led me to the presence of my Prince; and, come weal, come woe, I will stand by him! I say not that he has not his faults—for all are liable to err. But I *do* know that he has come to me in my Redeemer's name; that he has a good and kindly heart; that he is loving, affectionate, and gentle; that he aims to do the will of Him that sent him; and that he does it to the best of his ability. For these reasons I have faith in him; for these I will be steadfast to him: and never shall I utter a breath to tarnish his manly or ministerial fame! If I knew that he had a weakness which stood in the way of his success as an agent of our common Lord, I would point it out to him, saying, 'For this, our Prince and you are reviled;' and—so noble is he—he would put it, at once, away. But not knowing of it, and believing him to be a true and legitimate messenger from my Prince, I will receive him as such, have confidence in him, and treat him ever with the love, respect, and deference which are due to every envoy from on High!"

Isabella surveyed her cousin with smiling astonishment; never before had she seen her so energetic or impassioned, never before so brightly beautiful.

"Mirry is right," observed Mrs. Townsend, thoughtfully. "We have judged our pastor too severely."

The announcement, at this moment, of a visitor, interrupted and put an end to the subject.

CHAPTER XVIII.

One morning, Mr. Townsend received a letter from his wandering partner, announcing his approaching return, and winding up as follows:—

"I am pleased beyond measure to learn the results to the house of Samuel's piety. Pray, don't take this for humbug—I said to *the house.* Like you, my boy, I have an exalted opinion of *paying* piety. Still I like *Samuel's* piety for another reason: it is so genuine, and so rare. He is a great man, in his way—that is, a great *good* man; and I am not ashamed to say that I would give worlds to be like him. Make the most of that confession, old partner mine in business iniquity and humbug. Do you remember what a lacing the fellow gave me the first time I ever saw him, in the cars? I little dreamed, then, that my conqueror designed to take his business degrees in *our* house, and still less that the moral influence of his piety would be felt so sensibly upon its trade. And this leads me to an idea, viz.: *Is* the present system of fraud, falsehood, and humbug in business the *only* paying one? Is business *necessarily* wedded to that system? Is it not possible for men to do business on the square—as they and we all *profess* to do, but as they and we do *not?* The happy results of Samuel's movement answer the latter question in a manner which leaves no room for doubt; and I begin to have faith in it, although it upsets the views which I have entertained all along. Make the most you can of this confession, also. The fact is, partner, there *is*, after all, even in trade, a tremendous moral influence in Honesty, and it is a *paying* influence at that, depend upon it.

"I have a great desire to take hold of our young business reformer, and draw him out. You cannot conceive the width of the fellow's reputation. I hear of him everywhere. The dealers talk of him as of a great commercial wonder. Of course all this must tell, and I rejoice to learn that it *is* telling, largely, for the house. And so you are doing a tremendous fall trade? Good. How it must make our rivals groan! Honesty *pays*—eh? Thanks to Samuel! We must do the right thing by our young friend; but I know your business policy is founded upon correct views, and so I will not enlarge upon that point—a hint is sufficient.

"In case you should see fit to honor my return with one of my favorite *converzationes*, be kind enough to remember my gallery of living portraits. If any new ones have turned up in my absence, run them in. I wish to exhibit them to Samuel, and get his opinion of their merits. I am curious to observe the effect of tinsel in contrast with the legitimate article. You know my weakness—my propensity for drawing out character. I like to play upon little minds, and bring their humbug to the surface. I sometimes think that I am myself as great a humbug as the rest. But no matter. One must amuse himself.

"I shall be home on the 20th. You can make your arrangements for the *converzatione*, portrait gallery and all, accordingly. But pray don't invite anybody who is *respectable* except yourself, your fair lady, Miriam, and Samuel. I feel a deep interest in the latter, and wish to show him of what wretched stuff human nature is made up.

"An you love me, don't let that miserable bag of rubbish—Isabella—ensnare our favorite. Turn her over to her old flame, Brigham; *he* is worthy of her. They would make a *glorious* pair! If they should marry and be blessed with sons—what magnificent scamps *they* would be!

"We must make up a match between Samuel and Miriam.

Their guileless natures harmonize with and fit them for each other. I have long contemplated making Mirry my heir. If Samuel could only be brought to turn his eyes favorably upon her—and we might work it, I think, with your good lady's assistance—I would not only agree to leave her all I should be worth when I die, but I would put her in possession of half of my cash and property at once. She is the only being on earth, excepting Samuel, who has ever influenced my mind with pure thoughts—and *pure* thoughts are luxuries worth paying for. When I talked with Samuel in the car, the same happy feeling came over me which I always experience in my conversations with Miriam. What wonder, then, if, loving Miriam, I should also love Samuel, who possesses, in a yet bolder, grander, and more marked degree, the very qualities which render *her* so lovable.

"Samuel—Miriam!

"How I delight to repeat these words, to me so full of purity and sweetness!

"Say what we will, think as we may, partner, there *is* a grandeur, an elevating power, a hallowing influence, in religion, which we sordid sons of business know but little of—unhappily. As for myself, I am not ashamed to confess that when in the presence of little Miriam, or Samuel, I experience a sense of my own unworthiness, my own inferiority—more, I realize the comforting blessedness of their purer thoughts. It sanctifies me while I am near them, while I listen to them.

"Now, old boy, you, with all your humbug, all your worldliness, must have experienced this glorious feeling, also—because you are with them more, see them more, hear them more, and enjoy the luxury of their intimacy more. I almost—nay, I *do*—envy you these privileges; for it *is* a privilege to be admitted to the society, even for a few moments, of the good.

"And now tell me—partner mine in business humbug and iniquity—is not the principle, the institution or whatever it may be, which is capable of influencing minds like *ours* in that manner, of ridding us of our grossness and elevating us to a consciousness of temporary purity, hallowing us, as it were, with the *luxury of goodness*, WORTH GOING IN FOR, manfully, hand and foot, hip and thigh, heart and head?

"I know it requires courage to face the *thought* of it, greater to *resolve* upon it, and greater still to *do* it. But, partner mine, we are not boys, nor cowards. The pluck to think of it, *I* have, and to acknowledge it, too; but whether or no I have the stamina to go through with it—to face my Maker and tell Him I am a rascal, but that I repent and will serve Him, in future, like a MAN—is another question. I don't know *that* I have, and I cannot say *but* I have. Time will decide it.

"But how is it with *you?* I do not wish you to think me impertinent, but this I will say—*it is time you take the subject in hand!* Whatever we may say of it, whatever we may think of it, this trifling with the immortal part of us is *no joke!* I say this—*I*, Robert Crittenden—because I *feel* it; and the feeling has been growing on me ever since my conversation with Samuel in the cars. I cannot get over it. It forces itself upon me, by day, by night. It is with me a Presence—a Familiar. I tell you this—I, Robert Crittenden, who have seen the world, and studied it, and scorned it, for six-and-forty years.

"There *is* a vitalizing power, a hallowing influence, an arousing spirit—a stirring greatness—in religion. Believe it!

"I saw a dealer to-day. While conversing with him, an express wagon emptied five cases of goods at his door. They were opened in my presence, and laid out, for shelving, on his counter. They formed a goodly heap. The bill had arrived previously by post. The goods were examined piece by piece, and then stored upon the shelves. Every item was found to be correct, and every item *was* correct. The dealer showed me the bill—the goods had been purchased by his partner of Samuel—

at our house. I looked at them as I never looked at a bill of goods bought of our house before—with a feeling of honest pride, of stirring satisfaction!

"That bill of goods was an *honest* one! It had been made without a single lie; every piece in it had been sold at its *honest* worth. There was no paltry fraud, no petty falsehood, employed in making it up. From top to bottom, it was an *honest bill*, and —it was made at *our* house! At *our* house, where we neither lie nor cheat—NOW!

"Fancy my struggle to restrain my enthusiasm—to preserve my equanimity.

"That, partner, was the most glorious moment I ever experienced since I became a merchant. Ten years' profits could not have bought it. *I felt like an honest man!*

"John P. Townsend—I say it in all sympathy and kindness—have you ever had that feeling? Of late, even? If not, you cannot appreciate its *luxury!*

"Ah! partner—we sordid money dogs of business, when we barter our Honesty for a paltry Bill, give away a GREAT THING for a *very small* one! Believe it!

"Nor is this all. These country merchants, whom we city jobbers are so apt to regard as flats, *know* us, understand us, appreciate us! They are *not* the blind, silly moles we take them to be! Their eyes are sharp, their senses keen. They *know* us through and through. In backwoods parlance, they can 'tell a rascal by his *smell*.' When a drummer makes his appearance on their thresholds, they instinctively lock their tills! They eye him suspiciously, they listen to him incredulously. They understand the meaning of his oily politeness, of his assumed geniality; and duly appreciate both them and him at their *true* value. *They know city merchants and city drummers*, BETTER THAN CITY MERCHANTS OR CITY DRUMMERS KNOW THEM! Light your cigar with that—*after* riveting it in your memory.

"Well, while conversing with our friend, the dealer, to-day, who should come in, on a drumming call, but Mr. Wilson, of the firm of Gates & Wilson—one of our pretentious rivals. You know that house; you know its reputation for littleness, for lying, for gouging, for audacious humbug. Well—our dealer knew it, too! He had made bills of it, formerly, and found it out, and—remembered it. Wilson came in with his usual honeyed smile. One unused to him, and creatures of his kind, would have fancied him a shipwrecked brother, who had escaped from the Arabs, or some other murderous tribe, for no other object in the world than to embrace his relative, the dealer—he was so *very* glad to see him, and shook him by the hand *so* heartily! But it was of no use. The dealer understood him, the dealer knew him—right straight through. He received Mr. Wilson with calm, unaffected coolness; listened to him a few minutes, and then shook his head with a significancy which left the drumming gentleman without hope—surveying him the while with a slight curl of his upper lip, that betrayed his contempt both for the luckless worthy himself and the house which he represented. Mr. Wilson then retired, to drum elsewhere, with a pale hue around his lips, a mortifying glow on his cheeks, a ray of disappointment in his eyes, and an air not *quite* so genial as that which marked his entrance.

"This man represented a mean, dishonest house, and the dealer knew it. That was enough.

"I represented an honest house, and the dealer knew *it*, too.

"Mark the result:—

"Mr. Wilson went off with a flea in his ear, and the solemn consciousness of never selling another bill to *that* dealer.

"Mr. Crittenden went off, by invitation, to dine with the dealer, and with the pleasing consciousness that *his* house would make many another bill with that same country merchant, in spite of all the 'flattering inducements,' all the oily drummers, and all the tempting baits of other houses.

"Honesty *pays*, old boy! Believe it! Shall I tell you why? Country dealers *appreciate* it, and will, out of pure selfishness, if from no nobler motive, give their trade only to those houses who practise it.

"Another instance, in evidence. Two days ago I called upon a dealer in Schenectady. He was making up an order when I entered. When I mentioned my name and the firm I represented, he exclaimed—'Oh, yes—that's the *honest* house of which neighbor Miller has been telling us. There's a young man there, called Samuel Leland—better known by his given than by his surname. I intended to try him with this,' and he held up the order which he was writing out.

"You received that order, partner, by this morning's mail—or Samuel, rather, which is the same thing.

"You see, therefore, how the principle takes, and how it *pays*. But enough on that head—you have a discerning mind.

"And now, partner mine, one word:

"You and I are reaping the harvest of another's goodness, not our own. Should we not do something to manifest our appreciation of that goodness? Say, by a New Year's present of a round thousand or two to Samuel, the instrument of that goodness, and by a present of *ourselves* to the Divine Author of that instrument?

"I ask the first with confidence—the second with hope.

"Of one thing be assured: It is *time* we think this matter over! We are getting on in years; already the silver is around your temples, the dark is thinning and falling away from mine.

"Let us be MEN. Let us think *aright*—let us be brave and earnest—at least in our *latter* days.

"As our lights go out in the darkness of death, let them go

out gloriously—like great torches, not like small, mean, sickly lamps.

"Come, old friend—what say you? Shall we go up to Him with our thank-offerings, New Year's?

"Samuel—brave, simple, true-hearted Samuel, will show us the way!

"One word more. Do not fancy from the foregoing that I have given myself over to the High Principle of which I have been speaking, and of which Samuel and Miriam are such brilliant embodiments. I have not. But I am *thinking* of it. You will understand this when I tell you that I believe I have reached that intellective stage when the mind looks down with contempt upon common things as unworthy of it, and aspires to the highest range of human thought. That range, John, can only be attained by one ladder—Religion. *It* leads to themes which ennoble the intellect, strengthen it, expand it, and endow it with capacity to banquet on conceptions which are opulent with dignity and grandeur; themes which enable the mind to take broad, correct, comprehensive, and *comforting* views, because they start from the *right* point; themes which fill the mind with stirring glories, the heart with thrilling raptures! Do you understand me, now? Well, I desire to reach the *highest range*, and I propose to try if it can be done. Partner—friend—John! I should like your company and encouragement in the matter! What say you? It is not Robert Crittenden the merchant who asks this of John P. Townsend the prince of business men; it is Robert Crittenden's SOUL addressing John P. Townsend's SOUL. Friend and partner of many years! have you the *will*, and if so, the *courage*, to unite with me in the effort?

"To return again to business:

"How does Brigham relish the religious turn which the house is taking? It must make him shake somewhat around the knees I fancy—since he cannot but see that it is rapidly doing away with the importance of his 'extensive commercial influence.' I never could abide that man's teeth nor his airs. They sicken me. Let him make one, however, of the 'gallery.'

"This letter is long—too long, perhaps. But I could not help it. My heart had its story to tell, as well as my business.

"Yours affectionately, and in good health,

"ROBERT CRITTENDEN."

Mr. Townsend read the letter over carefully, and then put it into his pocket. In the evening he handed it to his wife, with the brief remark—

"A letter from Crittenden, my dear!"

Mrs. Townsend perused it twice, in silence and in thought. At the end of the second reading, she returned it to her husband. Their eyes met in the movement, and each inquired of the other:

"Well—what do *you* think?"

But neither made answer.

CHAPTER XIX.

A FEW evenings later, as they sat in the drawing-room, Mrs. Townsend observed that her husband's features wore an uneasy air.

" Anything happened ?" she inquired, at length.

" No, nothing of any great importance," returned the merchant, without looking up from his newspaper.

Mrs. Townsend regarded him for a few moments in silence, but did not repeat her interrogatory. Still she was satisfied that something *had* happened ; but as her husband did not, for some reason best known to himself, see fit to mention the cause of his soberness, she repressed her curiosity, solacing herself with the conviction that he would impart the secret of his own accord in due season.

A few evenings later, the merchant returned home with the same sedate air. He said but little during the evening, but on finding himself alone with his wife, he observed—

" We have got a dishonest clerk in the house !"

His wife looked at him in surprise.

" What makes you think so ?"

" Because I have been robbed," returned Mr. Townsend, impatiently.

" Of what—goods or money ?"

" Of both, it may be, for all I know; but at present I am only certain of the latter."

" Whom do you suspect to be the culprit ?"

" No one. But it is some one who is familiar with the money

drawer of my desk. Some one who—but, pshaw! What's the use of working one's self into a passion? I'll have him, whoever he is!"

"How much have you lost?"

"So far, seventy dollars. A trifle, to be sure; but yet too much to lose in that manner, by exactly sixty-nine dollars and one hundred cents!"

"I was not aware that you were in the habit of keeping your money in your desk."

"Nor am I. But my drawer gets pretty well filled during the day, before my cash account is made up, notwithstanding! Last Tuesday, when making up my cash for a deposit, I discovered a deficiency of thirty dollars. To-day, another of forty. Pleasant—isn't it?"

"Have you mentioned the matter to any one?"

"Only to Brigham and the book-keeper; but it will get out, of course."

An unhappy incident occurred the following forenoon in the packing department.

It was a busy day—right in the height of the business season—and the packing-room resembled a bee-hive. Bill Bradley and his assistants were driving away, as if for dear life. The vast basement floor groaned with packing-boxes—packing-boxes empty, packing-boxes filled, the latter marked and strapped (*anglice*, hooped), and ready for shipment. On a long table might be seen, at various distances from each other, heaps of miscellaneous goods—each heap being an "order"—all waiting their turn for the packer, Bill Bradley himself, who made short work with a pile the moment he approached it. In fact, the worthy packer had a genius for his business. He worked by system. His assistants laid out the orders—Bill Bradley himself packed them. The orders, large or small, as they might be, were laid in piles upon the sides of the long broad table, which, by the recent pressure of business, was continually kept full. Then stepping up with a box, or boxes, if the order demanded more than one, the gallant packer, his sleeves rolled up and his sinewy arms yearning for action, commenced making the tour of the table. It was a sight. The piles disappeared, one after another, like magic. Here is a great big heap, variously made up of cloths, de laines, flannels, cottons, silks, and prints of every hue. Bill Bradley approaches it, with the air of a conqueror, measures it with his keen, experienced eye, and cries out to the youth who supplies him with boxes, "Five cases, No. 3," and in another minute they are beside him. Now look at that order, and then glance in another direction for a few minutes. Now turn your head again, and look for that great big heap of goods. You see—what? A vacant space. The pile is broken up, packed, and lying snug and dry in those five cases which Bill Bradley is rapidly marking with a long slender brush thus—

SMITH & CO.,

Via John Jones, ABBEVILLE,
Charleston, S.C. S. C.

And the goods are ready for shipment.

"Here, John"—John is a porter—"hoist these up, and tell Billins—" Billings is the cartman of the house of John P. Townsend—"to hurry 'em down to the steamer right away. Quick. It's now ten o'clock, and she sails at twelve. Hurry!"

And the all-conquering packer moves on to the next order, which, being somewhat smaller than the other, disappears in a little less than no time; and then on to another, which is a great deal larger. Bill surveys it for an instant with a sharp, calculating eye. There are three long rolls of oil-cloth in the pile. They were bought elsewhere by the owner of the heap, and ordered to be sent into John P. Townsend's for packing with his other goods. The rolls were long, and required a large-sized box, which might be made to take in the whole pile. This the packer concluded at once to do. A case of the necessary size was picked out, and in ten minutes it was filled, topped, strapped and marked, and the packer moved on to the next heap, exclaiming—

"John—Bill, take this case ter the hoist-way, get it up on the walk, and tell Billins ter rush it down ter the Sea Queen, foot of Maiden Lane. She sails at three, and don't take freight after twelve. Hurry!"

But John and Bill, though stout fellows both, were not equal to the task. The box was too weighty. It mocked all their efforts to raise it, and they called upon the vigorous packer for help.

The latter met their request cheerfully. Once upon its "feet," it would be comparatively easy to work the case in any direction.

The stalwart packer had it in the desired position in an instant. Then bidding the others to steady it while he gave it its impulsion, he attempted, with a dexterous, energetic, half-jerking, half-oscillating movement, to urge the case towards the hoist-way. While thus engaged, one of his companions incautiously missed his hold. In an effort to recover it, he inadvertently pressed against the box while it was in motion. All saw the error, but not in season to avert its consequences. The untimely pressure deprived the case of its equilibrium, and urged it forward upon the manly packer, whom it forced before it to the floor, burying him beneath its ponderous weight.

The poor fellow uttered a loud, gurgling, agonizing scream, which resounded throughout the building, and fainted.

The startled clerks, followed by their no less startled customers, poured confusedly and throngingly down the broad stairway

—twenty hands removed the weighty case, and lifted the bruised, bleeding, and senseless packer from the floor to his old, familiar table. The stoutest-hearted of the crowd shuddered as they looked upon him. His clothes were rent, his limbs frightfully bruised, and his great, manly chest flattened, as if every bone had been crushed to powder. The livid paleness of his face was intensified by a crimson gush around his mouth and nostrils, through which the falling case had forced the blood in a fierce, sudden dash.

When the packer returned to consciousness, he found himself lying upon a narrow but comfortable bed, in a long, wide room, with a range of beds on either side—all, or nearly all, occupied by pale, wasted beings, in various stages of physical suffering. Here and there were nurses ministering to their charges: one rendering a pillow easier; another changing a bandage; a third feeding a tall, emaciated patient, who was sitting up and leaning for support against the head-board of his bed, his weak, nerveless arms hanging helpless from his shoulders, and himself with scarcely strength enough to open his lips to receive the refreshing broth which the attendant was giving to him, as if he were a little child.

The packer comprehended his situation in an instant: he was in the New York Hospital.

He tried to turn himself in his bed; but he discovered, to his utter amazement, that his will had no control over his body. He could not stir a hair's breadth. He was conscious, but he could scarcely be said to be alive. He had not even a sensation of feeling left. He made an effort to collect his thoughts, but in vain. The more he tried to reflect, the more confused he became. His head fell listlessly on one side, and remained so from utter inability to return: on perceiving which, a nurse approached, and raising it gently, propped it with pillows to retain it in its proper position. The packer's consciousness glided off into a soft, quiet slumber.

When he awoke again, he was still in a low stage of feebleness. He was conscious, nevertheless, of a certain measure of strength.

A surgeon approached, and surveyed him for a few moments in silence.

"How do you feel now?" he asked at length.

"Sore," answered the packer.

"Good! Feeling has returned to him!" mused the surgeon. "The crisis is over. He will live."

And with these thoughts the surgeon moved away to another patient, in a distant part of the ward.

The packer tried to think, and he succeeded; he then made an effort to arrange his thoughts, in which he was equally successful.

A nurse drew near. She had a mild, pleasant, motherly appearance.

"How are you now?" she inquired, sitting down beside the bed.

"Sore—sore all over," replied the packer.

"That is a good sign," remarked the nurse, encouragingly.

"Good!" said the packer, in surprise.

"Yes," answered the nurse. "But," she added, "you mustn't talk. The doctor won't allow it. It will weaken you."

"Stay," said the packer, as she was stepping away. "Only a few words. They will ease my mind. Do."

"In that case, I will humor you," said the nurse, resuming her seat. "But remember—only two minutes," and she took out her watch and noted the time.

"How long have I been here?" asked the packer.

"Ten days."

"Crazy, any?"

"A little."

"Any one been to see me?"

"Yes—your mother, and a young gentleman by the name of Leland."

"How often?"

"Your mother every other day, Mr. Leland every day. A good man, I think—a Christian?"

"A real one!" said the packer. "Yer orter know him!"

The packer paused. His breathings were feeble. The nurse observed him with an air of increased interest

"Your two minutes are nearly up," she said. "You had better give over."

"One word more," said the packer, earnestly. "Poor mother must be very lonely. She has no one to talk to her—no one ter care for her, but me. And I—I'm *down!*"

"Be comforted. Mr. Leland appears to be very good to her," said the nurse, in a soothing tone. "He always comes with her, and always takes her away. He is more like a son to her than a stranger."

"He is?" cried the packer, with an air of mingled gratitude and joy. "God bless him!" he added, energetically; "God bless him!"

"Time is up!" remarked the nurse, and she quietly moved away.

The packer looked after her a few moments, and then composed his thoughts. Three minutes later, his senses were wrapped in a soft sleep.

The surgeon and nurse returned. The former bent his ear towards the patient's head, and listened.

"He breathes well," he observed, rising. "He will mend."

And they left the packer to his dreams.

When the young man awoke, on the following day, he found a visitor on either side of his bed. On his left, seated on a chair, was a venerable and familiar female form, in black, her hat on, as if she had but recently come in. It was Mrs. Osborn, his adopted mother. She had a mild, matronly face, with an expression of rare gentleness and benignity. As the packer looked up at her, his eye detected a tear upon her cheek, and his ear caught the dying cadence of a sigh.

On his right was another face, fresher, younger—fairer, full of majestic beauty, and significant of unusual sweetness, gentleness, and serenity. From beneath the pale, thoughtful brow, looked two clear, dark eyes, beaming with tenderness and benevolence.

The packer glanced from the one to the other with an air of mixed gratitude and pleasure.

"Mother—Samuel!" he exclaimed. "I thank yer for this visit. Shake hands!"

With these words, he attempted to raise his arms from the coverlet, but the effort was followed by a sensation of pain so exquisitely excruciating that it forced from him a suffering cry.

"My dear boy," said the old lady, sobbing, "you mustn't stir. The doctor says so."

"It is true, Bill," said Samuel. "We shall not be permitted to see you, if it is found that our presence disturbs you."

"I'll be more careful," returned the packer. "Kiss me, mother."

Mrs. Osborn bent over him, and pressed her lips to his forehead with touching delicacy, as if she feared that even her breath might hurt him.

It was evident to Samuel that these two humble spirits were united by the holiest of all human bonds—sincere affection.

As the old lady resumed her seat, a cloud of anxiety darkened the poor packer's features.

"You are in great pain, Bill?" observed Samuel.

"In mind and body," returned the packer. "I'm hurt—I know *that.* I'm hurt badly. Yer can see it, and there aint no use in my denyin' it."

"No use at all, Bill," returned Samuel, kindly. "It would neither deceive us nor youself."

"Just so," returned the packer. "And besides, I don't want ter lie; it's agin my principles. I always like the honess truth—it makes a feller feel better."

"It is a good principle, Bill. Stick to it."

"Don't be afraid of me, Samuel. Yer see, it's *in* me—truth is. It's in my jints. I couldn't lie, no how—not even if I wanted ter. And that's what troubles me!"

"What do you mean, Bill?"

"Mother—" suggested the packer

"What is it, dear?" asked Mrs. Osborn.

"Yer will grieve over my trouble so," said the packer. 'Yer'll keep thinkin' that I am sufferin' so much—which is true. There's no mistake about it. It's true. But—"

"But what, dear?"

"Yer'll *keep thinking* of it, mother, when you *oughtn't* ter. Distressin' yourself, and breakin' your heart, about me. I know yer. You'll *keep* thinkin' of me!"

The poor old soul covered her face with her handkerchief and sobbed.

"And don't you want her to think of you, Bill?" asked Samuel.

"No," returned the packer. "That is, y-e-s. I want her ter think of *me* of course; but not of my trouble. Coax her not ter—won't yer, Samuel?"

"My dear boy!" sobbed the old creature.

"There," said the packer, "there yer are! Didn't I say so? Yer'll *keep* goin' on that way! Now if yer *wouldn't*, mother--if yer wouldn't! You see, mother, there's yer own trouble—the pallysis—yer'll aggravate *that*. And then what'll become of yer? Don't yer see?"

"Noble heart!" murmured Samuel.

"Now, mother," continued the packer, tenderly, "if yer would only promise not ter think *too* much of me, and more of yerself—I think I could get along better. I'm a man, yer know—a strong feller, too—and I can get through, and be up in no time; because there's a big foundation for my trouble to spread itself on. I'm young, full of vigor, and all that; and when the pains come along, I can stand 'em firse rate. But it aint so with you, mother. You're old and feeble; you've got the pallysis and the roomatics—the roomatics some, but the pallysis *bad*. Now, if yer'd only think of yerself a good deal, an' a little of me—say just enough to keep the old feelin' alive—I'd be satisfied, and I'd bear up tip top—I *know* I would!"

"My dear boy, you know I *must* think of you. I can't help it!"

"That's it," returned Bill, sorrowfully. "I know yer can't help it, mother—'cause yer've got a great heart. But if yer'd only promise me, before Samuel, here, not ter think too much of me, I'd get through quicker. There's so many things that yer can do, yer know, when yer find yerself givin' way too much about me. Yer can go and see some of the neighbors—Mrs. Weeks, for ins'ance, she's a nice woman—yer can go and talk with *her*; and then there's Mrs. Ellis, who lives up stairs—she'd be very glad if yer would only go and talk with her, once in a while. She's told me so—often. She likes you, firse rate. And then you can read—and then you can sing; and then read again. There's all them things yer can do, to keep from thinkin' too much of me. Don't yer see, mother—don't yer see?"

Samuel reflected. An idea struck him.

"Now, mother," continued the packer, coaxingly, "if yer think too much of me, yer'll forget all about yerself; and yer'll get thin, and weak, and wan, and unable to attend to yer pallysis and roomatics. Then what'll become on yer? And when I'm all right agin, and go home to see yer, there'll be no mother for poor Bill any more!"

"Oh, my dear boy, don't talk so! You'll kill me!"

"If you would only promise me ter take care of yerself, mother," said Bill. "But yer won't!"

"Oh, I will, my dear boy—I will," said Mrs. Osborn. "I will take *great* care of myself. Yes, I *will!*"

"But yer'll get so lonely sometimes, mother," said Bill. "Yer'll *let* yerself get lonely, a purpose!"

"No, my dear boy—I won't. I'll make myself comfortable —*very* comfortable—and—and—happy."

"But yer won't go and see Mrs. Ellis and Mrs. Brown; or if yer do, yer'll keep talkin' and thinkin' of me, all the time!"

"No, I won't, Bill, dear—not *all* the time!"

"But yer won't go and see 'em every day?"

"Yes, I will, my dear boy—if you wish it."

"I *do* wish it, mother!"

"I'll do it, then, Bill—yes, I will!"

"And take great care of yerself—*very* great care?"

"Very great care, Bill. I promise it!"

An air of triumph—of joy—illumined the pale features of the tender-hearted packer.

"Kiss me again, mother!" he said, falteringly.

Their lips met, and the tears of the poor old creature bedewed the cheeks of her loved and loving boy.

The latter, however, restrained the flood which was struggling to burst through his eyes, lest the object of his solicitude should impute it to his physical suffering.

At this moment, a physician approached.

"You must leave my patient for the present," he said. "He requires repose."

The old lady bowed, and rose. Samuel followed her example, and bidding the poor packer good-bye, they took their departure.

On reaching the street, Samuel called a cab, and after settling the fare, he shook Mrs. Osborn by the hand, bade her be of good cheer, and promising to see her again ere long, he returned to the store, where he arrived just in time to meet a customer, who, like the majority of *his* customers, had come to him because he had *heard* of him.

In the evening, Samuel posted to Mrs. Farley's. As he ascended the dark staircase, he caught the last stanza of a familiar hymn:—

"Sweetly may we all agree,
Touched with softest sympathy,
Kindly for each other care,
Every member feel its share.
Dum—dum—dum.
Many are we now, and one,
We who Jesus have put on:
Names, and sects, and parties fall—
Thou, O Christ, art all in all!"
Dum—dum—dum.

"She is ironing!" thought Samuel, as he heard the peculiar accompaniment. He knocked at the door, and the laundress appeared. Upon recognizing her visitor, she received him with her usual genial warmth.

The laundress entertained for Samuel a peculiar affection: the affection that one pure, artless spirit has for another, whom it knows to be equally as guileless as itself, and serving the same High Interest.

The young man guessed aright: his fair friend was ironing. He took a seat beside the table, and while she pursued her work, he related the details of the accident at the store, and of the interview at the hospital.

The laundress listened to his narrative with marked interest.

"And now, my dear friend," said Samuel, in conclusion, "to the object of my visit."

"Yes," said the laundress, encouragingly, for she understood the nature of the noble heart before her too well not to suspect what would follow; "go on."

"I want to ask a favor of you," said Samuel. "Bill is a good young man, and we ought to do something for him."

"True," said the laundress; "and I would be glad to perform my share."

"Ah! Mrs. Farley, you make me very happy! I expected no less of you, for you are one of *us*."

The laundress bowed smilingly, and Samuel continued:

"It struck me, while at the poor fellow's bedside this afternoon, that if we could only make him easy about the loneliness of his dear mother, that it would relieve him very much. Then I thought of you, as one who would willingly join me in an effort to secure him that relief; and so I have come to ask if you will kindly let the dear old lady reside with you until Bill shall get well?"

"Cheerfully—gladly," returned the laundress.

"Ah! madam, you make me very happy! It will be so consoling to Bill to know that his mother is not left alone, because calamity has stepped in between them for a time—to know that she is with one who understands her kind, pious heart, and will cheer her and be near her in case of trouble."

"So it will!" said the laundress.

"And then it will be so pleasant for the old lady herself," continued Samuel, "to have the company of one who can sympathize with her, talk with her, and pray with her."

"True, again!" observed the laundress. "And I will do all I can to lighten her affliction."

"Dear Mrs. Farley, you make me very happy! I will step

in at the hospital to-morrow morning, and tell Bill all about it. The knowledge will make his mind easy for the day, and enable him to bear his physical sufferings with resignation. In the evening I will call on Mrs. Osborn herself, and explain it all over, and if she consents—as I think she will, when I tell her that you are one of *us*—I will bring her here at once. And thus we shall save the poor lady from at least one night of loneliness and grief."

"Dear—dear!" exclaimed the simple-hearted laundress, "that will be something for the good soul!"

"So it will, Mrs. Farley. And now, let us see about her support."

"Oh, I will attend to all that, Mr. Leland," said the laundress.

"No, it would be unfair," returned Samuel. "Because I want to do something. Let us see. Suppose you give her your society, your sympathy, and your attention—and let me have the privilege of paying for her board? That would make it about even, and render it more satisfactory to our venerable friend herself, who would scarcely consent to owe everything to either one of us. Will that do, Mrs. Farley?"

"Oh, yes—since you wish it," replied the latter.

"Ah! madam, you make me very happy. And now let us come to the amount. Say four dollars a week?"

"Oh, no," returned the laundress, energetically.

"Six, then?" continued Samuel.

"No, not half, not a quarter of it. Why, how you run on!"

"A third of six," said Samuel, "would only be two dollars. The lady could not live on that!"

"Oh, yes, easily," said the laundress, "and on less too. Why it costs me but four dollars and a half per week, rent and all."

"But our friend is old," suggested Samuel, "and the aged want their little comforts. A cup of good nice tea now and then; a dish of chicken broth, too, and other things of which I know but little, but all of which *they* know and like. Say two dollars for the board, and a dollar for the comforts, Mrs. Farley?"

The laundress consented at length to this, and Samuel shortly after took his leave, congratulating himself, on his way home, upon an acquaintance with one who was so willing to lend a helping hand to the afflicted.

Of his own goodness, the young Christian never thought at all.

The packer awoke the following morning in great pain. His strength, however, had materially increased. His mind was clear, and moderately firm. He was conscious of his improvement; but he was impressed also with the conviction that a long siege of suffering lay before him. Between his present condition and his return to health, he beheld with his mental eye a dreadful interval. During that interval, what would become of his adopted parent? Relying ever upon his industry, he had saved none of his earnings. Anticipating no evil day, he had made no provision for it; and now, in his hour of trouble, to whom could his parent look for support? What would become of her? Who would care for her?

The packer groaned. Cold beads of sweat appeared upon his emaciated brow.

"Oh! if I had but thought of this before!" he murmured, in deep anguish. "If I had but considered it in time! Mother—dear mother—what will become of yer? What *orter* become of *me* for bringin' yer to this position!"

The poor fellow would have marched up to the stake at that moment if, by so doing, he could have rectified his error.

Another idea struck him. He was in the New York Hospital, an institution which expects three dollars per week from each of its patients. It is true the latter are not disturbed if they do not pay; still it is expected by the institution that each patient's bill will be paid, either by the patient himself or by his friends. Three dollars per week is a pitiful sum for board, nursing, and the best of medical attendance; but small though it be, it is a world of money to him who has it not. But this was not all. The packer was conscious that he received extra attentions, extra delicacies, extra medical care; and his good sense told him that those extras were charged as such—that, in fine, they were *added* to the three dollars per week. His good sense also told him that extras were never furnished unless they were specially ordered. *Who* ordered them? The packer himself did not. Some one must have done it for him. But who was that some one? His friend, of course! But *who* was his friend? The person who had introduced him to the Hospital. But who was that person? His mother? *She* had no money; moreover, she was dependent for her support upon himself. Some relative? Save his adopted parent, he had none. His employer? Mr. Townsend was only generous to those who could be serviceable to him. Who, then, was his unknown friend?

"Well," muttered the packer, "no matter. It's somebody. That's sure. But what does it prove? Simply this—that I, Bill Bradley—a hale, hearty feller of twenty-five—who have always had plenty of work and good wages—am now, in the hour of trouble, a dependent on another's charity! Well, that's pooty—that is! and poor mother, too, that I've allers pretended to care so much for! If I hadn't sense enough to lay by some'n for myself, couldn't I have cared a little for *her?* Won't," he added, forgetful of his situation, and talking aloud, "won't somebody come and give me a whalin'? I orter be laid out, right and left. Ugh! I'm a dorg—a fifer—a *thing!* Only let me get over this, once—that's all!"

"You are disturbed?" remarked a voice near him. It was that of the nurse, who supposed him to be raving.

"I am suffering," returned the packer. "One word: Who pays for my support here?"

"I'm not at liberty to say," answered the nurse.

"Why not?"

"Because nurses are not presumed to know anything about such matters."

"I s'pose so. But yer can tell me why I am tended to so carefully, can't yer? The other fellers in the ward are not looked after as I am."

"What then?

"A great deal. Somebody must have ordered it, or it wouldn't be so, would it?"

"That is true."

"There—I thought so. Now, who *did* order it?"

"Why do you ask?" inquired the nurse, surveying him attentively.

"For satisfaction," returned the packer. "Here's a big bill running up agin somebody on my account, and I wanter know who it is. Come, tell a feller, won't yer? I'll take it as a favor!"

"What good will the knowledge do you?" asked the nurse.

"It'll make a feller feel better—make me get well sooner."

"In that case, I presume I am at liberty to speak. Your friend is Mr. Leland."

"What—Samuel?" cried the packer. "Well! if I didn't suspect it! Samuel? Well—there! That takes me down! And yet, why should I be surprised? It's just like him!"

"Who is Samuel—Mr. Leland, I mean?" asked the nurse.

"What? Yer don't know our Samuel? Well—that's pooty—*that* is! I thought everybody know'd *him*."

"Are you able to tell me about him?" asked the nurse.

"Able? Yes, and willin', too. It does me good to think of him. It's better than medicine, or bandages, to see him, and talk of him. Listen."

And the packer related Samuel's career, from the hour of his entrance into "the house" until the day of the accident, as we have detailed it to the reader. How good he was, how manly, how benevolent, how gentle, unpretending, earnest, and upright. How he was loved in the "house;" what changes he had wrought in its business, and in the minds and habits of its people; of the religious meetings in the packing-room—of the tours among the poor; how many of the clerks had abandoned forever their previous vicious courses, and become good, manly-hearted, and manly-minded men—each of them exerting in their turn upon *their* friends, in greater or lesser degree, the same ennobling influences which Samuel had exerted upon *them*; and how these purifying influences were spreading, and deepening, and extending more and more—leading numbers, of rich and poor, from fraud to honesty, from falsehood to truth, and from *fashionable* to *genuine* religion. How he did all this in his simple, earnest, unpretending way—without noise, ostentation, or parade. How men spoke of him as of one among ten thousand; and how they said of him, that he presented, in his own person, a pleasing and impressive illustration of the wide and amazing moral influence which a single TRUE Christian is capable of exerting when he sets himself about it in EARNEST, *like* a Christian! And how it was remarked of him that whenever he talked with a person, that person always felt better after the conversation than before; that he never called upon a person without leaving a smile in the heart of that person when he took his departure; that the cheering influence of his presence was always felt and acknowledged wherever he went; that he never opened his lips to say a bitter or ungenerous thing; and that *whenever* he spoke, all around him were glad that he had spoken.

The nurse reflected.

"There he is now," said Bill Bradley, in a low voice, as he concluded.

The nurse turned around and looked at Samuel, who had just entered the ward, and was advancing, with a smiling face and a springy step, towards the packer.

"Good-morning, madam," he said, bowing; "good-morning, Bill. You are improving. What think you, madam—our friend, here, will soon be able to thank his surgeon for his kindly skill, and you, too, for all your watchful care—eh?"

"The surgeon speaks favorably of his case, sir," replied the nurse, catching the packer's eye, which said: "I told yer so—didn't I?"

"I am much obliged to him, and to you, too, madam, as it will enable me to make a good report at the store. Do you know, Bill, that the boys are all very anxious to hear how you are getting on? They ask after you, every day, with affectionate interest."

The eyes of the packer sparkled with mixed pleasure and pride.

"Do they, though, Samuel?"

"Every day, Bill; and many of them design calling up to see you. But I want to say a few words to you: something that will cheer you!"

The nurse considerately moved away to another part of the ward.

The packer looked up at his visitor, inquiringly.

"It's about your mother, Bill," returned Samuel. "What of her?" asked the packer, eagerly.

Samuel then related the substance of his interview with Mrs.

Farley, modestly omitting all mention of his own generosity, and winding up as follows :—

"If you think Mrs. Osborn would be happy in my friend's humble home, Bill, I will see her this evening and convey her there without delay. I will be answerable both to the lady and yourself that Mrs. Farley will spare no efforts to make her comfortable."

"I would thank yer, Samuel, for this," said the packer, in a broken voice, "but words fail me! Believe me, however—"

"You accept, then?" interrupted Samuel.

"With gratitude—"

"Ah! you make me very happy," cried Samuel. "I will see your mother to-night, and tell her how finely you are improving. She is a dear, good soul, and loves you very much. She is absolutely proud of you, Bill. Well, good-bye. There's a deal of business at the store, and I must be off. Keep your heart up like a hero—trust in our Lord and Prince, and all will yet be well. Good-bye!"

As he passed to the door, he whispered to the nurse—

"I need not urge upon you, madam, to be watchful of our dear friend. For every kind attention you pay to him, for every spark of pain you save him, for every hour that you bring him nearer to health, his tender-hearted mother will be grateful when sending up her pious thanks to God, while his friends will remember them in another way."

"I will do all I can for him, Mr. Leland—be assured of that," returned the nurse.

"Ah! thank you—thank you, madam. You make me very happy! What a field you have here for kindness, gentleness, and mercy! I could almost envy you the joy you must hourly experience in lessening your fellow-creatures' woes."

"There *is* a pleasure in it, Mr. Leland!" said the nurse. "For every spark of pain that we can save them, we find a satisfactory reward."

"In your own hearts?"

"Yes."

The young Christian looked at her mild, motherly face, and tenderly serene eye. An instant, and an air of joy mantled his own frank, honest countenance. He caught her hand, and pressing it, exclaimed—

"Sister! You are one of *us*. Ah! you make me very happy!"

"The pleasure is mutual, brother," returned the nurse.

"And thus, as we pass on to The Kingdom, we meet, now and then, a kindred spirit on the way. Ah, what joy!"

"We have many joys," said the nurse. "Our Prince is careful of His people."

"So very careful, and so kind! If men would but believe it! But I must away. Drop a word of our Prince, now and then, to our friend. His heart is but a little way from Him now. He would be a true soldier, if he should once put on the armor."

"I'll remember."

"Do—you make me very happy. Adieu!" the young Christian said, and was gone.

The following morning, Samuel returned to the Hospital, and notified the packer that Mrs. Osborn was under the protection of the laundress.

The intelligence was a healing balm to the poor fellow. It eased his mind upon a, to him, all-important point. From that hour he throve rapidly.

CHAPTER XX

"SAMUEL," said Mrs. Townsend, one evening, after tea, "have you anything particular on hand this evening?"

"Nothing so urgent that I cannot postpone it to another time," answered the young man; "providing I am wanted at home."

"You are always wanted there, truant!" said Isabella, with a coquettish pout. "Don't you say so, coz?"

"I presume Mr. Leland is at home as often as his duties will permit," returned Miriam, with her usual diffidence.

"You *presume!*" exclaimed Isabella. "Well, that *is* pretty! Why, you *know*, coz, that Samuel is *never* at home any more! To-night he is off to prayer-meeting, to-morrow among his poor, the evening after concerting with some of his fellow-clerks, in the packing-room—so uncle tells us—how they shall save one more poor soul from spiritual ruin, and another from temporal suffering!"

"I beg that you won't drag me into your conspiracy, 'Bel," observed Mr. Townsend. "The fact is, I was indiscreet in mentioning the secrets of the packing-room; but since you are so imprudent as to repeat tales out of school, I shall be more cautious in future!"

"That's a dear good guardy!" cried Isabella, patting him playfully on the cheek. "*Do* be cautious—don't tell us anything. We so *like* to be kept in ignorance of what is going on down there!"

"You have got one resource in case I fail," returned her uncle, laughing.

"Indeed?" cried Isabella. "Samuel himself? Pshaw! He won't tell us!"

"No," said Mr. Townsend, who delighted to torment her. "Mr. Brigham!"

"Mr. Brigham, indeed!" returned Isabella, with a charming pout. "Uncle—"

"Well, my pet?"

"You are a perfect tease!"

"But all this is apart from the main point," said Mrs. Townsend. "The question is, how shall we prevail upon Samuel to favor us with his company this evening?"

"That is the point, indeed!" cried Isabella, turning from her uncle, whom she had been playfully belaboring with her small, delicate knuckles.

"There needs no prevailing at all," observed Samuel. "Your simple wish is enough."

"Oh, Mr. Truant," said Isabella, shaking her finger archly, "it is well enough for you to say that, after you are caught; particularly when you know that you are wanted home all the time!"

"You have a merry heart!" returned the young man.

"If I have, no thanks to you, Truant!" said Isabella, in a tone which was artfully made up of mingled vivacity and feeling. "Here you are off every night among your suffering poor, and never give a single thought to the suffering poor at home!"

The merchant and his wife exchanged a glance, which said—"She is after him again!"

Miriam was pale. An air of anguish was visible in her features. Her uncle observed it, and came up to her rescue.

"If a certain gentleman should hear you say that, 'Bel!" he cried, laughingly.

Isabella understood him, and retorted—

"A certain lady don't like to be tormented about a certain

gentleman, guardy, because that certain lady feels no interest whatever in what a certain gentleman may think!"

"Mr. Brigham," said a servant.

Isabella bit her lip; the merchant and his wife smiled; Miriam experienced a sense of relief, and Mr. Brigham entered the parlor.

"How d'ye do, Brigham?" said Mr. Townsend. "You have come in quite opportunely. We want you to settle an important question."

"Ah! you are very good!" remarked the confidential clerk, seating himself. "But I hope it won't detain us long."

"Us!" repeated Isabella.

"Exactly," returned Mr. Brigham, surveying her with his half-pent eyes. "Don't you remember our engagement? The opera!"

"Dear me!" said the young lady. "How very shocking! I had forgotten all about it!"

Mr. Brigham's lips became livid.

Mr. and Mrs. Townsend regarded Isabella with astonishment. They were wholly unprepared for this rudeness even in their whimsical niece.

"We have still half an hour!" suggested Mr. Brigham, referring to his repeater.

"Oh! I could never dress in that time!" answered Isabella. "Besides, I have no inclination to go. I detest the opera!"

"A recent conversion, I apprehend!" observed Mr. Brigham, showing his teeth.

"No!" rejoined Isabella. "I have never regarded it with favor. If I have appeared to do so, it has only been to accommodate my friends. But we must not always be frivolous, even to please them!"

"Good!" thought Mr. Townsend. "That's another bait for Samuel!"

"In that case," bowed Mr. Brigham, "I have not a word to urge." Then turning to Samuel, he said, with an ill-concealed sneer, "I believe you are not partial to the opera, either?"

"Not very, sir!" returned Samuel. "I judge every institution by a single standard; and that standard condemns the opera."

"Yes. The standard of the Church!" said Mr. Brigham, derisively.

"Yes, sir—in effect. Specifically, by the query: 'What good does it perform?'"

"It cultivates music, art, and taste," said Mr. Brigham, with the cynical air of a Solon; "benefits trade by giving employment to thousands, and—"

He paused, as if in chase of an idea which had suddenly escaped.

"Corrupts the morals of its auditors!" said Samuel, finishing the sentence for him.

"A stale idea!" remarked Mr. Brigham.

"It may be, but yet a correct one."

"You flatter yourself, sir!"

"By no means. I put forth the statement not for its novelty, but its truthfulness. Minds whose opinions are governed by the One Code, look upon evil things in the same light, through *all* ages. What can be said of an institution which enervates the minds and morals of its own professors, but that it is a bad one? It is true, a singer appears now and then who is up to the average line of virtue, honesty, and integrity. But such instances are the exception—the very reverse being the rule. Who will stand up for an institution which employs the divine art of music to allure unsuspecting minds to an exhibition which undermines the modesty of woman, familiarizes her with bawdy sentiments, and uproots the holy principles which were implanted in her heart in her childhood? Which exhibits woman in a garb that deprives her of every vestige of purity, and makes even of the spectators smiling aiders and abettors in her shame?"

"Stiff-necked cant and religious drivelling!" sneered Mr. Brigham.

"Call it so, if you will. You are entitled to your opinion, and I to mine. But answer me this. Would it not humiliate you, would it not empurple your cheek with shame, to see your mother or your sister flaunting in the immodest garb of a ballet-dancer, or an opera-singer, *in the street*, or even in a drawing-room?"

Mr. Brigham made no reply.

"Transfer her, in the same revolting garb, from the street to the stage, would the change make her the less immodest or revolting, or your blush less humiliating or less burning?"

"You are taking too great a liberty, sir," said Mr. Brigham, drawing himself up, "in supposing that either my mother or my sister could descend to a level with people of that sort!"

"Excuse me," returned Samuel, "I had no idea that you could be offended by such a comparison. It would be no more improper in your relatives to outrage woman's delicacy than in mine, or any other man's. The outrage is still an outrage, by whomsoever performed. Nor is it any the less shameful because it is supported by the world!"

"And so you, like all religionists," said Mr. Brigham, desiring to shift his position, which was not at all flattering, "are opposed to all amusements?"

"No, sir; only to those which, like the opera, make use of Art to sap the foundations of Morality!"

"One thing is certain," said Mr. Brigham, with a mocking bow—"you are in a glorious minority!"

"I regret it," returned Samuel. "But I would rather be in the minority of Right, than in the majority of Wrong!"

"Come," said Mr. Brigham, "that is a heroic phrase!"

"Perhaps you can entertain us with a better!" said Isabella.

"Excuse me!" returned Mr. Brigham, showing his teeth. "I am not an actor!"

"What a pity!" cried Isabella. "You would have made such a capital 'villain!'"

"Ha! Miss Landon!" returned Mr. Brigham, in a voice which resembled a serpent's hiss, "a 'villain!'"

"Yes, sir," answered Isabella, with freezing calmness.

The half-pent eyes of the confidential clerk glittered, through their fringes, up at the speaker, for a few moments, with an expression of the most intense malignity. Then, as if conscious of the impolicy of exposing his feelings, he gradually softened the glance, and said, laughingly—

"To be as facetious, severe, and capricious as she pleases, is the prerogative of beauty!" Then, without giving her time to reply, he turned to Mr. Townsend, and said—"The question which you were about to put was—"

"This," said the merchant. "Whether a man should go abroad in search of heathen, while there are heathen in his own house?"

"What *is* guardy up to?" asked Isabella, in a whisper, of her aunt, who answered her with a dubious shrug.

"I should say look at home first, by all means," replied Mr. Brigham, wondering at what lay hidden beneath the query.

"There, Samuel," cried Mr. Townsend, "all are against you—even Mr. Brigham!"

"I should be sorry to have Mr. Leland rank me among his enemies," said Mr. Brigham, with a nervous tremor of his lips, which was observed by all except Samuel himself.

"It would give me great pain to be aware that I had *any*," returned Samuel.

"Good! I find I am not suspected!" muttered the confidential clerk. Then resuming his vein of irony, he said, aloud, "A man of merit, however, cannot expect to pass through life without finding foes at every step."

"In that event," said Samuel, "an obscure individual like myself may reasonably look for an exemption from so trying a lot."

"That," said Mr. Brigham, "would be confessing to an acknowledged absence of all claims to superiority!"

"Yes, sir. I pretend to no such claims."

"Excuse me," said Mr. Brigham, showing his teeth, with him a sign that he designed to be very cutting, "I had a *contrary* idea!"

"I regret to hear it, Mr. Brigham," replied Samuel, suppressing, with a heroic effort, his rising blood. "I have no desire to be considered what I am not. I regard pretension of every kind with abhorrence. It is unworthy and superfluous. It deceives no one, and least of all, those whom it is designed *to* deceive. A man of conscious or confessed merit has no need of it. Gold will pass for its own honest value, without the aid of brass. While all the pretension in the world will not make a man of merit of one who *has* it not; and still less will it enable him to pass *for* a man of merit. The world, if it be not over wise in great, has a keen eye for *little* things; and when a small mind comes with a flourish of trumpets before it, the latter detects its flimsiness in an instant, and greets it with a scoffing roar. For these reasons. if for no other, I should always avoid pretension!"

"But for which of your reasons, Mr. Leland?" pursued Mr. Brigham, ironically. "The first or the last?"

"That is pressing the question rather too closely, I think," returned Samuel. "Nevertheless, I will answer it."

"If you will be so kind!" said Mr. Brigham.

"In this way," said Samuel. "If I desired to be thought a man of talent, in sarcasm, for instance, I would return you sneer for sneer. (Mr. Brigham reddened.) That I *have* not, implies one of two things—either that I am unable, or unwilling, to do so. I confess to the correctness of both!"

"Bravo, Samuel! Give it to him again!" cried Isabella.

"'Bel!" said her aunt, in a reproving tone.

"Oh, if the gentleman is unable to defend himself—" began Mr. Brigham.

"Excuse me, sir," interrupted Samuel, "I was not aware that I had been attacked."

"Good again, Samuel!" cried Isabella, clapping her hands. "What a giant he must be when his heaviest blows scarcely ruffle the air!"

"Oh, if I must face two such *master*-spirits," sneered the confidential clerk, "I shall retire from the combat altogether!"

"The only way by which you can save the remnant of your reputation!" laughed Isabella. "When a man is defeated, it is a glorious thing for him to be able to say, 'I retired to avoid my enemy's *last* kick!'"

"You are very good!" said Mr. Brigham, showing his teeth. "It is no disgrace to retire before the advance of so pitiless a reinforcement!"

"A stranger would suppose," said Samuel, good-humoredly, "that we were a trio of enemies, and not friends. Let us drop our personalities, and talk in a pleasanter strain."

"Speak for yourself, sir," said Mr. Brigham, drawing himself up. "As for me, I neither dread your personalities nor your logic!"

"Hear him, aunt!" cried Isabella. "And he was himself the first and only one to exhibit bile!"

"You appear to enjoy rating me to-night, Miss Landon!" said Mr. Brigham, biting his lip.

"Oh, no—you flatter yourself, sir!" answered Isabella, jeeringly. "I rate you without any pleasure, I assure you!"

"If my presence is offensive—"

"Oh, no—don't think so, sir; pray, don't!" cried his tormentor, with a pitiless smile. "Your presence, like your conversation, is altogether *amusing!*"

The confidential clerk turned absolutely livid.

"I fear," said Samuel, "that I have, without meaning it, been the unhappy cause of all this!"

A general murmur of admiration greeted this noble offer of the young Christian to take upon himself the blame of the jarring cross-fire.

Mr. Brigham started. He saw in an instant that his only chance of salvation from the contempt of all present consisted in a speedy and manly change in his tactics.

"I will not be outdone in magnanimity," he said, extending his hand to Samuel, with a show of deep feeling. "Forgive me for what I have said, and attribute it not to an ungenerous heart, but to a hasty head!"

"Ah!" cried the young Christian, returning the pressure, "you make me very happy! How much better this which warms us, than cutting words which wound!"

"May I hope for forgiveness from you, too, Miss Landon?" added the confidential clerk, approaching her.

"If Samuel is willing to overlook your fault," returned Isabella, calmly, "I don't see why I shouldn't!"

This was said in a tone which impressed the confidential clerk with a conviction that the speaker fully comprehended the character of his repentance. Nevertheless, he deemed it most politic not to appear to have understood aught beyond her words.

"You are very good!" he said, with a low bow. Then resuming his seat, he muttered to himself in an under tone, "*My* time will come by-and-bye!"

"How much better," said Mr. Townsend, in his pleasant way, although he believed about as much in the honesty of the confidential clerk's sincerity as his niece did, "to dwell in peace and concord, than, like mad dogs, in snapping and snarling at each other!"

"It is much pleasanter, and more becoming, at any rate,' remarked his lady.

"As for me," said Isabella, "I do so love a good jolly fight, once in a while! It makes me feel better for a week!"

"So that," laughed her uncle, "for you to be perfectly happy, it is essential that you should have a game of sharps with somebody once every seven days!"

"Uncle—"

"Well, my pet?"

'You are a tease!"

"In that case," smiled Mr. Brigham, "I shall know how to take you in future."

"Mr. Brigham—" said Isabella, shaking her finger playfully.

"Miss Landon?"

"You are a torment."

"I'm sure, 'Bel," said Mrs. Townsend, "you will have no right to complain if we give you a wide margin when you undertake again to be satirically severe!"

"Aunt—"

Well, my dear?"

"You are a plague!"

"Come, come," laughed Mr. Townsend, "when one's wife is attacked in that way, it is a husband's duty to come up to her rescue. Now, miss—do you know what you are?"

"Pray, sir, what am I?" demanded his niece, placing her arms a-kimbo, and marching up to him with an air at once so full of hoyden mischief and mock earnestness, that it plunged all present into a roar. "What am I?"

"You are—"

"Well, sir!"—shaking her head like a little old woman, who

was chuck full of spirit, and was facing another little old woman who had been taking down her clothes-line, and was adding to the enormity by uttering some cutting things—" why do you pause? If you have got anything to say, spit it out!"

"You are—"

"Well, sir—what?"

"The prettiest, pertest, sauciest, and most independent patron of dry goods that resides in Fifteenth street!"

In another moment both uncle and niece were engaged in a fierce battle, which terminated in favor of the latter, who waved her handkerchief over the head of her enemy with three cheers, and then with an "Alone I did it!" she returned with the majestic air of a victor to her seat, to the tune of "See, the Conquering Hero Comes," which was whistled by no less an individual than the great defeated himself—her uncle.

"Bravo!" cried Mr. Brigham, applauding vociferously; "bravi—bravissimi!"

"You have a merry heart!" cried Samuel, who could not help admiring the young lady's charming vivacity.

"And such a coquettish swing!" added Mr. Brigham, mimicking her walk.

"Ah! well," laughed Mr. Towesend, "it is fortunate we are not all young men; or that merry heart and that coquettish swing might be the death of some one! And that reminds me—"

"Of what, guardy?" asked Isabella.

"That we shall have a *converzatione* here on the twentieth. Brigham, my boy! consider yourself invited."

"You are very good," returned that gentleman.

"And poor me, guardy?" said Isabella.

"You are already set down for it, per order."

"By whose order, I should like to know!"

"Mr. Crittenden's!"

"Good! He will be home, then! Bravo! what a time we'll

have in tearing each other to pieces! Mr. Brigham, look out for yourself!"

"Nay, I shall assist in the massacre," answered the confidential clerk, with a grand display of his eloquent teeth.

"In that case, I shall look out for myself!" cried the imperial beauty. "Dear—dear! what slashing there will be! We always do have such jolly times at Mr. Crittenden's *converzationes!*—But, guardy—you forgetful man!—how about Samuel?"

"How very pat she is with that hated name!" muttered Mr. Brigham, in an under tone.

"Samuel is invited, of course, and Mirry, and all the rest of us, and—that's all!"

"In which case," laughed Mr. Brigham, "I shall be off."

"Oh, cruel man!" cried Isabel, striking an attitude, "tear not thyself away!"

"What—so soon?" demanded the merchant. "It is scarcely ten!"

"Nay, half after!" returned Mr. Brigham, consulting his repeater. "Good-night!"

"And a good riddance!" thought Isabella.

The departure of the spirit of discord—Mr. Brigham—was a sensible relief to the party, and the evening passed away pleasantly.

CHAPTER XXI.

UPON reaching the store, one morning, Samuel took up a morning paper, the New York Satanic Chuckle. While glancing through its editorial columns, his eye was arrested and his mind disturbed by the following characteristic article:—

"ASTOUNDING FRAUD—CONSTERNATION AMONG THE CASHIERS—A SPLENDID LIVE SPECIMEN OF THE CODFISH ARISTOCRACY—FASHIONABLE PIETY AT A DISCOUNT—RICH DEVELOPMENTS.—In another column will be found the particulars of a rich scene which came off yesterday at the Tombs. Mr. John Rankin, Cashier of the —— Bank, was arrested by officer Bowyer, one of the aids of the Chief of Police, charged, on the complaint of Mr. Peter Leslie, President of the Bank, with having embezzled, from time to time, within the last eight months, various sums from the Bank, amounting in all, as nearly as can be ascertained, to between $75,000 and $80,000, and also with having made false entries in his accounts for the purpose, to use a delicate phrase, of concealing his *deficiencies.* According to our reporter, the appearance of the prisoner, when brought by the officers into court, whither he was followed by a motley crowd of street and other loafers, among them several bank officers, who seemed to enjoy, with wonderful zest, the woe-begone air of this specimen of their number, was ludicrous in the extreme. He was very much agitated; so much so, that it was with great difficulty he could stand upon his feet. He was, by turns, pale and red. His teeth chattered, his hair rose up with mingled shame and terror, and his whole aspect was that of a man who desired the earth to open and swallow him up. The poor devil was, in fact, in the highest state of excitement. His white neck-cloth was turned awry, the tie being on a line with his ears. He was bewildered, confused, stupefied. The evidence against him was so strong that the magistrate fixed his bail at the sum of $50,000; but as no one appeared willing to run the risk of bailing the prisoner in that amount, he was locked up without further ceremony. It appears that the cashier has, for nearly a year past, been a constant *habitué* of Pat Hearne's extensive gambling establishment, on Broadway, at which famous hell he is said to have lost every dollar of his own, as well as of the successive amounts which, it is alleged, he abstracted from the Bank. He is said to be the father of a large and interesting family, who, it is needless to add, are thrown into the profoundest consternation and affliction by the culpability of their head. The prisoner has been living in splendid style among the codfish aristocracy, of which delectable order he was, up to yesterday, a very prominent member. We also learn that he is a very pious and leading member of the Rev. Dr. Engold's church, where he is said to hold a pew at the very moderate rent of eight hundred dollars!

"P. S.—Since the above was written, the prisoner has given the finishing touch to his guilty career, by adding to his previous catalogue of crimes that of self-murder. The keeper, Mr. Sniffen, upon looking into the prisoner's cell, at twelve o'clock last night, found him lying upon the floor, weltering in his blood. He had succeeded, with the assistance of a small pocket-knife, which was found near him, in opening a vein in his left arm, and had bled to death. When discovered by the keeper, life was extinct—thus furnishing another chapter to the great volume of human folly. So we go!"

Samuel was shocked; not more at the frightful picture which the article presented of a soul reeking with the smoke and freshness of its guilt, rushing, madly and unrepentant, up to the stern bar of its Creator, than at the cold-blooded tone of the article itself—as if its writer were a second Satan, and chuckled over the sinful tendencies of poor humanity; as if he enjoyed the opportunity which the subject afforded him to banquet, with devilish mockery, upon a fellow-creature's ruin, upon the complete overthrow of another soul; as if he gloated over the havoc which sin was making in society; as if John Rankin's crime, John Rankin's hypocrisy, John Rankin's suicide, John Rankin's eternal spiritual destruction, and the shame, humiliation, grief, and temporal distress of John Rankin's widow, and John Rankin's little ones, together with all the John Rankins, past, present, and to come, and all the iniquity of the age, and the swiftness with which the age itself, and all of it, and all following it, were driving, pell-mell, to everlasting destruction, were—all summed up in one—a great, philosophic, side-splitting JOKE!

The paper fell from the young Christian's hand.

"Ah," he murmured, with an air of pain, "how the press needs purifying! If I thought, now, that the heart of that bad man could be reached by a letter, or by a personal appeal! But, no," he added, after a few moments of further reflection, "both would be useless. He would sneer at them, as he does at the lightning speed with which men are hurrying to *his* Master. Who sees his fellow-creatures struggling in the gulf, and instead of putting out his energies to their rescue, *mocks* at them—"

"Samuel," interrupted Charley Gibbs, "a dealer from Norwich, New York, desires to see you. Another new customer!"

The day wore away, and evening came. Tea was over, and Samuel put on his hat.

"Are you going out?" inquired Mrs. Townsend.

Samuel replied in the affirmative.

"You are never at home any more!" observed Isabella, with playful petulance. "Why can't you spare us an evening, you naughty truant?"

"Business!" replied Samuel, with suggestive brevity.

"Important?" asked Isabella.

"My MASTER'S!" returned Samuel.

The ladies, followed by Mr. Townsend, passed into the drawing-room, and Samuel into the street.

"Something is on his mind," remarked Mrs. Townsend, seating herself by the centre-table.

"He's pondering over that sad affair of Mr. Rankin's," said Isabella.

"What makes you think so?" inquired her uncle.

"Because he appeared to listen with so much interest to our discussion of the subject during tea."

Miriam made no remark. She was reflecting upon the unhappy position of the suicide's family, and considering what she could do to mitigate the severity of their affliction.

At this moment Mr. Brigham was announced. But as nothing of any importance followed that worthy's appearance, we shall follow our hero, whose every word, and thought, and act, always had a meaning and a purpose.

Samuel sped down to Tenth-street. His step was hasty, his brow thoughtful, and his general air pregnant with earnestness. In ten minutes he was standing at the door of his pastor's, with his hand upon the bell-pull.

A servant answered the summons, and upon learning whom he desired to see, showed him into the parlor.

Samuel seated himself, and looked down musingly. He had called upon a, to him, important business; a business which required delicacy and nerve; which might be regarded as offensive; which might be construed into an insult; and which might make an enemy of a friend. Nevertheless, he felt that his motive was a good one, and he determined to face the subject manfully.

"Help, Lord—help!" he murmured, reverentially. "Be Thou with me in this, as in seven others of its kind—for Thy dear Son's sake!"

A ray of light, filling him with its radiance and warmth, glowed in the young Christian's heart, and he knew that his prayer had been heard and answered.

His countenance beamed with mingled gratitude and joy.

"Thou art with me! I feel Thy stirring Presence. Glory to Thee!—glory!" he murmured.

An approaching step echoed upon the soft, spongy carpet. Samuel raised his head.

A tall, graceful, dignified, and well-made personage—with the bearing and manner of a gentleman, and the calm, thoughtful air of a student—stood before and was looking down upon him with a glance of paternal benignity.

The Rev. Mr. Engold was what is termed a fashionable preacher. That is to say, he was the pastor of a fashionable church, whose congregation was made up of wealthy and fashionable people, who did not object to pay him four thousand dollars per year for his professional services, because *they* could afford to pay him that amount, and because *he* WAS WORTH IT. Mr. Engold was a ripe scholar, an acute thinker, and a graceful declaimer. Possessing the refined instincts of a gentleman, he was mild, courteous, and dignified in his deportment. Endowed with a large mind, he was noted for the depth and comprehensiveness of his views. Gifted with a noble heart, he was naturally chivalrous, and humane. But being of a delicate, sensitive, and retiring disposition, he rarely ventured abroad, except when called upon by his professional duties, preferring the companionship of his family, and the privacy of his study, to all the society in the world.

The clergyman pressed the hand of his visitor with mingled dignity and kindness.

"I am happy to see and welcome you, brother," he said. "I should be glad to have you visit me oftener than you do. But knowing the character of your time and occupation, I presume I must forego that happiness. I received from you, to-day, a note stating that you would call upon me this evening, in the hope of finding me at leisure."

Samuel bowed.

"Permit me to add," said the clergyman, with an encouraging smile, "that you could not have chosen a happier time."

"You are very kind," returned his visitor, gratefully. "I have come," he added, "to counsel with you upon an important topic:—*Earnest preaching.*"

"An important topic, indeed, and one which it will give me much pleasure to converse upon."

"You make me very happy! I want to talk with you upon it in a way which will do us both good; in a way which will warm both your breast and mine; in a way which, whatever I may say, will not lessen me in your esteem, nor deprive me of your friendship."

"Say on, sir," said the clergyman, betraying, in spite of himself, a slight degree of surprise.

"I want," pursued Samuel, who was somewhat disturbed by the change in his pastor's manner, "to talk with you in a cordial, brotherly tone—like two hearts that love and esteem one another, and who would not dream for an instant that either *could* have for the other any but the highest, purest, and tenderest good-will!"

The clergyman regarded his visitor for a moment or two in silence, and then said, in a voice at once frank and reassuring—

"One word! I enjoy the acquaintance of a young man who is noted for his rare devotedness to his Redeemer. It is said of him, that he has never spoken an unmanly or unchristian word; that from his lips come forth, daily, utterances which put to shame the loftiest of human wisdom; that he never enters a room without imparting to all in it the sunshine and the odor of his own pure, artless spirit; that he wanders, like a spirit of good, among the haunts of the vicious and outcast, and persuades their votaries, one by one, back to virtue and morality; that he glides from garret to cellar, and from barrack to hovel, among the poor, who love and revere him, as their only true earthly counsellor and benefactor—bringing food to the hungry, raiment to the naked, money to the impoverished, medicine to the ill, encouragement to the despairing—procuring work for the capable, advice for the troubled, consolation for the afflicted, credit for the creditless—wiping off the little debts of the ill and broken, putting sound, practical thoughts into the minds of the shiftless, giving tone, strength, and direction to the wavering:—and leading all, step by step, like little children, up to the feet of Jesus."

"You know of one like that?" cried Samuel, with an air of mixed wonder and delight. "A noble heart! A gallant heart! A TRUE man! Oh, sir, acquaint me with him, too!"

The clergyman smiled, and continued:—

"This young man is not my friend alone, but every one's who is in trouble, in error, or in need. Of himself, he thinks never; of the service he can be to his Prince and his fellow-beings—always. Knowing of the immeasurable happiness which follows upon a familiar acquaintance with his beloved Redeemer, his every thought is given to bringing his fellow-men to a participation in the same happiness, early and at once."

"A noble heart!" cried Samuel, joyfully. "How I long to know him! He could teach me what to do, to better serve our Prince. You will introduce me to him—will you not? Oh, what great things we could do together for the extension of our Master's kingdom!"

The clergyman went on, as if he had not heard him:—

"My young friend is inspired from time to time with noble conceptions of noble enterprises."

"Ah! sir, how could he else, when he is in the confidence of our Prince?"

"He has planned an organization, which is made up of young clerks in his own business—of young clerks, who will be future merchants. The object of this association is three-fold: first, to imbue each of its members with a firm determination to do business upon the single principle of strict honesty, when they shall themselves become merchants, and to adhere to that principle throughout their clerkships; secondly, to become active, energetic followers of their Prince—to bend their minds and hearts to the bringing of men to Christ, to helping those who cannot help themselves, to scattering messages of salvation, to rescuing their fellow-beings from temporal want, mental darkness, and spiritual misery; and, thirdly, to spare no pains to urge their acquaintance in the same business to start similar associations in their respective houses, and thus lay the nucleus of a future generation of *Christian Merchants*, whose every transaction shall be governed, not by the law of Greed, but by the Law of God!"

Samuel blushed. He began, at length, to comprehend the original of his pastor's portrait.

The latter smiled quietly, and added—

"This young man's ideas work: because they are suggested from On High. His association, which was begun with six, now counts seventy members, who are engaged in various houses in the dry goods trade; all of them Christians—brave, earnest, self-denying youth—and all exerting an influence for good in their respective establishments. Think: seventy *true* Christian men, working together to lay the foundation of their Master's Church in their own branch of Commerce, and looking forward, like true men in the Lord! to the time when every house in the Dry Goods Trade shall be a branch, an arm, and a pillar of the One Temple! Seventy leal subjects of Our Prince, and all partaking of the gentle, fervent, humane spirit of their leader! What may they *not* perform! Every otherwise unemployed moment in the day is given to kind suggestions to their fellow-clerks to come up and find joy in the work of the Lord. In the night—look for these gallant youth! Once a week, they meet in the packing-room of the house where their leader is employed, to report the results of their labors for the week, and to renew their strength with fresh draughts of exhilarating prayer. *Five* nights in the week, they scatter, sometimes in couples, but in the main, singly, and apparently disappear. Would you know whither they go? Listen: There are in this great city districts around which Poverty has drawn a cordon which forbids the ingress or egress of all save the *lowliest* poor. The tenements in these districts are old, broken, and decayed. Each apartment in these tenements is the abode of an entire family, made up sometimes of only two, but oftener of six, persons: so that each house of three stories not unfrequently gives shelter to fifty wretched beings, who, nine times in ten, know as little of God as of cleanliness or comfort. From cellar to garret, they nestle in swarms, amid squalor, dirt, ignorance, disease, and misery. Say there are five hundred houses—in some, the number is greater!—like these, in each of Poverty's districts—what a field for the philanthropist and the Christian! Come night, and look for the seventy! They are toiling up the broken stairways of these tenements—halting at every door, leaving advice, encouragement, tracts, Bibles, bread and money to the inmates of each, as their wants may suggest; getting one work, giving to another help, another encouragement, and inviting all to go up to Him whose smile makes equal or poverty or wealth; bringing joy to the hearts of all, and leading now one, and then another, to His feet. Ah! who shall measure the pangs assuaged, the suffering averted, the sweet counsels given, the bitter thoughts removed, or the hearts led from darkness up to light, by this noble Christian band!"

Samuel was blushingly silent.

"Recently," continued the clergyman, "the leader of this glorious organization, zealous ever in the promotion of the operations of his Redeemer, has undertaken another task—to arouse the pulpit to an *earnest* prosecution of *its* work. But here I must pause: for save a few stray rumors, which may, or may not, be authentic, I know but little, but of which I should be glad to be wholly informed. I have gone over these facts in the history of my young friend, to show you, sir, that I appreciate the character of him who says to me that he desires to converse with me upon an important topic, and that he does not wish me to take offence, since offence is in nowise meant, at whatever he may say. Let me add, that in the breast of Henry Engold, whatever may be thought or said of him in the world, there beats a heart whose every throb is for Humanity and God!"

"Ah! sir," cried Samuel, who was visibly distressed, "never have I, for one moment, doubted the motive of your work—never, for one moment, your loyalty or well meaning!"

"I thank you, sir!" returned the clergyman, gratefully. "And now that we understand one another, let us converse frankly, bravely—not like men, talking to each other's ears, but, like Christians, to each other's hearts!"

"You are very kind, sir! How, in that noble suggestion, do I recognize the pure ore, the sterling ring, of a brother!"

"Let us be frank, brother!" said the clergyman, in a voice whose quivering tone was accompanied by a moisture in his eyes. "Come, begin."

Samuel was disturbed; but mastering his emotion, he said—

"The human heart, my brother, is like the field of a husbandman, who rooted out all the weeds and stones, who ploughed well, sowed well, and reaped a rich harvest for his pains. The spiritual husbandman who would glean well, must plough well, and sow well, or his harvest will be scant."

"That is true!" observed his auditor, after a few moments of reflection.

"My brother," said the young man, solemnly, "thou hast labored long upon thy field."

"I have. Go on. Spare me not!" said the clergyman.

"Thou hast seen the rocks and the weeds?"

"I have."

"My brother, what hast *thou* gleaned—my brother, where is *thy* harvest?" said the young Christian, mournfully.

The clergyman started, and turned pale.

"*My* harvest?" he stammered.

"Thine?"

The clergyman stared at his interlocutor, and breathed hard.

"Here," said the young man, drawing a paper from his pocket, opening it, and pointing, with a sad but firm gesture to an article upon the editorial page, "read that!"

The article was that which Samuel had read in the morning, concerning the defaulting cashier.

The clergyman had already perused the details of the sad affair in another journal. He ran his eyes, nevertheless, through the editorial in question—blushing at the sight of his own name—and trembling with mingled scorn and indignation at the low, scurrilous, mocking tone which pervaded the article itself.

"The concoction of a beastly and malignant mind, which appears to revel in the consciousness of its own and others' evil!" he observed, as, with a nervous shudder, he permitted the paper to slide through his fingers to the floor. "I hope, Samuel—but no, why ask such a question of *you?* You *could* not be a regular reader of so infamous a sheet as that?"

"You are right, my brother—I could not. I saw it by chance, this morning, at the store, for the first, and, as I hope the last time! I brought it with me, in part that you might see how Satan's chief organ—for I hear that of all ribald journals, *it* is the most widely read—chuckles over each new evidence of weakness in humanity, and every fresh instance of degeneracy among the people of Our Prince; and in part that you might yourself see the fruits—not yours alone, my brother, for the style was begun and sanctioned by custom long ere you were born! but—of a kind of preaching which is doing more for Satan and less for Christ than men dream of—aye, even more than that dark chuckling thing upon the floor!"

"Me, brother!" cried his agitated pastor, staring at him in mingled mournfulness, reproach, and bewilderment. "You accuse me of coldness, indifference, neglect—*me!*"

"For none of these!" returned Samuel, gently. "O, no—for none of these! And yet—*the* FRUITS!"

The clergyman breathed hard and audibly.

"The fruits?" he repeated.

"John Rankin, thief, gambler, and self-murderer—Peter Jones, fraudulent bankrupt, and betrayer of his own wife and child—Mrs. Jane Clarke, his paramour, the willing violator of her own marriage vow—"

"Hold, in mercy, brother! What could do I for these? Their own hearts were set on evil!"

"I say unto you, my brother—ah! I say it not unkindly!—that these are not *all* of the members of your church who have fallen or will fall!"

"How know you the latter?"

"By that standard which deceives not—Want of piety!"

"In *my* people?"

"Ask your heart, my brother, how many in all your congregation meet the *Christian's* mark?"

The clergyman reflected, and his brow became clouded with an air of pain.

"I would not judge!" he said, rising and pacing the floor in deep agitation.

"Giving to its two hundred members and its four hundred pew-renters every generous latitude—how many evince a solemn, earnest interest in their own salvation, and in the extension of their Redeemer's Kingdom? How many?"

The clergyman resumed his seat, and shading his eyes with his hands, breathed hard, but made no reply.

"Shall I go on?" asked Samuel, mournfully.

His auditor made a sign in the affirmative.

"I will answer for you," said the young man, touched to the heart by his pastor's sufferings. "There are *five*—five only who give hope that they are of the Ransomed. Oh, my brother, how small a number, from so many! And of these five, four were leal subjects to Our Prince ere your coming as their shepherd; while the fifth was blessed through the instrumentality of another in a neighboring city. My brother—my brother! The weeds and the stones in the hearts of your people have been *sadly* rooted out!"

"Nay," said his pastor, hoarsely, "you are unkind! You chide me for no fault of mine. I have preached and prayed—I have suggested and advised. What *could* I do *more?*"

"Listen, brother: To the great work of upbuilding the Temple of our Lord, able men come up every year in thousands. Many enter the grounds, but only a few are of service. Not because the unthrifty have not thews and sinews like the thrifty, but because they do not come up like *workmen*. They toil, and toil, and toil, but their united labors are as naught to the advancement of the common cause. They work, and work, and work; but at the end of the season, they cannot point to a stone that they have laid, to a pillar that they have raised, nor to a beam that they have set. And yet they know that they have labored, faithfully and hard, eagerly and long. They look around, in doubt and dismay, for the fruits of their labors, but find them not. They rub their eyes, and look again; but with no better success than before. There *are* no fruits; or if there be, they are lying aside among the spoiled castaway refuse—which any stranger is free to come in and take away. And why? Because the unthrifty toilers *worked not with their Master's tools, but*— THEIR OWN!"

The clergyman started up, and paced the apartment as before, in profound agitation.

Samuel observed him, and went on:

"Our Prince is the kindest of all masters. When He invites His people to come up to His work, He provides them with fitting tools—tools which are reliable, and easy to the hand. Who uses them, gains ground; who discards them, and takes up others of their own, advances *not.* Neither the arches nor the walls, nor yet the pillars, nor the altar, nor any part soever of *His* temple, can be worked with implements wrought by *human* hands!"

"Go on, brother. Strike deep and spare not!" cried the clergyman, who was pale and trembling, but yet firm and decided in heart. "It is my conscience which you are addressing, and not me! If I have been unthrifty, 'tis time that I should change; for 'tis my desire to *advance* my Master's work, and not retard it by standing in the way, or making work which shall be cast aside. I affirm it before Him and you, that my heart is eager and willing for His cause!"

"I think it, and know it, dear brother," said his visitor, taking his hand, "or I had not spoken as I have!"

"I thank you for it, brother!" answered his pastor, returning his warm pressure. "And now, go on! I submit frankly to the justness of your reproof, and receive your counsel as generously as it is meant. Proceed!"

"Nay, not now," said the young man, with an air of deep tenderness and sympathy; "you are pale, agitated—"

"No matter," returned the clergyman, with a grateful smile, "I am all right *here*, and I will go through with this like one whose only fear is of his Maker's frown. Go on, my brother! You have spoken bravely, nobly, manfully, and I esteem you for it the more. Go on! The storm which you have raised in my breast, it is fit you help me to allay, or I shall suffer more than I can bear—more, let me hope, than I deserve, seeing that my error has come not so much from a weak or wilful heart, as from a want of thoughtfulness in head! Go on!"

"I thank you, brother. There are two kinds of preaching—that which keeps the *preacher* before the minds of his auditory, and that which keeps the *subject*. The former is man's tool, the latter is of God. The first may fill the pews with *renters*; but the second does better, for it fills them with honest *converts*. Every pastor should aim to so preach that his own individuality shall disappear in his *subject*, and naught be left upon the minds of his hearers but the goodness of their Redeemer, the solemn consciousness of their own peril, and the imperative necessity of immediate repentance. Every discourse that does not this, may be faultless and masterly as a *composition*; but as a *sermon*, it is a mournful and humiliating failure."

"I confess to the truthfulness of this," said the clergyman, frankly. "But reflect. The class for whom I preach are the most worldly intelligent. Should I abandon the eloquence of talent, and the polish of the scholar, they would abandon my church, and I should be left to empty benches—thereby depriving me of the means of reaching their hearts at all."

"Nay, hold on to both with a firm hand! For who so deserving of our *highest* talents and accomplishments as Our Redeemer? What topic calls so imperatively for the mind's *choicest* jewels as THE DIVINE MESSAGE! Only so employ these jewels in their setting, that the world shall see that they are set to beautify the *Message*, and not the *preacher*."

"Surely, if I know my heart, that is my *intent!*"

"But the world don't see it so! Herein the error, and the necessity of a struggle which shall enable the world to see, at a single glance, your *aim*. When men can *see* THAT, they will give heed the quicker to the Message which you bring. For men's hearts," added his visitor, with a mournful smile, "are cold, suspicious, and wilfully incredulous things. Who comes to them in Christ's name, must be simple, earnest, and dignified, *like* Christ, or they will none of him, when he would speak to them *of* Christ. The *man* first—his message afterwards. As they are satisfied of *him*, so give they ear to the message that he bears. Say they find, by watching—for they *will* watch, yea, and suspect him, too, and that for a long time!—that he is a mere utterer of words, and that his daily deportment corresponds not with his professions, they will listen to him as to one who believes not himself what he is saying,; nor will *they* believe it either, and thus become lost, because they cannot and do not believe in *him*. But let them once discover that he is himself true—that he calls up his great eloquence and rare scholarship simply to lend beauty and attractiveness to the grandeur of his Theme, and not to call their attention to himself, *then* they give attent ear, for the first time, to the *Message*, and are saved, because they have at length gained confidence in the *man!* Therefore it is, when our preachers are neglectful or forgetful of this distinction, that no blessing follows their labors, let them struggle with what zealousness and unceasingness they will!"

"You are right, brother. I see it, feel it, and thank you for the suggestion. Rightly is it said of you that you never enter a room without leaving better and juster thoughts than prevailed there before your coming. Again, I thank you; knowing as I do that you have only spoken for my good, and that I might see why I have not done more of good to others heretofore. But enough, I shall strive to take advantage of your kind counsel; and by my deportment in the future make some atonement to men and Our Master for my unintentional error in the past!"

"Oh, sir," cried his visitor, "you make me very happy. I knew you would say this, and resolve this, ere I came; and it fills me with glad joy to learn that I did not misjudge the spirit of my pastor. And besides, I was assured, by our Lord, in answer to a petition, that He would be with me in this interview!"

The clergyman looked with an air of mingled love and reverence upon this man, whose purity, gentleness, and piety of heart enabled him to hold a conscious intercourse with GOD.

"When was this?" he asked.

"A moment ere you entered," returned Samuel.

The brow of the worthy clergyman brightened, and his frame trembled with a feeling of ineffable delight.

"Joy—joy!" he exclaimed. "Our Lord visited you in my house? Oh! does not that prove that He, in His great goodness, kindly remembers His unworthy servant, and that He will bless my resolution? Glory to Thee!" he added, with a grateful gesture; "glory—glory! Never shall I cease to do Thy will—nor to praise Thy holy name!"

"Let us praise Him together!" cried Samuel, with emotion.

"Aye, as one heart!" said his pastor.

And both fell upon their knees, and stretching up their hands, burst out—

"Glory to God on high!
Let earth and skies reply,
Praise ye His name;

His love and grace adore,
Who all our sorrows bore,
Sing loud for evermore,
  Worthy the Lamb.

Jesus, our Lord and God,
Bore sin's tremendous load,
  Praise ye His name;
Tell what His arm has done,
What spoils from death He won:
Sing His great name alone,
  Worthy the Lamb.

While they around the throne,
Cheerfully join in one,
  Praising His name;
Those who have felt His blood
Sealing their peace with God,
Sound His dear fame abroad,
  Worthy the Lamb.

Join, all ye ransomed race,
Our holy Lord to bless;
  Praise ye His name—
In Him we will rejoice,
And make a joyful noise,
Shouting with heart and voice,
  Worthy the Lamb."

CHAPTER XXII.

The second Sabbath following the young Christian's interview with the "fashionable preacher" was an important one in the history of that gentleman's ministerial career, as well as in that of his church. Samuel had, meanwhile, seen the trustees, together with many of the members of the church, and obtained a pledge from each to lend their assistance to their pastor in his endeavor to wake up his people from their surface piety, and imbue them with a solemn sense of vitalizing grace. The parties were faithful to their promise; and they were careful to prepare their acquaintance in the society for the event. This preparation led, of course, to considerable conversation; the conversation to religious discussion; the discussion to a general resurrection of long dormant ideas; these to a certain degree of self-examination; and this to not a little religious feeling: all of which resulted in a universal determination to sustain Mr. Engold in his new effort to arouse his congregation from their spiritual palsy.

The momentous day at length came round. The church was filled to its utmost capacity with an assemblage of brilliant, but, in the main, irreligious intelligences. The trustees, most of whom possessed only a faint knowledge of their Redeemer, shared in the general wish that the day might not pass away without blessing—somebody. As for themselves, they didn't think that genuine piety would pay—*them!* They had a notion that "the *real thing* was *hardly* the thing for—*them*." "They were in business; and the pressure of *competition* IN business would not allow it; and, besides, society would scout at a man who was *really* pious." And they—*they* lived *in* society. Um! Independently of these considerations, they had always *professed* to be religious; and it would "hardly do" to *permit* themselves to be converted, because that would have the effect of unmasking them, and of showing them up in their true colors; and so, on the whole, they thought that, so far as they were themselves concerned, the "real thing" wouldn't pay—just yet. One of these days, when their pecuniary circumstances—that is, their business—should render them a *little* more independent, they meant to give the subject some serious consideration; because *then* they would be "in a position" to "do as they pleased," and to "act upon their convictions." But, "at present" they "couldn't *afford* it," and, therefore, it "wouldn't *pay*." And so, as they could not hope for *themselves*, they hoped, *very* heartily, for—*somebody else.*

The *members*, whose piety was about as deep as that of the trustees, were equally as concerned for the welfare of—*others.* They didn't think that they were themselves in any very great spiritual want, because they were *already* within the ark—so far as the world knew. But then they designed to be *really* so—at some future time. Just then, however, as they were in business and society, and as neither business nor society would permit a person to be *very* pious, they thought that they were *about as* pious as they could *afford* to be. But there was Mr. Smith, who had *retired* from business, and had now nothing to do but to amuse himself—*he* COULD afford it, and they really hoped he *would.* Then there was Mrs. Griggs, a rich widow, who had "got off" her daughters, and who had, therefore, no reasonable excuse for humbugging the world or herself any longer, *she* MIGHT take hold of the real thing in *earnest,* and they trusted that she would. Mr. Lester, too; *he* was rich enough—worth three or four millions, at least—and he could *afford* to go into it, and they hoped and prayed that he wouldn't neglect the opportunity. Mrs. Allen could afford it also. She was the wife of a really pious man, who would give worlds for her conversion. She had no daughters to work off; was in easy circumstances—worth some eight hundred thousand or so, and with nothing on earth to prevent her from doing just as she pleased; and she might throw off her transparent humbug, and take hold of the real thing, just as well as not. *They* would, if they were in her place—quicker! As for themselves, they intended to do so, one of these days, *any* how; that is, when they were a little richer, a little older, and a little more tired of the humbug of society. Why, then, couldn't the Smiths, the Griggses, the Lesters, and the Allens pluck up, as *they* designed to do when they should be as rich and old *as* the Smiths, the Griggses, the Lesters, and the Allens, and as every really sincere person who was old enough, and rich enough to afford it, *ought* to do?

As for the retired Mr. Smith himself, he thought, now that he was rich and could afford to do as he pleased, that he would amuse himself by studying society. He opined that it would be time enough to take hold of the real thing after he had got through with his amusements. At present, however, the surface article would "answer his purpose" very well. The real thing might interfere with his plans, and hurt him; and as he was now in the possession and enjoyment of his plum, he didn't want to be interfered with, nor hurt, either. Still, as he felt an interest in the Lord's business, he was not "unwilling" to "lend his influence" to the Holy Spirit in "pushing things on."

Mrs. Griggs thought that, now that she had got off her daughters, the next best thing she could do would be to get *herself* off. She had several gentlemen in her eye, and as she was blessed with a large stock of self-confidence, she flattered herself that she could wing either one of them, easily, when she had once made up her mind which to aim for. After that should be accomplished, she proposed to throw aside her convenient piety, and embrace the genuine article with all her heart. To be sure she felt a lively interest in her Redeemer's affairs, and she would cheerfully do all she could, so far as her influence would go, to advance them; but she had her own affairs to look after, and she should, of course, have to give *them* "the preference." There were the Townsends, however: *they* had no special object in the way, and they might as well drop their surface humbug as not, and she would be glad to see them do it. A little of the real thing would do *them* good. And the Johnsons, too—*they* were in want of genuine religion about as much as anybody she could name; and if they would only consent to "take it up," she felt quite sure that it would be a great blessing, not only to themselves, but to the world.

Mr. Lester had an idea that three or four millions were nothing. If he had eight, now, or even six, he thought that he might perhaps persuade himself to drop his easy piety, and take hold of the real thing with his whole heart. But at present, he couldn't afford it. He was too poor. Besides, if he should attempt to do so, he couldn't succeed. His heart was upon his money, and upon the three or four other millions in perspective. He thought that some of the *young* men might yield to whatever influence should come down from above—*easily*. They had no money, and no prospect of any—that is, in comparison with amounts like his. Therefore, having nothing to give up, no sacrifices to make, they might as well take hold of the real thing as not. *He* would, if he was in their position—right quickly.

Mrs. Allen wasn't tired enough of the world yet, to take hold of religion in earnest. She found herself comfortable. Society's piety agreed with her very well—for the present; she had no desire to go over to the real thing—just yet. She meant to do so, at some future day, but that day had not yet dawned. But, of course, it would come one of these days, and *when* it came she meant to be prepared for it. But at present she felt no disposition to depart from her usual course. She liked society, and society's dear, easy ways, too well for that. But then all people were not like her. Some people *needed* real piety more than others. There was Mrs. Jenkins, for instance, and Mrs. De Witt too. A little *genuine* religion wouldn't hurt *them* a bit. But as for herself, she didn't see any absolute necessity of it, just then; and until she did, she thought she could get along very well with the kind of piety that she had.

The Townsends didn't know what to think. They had an impression that there *might* be something in religion, but they were not sure. Of course they *affected* to believe in it—*everybody* did—but they were not so certain that it wasn't considerable of a humbug, after all. Those who pretended to believe in it most, were, so far as they knew, specious rascals, who only used it—for their own purposes. Still they were not unwilling to see their acquaintance take hold of it; but as for themselves, they didn't think that it would hardly pay.

The Johnsons didn't give themselves any anxiety about the matter at all. While they did not absolutely disbelieve in religion, they had an idea that it "wouldn't answer" for them to go into it any further than they had already. It "wouldn't do." The old gentleman's business—money "exchanging" and selling lottery tickets on the sly—wouldn't admit of it. So where was the use of "touching it?" Nevertheless, as the old gentleman had a "good feeling" for the "Church," he had "no objections" to seeing a better state of things in it. He "deplored" surface piety as much as any man; but what could he do? If he should take hold of the real thing, his conscience wouldn't permit him to continue selling policy tickets; and what would become of him and of his family, if he were to give *that* up? No; it wouldn't do. Surface piety was "about as far" as he could go, or his family either. Nevertheless, he lived in hope that a few more years would put him in a position to do as he liked; and when that time came round, he meant to take hold of the real thing like a man, and persuade his family into the same course also. In the meanwhile, he was "quite willing" that other people should do just as *they* pleased, in the matter; nay, more—he would "encourage" them and religion too, all he could, "conveniently."

The unconverted pew-renters, never having put on the robes of convenient piety, were considering whether they could afford to *receive* the Holy Spirit, in case it should conclude to visit them! They had their opinion of the *members'* piety, and thought that if they should themselves be influenced into an open profession of religion, that *their* piety would be of a *little* different character to that of the pretentious "members." But upon "looking at the subject in all its bearings," they did not believe that they could afford to be *very* pious—just yet. Business wouldn't allow it—Society wouldn't allow it; and if Business and Society wouldn't, *what* WOULD? To be sure, they could easily afford to be as pious as the *members*, but then they didn't regard *that* kind of piety as of any *very* great importance. It is true it might help one some in business, but not *very* much—and a little in society, too, but not so *very* greatly, seeing that they were already *pretty* well established in the one and tolerably well received in the other. On the whole, they didn't think it was *much* of an object! In fact, with their view of what religion DEMANDED of its *professors*, they were inclined to believe that they had no *very* great desire to *become* professors—just at present. Still they thought that it would be a "capital thing" for certain of their fellow pew-renters, and particularly for many of the *members*, to be "touched from On High." *They*—the members—wanted "something of *that* kind" *very* much.

The strangers—and there were many of *them*—having come simply out of curiosity, were there to "take the chances." They anticipated "something rich," because their friends among the members and pew-renters had informed them that Mr. Engold—of whose eloquence and finished rhetoric they had often heard—was going to make a "great effort" on that Sabbath, and they wanted all their friends to be present:—not so much for any great good that might come of it, but just to let their friends see what a "powerful man" their pastor was when he felt disposed to "let himself out." And so the friends—that is to say, the strangers—had come to see Mr. Engold "let himself out."

But notwithstanding all this, there were many in the congregation who had given no thought to the matter at all, and who, like the strangers, were ready to "take the chances." If the sermon should prove a rouser, well; if it should elicit their admiration, well; if it should wake them up, well; if it should storm their hearts, and set them in flame, well; and if it should only serve—although they had their doubts of *that*—to put them into a quiet doze—well.

And yet all hoped that good would result from the discourse to—somebody.

The Townsends were in their pew, looking very pious, and aristocratically humble.

Isabella Landon, knowing that it was going to be a great day in the church—that is to say, that an unusual number of strangers would be there—and having spent three hours at her toilet, in anticipation of several new conquests, was looking as killingly meek and interestingly pious as a young lady could be expected to look, who had nothing in life to do except to patronize herself and "assist" society in its general exhibitions.

Miriam Selden—who, poor, unsophisticated thing! always thought that God's house was the last place in the world in which to make a "display"—was so neatly but plainly dressed, that she might easily have passed for some obscure person who had got into the church either by mistake, or through the carelessness of the sexton.

Samuel was making himself useful in helping strangers to seats, and in tranquillizing some late members and pew-renters whose slips had been coolly taken possession of by certain earlier individuals, who, having inherited an unusual share of self-confidence, had no notion of waiting to be invited, but walked right in, seated themselves comfortably, and closing the door, looked around them with an air of easy independence and ineffable satisfaction.

As the time drew near for the opening of the morning service, all eyes were turned anxiously towards the pulpit. But the pastor had not yet made his appearance. Could the congregation have looked into the ante-room, they would have seen him upon his knees, fervently imploring his Master to be with him in his approaching effort to penetrate the hearts of those of his charge who were "too poor" to afford the Saviour of men a single solemn thought, when they desired so much for themselves.

At length there was a fluttering of silks and feathers in the brilliant auditory; a general smile of mingled joy, pride, and satisfaction; a quick, hurried breathing of enthusiastic hearts; a low whisper of "There he is!" and—

Mr. Engold was in the pulpit.

He was pale, but self-possessed. As he rose, in prayer, a thrill of hopefulness and affection swept through the congregation. The impressiveness of his air, the earnestness and humility of his manner, the scholarly tone of his features, the manly grandeur of his general deportment, and the mild benignity of his glance, subdued all hearts, like an invisible power, and bowed them into a, to them, novel feeling—meekness.

The clergyman spoke; and every heart was touched as with an electric shock: for his tone and manner told his auditors that he was communing with JEHOVAH like one who was conscious WHOM he was addressing!

A sense of awe, humility, and human impotence crept over the assemblage.

A solemn stillness, broken only by the voice of the petitioner, reigned throughout the temple.

Not one in all the throng, that did not feel the sacredness of the place.

It was a touching, contrite, and humble prayer—without a solitary grain of affectation, heaviness, mannerism, or monotony, for the smallest or lightest mind to carp at.

It suggested nothing but *itself*—a prayer from an humble heart to its dear Creator!

It was not with the artlessness of a child—but the appeal of a great manly heart and a noble intellect bowed down to a sense of their own nothingness when in the presence of Almighty GOD.

A stirring, thrilling, awe-subduing prayer—which made beauty forget her beauty, wealth its millions and its pride, ambition its feverish dream, disappointment its sorrow, envy its bitterness, and display its littleness.

At its close, the assembly experienced a grateful sense of relief: they felt that for that brief season of sincere humility they had been rewarded by a refreshing shower from On High!

The hymn that followed was not, as formerly, confined alone to the choir. Every voice joined in it with spontaneous and enthusiastic acclaim.

The sermon was a bold, eloquent, and startling picture of man's relations to his Creator. It was presented with all the earnestness of the ambassador, all the eloquence of the man, and all the cultivated rhetoric of the student. Ere long, the auditors lost sight of the scholar, the man, and the ambassador: one by one they disappeared from their minds, which then became absorbed by the solemn grandeur of the Theme. From that moment they beheld but three objects:

Their Maker's greatness;

Their Redeemer's goodness;

Their own unworthiness.

From that moment loomed up before them the startling and unflattering facts:

That THE LAW of God is absolute and pitiless, but that—*it must be met;*

That it can only be met by faith in the Redeemer, and by thorough and earnest repentance;

That this faith must be given, and this repentance be worked out by men during life;

That at death the chances of mercy cease;

That there is no repentance *after* death;

That whoso neglects or refuses to comply with the requirements of THE LAW, while in the flesh, thereby pronounces his own condemnation, because

THE LAW *must be met!*

And from that moment this haughty, supercilious, self-sufficient throng forgot their wealth, their exclusiveness, their pompous littleness, and their inability to "afford" the "real thing." They forget everything but their Maker's greatness, their Redeemer's goodness, their own sinfulness, and—the pitiless rigor of THE LAW! O, how for one long hour they sighed, and wept, and trembled over their previous paltry views! How for one long hour they listened to The Message as it fell from the lips of the preacher! How for one long hour the thunders of Sinai rattled through their quaking hearts, shook the starch out of their proud blood, and the fire from their insolent eyes! How for one long hour the members took shame for their *surface* piety, the pew-renters for their *want* of piety, the strangers for their churchlessness, the retired Smiths for their selfishness, the Mrs.

Griggs for their unworthiness, the Lesters for their greediness, and the Mrs. Allens for their littleness! How for one long hour all forgot whether they could, or could not, afford to *patronize* their—REDEEMER!

At length the voice of the envoy ceased; the wrapped throng drew a long breath, and—each *forgot* to look at his neighbor.

The doxology—ah! how soft and broken were the voices of the flaring assemblage as they joined in *that!*

And *how* meekly and reverently all bowed their proud heads during the benediction!

And then, how, like mean, guilty things, they slunk from the sanctuary!

But, not all—no, not *all!*

Here and there, still remaining in their seats—their heads bowed upon their breasts, or else upon the pew-tops—their frames moving convulsively—tears of shame, and grief, and wretchedness gliding down their pale cheeks, were many in penitential agony. A few of them in life's bright spring-time; some in its sweet summer; and others in the various stages of autumn. Among them the veriest veterans in society's convenient piety, society's easy indifference, and society's smiling heartlessness. And—of all the world!—Mr. Smith, Mrs. Griggs, Mr. Lester, Mrs. Allen, and Mr. Johnson, with two score others of their kind, and one score more of weepers who had never, until then, given a single honest thought to aught but—themselves!

The pastor—his eyes dewy and his voice tremulous!—invited them all to the altar, and all went forward, but—*two!*

Mr. and Mrs. Townsend!

The Holy Spirit, in its descent, had looked upon them kindly, and bathed them, among others, in the rich sunshine of its smile; but—they resisted. They wept, but—resisted.

"Dear aunt," whispered a gentle voice imploringly, "be brave

—be firm. Come forward—God will make you happy. Struggle not against Him. Our Prince waits to bless you!"

No reply.

"Dear friend," whispered Samuel, gently, in the ear of his employer, "falter not—resist not the Holy Ghost. Rise, come forward, and partake of the rich blessing which is about to descend upon the brave hearts kneeling at the altar. Come, and enter upon a new existence. Come, and peace will reign henceforth in your heart. Come, Jesus is waiting. Come, and be happy!"

No reply.

The young Christian moved away with an air of pain towards the altar, and then his features became radiant with indescribable delight, as he beheld the small multitude of brave hearts that were kneeling there.

Here let us pause; for there are things which may be seen and felt, but—not told.

Uncover, sir—uncover and halt gently, you who are passing by; for this temple is now hallowed and made holy by a visitation from On High. Look reverently—*feel* reverently. For—this in your ear!—within are three-score and five of humble penitents, kneeling at the feet of JESUS! Three-score and five of humble penitents, saluting their Saviour, in sincerity and humility, for the first time! Three-score and five of humble penitents—young, middle-aged, and gray-haired—are sobbing; sobbing, sir—think of that. Great manly and womanly hearts—sobbing and crying, like little children over some very joyful or heart-breaking thing. And struggling, too—many of them fiercely, but all of them earnestly—with Evil, the greatest enemy of all their lives, and of yours and mine, too, sir—and calling on their Prince for help, and *getting* it, and promptly, too, and kindly: for who called ever upon HIM in vain?

Three-score and five of thinking, reasoning beings upon their knees! Warms it not your heart with solemn, stirring fervor? Shakes it not your blood, heating it and expanding it till every vein seems as if about to burst with proud, grateful joy? Three-score and five upon their knees to HIM, the only one in all the universe to whom that posture's due, and who never lets His people rise again until He has made them happier, by more than twice ten thousand times, than they were before they bent them down. Three-score and five—shout, shout!—for each and all of them are now registered Above; mansions are even now preparing for them There; and cherubim and seraphim are rejoicing o'er them, There; and they will sleep to-night the peacefuller for this, and rise again the better for it on the morrow; and have new thoughts, and better and kinder ones, for it, too; and they'll march along life's pathway, from this hour, with a firmer and surer step; and be ever, from this day, so full of joy and comfort, so abounding in hope, confidence, and gladness, that you will know them for what they are—

Of the *Ransomed*—the REDEEMED!

CHAPTER XXIII.

THE good work went on. For many weeks it was like the gathering in of a great harvest. Members, pew-renters, and strangers awoke in large numbers, repented, and found peace. Society's Church lessened day by day, Christ's as rapidly filled up. It was a season of great joy to many; but not to all. Society's Church neither wanted a too familiar acquaintance with The Redeemer, nor would accept it. At first they regarded the revival with favor. It was a novelty; it would amuse them; it would interest them; it would pass away, in a short time, like any other novelty; and it would enable them—Society's party—to say, complacently, that they were pleased with it, because it gave them an opportunity to evince their interest in The Church. But they discovered, at length, and to their horror, that "the thing" was getting to be "utterly unbearable." Instead of passing away in a few days, it CONTINUED—gathering new life and fresh strength at every step, and there was no telling when or where it would end. This was all well enough for those who desired to be converted, and to take hold of the real thing; but as for themselves, they had no such wish; they were satisfied as they were; they didn't want so many strangers there every Sunday; and they *did* want the "agitation" brought to a close. But on finding that their desire was by no means likely to be heeded or gratified, they came out, took a bold, firm stand, and declared that "They wouldn't put up with 'the nonsense' any longer." They styled themselves The Exclusives, called the revival The New Movement, and stigmatized the converts as The New People.

The Exclusives were, however, in a glorious minority—the New People outfigured them two to one. But, no matter; they flattered themselves that they made up in consequence and respectability for what they lacked in number.

The New People went on, meanwhile, as if there were no such individuals as Exclusives, or "exclusive" sentiments in the world. The pastor continued to do the will of Him who sent him, and the Car of Grace rolled on in triumph.

The Exclusives were fierce, supercilious, and scornful. They would have nothing to do with the New People. They had no sympathy with the New Movement. They disliked the pastor's new style of preaching. They couldn't stand it, and wouldn't. It "disturbed them;" and they "wouldn't be disturbed." Some got enraged, and cleared out altogether; declaring, as they departed, that "they wouldn't patronize any church where the society was not more select." Others remained, affirming, through their leader, a Mr. Wells, a retired army officer, who was very rich, very proud, very obstinate, and very exclusive, "that they would not submit to aggression; that they would not yield an inch to the enemy—the New People; that they would maintain their rights; and that they would break up the New Movement, and kick out the disturbers, or perish." But notwithstanding the opposition of The Exclusives, the New Movement continued to prosper, and the New People to increase. The Exclusives waxed wroth; some followed the example of their predecessors, and retired in disgust; but those whose pride inspired them to remain, formed still a goodly body. What most enraged them was the fact that every time a pew was thrown up by a retiring member of their party, a dozen or more of the strangers in the ranks of the New People stepped forward with alacrity, and vied with each other, in their mild, brotherly way, for the privilege of obtaining it. The Exclusives swelled and reddened with indignation.

But, some how or other—one would hardly believe it, but things will work very oddly, now and then!—The HOLY SPIRIT was *stronger* than the *Exclusives;* and its work went on in spite of all the latter could do to arrest it. In less than six months from the commencement of the revival, nearly two-thirds of the old surface members and pew-renters had taken up arms for their Redeemer; not passively, but with energy and enthusiasm. All this, in the estimation of the Society Christians, was exceedingly aggravating. But worse followed. They wanted the *Exclusives* to come over to Christ also. "Come, and partake of our great happiness!" they exclaimed. "Our Prince is a kinder Master than Society's, and makes His people happier. Come—do!" Now, language and conduct like this were perfectly exasperating to the Exclusives. They didn't go to church for any such purpose. What they wanted was—to be let alone; and if the New People wouldn't let them alone, and respect their quiet, dignity, and exclusiveness, they would take steps to compel them. Now, was there ever anything more outrageous? To disturb nice, quiet, respectable people like them! It was shameful—positively shocking!

But if the New People would only have stopped here. But they wouldn't—no, they wouldn't. They were too "low," too "vulgar" for that! Instead of being satisfied with their own happiness, they had a grovelling desire to see everybody else happy as well. Instead of minding their own business, like respectable, well-bred persons, they acquired a propensity for meddling with other people's affairs. "Have you become acquainted yet with our dear Prince?" they would impudently inquire of all their friends and neighbors; "if not—do come with us, and see how good, how kind a friend He is, and how full of joy He makes all who call on Him. *Do* come!" Now, what business was it to these impertinent meddlers, whether their friends and neighbors were happy or not? Isn't this a free country? And hasn't a man a perfect right to do as he likes—and be as happy or miserable as he pleases? It's a pretty state of things, when a man's private affairs are to be meddled with in this insolent manner! Isn't a man's house his castle? Isn't it sacred from intrusion any longer? And can't he go to church, and sit down in his own pew, without being exposed to impertinent inquiries, or impertinent interlopers, any more? Answer these questions—will you? What is it *your* business whether I have a familiar acquaintance with The Saviour or no? He died for all men—didn't He? For me, as well as for you? Come, sir—go away from here, with your impertinence. *Clear out!*

It was that Samuel who started this gratuitous meddling, and upon him rests all the blame and the shame of it!

"If," observed Mr. Wells, as the Exclusives discussed their grievances among themselves, "that young emissary of mischief had never been admitted into our church, we should have had none of this. Everything would now be going on smoothly, orderly, and respectably!"

And the ex-army officer fumed and looked daggers.

"Right!" observed Mr. Eastlake, another of the Society party. "And it is well for him that he is no longer among us, or I should move for his expulsion! But it's always the way with these young religious enthusiasts. Let one of them once get into a respectable church, and its peace, order, and respectability are gone forever!"

"They are never easy," sneered a third, "until they have got everybody by the ears, or on the stool of repentance, which is the same thing!"

"For my part," said another, a cotton-broker, "I was always fearful of that young man. You all, at that time, called him a saint—but *I* didn't! No. I perceived danger in him—he carried it in his eyes!—the first time I ever saw him! It is well he is gone!"

"Yes," said the ex-army officer, "but he has left two hundred of his like behind him. There's hardly a man among the enemy —the New People—that isn't imbued with his meddling spirit!"

The New People certainly *did* behave most shamefully. Instead of being satisfied, like decent, respectable persons, with hearing The Message themselves, and taking advantage of it, and enjoying it nicely, comfortably, selfishly, sensibly, and exclusively, when they alone paid for it—they must go around, evenings, among their friends, and invite *them* to come and hear it, too! Nay, they even stooped so low as to yield up their own pews to strangers and invitees, and were mean and spiritless enough to sit or stand themselves, anywhere—everywhere—wherever they could! Could anything exceed *that?* Did one ever hear or see of anything so "low," "shocking," and "outrageous?" It made the Exclusives "fairly sick!" But there was still a lower deep for these abominable wretches. They even carried their enormity so far, at times, as to ask *the Exclusives* to be "kind enough to make room" in THEIR pews for some of these "strangers, loafers, and vagabonds," "whom nobody knew," and "whom nobody wanted to know!" Now, reader, we put it to you as a decent man or woman—as one who knows the meaning of good breeding and individual rights—did you ever, in all your life, hear of such a solemn outrage? Isn't it almost enough to tempt one to publicly protest against the insolence of high-handed fanaticism? To be sure, the "loafers and vagabonds" dressed well enough, looked well enough, and behaved well enough. But what then? Were these any reasons why they—the Exclusives—should let them into *their* pews, and incommode *them*selves? Now, reader! *now*—be candid! We put it to you, as a reasoning, thinking, respectable person!

Mr. Eastlake was dignifiedly indignant—and very properly! Don't *you* say so? *He* spoke out like a man—like an Exclusive! He declared, at a church-meeting, one evening, "that when he rented a pew in a church, he rented it for *himself*, and not for other people. More than that—he didn't mean that other people should have the use of *his* pew while it *was* his. (Wasn't that spunky?) When his year should expire, he was perfectly willing that the New People should take the pew, and do just what they pleased with it. But *till* then, he meant to hold on to his own!"

Hurrah for the Exclusives! Hurrah—hurrah—hurrah!

Mr. Benedick "was grieved to say, that he had no sympathy with the New Movement. It disturbed his equanimity, and he—didn't like it. When he rented his pew, everything was orderly, respectable, and exclusive. (Hear, hear.) Everybody attended to their own affairs. The pastor was quiet, graceful, and mild. There was no commotion, no intrusion. Everything went on harmoniously. But the New Movement and the New People had changed all this. In fact, everything had undergone a revolution. The church was crowded every Sabbath with strangers, of whose antecedents or standing in society nobody knew anything. (Hear, hear.) They might be respectable, and then again they might not. *He* couldn't and wouldn't take it upon him to say. (Sensation.) But of one thing he was certain: He knew nothing of them himself, he didn't wish to know anything of them, and what was more, he wouldn't associate with them. (Loud applause—reader, join in.) The pastor, too, displeased him. He didn't enjoy him as he used to, prior to the New Movement. *Then*, Mr. Engold preached to suit him. At present, and ever since the New Movement, he didn't; and that was the long and the short of it. He—Mr. Benedick—was a business man, and he was accustomed to speak out, frankly and boldly, just what he thought. His frankness might be regarded by others as a weakness; if so, all he had to say was, that he gloried in it. (A proper spirit! Go it, old gentleman!) The change in Mr. Engold's preaching was everything but satisfactory to him— the speaker. It might please *other* people—he had nothing to say as to *that;* but it did not agree with *him:* and he would not sit under it. If anybody wanted his pew, they could have it—when his year was up!"

Mr. Wells, the ex-army officer, "fully agreed with his dear friend, Mr. Benedick. He believed that the time was come when every man who had any regard for society, should take a firm stand against this wild, stupid, and unnecessary fanaticism in the Church. If there was an institution on earth which should be exempt from undue agitation, it was the Church. Let undue agitation once enter the Church, and where is its dignity? Without dignity, what would the Church be? Like a fortress without guns! How nicely, orderly, and respectably everything went on in their church before this new agitation came up! And *since* then, what has been the story? Agitation—agitation—agitation! Old members and pew-renters disturbed, agitated, and rendered, for a time, half-insane—strangers flocking in, in hundreds, joining in the agitation, and then taking sides with the New People! And who *were* these strangers? Who would vouch for their honesty and respectability? *He* wouldn't! (Sensation.) Who *wanted* them? *He* didn't. (Loud, tempestuous, and heart-stirring applause, in which the reader is very respectfully requested to join, in case he or she should happen to be an Exclusive—if otherwise, don't take the trouble.) No, what he wanted, was a deliverance from all undue agitation in the Church; the exclusion of all strangers; and a return to the easy quiet of old times. (Deafening cheers.) If he couldn't have these, then it was time for him, and all who shared in his sentiments, to withdraw, at once, and forever, *from* the church, and leave it to the disturbers, the interlopers, and the undue agitators! If anybody wanted his pew, they could have it—right away!"

Twenty of the interlopers stepped up at once, and eagerly requested the privilege of taking it off his hands.

The ex-army officer surveyed them silently, and—bit his lip. Then, with the quiet remark, that "they couldn't have it!" he sat down—very indignant, and very red.

But—somehow or other—how singularly things *will* happen sometimes!—the ex-army officer, turned traitor to his party! He, coolly, openly, and deliberately, went over, on the following Sabbath, to the ranks of the enemy—the New People, who received him very warmly, and thanked him very kindly, for coming up to the help of their Prince. The Exclusives could hardly credit their eyes, when they saw the old gentleman, tottering, like a crushed, broken, trembling, weeping man, up the aisle, and falling on his knees at the altar, with the touching, abject air of one whose last hope was gone; his hands clasped in agony, and hot tears falling from his sweltering lids in a perfect gush. They would never have believed it of him—never!

And yet the brave old soldier was there, with near a score of others, calling, in piteous tones, for help and mercy at the hands of The Ever Kind!

Oh, what a thrill of joy darted through the frames of the New People at the sight!

And how virtuously indignant were the Exclusives as they looked upon the hoary traitor! Oh! how they would have liked to tell him their opinion of his base desertion!

From that hour the Church of Society—the Exclusives—had no deadlier or more unsparing foe. He would walk right in among them, and carry off a willing prisoner in each hand. He would treacherously call upon them individually at their houses, and capture them in that way. When he failed in all of his own manœuvres, he would drop a line, secretly, to Mr. Engold, and make him an accomplice in his nefarious work: the lines running in the following laconic style:—

"MY DEAR PASTOR—Fire a red-hot shot, next Sabbath morning, from 1st James, 22d verse. A certain man in the ranks of the enemy requires raking; and a red-hot shot from that gun will demolish him.

"Yours, affectionately,

WM. WELLS."

So that, instead of taming down his proud, military spirit, his acquaintance with his Prince reawakened the old soldier, and imbued him with all his ancient fire. In less than a year after he had become one of the New People, the veteran, to use his own expression, "had, with the help of JEHOVAH, made such a breach in the ranks of the enemy, that they scarcely knew whether to strike their flag, or fly!" Some chose the first, others the second alternative; but in the end, the Exclusives disappeared: or, if they remained, they were very careful not to show their colors. Among those who held out to the last, and then threw down their arms and asked for quarter, were Mr. Eastlake and Mr. Benedick; both of whom, as the gallant old soldier expressed it, "were struck down by a red-hot shot from Hebrews—thirteenth chapter and second verse!"

And now, let us go back to our narrative, with the confidential understanding that the incidents in the next chapter took place some two weeks after the commencement of the revival.

CHAPTER XXIV.

The twentieth of December was a great day in the great house of John P. Townsend. The store, book-keeping, and packing departments were in a ferment of mingled pride and joyful enthusiasm. All this was brought about by a simple incident: *the return home of the silent partner*. His wanderings were over. His health was completely restored. He was in high spirits. He looked tip-top, and his appearance was hailed throughout the establishment with stirring gladness. He had been around to, and shaken hands with, everybody in the house. He had imparted his own happy feelings to everybody in the house. He had expressed the heartiest satisfaction with the business and individual conduct of everybody in the house. He had declared that he appreciated what everybody in the house had done for the house. He had backed this up by stating that when New Year's came he should remember everybody in the house. And he had also told everybody that he had now concluded to stay at home, and help all hands in pushing forward the interests of the house. And great was the glee at all this of everybody in the house: for the silent partner had ever been the most popular of the firm with everybody in the house. Therefore, although laboring under the pressure of a heavy flow of business, and although everybody in the house had just as much to do as they *could* do, the twentieth of December was, to everybody in the house, like a great gala-day. Everybody was smiling at everybody, all day long; everybody was in great spirits, all day long; everybody was shaking hands with everybody, almost all day long; and that house was the happiest house in all down-town, all day long.

And when night came, everybody went home to tea, in the very highest state of satisfaction with themselves and everybody else in the world—apparently.

There was *one* gentleman, however, who was not in such *very* great glee, after all—Mr. Brigham. He *didn't* like the silent partner's permanent return; because he knew that Mr. Crittenden had concluded upon this step from a conviction that the new movement, had rendered further "travelling" wholly unnecessary. He knew, also, that he was himself somewhat *less* than a favorite with that gentleman, and there was no telling where his lack of favor in that quarter might terminate. He didn't like Samuel's position in the silent partner's mind, either; nor that young gentleman's position at a certain house in Fifteenth street; nor his position in the heart of a certain young lady who dwelt in that house; nor his position in the minds of the city and country trade; nor yet his position in the minds of his acquaintance generally—because, for a few of these reasons, Mr. Brigham was himself rapidly becoming a mere nobody; and because, for all of them put together, he felt that he would like to bite a certain young gentleman in some way that would give him a great deal of real *piercing* PAIN.

These were, doubtless, the grounds of the remark which the confidential clerk permitted to glide through his teeth, while on his way from the store to his boarding-house:—

"I have laid the train: why should I hesitate to fire it? A flash, a smoke, a crash, and—ruin, out of which, if he can come whole again, let him!"

It was to be a great night at the Townsends'. There was to be a party there—that is to say, a few knowing people were going to amuse themselves at the expense of a few other people whom they believed to be everything but knowing—although the latter were, in their own estimation, very knowing people, indeed.

And so one of the knowing ones—that is to say, one who innocently flattered himself that what he did *not* know, was not worth knowing—was refreshing his mind with a string of compliments, which he had been a whole week in preparing, for his guests. These little things would serve a double purpose: to flatter the mental weaklings for whom they were designed, and to glorify, in a small way, the little mind that uttered them—that is, add to his previous reputation for affability, generosity, wit, and urbanity.

Mrs. Townsend, whose chief error lay in a superabundance of talent, was impressing upon herself the propriety of guarding herself from all *unnecessary* observations: a great idea, of which only few comprehend the value of. "For," mused Mrs. Townsend, "the great art of life is, not to talk one's self, but to make others talk; if they utter pearls, they are thenceforth yours, as well as theirs; if they utter trash, you know at once the measure of their minds—a valuable knowledge *sometimes*. While, if you are silent, no one can sound *your* mind. I have found that it is sometimes an advantage to not let others know the measure of *my* mind!"

The lady was right. Not to know how to talk, but how to be silent—or rather, how to preserve one's self *from* talking in the *wrong* place, is a study worth cultivating.

Isabella was, with the assistance of her maid, preparing for a regular massacre.

"How many conquests do you count upon to-night, miss?" asked the girl, who found that a little flattery, now and then, helped her wardrobe.

"Have done with your nonsense, do!" answered her young mistress, with everything else but a frown.

"You'll make twenty—I'm sure of that, at least!" pursued the attendant. "For you never looked so brilliant before in all your life. You are perfectly irresistible!"

"Nonsense! You are quizzing me. And you know I detest quizzing."

"I don't mean anything of the kind, miss. I know my place better than that! But this I will say: if you don't break some hearts to-night, then it will be because there are none *to* break!"

"Pshaw—nonsense! There's nothing very unusual in my appearance to-night."

"That may be your opinion, miss: but it isn't mine—I'm sure. Wait till you sail in among the company—that's all. There won't be any sensation—oh, no! The ladies won't bite their handkerchiefs for spite—oh, no! And if Samuel don't feel a fluttering under his waistcoat when he sees you—"

"Do stop your quizzing!" interrupted her mistress, surveying herself, with a well-pleased glance, in her toilet mirror. "'And that reminds me,' as guardy says, that I shan't want that dress which I wore to-day, any more!"

"I'm very much obliged to you, miss. You are so good! Dear me! how splendid you do look! How I *should* like to be in the drawing-room when you sail in!"

Poor Miriam was considering how she could contrive, during the evening, to avoid observation.

She thought that she would put herself under the protection of Mr. Crittenden, who understood her. In case that gentleman should be otherwise taken up, she had hope in her aunt; failing in the latter, she would do what she could for herself.

"Perhaps," she murmured, in conclusion, "perhaps Fanny Adriance, may not be *wholly* monopolized by her intended, and will kindly give me a part of her attention!"

In the meanwhile, Miriam, who was never much given to display, was arraying herself in a dark purple dress, which was just showy enough to evince her willingness to step a little out of her usual plainness, for the sake of pleasing her friends, and yet sufficiently modest not to do violence to her own simple taste.

Mr. Crittenden was felicitating himself, in advance, upon the enjoyment which he should derive from his portrait gallery, the pitiful figure that each of them would make in the presence of his sterling favorite, and seriously resolving that this should be the last time he would attempt to amuse himself over the weaknesses of his fellow-creatures.

Samuel, who knew nothing of Mr. Crittenden's anticipations from the *converzatione*, and still less of the part which that gentleman expected *him* to play in it, had given but little thought to the subject. He fancied that he had been invited simply out of courtesy, and that whether he was present or not would be of but very little consequence. Still, as he had not declined the invitation, and as that might possibly be viewed by his friends in the light of an acceptance, he concluded that he would look in upon the party some time in the course of the evening, and make his escape at the earliest excusable moment. With these reflections, he stopped, on his way home, at the laundress's, partly to pay his respects to Mrs. Farley herself, but mainly to see his little friend, Bob, who had been for some weeks in a state of decline.

Samuel found the laundress ironing, and little Bob sitting up, on a low chair before the stove, watching with his large, brown, thoughtful eyes, the bright shining coals, and dreamily shaping them into a thousand fanciful figures. The poor boy was reduced to a mere shadow; and the glare which was thrown from the stove upon his wasted frame, gave a painful prominence to the hunch in his shoulders, which rose almost on a level with the top of his large but beautifully formed head.

It was about seven o'clock, and the kettle was singing on the stove.

"I hear some one on the stairs!" observed the laundress.

"It's Samuel," said Bob, listening. "I know his step."

A moment later, and the young man was shaking hands with the laundress and little Bob.

"How are we to-night?" asked Samuel, taking the lad on his knee, and stroking his dark locks with tender playfulness.

"Pretty well," answered Bob, in a clear but feeble voice.

"Have we been a good boy?"

"*Pretty* good," said Bob. "Haven't I, ma'?"

"Very good!" replied the latter, taking a fresh iron from the stove, and giving her boy a cheering smile.

"That's a dear little heart!" cried Samuel, patting him affectionately on the cheek. "I've brought him a pretty little book, which is ever so full of pictures, and a nice little pair of gloves, which will keep his little hands ever so warm, and a little coat to go to church in when he gets well, and a funny little dancing-jack, which will make him laugh ever so much—and all for his Christmas. See!" and breaking open a small bundle, he held up the articles of which he had spoken. "And now what is Bob going to give Samuel for *his* Christmas—hey?"

"Dear—dear!" cried the laundress, "aint they nice?"

The child surveyed the things for a few moments with silent but chastened delight. Then putting his little thin arms around the young man's neck, he hugged him with a tight, emotional grasp, and uttered a low sob.

The laundress started, and asked soothingly: "What is it, darling?"

"Tell Samuel what the matter is?" said the young man, who could feel the heart of the child throbbing violently against his own. "Bobby will tell Samuel what the matter is—won't he?"

"Bobby will never wear his new coat!" replied the child. "Bobby is going away—to Jesus—up in heaven!"

The laundress and Samuel exchanged a sad glance. The former turned pale; a feeling of faintness crept over her, and staggering to a chair, she veiled her face silently with her apron.

"What makes Bobby think so?" asked Samuel.

"*I* know!" said the child, shaking his head.

"And won't he tell his Samuel?"

"Samuel knows, too, and so does ma', and aunty, and Bill!"

"Aunty" was Mrs. Osborn, and "Bill" her adopted son, who, ever since his recovery, had become a very frequent visitor at the laundress's.

"Are you sure, Bob?"

"Very sure," answered the child.

"But you are not afraid to go to Jesus—are you, Bob?"

"No; but I'm sorry. I don't want to go alone. If you and ma', and aunty, and Bill, would go with me, I'd like it very much. It would be so pleasant!

"Ah! well, Bob, we'll come by-and-bye."

"By-and-bye? When?"

"In a few years. Perhaps in a few months. Who can tell?"

"Why can't you all go when I do? The Lord will let you in—won't He?"

"O yes. But we must wait until He calls us. He calls those first whom He loves the most."

"Does He? And is that the reason why He calls me first?"

"I presume so," said Samuel, with a cheerful smile. "But it's a great thing to be called to Him *early*. You ought to be very grateful for His kindness?"

"I guess I ought—and I *am*, too," said Bob.

"Because," said Samuel, "when He takes you Up There so early, He saves you from twenty, thirty, perhaps fifty years of trial, suffering, and sorrow."

"Yes, and from the bad boys who hit me and call me names," said Bob. "Dear, dear—*aint* He good?"

"Very. Don't you love Him?"

"I guess I *do!*"

"And you won't be sorry any more?"

"No; but still I'd like to have you and ma', and Bill, and aunty, go Up There, too!"

"Oh, we'll come, in time!"

"Right away?"

"No; one of these days."

"All together?"

"No; one after another. But by-and-bye, we'll all be there. And then we shall never be separated again."

"Never—never at all?"

"Never. We'll live together among the angels; and we'll see God, and Jesus, and all the angels, every day, and be happy all day long, forever."

"And father, too?"

"And father, too."

"Dear, dear—won't *that* be nice!"

"Very nice, Bob. And so you won't be afraid or sorry any more—will you?"

"I guess I *won't.* I'll be *ever* so happy and brave."

"And when you come to go, you'll be joyful—won't you?"

"I guess I *will.*"

"Because," said his friend, "we ought to be *very* glad when we are going up to see God and Jesus."

"So we *ought!* And when I get Up There, I'll ask God to let you all come up, too—right away!"

"You are a dear good boy!"

And in this strain the child-boy and the child-man talked on for an hour or more, by which time little Bob fell asleep in the arms of his gentle friend, who then yielded him to his parent, who quietly bore him to the inner chamber and put him, with a soft kiss, to bed.

"You must keep your heart up, dear madam," said Samuel, with a cheering smile, as the laundress, pale and agitated, returned to her ironing. "Let this console you: Your flower, when once the petals of his spirit close up here forever, will blossom again, eternally, and brighter and more beautiful than ever, in the Better Garden! Weep not—rejoice, rather; thanking Him, for

His great goodness in taking to His bosom your darling, whose gentle spirit is wholly unfitted for a rough, stormy world like this, where rude hearts are many, and kind ones but few!"

He had touched the right chord; and the sorrow in the poor mother's eye was succeeded by a smile.

"He will pass away gently," continued Samuel. "Like the breath of the night before the light of the morning; and the light of *his* new morning will be that of the Happy Land. Take comfort from that!"

After an hour of pleasant converse, the young man took his departure, leaving the laundress happier than he had found her—yea, even cheerful in her resignation to the Divine will.

It was half after ten o'clock when Samuel reached home. Upon entering the drawing-room—which was a-blaze with light, beauty, wit, and talent—he was greeted by Isabella, who broke off an interesting discussion with an eminent legal gentleman, upon the rights of the people to defend themselves at the bar, and rushing forward, exclaimed, as she playfully secured the new-comer by the collar—

"So, Mr. Truant! we have got you at last, have we? Come up here, sir, and make your peace with this gentleman, who has been wondering all the evening at your absence!"

And she led the blushing loiterer towards the left corner of the apartment, where Mr. Crittenden was holding a sort of little court of ladies and gentlemen, whom he was charming with a witty account of a fanciful new continent, which had recently been discovered by a fanciful navigator, while making a fanciful voyage of discovery around the world.

"So, sir," said Mr. Crittenden, pressing him warmly by the hand, "we had begun to fear that you had forgotten us; but now that we have got you, we shall do with you as Her Majesty of Spain does with the Isle of Cuba."

"How is that?" asked Isabella.

"Cherish him as the apple of our eye, and—hold on to him! And now, ladies and gentlemen, permit me a few words with our dear friend here, who is, we doubt not, very anxious to propitiate us for his prolonged absence."

"But you forget, naughty man," said Mrs. Townsend, playfully, "that we are all dying to hear whether the navigator ever married the handsome widowed queen of the new continent."

"Well, upon my word! I can't say positively," returned the narrator; "but I have a sort of an indefinite idea that he did; that he became king, that he lived to a good old age, and that he then died, and immediately, like all of the inhabitants of that delightful country, came to life again quite a handsome young man, and his queen quite a likely young woman; and that they both lived on happily to another ripe old age, and then died again, and then came to life once more, younger, handsomer, and happier than ever, and then went on together to another old age, in which condition they were at last accounts, which stated that they were in daily expectation of again dying and again turning up young, and beautiful, and rich, and loving, as before. There! if that isn't giving the lovers good measure, I don't know what is!"

"I say," cried a spruce old bachelor of sixty, who had been favoring a spruce old single lady of sixty-five, with ringlets like those of a young boarding-school miss, with his private opinion of the disastrous effects of salt, and stating it as his belief that that article had a tendency, in time, to ossify the human system, "a great country that! Have you any idea when the next steamer starts for it?"

"Yes, Mr. Jessup; as soon as the next one comes in!"

The laugh that followed this gay rejoinder informed the spruce old bachelor that he hadn't got *very* far ahead of the witty narrator of the wonderful continent, and he quietly resumed his impressions upon the salt question.

In the opposite corner, near the window, Charley Gibbs was

explaining to Miriam and Fanny Adriance—the latter a young lady of twenty, rather *petite* in feature and figure, and remarkable as much for the mildness of her manner as for the goodness of her heart, which latter was unalterable in its affection for Charley—how near he was towards "bringing obstinate old guardy to terms,"—how soon he expected to come into possession of his money, and how his lawyer had told him that a few hundred dollars more would settle the old gentleman's hash so completely that, figuratively speaking, he wouldn't have the first fraction of a leg to stand upon.

On Miriam's right sat Mrs. Townsend, discussing the merits of modern literature with a gentleman, who—but let us listen to Mr. Crittenden, who is now opening his gallery of living portraits to his young friends.

"That individual who is conversing with Mrs. Townsend is a Mr. Sly, of the great publishing firm of Sly & Slocum—a house which has been remarkably successful in flooding the country with books and pamphlets which corrupt, demoralize, and destroy every mind that is unfortunate enough to come in contact with them."

Samuel shuddered.

"A dirty dog!" he observed, surveying the head of the great publishing house with an air of mingled uneasiness and disgust.

"Oh! my dear boy, you mustn't say *that!* Why, sir—Mr. Sly is a *respectable* man—has a pew in the church; is sometimes *affected* by the sermon; is regarded as one of our good citizens; is admitted into society; is taken by the hand by very worthy people; never feels ashamed when he surveys himself in his mirror; lays down at night without trembling; wakes up in the morning without creeping; looks his wife and children in the face without blushing; eats his food without fear of choking; walks down to his business as if he were a decent man; and sends out, every week, from five to fifty thousand books and pamphlets, every one of which effectually uproots the last vestige of virtue, purity, and morality, from the hearts of from five to fifty thousand persons. But what then? What is the moral destruction of from five to fifty thousand hearts per week—a small army of ruined souls per year, eh?—to Messrs. Sly & Slocum, so long as Sly & Slocum make money by the operation—eh? Why, sir, Messrs. Sly & Slocum—their one house alone—do more, in a single year, towards manufacturing candidates for brothels, gambling hells, rummeries, race-courses, and ring-fights—filling our penitentiaries and state prisons, and hurling destroyed souls into the Everlasting Gulf, than you could count in the same period, providing you should count sixty a minute and work ten hours per day. This one house alone neutralizes and undoes, in a single week, the Sabbath labors of a thousand faithful clergymen. This one house alone creates more work for our Bible, Tract, and Home Missionary Societies, than the natural sinful propensities of a half million of people. This one house alone cuts out more labor, in six days, for our courts of justice—makes more thieves, pickpockets, housebreakers, and general felons—breaks up the honor, peace, and concord of more families—familiarizes more young men and women with the frightfullest of all sentiments—and drives more half-witted creatures into the broad gulf of vice and crime, than the entire pulpit could retrieve in a year! Now, sir, I ask you—as a thinking, reasoning being—how the soldiers of the Cross can *expect* to accomplish much permanent good, while houses like Sly & Slocum's are permitted to exist! The souls that *they* draw near to heaven on the Sabbath, Sly & Slocum drag down again, during the week. Sly & Slocum, alone, by simply publishing a single filthy book—which their extensive business facilities enable them to scatter in copious showers over the length and breadth of the land—can sit behind their desks, and put to rout a whole army of Christ's warriors. And what is more—they *do* it, sir—do it, every week in the year!"

A sensation of sickness crept over his auditor, who became pale, faint, and nervous.

"You are ill?" said Mr. Crittenden, anxiously.

"I'll be better in a moment, sir. You make me shudder with your dreadful pictures!"

"Shall I soften them for you, my friend?"

"No; but let me think a moment. You oppress, bewilder, terrify me. Come with me a moment up stairs, to my room."

"For what?"

"I want to pray to my Prince for these two miserable men—for Sly & Slocum!"

"My dear friend—you are in error. Sly & Slocum, and all of their kind, are *past* praying for! Why, sir—they are not even human! Wretches whose daily bread is obtained, by destroying souls at the rate of from five to fifty thousand per week! Why, you must be mad to think it!"

"Oh, no, Mr. Crittenden—it is *they* who are mad, *you* who are in error. *All* men are human, however *in*human they may act. Let us appeal *to* them, and *for* them, as if they had never done an inhuman thing in their lives, and then the human part of them will come out. Humanity will stand up at the call of Humanity. And therefore I will pray for these men before I go to bed, as if they were human, and not as if they were mad beasts. And Our Prince, who is very kind, very generous, and very merciful, will plead kindly for them to His Father, who will touch them with His mercy, and stir them out from this mad, horrid work!"

"Ah!" said Mr. Crittenden, shaking his head, and smiling at the young man's simple earnestness, "you don't know these men!"

"But I *do* know the goodness of my Prince, and the Power of my God!" replied Samuel. "Come, dear friend—let us, who see their dreadful course, make an effort for these two men, who cannot see their own madness."

"What can we do?" asked Mr. Crittenden, smiling, in spite of himself, at the young man's simplicity and faith.

"Many things," replied Samuel. "Let us pray for them—that must be the first step. Then let us call on these men, and tell them of the exceeding wrongfulness of their course—asking our Redeemer, on the way, to come up to our assistance in the effort. Then I will find out their pastors, lay the case before them, and invite them to make a special effort for them in their next sermons. Then we must assist the pastors by our prayers—Our Prince will assist us all—and Our Father will send down His Holy Spirit to visit Sly & Slocum, and knock stirringly at their hearts. Then these men will see the monstrous wickedness of their business—then they will give it up—then from five to fifty thousand souls, per week, will be unvisited by their insidious books and pamphlets—then the work of wickedness will be, in a measure, stopped—then the good books which are published by good houses will be widelier read—then the wholesomeness of *their* better sentiments will take an easier and firmer hold upon the public mind—then the labors of our Prince's warriors will not be in vain—then hearts that have wandered from their Father will return—then hearts that have never known Him will come up—then men will be saved, and our King and Prince be glorified!"

"Ah, Samuel," smiled Mr. Crittenden, "your enthusiasm runs away with you!"

"No, my friend, it is your want of *faith* that runs away with *you!* 'Enthusiasm?' Know you not that all things are possible to HIM, and to His people, when they work with faith *in* Him!"

Mr. Crittenden pondered a moment. He remembered the great change in the business in his own house—the packing-room society—the vast good accomplished by its members—the great revival in the church of Mr. Engold, who, like Samuel, was an enthusiast in faith—and the amazing spiritual results which followed in the wake of this young Christian wherever he went, and whatever he undertook to perform, and he replied—

"You are right. I take back my observation. Faith is equal to anything, however difficult."

"Because," added Samuel, "the power of Him in whom we *have* faith is greater than that of all the universe—let alone that of one or two of its smallest atoms."

"But you overlook one thing," said Mr. Crittenden. "Sly & Slocum, although the principal, are not the only wretches engaged in this frightful business."

"No?" said the young Christian, mournfully.

"No. There are a score of them."

"What! Twenty houses engaged in sending out weekly from five to fifty thousand messengers to corrupt the hearts of the people?"

"Even so many."

The young Christian was shocked. As before, a sickening sensation crept over and unnerved him.

"What wonder that society is false, rotten, double-minded, and corrupt?" he exclaimed, mournfully. "What wonder that our Redeemer's soldiers grow weary and disheartened—with all these insidious serpents working against them, and neutralizing the effects of their labors!"

"You despair, then?" said Mr. Crittenden.

"Despair? No! Were there a million, the great power of THE KING would be greater than the million! How much for hope, then, have we, when the sources of this vast evil are only a paltry score! Come, we must give our energies to this work. These channels of corruption must be dried up. This vast under-current of corruption must be arrested."

"How?"

"By the might of Jehovah! There is no other way. We must

take hold of each house separately; call on Our PRINCE for aid, on The KING for mercy, and *at it!*"

"When?"

"Right away! For HIS service, no time like the present!"

"Wait a moment," said Mr. Crittenden, catching the young man's enthusiasm. "Give me two weeks, in which to arrange some private matters, which have been neglected by my long absence, and I'll enter with you, heart and hand, in this great work. In the meanwhile, we can be gathering a list of these firms, learning the names of their pastors, and laying our plans for the campaign!"

"Agreed, sir!" cried Samuel, warmly pressing his hand. "O, my dear friend," he added, "you do not know the joy—the *exceeding* great joy—in campaigning for THE LORD. All other pleasure is as nothing to it—all other joy is but barrenness to it—all other enthusiasm is as dullness before it!"

"Enough, Samuel," said Mr. Crittenden, returning the pressure with equal warmth, "we understand each other!"

"Ah! sir, you make me very happy!"

"'Tis well," said Mr. Crittenden, in a disturbed voice. "And now, let's see the miserable rubbish with which Messrs. Sly and Slocum are doing such service for Satan." Then directing his voice at the publisher, he said, in a tone which could not fail to arrest general attention, "Excuse me, Mr. Sly, for interrupting your discourse with my fair friend, but I have been mentioning to this gentleman, who was ignorant of it before, the vast business resources of your house, and the extraordinary sales which you effect upon your publications. Will you be kind enough to give us some of the names of your most popular works?"

All eyes were immediately fixed upon the representative of the great house of Sly & Slocum.

"With great pleasure, sir," answered that worthy—a short, slender-bodied gentleman, with broad shoulders, a low neck, a very high-pointed collar, a flaming neck-cloth, a long face liberally bespattered with tell-tale blossoms, deep-set eyes of a grayish blue, square, heavily projecting brows, and a low, flat, slanting forehead, with light hair pomatumed into dark, and falling around the cheeks and back in an equal length. "With great pleasure, sir," he repeated, with a gracious wave of his gloved hand. "The chief publications of our house are, 'The Deserted Chambermaid,' 'The Dashing Exploits of Illustrious Highwaymen,' 'The Illustrious Pugilists; or, the Bruising Boys of Young America,' 'The Lives and Adventures of Illustrious Freebooters,' 'Lucy the Hard 'Un; or, the Marvellous Exploits of a Female Highwayman,' 'Tom Briggs, the Black Rover of the Ocean Main,' 'Owley Bill; or, the Fearless Burglar,' 'Daring Sarah, the G'hal of the Red, Red Locks,' 'Sam Swipes, the Heroic House Thief,' 'The Beautiful Cigar-Seller; or, the Handsome Libertine,' and 'Betty Williams, the Orphan Girl; or, the Key to Easy Crime.'"

"A rare selection, sir!" observed Mr. Crittenden.

"Well, yes!" said Mr. Sly, with the air of a man who was a capital judge. "Pretty fair! We understand these matters, a little, at *our* house!"

"So I perceive, sir! Are you a married man, Mr. Sly?"

"I believe so," answered Mr. Sly, who could not see the sarcasm in the question.

"A father, too?"

"I think so," answered Mr. Sly, wondering what connection could exist between his being a husband and father and a member of the great publishing firm of Sly & Slocum. "Two children, Mr. Crittenden."

"Ah! indeed? What do you propose to make of them? Publishers?"

"If they should live; which I presume they will, for the Slys are a healthy stock."

"Very healthy, indeed!" remarked Mr. Crittenden. "Will you bring them up in *your own* house?" he added, quietly.

"That is my design," replied the publisher. "Our house is generally regarded by the trade as a pretty good school!"

"No doubt, Mr. Sly—no doubt! In fact, of its *kind*, it may be almost said to be unrivalled!" observed Mr. Crittenden.

"Our *competitors* think so!" ventured Mr. Sly, with modest wittiness.

"And they think very justly, no doubt. That is all, Mr. Sly!"

The publisher bowed as graciously as before, and resumed his conversation with Mrs. Townsend, perfectly unconscious of the loathing with which he was regarded by all in the apartment.

"So," said Mr. Crittenden to Samuel, "you see that there is work before us. That individual, as you perceive, is so hardened in vice, that he cannot see even the *infamy* of his business! What can religion do for such a man?"

"Reform him!" said Samuel.

"But only think of the depravity of the creature's heart! He sees no shame even in *proposing* to bring up his sons to the same beastly business!"

"God's power is greater than this man's depravity."

"Let us hope so."

"I know so," said Samuel.

"So be it. But now let me call your attention to that slender gentleman who is engaged with Mr. Townsend. He, too, is a great man in his way, and remarkable for having achieved an immense fortune in three short years."

"In what way?"

"Fancy banking. He started, one after another, three separate banks, which failed, one after another, without redeeming a solitary bill, leaving the note-holders absolutely minus, and himself so poor that he didn't know, for a time, what to do—with his money!"

"And is this man received in society?"

"Certainly; and in the church, too: and he is a very exemplary member, I assure you!"

"Pray, don't talk so," said Samuel. "It pains me. You ought always to remember that there are two churches—Christ's and Society's; and when you say of a known knave, 'He is a member of the Church,' please add, 'not of Christ's, but Society's.' In this way, our Redeemer's people are saved from undeserved reproach, and society receives due credit for its own. Who is that gentleman on the left of the banker?"

"That, sir, is a Mr. Morehead; a remarkable specimen of industrious littleness. He can tell you to a hair how many letters there are in the Bible; how many seams in a coat; how many pairs of pantaloons are probably made up throughout the world in a year; how many cigars are smoked, how many whiffs taken from them all, the aggregate of the ashes made by them, the number of farms which the cigars would have bought, the number of clouds which the smoke would naturally form, and the number of acres which the ashes would cover; the number of hats which each man wears in a lifetime, the number which have been made since the deluge, and the number which will probably be made between this and the end of the world."

"But of what service is all this waste of thought and calculation?"

"To help show to what absurd littleness minds will bend themselves when endowed with noble faculties. The principal enjoyment which this man finds at church is in counting the number of attendants; the number of frock and the number of dress coats; the number of hats with a certain kind of feather, and the number with a certain kind of trimming; how many wore silks, how many satins, and how many ginghams; how many were over, and how many under, a certain age; how many had silk, how many yellow, how many white, and how many green, purple, or black kids; how many sentences, words, and letters were in the prayer, how many in each hymn, and how many in the sermon. Ask him what is the principal business of life, and he will answer, To make statistics. When he goes home, his first movement will be to figure out the probable number of subjects that were discussed here to-night, the number of sentences and words spoken, the number of letters in all, and the comparative amount of nitrogen and oxygen consumed in their utterance."

"How absurd! Why can he not be induced to devote a fraction of this vast labor to some useful purpose?"

"Because his mind can only comprehend little things. And yet the simpleton innocently fancies himself gifted with comprehensive views! Should you fail to answer promptly his question of How many tobacco quids are used up and fired away throughout the world in a single year, or, How many breaths are drawn by a man in a lifetime of sixty years, he would triumphantly set you down for an ignoramus without a particle of intelligence! His companion is the celebrated Mr. Ruffin."

"Celebrated? For what?"

"'Ruffin's ale!' What? Never heard of *it*, or *him?* Why, man—you are behind the age! Ruffin's ale—a rival to Barclay and Perkins of England—poisons, swills up, and sends to death, one hundred thousand men per annum. It is strongly recommended by nearly all of our best physicians, because it—*helps* THEIR *business!* They endorse wines, and gin, and French brandies from the same *worthy* motive. Nay, my dear boy! you must get rid of that habit of shuddering, when you hear of these things—it is very impolitic and impolite, believe me! Why, sir, Mr. Ruffin is a rich man, a respectable member of society, and a member also, in good standing, of the church of —— society. You see I improve upon your suggestions!"

"That gentleman on Mr. Ruffin's left?"

"Is a Mr. Snillwick—a remarkable man; a perfect study. We call him the Straw Watcher."

"Why so?"

"He is a successful politician; always in office. Has been three times in Congress; five times in the Legislature, twice in the Mayoralty, and four times in the Common Council, of which he is now a member."

"Whig or Democrat?"

"Neither. He is simply a Straw Watcher. He started in his political career as a Democrat. A brief season, and the democratic stock declined: whigism mounting in its place. He watched the straws, changed in time to rise with the new tide, and when whigism rose, Mr. Snillwick was a brave and active Whig. A few years, and the political wheel took another turn; then Nativism was up—and so was Mr. Snillwick, elected by a large majority. By-and-bye, the old parties united to rout the Natives. Mr. Snillwick watched the straws in time, met the changes as they came, moved gradually and noiselessly, and when the Democratic Whigs turned in their elected candidates, Mr. S. was among them, smiling and rosy as ever. By-and-bye, the political current veered in the Democratic direction; the wires were pulled to arouse the masses; rum, circulars, flaming handbills and tickets were freely distributed; Irish, Dutch, and Germans were invited to rouse up like men and strike a gallant blow at the polls for their fatherlands and freedom; the native-born were appealed to, in stirring tones, to stand up for the land for which their sires fought and bled, and the Democratic nominees were elected with enthusiastic acclaim — Mr. Snillwick coming in some thousands ahead of the general ticket! And so on, throughout all the political changes of thirty years, Mr. S. has been true to his one great principle of—watching the straws! Hence, he is ever on the winning side. This would be a fine lesson for you, my boy, if you were one of the great herd who bend all principles into the principle of Number One; but as, fortunately for yourself, you are not—the lesson will be lost upon you. For the great secret of success in the world, whether in politics or whatever business, lies in Mr. Snillwick's motto: To watch and follow the straws!"

"And society, knowing this man's want of principle, is willing to receive him?"

"Certainly, and with open arms; and the Church also—that is to say, Society's!"

Samuel looked down, mournfully.

"Society," continued Mr. Crittenden, "is so much accustomed to knavery, faithlessness, and utter selfishness in politicians, that they now look for these things in them as a legitimate matter of course. The chief business of a man in office is, not to keep his oath, but to break it, a hundred times a day, if need be; not to study the people's interest, but—his own. And if, after leaving office, he leaves it poor, society looks upon him with mingled pity and contempt. 'What!' it exclaims, 'not fill his pockets—not plunder the people's treasury while he had a chance! He is *soft!*' And then society sneers at him, turns its back upon him, and brands him for a fool! 'The business of a politician,' says soeiety, 'is to do his duty, his whole duty, and nothing but his duty; and his duty, his whole duty, and nothing but his duty, is—to rob!' When he fails to do *that*, society declares that he has *not* done his duty, and drawing itself up, with virtuous indignation—*cuts* him!"

"I do not believe this," said Samuel, looking up.

"Why not?" asked Mr. Crittenden.

"It does not tally with my observations," replied the young Christian. "Let us look at it once. You are yourself one of society. Now, sir, would *you* cut the society of a man who was noble enough to resist temptation!"

"Of course not."

"You would honor him, rather?"

"Certainly."

"Well, you represent a very large body of society; and that is the only body whose opinions are of weight, and whose countenance is an honor to the recipient—because the individuals composing it are themselves noble, honorable, and good. As, in the Church, there are two kinds of Christians—Christ's and Society's; so in society there are two bodies of sociates—the thoughtful, dignified, and influential, who examine everything by the light of principle; and the unthoughtful, undignified, and uninfluential, who examine nothing, and care only for money, show, and frivolity. But the latter, although they may be the larger body of the two, are not Society itself, any more than Society's Christians are The Church. Therefore, if it be a slander upon the people of our Prince to say of a bad man, 'He is a member of The Church,' because he has a pew or is found at the communion-table in one of God's temples—so is it equally a slander upon society to call these latter of society because *they* call themselves so, or because they are sometimes found in it."

"My dear boy," cried Mr. Crittenden, "you are—I don't know what! There is no getting along with you. You won't look at the world as it is, but as you wish it to be. You are always taking the better view!"

"Because," returned Samuel, "the *better* view is always the *most just!* The world is not so bad as you would represent it. It is wicked, I admit—very wicked, but it is willing to be better—*very* willing—if men will only speak to it kindly, and not sneeringly, and give it credit for *the good that it has.* It is *thoughtlessly*, not *wilfully*, bad. Speak to it as to a *brother*, and not as to an *enemy*, and its goodness will gush forth like a torrent, and amaze and enrapture you with its quantity and richness! It is true that now and then, one will rise whose heart is exceedingly difficult to reach; but patience and *continued* kindness will penetrate to it *in time.* So, all along The Pathway, the better view works the *happiest*, and *the best!*"

Perhaps so," said Mr. Crittenden.

"Nay, you will know it, once you take up arms in earnest, for Our Prince! You cannot conceive what a vast storehouse of new and comforting thoughts He kindly puts in the hearts of His people!"

Mr. Crittenden smiled at the young Christian's enthusiasm.

"Well," he said, "I'll not contradict it. And now, let me call your attention to that lively, mercurial gentleman who is amusing that small knot of ladies by the mantel."

"Who is he?"

"A witty gentleman; very witty—always cracking a joke at somebody or something. Is always very ready, very funny, and very cutting. Is into everything and everybody; a perfect battery of broad humor. Spares neither God nor man, religion nor society, and thinks the highest use to which he can turn his mind is to sting somebody in a way that will make the world laugh!"

"Of what benefit is such a man?" asked Samuel, with his usual simplicity.

"To keep society in a ferment and away from Thought. He helps the filthy publishers, the fraudulent bankers, the beer-makers, and the knavish politicians, to persuade men that there is nothing serious in life except humbug, bitterness, vice, and frivolity. He is never happy save when witty; and every joke stings some *one*, and makes a thousand or more roar. He flings a joke at a picture, and the unfortunate artist is from that moment miserable and unhappy—perhaps a ruined man. He throws a jest at a singer, who is thenceforth a nobody; at a clergyman, and the heart of a good man is pained, his friends grieved, and his influence for a time lost. But what then?—the witty man has amused himself, showed his contempt for one of Christ's workmen, and induced a thousand others to unwittingly abandon their respect for a sacred calling. In this way he helps, little by little, to lessen the world's confidence in everything high and good."

"He is a writer, then?"

"Yes--the editor of a witty paper, *The Jolly Sneerer*, which, with *The Satanic Chuckle*, and *The Felon's Hue and Cry*, are the chief organs of the Sin-King for corrupting the thoughtless of our Metropolis, and sweeping from their minds every vestige of respect for good men and good things. Take care—you are shuddering again!"

"You make my blood creep with your statements. Why don't some great good mind attempt to reform the editors and publishers of those journals?"

"Because it would be impossible."

"You forget that he would have GOD and CHRIST upon his side!"

"Well, well; I yield. You have such an original way of removing obstacles—a way so entirely new to me, that I cannot urge anything against it. Do you see that gentleman who is wiping the sweat from his forehead?"

"Certainly. Who is he?"

"Another great man—in his way. He is the notorious Mr. Lifferts. What, you never heard of *him?* My dear boy, where *have* you kept yourself! Not to know Mr. Lifferts is, as Shakspere says, 'to argue thyself unknown.' Mr. Lifferts keeps a vast palace where respectable promenaders can drop in and partake of a cup of tea, chocolate, or coffee, nicely intermixed with—brandy, gin, or whisky, according to their tastes. In this way, he, every year, gently prepares thousands upon thousands of our young women and young men to take their liquor *without* the friendly aid of coffee, chocolate, or tea! And in this way he contributes *his* share of victims to the general maelstrom. His saloon is the primary school where our young women and young men take their first lessons in rum-drinking. It is he who fits them for the regular bar-rooms and corner groceries. An important individual—eh?"

"Who is that gentlemen on his left?"

"Another contributor to the great cauldron: a *retired* bankrupt, who defrauded his creditors out of a round million, and now amuses himself by reading his favorite journal, *The Satanic Chuckle*, smiling over the ruin of those whom he rendered penniless, and in maintaining a splendid position in society and society's church—thereby convincing men that neither the Church nor society frown upon the conduct of great rascals: thus destroying their confidence in both."

"That gentleman who is talking with Isabella—"

"Is a hardware dealer, a member of society's Church, and is remarkable for never having uttered a pleasant word in his life. He is generally feared, and thoroughly disliked."

"For what?"

"His acrimonious spirit. He takes a special delight in displaying his venom, and uttering bitter sneers. He has a quick eye, and always looks at things in their most hideous light. His name is Griscom, but he is better known as 'the sarcastic gentleman.' He takes great pleasure in railing at those things which pure minds regard with reverence."

"That old gentleman who is conversing so snappishly with that old lady in ringlets?"

"Is a Mr. Jessup—a cotton-broker. He is a bosom friend of the sarcastic gentleman, and is generally known among his acquaintance as 'The Little Wasp.' He is very rich, and very bitter, and enjoys himself by stinging people."

"Who is that gentleman behind him?"

"A Mr. Whipple; a gentleman of leisure; who has nothing to do but to amuse himself, and finds that very hard work. His father left him three hundred thousand in cash and property, and—nothing else. He is without a mind, a hope, or an aim. He finds talking very hard work, and talks therefore only when compelled. He is very fond, however, of being looked at by the ladies most of whom think him handsome, because his fortune is. Observe, there are three young twenties and two twenty-fives struggling with each other to catch his attention. But their labor will amount to nothing. He is too indolent to feel an interest even in black eyes. Still he has been known this evening to make a remark."

"Indeed!"

"Yes, concerning our friend Miriam. He thinks 'she might suit him.'"

Samuel turned slightly pale.

"What do *you* think?" asked Mr. Crittenden, noticing the change in his features.

"I would rather see Miss Selden wedded to a worthier man," replied Samuel, growing paler than before.

"Bravo!" mused Mr. Crittenden. "I know the secret of *your* heart, my friend!" Then speaking aloud, he said—"One thing is certain: Miriam will not marry one who is *un*worthy of her. She is too good for that! By-the-way, her cousin shines out to-night. She is decidedly killing!"

"Miss Landon shows well in a drawing-room," returned Samuel, tranquilly.

"Good! Mirrry may laugh at the rivalry of her bold cousin. My darling is safe!" mused Mr. Crittenden.

"Pray, who is that gentleman with the moustache, who is conversing in the corner, there, with that middle-aged lady?"

"An important contributor to the social cauldron. That, sir, is one of the arrantest scoundrels that ever had the *entrée* of society."

"His business?"

"That of a professional libertine! My dear boy! what is the matter? You are shuddering again!"

"It is a weakness to which I am liable when in the presence of deliberate evil," replied Samuel, his mild, manly features overshadowed with an air of mingled pain and horror. "And is this bad man received in society, like the rest?"

"Certainly; and in society's church, too."

"One would think that even society's church would not countenance a beast," observed Samuel.

"Quite a mistake. Society's church will receive any one who has money."

"This man is rich, then?"

"He is rated at one hundred and fifty thousand, which he will come into possession of at the death of his father, who is marching rapidly to his grave with consumption."

"Is *he* a converted man?"

"He has been a member of society's church for twenty years, but was never very particular about other people's rights or feelings. When he dies, the everlasting gulf will be richer in its population by one great rascal."

"Can nothing be done to save him *before* he dies?" asked Samuel, naively. "Our Prince is very good, and His Father very kind, you know."

"I think not," replied Mr. Crittenden. "The old fellow is a proud, harsh, spiteful old codger, who never did a generous thing in his life. He has an idea that all the world was made for himself. He is cruel, selfish, and sordid, to the last degree. He regards religion as a capital thing to make money out of, and believes that it was projected by men, in the beginning, for no other purpose. He regards prayer and preaching as so much machinery to sustain an institution whose principal object is to keep the world in order. He has no belief in its divine origin. Future happiness and future punishment he regards as all fudge. He is not certain of it, but he inclines to that impression. And this, my dear boy! is the private belief of three-fourths of society's church. There—you are shuddering again!"

"You do not mean this!" said Samuel, uneasily.

"I do, most certainly."

"There is no foundation in the Bible for any such frightful doctrine."

"You forget that society's church never read the Bible, and care as little about what it teaches as they do for what becomes of their next-door neighbor."

"But why deceive themselves with so absurd a doctrine?"

"Because it is a very satisfactory one. They do not desire to change from their present way of doing. They find surface honesty, surface genuineness, surface piety, and humbugging each other, very pleasant, very amusing, and very gratifying. Hence, a doctrine which will favor or admit of their continuance in humbug, is very acceptable. This is the main reason why clergymen meet with so little success among our fashionables, who do not wish, and will not allow themselves to be converted. They want a doctrine which will permit them to do as they like; when they can't find it in the Word of God, they look for it in the word of society, and *there* they find it!"

"Dear friend, you draw frightful pictures!"

"Do you doubt their accuracy?"

"I cannot do otherwise."

"In that case, I must bring up a witness!' observed Mr. Crittenden, playfully. Then slightly elevating his voice, he said, "Mr. Griscom—one word!"

"With pleasure," answered that worthy. "What is it?"

"My friend, here, is anxious to know the materials of fashionable society. Will you, who understand the subject so well, be kind enough to enlighten him?"

"Fashionable society," said the sarcastic gentleman, "is made up, in its males, of men who have not yet failed; in its females, of women who still have credit at Stewart's, on account of the undiscovered insolvency of their husbands."

The tittering of the assembly told the speaker that he had made a hit.

"Anything more in my way?" he asked, patronizingly.

"Nothing just now, Mr. Griscom," answered Mr. Crittenden. "Thank you!" Then turning to Samuel, he said, "You see I am not very wide of the truth in my pictures!"

"Your witness is one who enjoys a fling at the poor prisoner at the bar!" returned Samuel, with a mournful smile. "Hence, his testimony is of but little account."

"My dear boy! you have the hopefullest of hearts."

"And why should not *you*, Mr. Crittenden? What good in *railing* at evils? Why not make an effort either to lessen, or to remove them altogether? Say you should see a child running wild on a Sabbath morning in the street? Would you find any satisfaction in scoffing at the carelessness or indifference of its parents? How much better, how much more gratifying, to take it by the hand, and lead gently it to some Sabbath school, where it would hear of good things, which might change the whole tenor of its thoughts, the whole tone of its future? I have never seen the beneficial effects of a sneer; but I *have* seen, and experienced, great joy in witnessing, the good results of *effort*. And therefore I am hopeful. Come, dear friend—let us not scoff at men's blindness or infirmities, but do something which will help them to see better and to get strong. They will thank us for *that;* but they would hate us for the sneer."

"Nay," said Mr. Crittenden, "they would neither thank you for your kindness, nor appreciate the nobleness of your motive."

"If *they* would not, HE would!"

"There you are again!" observed his companion, with a laugh. "What is the good of bringing up one's knowledge of the world before *you!* Why don't you give a poor fellow a chance?"

"You won't give *yourself* a chance! You always start from the wrong point. Take a Christian's, instead of a worldling's view of these things, and you will always come off with satisfaction to your inmost heart. But we have wandered away from the libertine."

"And fortunately. He completes my gallery of living portraits. I have called your attention to them, to show you what a dirty set of dogs are arrayed in society on the side of evil. These rascals, and the professions which they represent, are the leading contributors to the cauldron of social vice and error. These are the creatures who keep society in its present corrupt state. Were it not for a vicious literature, which undermines the morals of all classes; for little minds, who make great ado over the smallest and absurdest of human aims; for society's gross error in admitting known knaves into its circle; for the dirty dogs, who *manufacture* poisonous drinks; for the unprincipled beasts who, in their gorgeous saloons, educate the people up to easy drunkenness; for the base rascals who sell this poison in its naked form; for the mean witlings of the press, whose highest ambition is to sneer at Jehovah, and everything which bears a show of goodness; for the Satanic Chuckles which pander to and keep alive the lowest of all human ambitions, and the vilest of all human thoughts; for dishonest members of the Church, who destroy men's confidence in, and respect for, religion; for wealthy idleness, which leads wealthy thoughtlessness to believe that man's highest destiny is simply to amuse himself, and to cultivate selfishness; for society's blunder in not branding libertines as the worst of felons, or destroying them like other serpents, instead of admitting them into the drawing-room or the Church; for society's great error in not avoiding all scoffers at religion, honesty, or purity, as it would any common lunatic whose freedom and want of sense were dangerous to the common weal:—but for these, the world, aided by a noble pulpit, and a noble literature, would soon banish all minor evils, and right itself."

"Very true, sir," said Samuel. "And now that we know

where the fountains of all this mischief are, let us go to work and dry them up."

"*Us?*"

"Certainly. Let us at it, in the name of our King and Prince. With Them on our side, we shall be equal to a whole army!"

Mr. Crittenden looked with mingled amazement and admiration at the sublime confidence and marvellous faith of the young Christian. Then extending his hand, he said, with emotion—

"I am with you, henceforth, in your great enterprises. Command me, sir, as your lieutenant. From this hour I am a campaigner for Our Lord!"

"Oh, sir! you will find His service so very easy, sweet, and good! Oh, what great things we'll do together for His cause! You—you," he repeated, in a broken voice, "you make me *so* happy—happier than I can express!"

They shook hands, warmly.

"Hark!" said Mr. Crittenden, "the conversation is becoming general. We must take part in it. Who knows how a good word from us, to-night, may tell in the future for Our Prince!"

"The right spirit, sir!" said Samuel, joyfully.

"Hark! They are attacking Him now. The fight is begun—perhaps to try our zeal. Who knows? We must mingle in the fray. HIS service!"

"Wait a moment," said Samuel, gently. "Let's bide our time, till we can deal a telling blow."

"Agreed!"

"Life," said Mr. Sly, in answer to a query from Mr. Jessup, "is a small affair of fifty or sixty years."

"What do you think of it, Mr. Townsend?"

"Life," answered that gentleman, "is simply a bitter jest."

Mr. Crittenden pressed his companion's arm.

"You do not believe *that!*" said Samuel, stepping forward.

"No? Why not?"

"Simply because it is not true."

"Really, Mr. Leland," said the merchant, drawing himself up, "you are very complimentary!"

"Young men, with neither knowledge nor experience, are so *very* wise!" observed the cotton-broker. "Let's see," he added, looking around at the company to catch their attention and invite their admiration, "there's a glorious old proverb—'The young man is proud in his little wisdom and self-conceit!'"

"You have quoted the proverb well, sir," said Samuel, calmly. "But there is also another—I mean it not unkindly—which runs thus: 'Wisdom follows not always with gray hairs!'"

The cotton-broker blushed, and eyed the young man spitefully.

"There is a higher and *better* wisdom than that which comes from a long and bitter experience with the world," said Samuel, observing his glance with pain. "Who has not learned *that*, though he have learned all things else, has learned nothing. The little child who has a single grain of faith in it, or has been favored with one lone glimpse of it, is a giant to him in knowledge, though he bear above his brow the baldness or the silver of whole centuries."

"Yes," sneered the cotton-broker, "cant!"

"No," returned Samuel, with mild impressiveness—"Truth, which neither the young man's pretensions, nor the old man's experience, can set aside. What is the value of that experience which teaches us faith only in—*our own* wisdom? The man who has expended a long life in seeking wealth among the mountains, talks learnedly of their barrenness; and smiles incredulously when he is told that another, who has gone over only a fourth of their surface, has picked up a pocketful of rubies. And yet the rubies were in the mountains when *he*—the man of many years—went through them. That *he* did not find the precious stones, was not that he had no eyes, but because he did not turn them in the *right direction.* Now, I put it to your candor—are the rubies worth one mill the less, because *another* found them?"

"Ha, ha! ho, ho! he, he!" said Mr. Jessup, with his usual facetiousness. "Very clear, indeed! Reminds me of a certain little Solomon who always had a funny way of putting on great airs when indulging in the most oracular of—commonplaces! And now, sir, allow me to put it to *your* candor: What"—twirling his gray beard with derisive deference, "has your marvellous sagacity discovered, that I have not?"

"One thing important: respect for truth, let it come from whatever well," replied Samuel. "Life is *not* a bitter jest. But if a man *will* look upon it in that light, he loses all the delicious sweetness of the *better* view. From childhood to old age, man's life is a perpetual *succession* of solemn compacts—with his parents, love and obedience; with his teachers, application to his studies; with his playmates, gentleness and fairness; in riper years, with society, courtesy; with business, diligence and prompt honesty; with the State, faithful citizenship; in peace, prompt service in her hour of peril; with the partner of his days, confidence, faithfulness, and love; with the world, concord; with himself, earnest manliness of thought and action; with his Maker, pure allegiance and love. Who *keeps* these compacts, finds life no bitter jest, but a thing of earnestness, of beauty, peace, and joy—a tranquil stream, bearing him gently on to the green shores of the Bright Beyond!"

"I yield," laughed Mr. Townsend. "The compacts floor me!"

"Our young friend," sneered the cotton-broker, "reminds me of my pastor, who is always prepared with a capital homily, which will do for any enemy that comes along."

"Does he favor *you* with many?" asked the witty editor.

"Every time he sees me."

"Then you are one of his enemies?"

"Sir!" exclaimed the cotton-broker, reddening, "you are—"

"Quite cool—which, I regret to say, you are not!" laughed the witty editor. "The fact is, Mr. Jessup, you are giving yourself a great deal of unnecessary heat. The room is already hot enough, and if you add to it, uselessly, you will render us all exceedingly uncomfortable."

"Sir—you are a—"

"Now, don't—don't, Mr. Jessup, I beg of you; or we shall be compelled to hoist the windows, and that, at this season, which is very inclement, might prove dangerous. You know how easily young people catch cold!"

The cotton-broker gnawed his lip quite fiercely; but disdained to reply.

"Talking of preachers," said the witty editor, "did any of you ever hear the learned Dr. Aston?"

All declared that they had "never had that pleasure."

"He is a very learned man," continued the witty editor "Mr. Ruffin, he would suit *you* to a T."

"Ah, indeed?" said the beer-maker, quite delighted.

"Yes, sir. He is so learned!"

"How learned?"

"*Almost* learned enough to explain the Scriptures so his congregation can *understand* them, but—not quite!"

"And how would that suit me, sir?" demanded Mr. Ruffin, sternly.

"Because," said the witty editor, "it would be well for a man of your business, when he gets up to the *last* Bar, to be able to say that he didn't understand the Scriptures!"

"Sir," said the beer-maker, "your wit is a good deal like your paper—very low and vulgar!"

"Observe how Satan's people appreciate each other!" whispered Mr. Crittenden to Samuel.

"And *your* wit," returned the editor of *The Jolly Sneerer*, "is a good deal like your ale—very flat, stupefying and insipid!"

The beer-maker imitated his illustrious predecessor, the cotton-broker, by disdaining to reply.

The witty editor looked round him with the air of a conqueror, and taking courage from his double triumph, he concluded to finish off with Samuel himself.

"I believe, Mr. Leland," he said, "that you have some acquaintance with the pulpit?"

"A slight *acquaintance* but a very great *respect* for it, sir."

"Ah! *that* is owing, I apprehend, to your education. Now *my* acquaintance with preachers is more extensive than my respect for them!"

"That, sir," replied Samuel, quietly, "is owing to your *want* of education!"

The laugh that followed this quiet rebuke informed the witty editor that he had not won his proposed victory—exactly.

"You got a benefit that time, Mr. Impudence!" chuckled the cotton-broker. "You will draw in your horns now, I presume!"

"And hide your diminished head in some out-of-the-way corner," added the brewer, enjoying his enemy's discomfiture. "Shall I give you an order for a glass of my ale?"

"Pardon me," returned the witty editor, "I am very particular about what I drink. It is a weakness, I know; but I can't get over it!"

"You don't like anything insipid?" sneered the cotton-broker.

"No, sir—nor *old*, either!"

"Then, I presume," returned the cotton-broker, with an air of spiteful triumph, "that you never read your re-vamped jokes in your own paper!"

The witty editor turned livid, and, in his turn, disdained to reply.

"Mr. Griscom," asked Isabella, at the suggestion of her uncle, who desired to keep up the excitement, "what is your opinion of modern religion?"

"If that fellow grows impudent," whispered Mr. Crittenden, "you must take him in hand!"

Samuel nodded, and bent his eyes upon the party addressed.

"Modern religion, Miss Landon," said the sarcastic gentleman, with a knowing sneer, "is a hum—bug!"

"Why so, sir?" demanded Samuel. "There is no difference between the Church of to-day and the Church in the days of the Apostles. We believe as they believed—what Christ taught. How, then, is modern religion—which is simply the same as that of the earliest times—a humbug?"

"Because it *is!*" was the *logical* reply; "because its humbug is visible to the dullest eye; because for whatever may be dragged up in its favor, more can be adduced to prove that its evil more than counterbalances its good!"

"I hope, Mr. Griscom," said Samuel, "you will not forget in whose presence you are saying this!"

"In *whose* presence, sir!" demanded the sarcastic gentleman.

"In your MAKER'S, sir! In your Maker's, as well as in that of another who will record every unjust word that may be uttered here. Pray, do not consider me impertinent or obtrusive: I speak not in the spirit of either. But I will take it as a favor, if you will kindly refrain from making any unfair strictures upon an institution which was planted by the hand of God, and which draws its vitality from His Son!"

"I have a very high respect for *you*, Mr. Leland," sneered the sarcastic gentleman, "but a still higher regard for—freedom of speech! As to the recording angel, and all that nonsense, it will do to frighten children with, but not *me!*"

The character and tone of this reply precluded the necessity of a reply; and Samuel resumed his seat with an air of pain.

"You say, Mr. Griscom," ventured Mr. Townsend, for the purpose of drawing him out, "that modern religion is a hum bug. Wherein?"

"Wherein?" repeated the sarcastic gentleman. "In everything that we can see of it; what we *cannot* see of it, I have nothing to remark upon, lest," he added, with a sneering glance at Samuel, who was conversing in a low tone with Mr. Crittenden, "the recording angel should make a serious entry opposite my humble name!"

"Come, come, Griscom, my boy," said the cotton-broker, derisively, "draw it mild! We must have some respect for our young friend's *tenderness*—here!" he added, pointing, with a quiet chuckle, to his head.

"A poor joke!" remarked Isabella, scornfully, "and as venerable as its maker!"

"Nay, miss," returned the disconcerted cotton-broker, with a malicious smile, "I was not aware of *your* touchiness in that direction, or I should have had mercy upon your—*weakness!*"

Isabella flushed to her very temples, but mastering her temper as quickly as it had risen, she returned, in a low dulcet tone, which was the more cutting for the peculiar smile with which it was accompanied—

"Pray, Mr. Jessup, don't spare your wit, which is perfectly pointless; but *do* save me from the humiliating consciousness that you *could* have the least consideration for *any* lady, and least of all for *me!*"

"Nay, Miss Landon," returned the cotton-broker, with a malignant sparkle, "*I* have no design of entering the lists for so amiable a heart, I assure you!"

"You give me a new lease of life, Mr. Jessup!" said Isabella. "The bare thought of having so young and spruce a cavalier in my train, would make me die of—laughter!"

This fling at his wrinkles rather disconcerted the snappish old bachelor, who replied—

"Old age is respectable, miss!"

"Very true, sir, when it does not aspire to be thought *young; then*, it is simply ridiculous!"

With these words, Isabella turned her back upon the old gentleman, and opened a conversation with Mr. Brigham.

Mr. Jessup smiled, and—bit his lip.

"But all this," said Mr. Townsend, for the double purpose of directing attention from the defeated old bachelor, who looked as if he was sitting upon nettles, and of pitting his young favorite, who had no suspicion of his design, against the sarcastic gentleman, "all this is apart from the main question. Mr. Griscom affirms that modern religion is a humbug in all its visible points. Now a charge like that, coming from so keen an observer as Mr. Griscom, is entitled to consideration. But then, again, although I have the highest respect for Mr. Griscom's vast discerning powers, I, for one, must be permitted to doubt the accuracy of his statement, unless Mr. Griscom shall see fit to favor us with the proofs. In that case, indeed—as who can resist conviction?—I might be tempted to take the same stand."

"You have too much intelligence for that!" said a low, sweet voice on his left.

"We'll see about that, Miriam, by the time our satirical friend gets through!" answered her uncle, in a laughing whisper.

"Men," said the sarcastic gentleman, with the air of one who knew all about it, and more too, "men join the Church from one of two motives: either to extend their business, or to secure a social position. When you see an individual becoming what the world calls pious, you may safely set him down as having a design which a reputation for piety will assist him in carrying into effect. In fact, it is a good rule to go by, that The more religious a man is, the greater is his knavery. I always avoid a pious man, for fear he will pick my pocket. I may be wrong, but I cannot help it. I have seen the world, and studied it; and I flatter myself I have not studied it in vain."

"How old are you, sir?" asked Samuel.

"Fifty years," answered the sarcastic gentleman.

"And that is the sum of your wisdom! Heaven help you!

Why, sir, there are little children in our Sabbath school who know more than that!"

"Ah, indeed!" said the sarcastic gentleman, showing his teeth in a sardonic laugh. "Little children?"

"Little children, sir—who have learned how to cherish and reverence an institution which, apart from its higher claims, teaches them to protect the helpless, to heal the sick, to clothe the naked, to forgive their enemies, and to do good unto all men."

"Very pretty things to—*preach!*" sneered the hardware dealer.

"And very comforting to *practise!*" returned Samuel.

"Perhaps you know of some who do that!"

"All of God's people do it!"

The hardware dealer laughed outright.

"You are a very amusing individual!" he observed, derisively. "We have six hundred members in our church, and I have yet to learn that they disturb themselves *very* seriously in that way!"

"There is a vast difference between the facts in the Church and the facts in your mind, Mr. Griscom! If you take no pains to get at the *real* ones, you cannot expect that they will force themselves upon your notice. And yet there are more exemplars of practical Christianity among your congregation than you have any idea of. I am myself acquainted with seven; all of whom are noble monuments of Christian goodness!"

"Fudge!"

"O sir, why do you discredit this, without first making some inquiry concerning it?" said Samuel, reproachfully. "Why doubt the existence of love, meekness, gentleness, benevolence, and single-minded piety, because they do not come under your own observation, and because they do not appear in the channels in which *you* move? Take a stroll in *their* channels, and you will find them abundant as the stars."

"My dear Mr. Leland," smiled the hardware dealer, ironically, "you have a fertile imagination. It is so singular that you should see so much more in your eight-and-twenty years than I have been able to discover in fifty; and mine are *inquiring* eyes, believe me!"

"Oh, sir," returned Samuel, "why persist in a disbelief in human goodness—why draw a wilful veil between your mind—bright only with deceptive views, and the real? Man of fifty years!" he added, in a tone which electrified the assembly, "you have wasted half a century in profitless and ungenerous work. What evil has God heaped upon you, that you should wage war upon His institutions? What injury has my Prince inflicted upon you, that you make mock of the goodness and fidelity of His people? What wrong have Mankind done to you, that you should sneer so pitilessly at their weaknesses? Man—man! have you no HIGHER aim than to play the *scoffer*? What enjoyment find you in it—what benefit—what good? Whom does it help, relieve, cheer, or strengthen? Compare yourself, sir, for one moment, with all your wealth, experience, and worldly knowledge, with the humble Christian craftsman, who, for love of his Redeemer, fills up his basket every Saturday night, and wanders from chamber to chamber of the yet poorer, making sad hearts glad, and feeble ones strong. Contrast the happiness of that poor toiler on his errand of mercy, with that which comes to yourself from your bitter mockery, and say which is the truer!"

A murmur from the assemblage told the hardware dealer that public opinion was rather setting in against him. That worthy, however, was perfectly undaunted. Like all sarcastic individuals, he gathered strength from defeat.

"You are, I believe, a pious man?" he said, with a sneer.

"I profess to serve my Maker," said Samuel.

"Ah! you only *profess* to do so?"

"I endeavor to do so in fact, as well."

"Ah! yes," returned the hardware dealer, ironically, "they will all tell you that, when cornered; those who connect themselves with the Church to serve their pockets, they who attach themselves to it for the purpose of smuggling themselves into respectable society, and all!"

"For which of these two objects did you join the Church, sir?"

"For neither," answered Mr. Griscom. "I connected myself with it in order to study the humbug of modern religionists, from the knowing little children upward!"

"A singular motive, I will not say a praiseworthy one! How long have you been a member of the Church, Mr. Griscom?"

"Before you were born, sir!"

"And in all that time you have been analyzing the Church, studying the Church, and found nothing in it, but—"

"Cant and humbug!" broke in Mr. Griscom, with a sneering laugh, which he designed to be very knowing, very bitter, and very crushing.

Samuel regarded him, for a few moments, with astonishment.

The sarcastic gentleman smiled with an air which seemed to say, "Aha! I've demolished you at last—have I?"

But Samuel did not appear to be conscious of having been demolished at all.

"And you have been studying the Church over twenty-eight years, Mr. Griscom," he said, "and found in it nothing but cant and humbug!"

"Nothing more, Mr. Leland, I assure you!" returned the sarcastic gentleman.

"And you say that to me, sir, and to this assemblage of intelligences?"

"To you and to them, sir! I am not one to go back of my word. My ancestors fought in the Revolution, sir!" said the sarcastic gentleman, loftily.

"What has the latter fact to do with the case in point?" asked Samuel.

"That I am not to be trifled with!"

"Who is trifling with you, sir?"

The sarcastic gentleman turned pale. He discovered that he had made a very stupid remark.

"I stand ready to maintain my position!" he said, doggedly.

"Prove it, then, sir," said Samuel. "I am interested in its establishment, if it can be established; and in its refutation, if it cannot be established."

The hardware dealer was silent for a few moments. At length his countenance brightened, under the magic influence of a fresh idea. His eyes sparkled. Already his lively imagination enabled him to behold his opponent writhing in the humiliation of an overwhelming defeat.

"I will favor you with a *few* evidences of the weakness of your ground," he said, "or rather with a few pictures of certain of your friends, who were, like yourself, clamorous for the rights of the Church, and absolutely majestic in their piety!"

"Bravo!" whispered Mr. Brigham to Miss Landon. "The gentleman is spreading himself. Now for something tremendous—"

"Like *himself!*" answered Isabella, "or," she added, "like *you!*"

The confidential clerk bit his lip.

"I am waiting, sir," said Samuel.

"And you will not have to wait long, my friend, depend upon it," returned the hardware dealer, with an air which implied that, now that he had taken the young man in hand, it was his intention to make short work with him.

The assembly pricked up their ears, and looked at each other.

"Now we are going to have fun!" whispered Mr. Townsend to his wife.

The latter nodded, and glanced at Mr. Crittenden, who smiled, and glanced at Miriam, who was regarding the hardware dealer with an expression of pain.

"I will give you a few pious samples," said the sarcastic gentleman, by way of an introductory flourish. "There was, to begin with, your old and dear friend, Mr. Jones, who swindled his creditors out of two hundred and twenty thousand dollars, deserted his wife and child, and wound up by running off with another man's wife, the mother of two highly interesting children. *He* was a *very* pious brother—one of your trustees, in fact—carried around the plate, and was remarkably fond of prayer-meeting. Indeed, the fervidness of *his* prayers used to throw those of his brethren into the shade. In that respect, sir, they were almost equal to your own!"

Samuel made no reply.

The hardware dealer wreathed his lips into a patronizing smile, and continued:

"You asked me for the proofs, sir, and I feel bound in honor to produce them!"

"Go on, sir!" said Samuel, calmly.

"Then there was your other dear friend and pious brother, Mr. Rankin," said the sarcastic gentleman, in a tone which sent a shudder through the assembly. "He, too, was a bright and shining light. He used to make the softest, mildest, sweetest of prayers, and walk from prayer-meeting to a—gambling-table. He was *so* pious that he paid eight hundred dollars a year for his pew; not to be talked about—O no, but simply because he was so *good!* At church, on Sunday, who so devout as 'dear brother Rankin!' During the sermon, who so contemplative! 'Ah,' said everybody, 'brother Rankin is piously weighing the words of the preacher!' All a mistake. He was merely considering how high he should make his stakes on Monday night! When the congregation saw a tear in his eye, they innocently attributed it to the touching eloquence of the discourse; but it proved, after all, to be simply a tear to his losses at faro on the evening before! He carried around the plate, too, and was so unctuously pious that everybody said of him, 'He is a saint!' Well, it was subsequently discovered that this saint was, in plain language, a miserable thief, a private blackleg, and a fast liver—on other men's money. In the polite phraseology of our times, he was a 'defaulter' to the tune of seventy-five or eighty thousand dollars. To conclude the catalogue of this pious worthy's crimes, he committed suicide—piously leaving his wife and children to the parental care of the—alms-house!"

"Go on, sir," said Samuel.

"*Certainment!*" said the sarcastic gentleman, with mock-graciousness; "but I warn you that it will take me till morning to get through."

"No matter," returned Samuel, calmly. "Go on, sir."

"Oh, if you will have it so, Mr. Leland, you shall be accommodated to your heart's content. Then there is Mr. Wilson, of the dry goods firm of Gates & Wilson. He was always *so* good, and *so* glad to see you. Why, sir, one would suppose that that man was the blood-born brother of all mankind, he was always so delighted to see everybody. How he would weep over the preacher's eloquent pictures of Christ's sufferings, or a sermon on the poor! In fact, he was always in tears. How he would press a sister's hand, and talk to her of the delights of heaven; and how fond he was of inviting himself to their houses to pray for and with them! And with what pleasure he made the acquaintance of every new member of the church; how particularly he inquired after their own and their family's healths, from the antique grandmother down to the last little contribution; how affectionately he invited everybody to call and spend the evening with his family, always taking care to let you know that he himself was never at home; and how cordially he invited himself to everybody else's house, and, when there, tenderly inquiring how much you paid for every article in it, whether you got it at a 'bargain,' a polite way of learning whether you paid cash for it, or got it on tick; what your rent stood you in, and whether the landlord was inhuman enough to demand security, and if so, who was the kind friend that stood by you in that trying moment—where you came from, how many there were in the family, together with the amount of property which had already been, or was to be, divided amongst you—all of which information he carefully recorded, if not in a book, at least in his memory, for future reference! And then, as the breath of misfortune came in your path, how ready he was in—turning his back upon you, and in wondering what you meant by bowing to, or calling upon him—*him*, a perfect stranger to you! Well, Mr. Leland, this dear friend and pious brother of yours—or rather his firm, which is the same thing—failed yesterday, doing his dear creditors, as one of them informed me to-day, out of a cool two hundred thousand!"

His auditors stared at one another. The party spoken of was known to nearly all present, and the news of his failure took them by surprise.

Mr. Crittenden glanced at his partner—the latter returned the look with a sly sparkle of business joy. The bankrupt house was one rival the less to the great house of John P. Townsend!

"That firm has, for a year past, been offering me very tempting inducements to change houses," mused the confidential clerk. "And they have caved in at last, for all their craft and honey! Well, I've been expecting it for some time!"

"Have you done, sir?" asked Samuel.

"That is as you please, sir," answered the sarcastic gentleman. "If you wish for any more, be kind enough to signify it. I am not exhausted, I assure you!"

"Go on, sir," said Samuel.

"There is another of your dear friends, Mr. De Witt. The sleek, fat, pious Mr. De Witt, who always found so much comfort in prayer, and yet who never looked upon an acquaintance without considering how much he could make out of him. The wise, knowing, crafty Mr. De Witt, who, as everybody thought, had grown rich upon his judicious mixture of rascality and religion. He, too, used to make long prayers; he, too, was so charmed to cultivate loving friendships with his dear brethren; and he, too—the oily, well-fed rogue!—carried around the plate, into which, as everybody knew, he never himself dropped a sixpence! Well, sir, this dear, delightful, pious rascal hung himself this morning, owing a credulous and 'done' world between three and four hundred thousand dollars!"

All started at this announcement.

"Is that true?" asked Mr. Townsend.

"I learned it from one of his brothers-in-law, on my way hither," replied the sarcastic gentleman, who appeared to be perfectly delighted at the sensation which had been created by his last gun.

"Did Mr. De Witt owe you anything?" asked Mrs. Townsend, in a whisper.

"Not a dollar," answered her husband.

Mrs. Townsend breathed easier, and then glanced at Miriam. Both were thinking of Mrs. De Witt's treatment of her sister—the helpless Mrs. Jones.

"Poor creature!" murmured Miriam, sympathizingly. "How hard she will find poverty—she who could not endure prosperity! I must do something for her!" And she began to think how she could serve the widow, without wounding the latter's pride.

Mrs. Townsend's idea was as follows:

"Thank Heaven! that odious creature will at length taste of a little of the bitterness which she administered so freely to her sister!"

Isabella was quietly thinking of the sensation which the affair would create the next day, when it should be reported, with all the interesting details, in the newspapers.

Mr. Townsend was silently congratulating himself upon his good fortune in not "doing" a note of the defunct's which had been tendered him some two or three days before.

Mr. Crittenden was considering how utterly unfit society and society's church had rendered Mrs. De Witt to grapple with poverty.

Samuel was pondering, with a shudder, upon the chances of the soul which had precipitated itself, reckless and unrepentant, into the presence of its Judge.

The sarcastic gentleman was felicitating himself upon the stir which he had produced and the triumph which he had achieved over his opponent.

The little publisher was wondering how a series of volumes upon the "Lives of Illustrious Suicides" would go, in the style of the successful "Illustrious Highwaymen" and "Illustrious Pugilists."

"This is a very shocking affair!" said the brewer, gloomily. "I don't like it!"

"I hope it don't touch *you*, sir?" said the hardware dealer.

"But it *does* touch me, Mr. Griscom, and very seriously, too, sir. What right had that rascal to hang himself before seeing me? The scoundrel—the base, ungrateful scoundrel!"

"Hold, sir!" interrupted Samuel. "You forget: you are speaking of the dead!"

"Dead or alive, sir," cried the brewer, foaming with rage, "the rascal owes me ten thousand dollars, borrowed money. He had it from me last week, stating that he only wanted it for thirty days; and now—why, it is perfectly frightful!"

"Take it cool, take it cool," laughed the witty editor. "The public will drink back your loss in Ruffin's Ale, before the thirty days shall be up !"

" And besides," said Mr. Sly, with the air of a man who desired to make an impression, " there is a large profit in ale."

" How do you know that, sir ?" demanded the brewer.

" I figured it out, once," returned Mr. Sly ; " and finding the profits so heavy, I was within an ace of going into it."

" And what, sir, may I ask," inquired Mr. Crittenden, " influenced you from taking up so *praiseworthy* a business ?"

" The still greater profits in book publishing !" chuckled Mr. Sly.

" I have always heard that book publishing was a poor business," remarked Mr. Crittenden.

" On the contrary, sir—that is to say, for a certain class of books !" said Mr. Sly.

" Your own, for instance ?"

" Yes, sir," said Mr. Sly, with becoming modesty. " We understand how to make publishing *pay*."

" Anything for money—eh, Mr. Sly ?" said Mr. Crittenden, dryly.

" Men must live, you know !" faltered that worthy, looking exceedingly foolish.

" Why, what are you doing, Mr. Chipp ?" asked Mr. Townsend of the witty editor, who was pencilling rapidly on his tablets.

" Sketching for my next number the portrait of the first instance on record of a blushing publisher !" answered the witty editor.

" Add under it," said the cotton-broker, who fancied he was letting off a clever thing, " that he is a sly fellow—very sly ; but that he never could see when he was a butt !"

" Sir !" growled the little publisher, looking exceedingly fierce.

" Well, Mr. Sly," asked the cotton-broker, with a supercilious stare, " what is it ?"

"No matter!" said Mr. Sly, in an humbler tone. "I presume you were only joking."

"O, you presume *that?* Indeed! Happy man!" returned the cotton-broker, derisively.

The little publisher crimsoned to his temples, and wished himself a thousand miles away.

"After all," whispered Mr. Crittenden to Samuel, "society appreciates rascals at their just value, and compels them, now and then, to submit to the most abject humiliations."

Samuel was about to reply, when he was interrupted by the hardware dealer, who was in nowise inclined to leave the result of his fancied triumph over the young man in doubt.

"I apprehend, Mr. Leland, that you have had quite enough of the contest which you were so eager to enter?" he said, in a voice which turned all eyes upon the latter.

"Save a vast flow of bitter, rambling sarcasms, and three or four dreadful pictures," returned Samuel, "I have heard nothing from you tending to establish your position."

"Dear me!" said the hardware dealer, ironically.

"Perhaps, Mr. Leland," said the cotton-broker, "you can favor us with something in support of your own?"

"Why, sir, a child could do that!" returned Samuel. "Religion—modern religion, if you will have it so—stands, happily, in need of no argument to sustain it. It is its own great advocate; and the evidence of its truthfulness and power lies in the visible happiness of its people, and in the joy which it confers upon all who embrace it. I shall therefore trespass neither upon your intelligence nor your patience by a waste of unnecessary words. But, with your permission, I will draw a portrait of an every-day exemplar of the fruits of the *want* of religion in a single individual."

"Hear—hear!" creid the hardware dealer. "All those who have never been pious—hear; all those who are not pious—hear;

and all those, of whom I am one, who never expect to become pious—hear !"

Samuel surveyed him, for a few moments, with an air of painful surprise.

"One of these days, Mr. Griscom," he then said, "you will learn that every sneer and sarcasm which you utter, outrage your own dignity; that they are ungenerous and unworthy; and that they are the issue only of bitter and self-blinding minds."

"Well," returned the incorrigible hardware dealer, "I am willing to wait until that happy period shall arrive. In the meantime we'll take your portrait of a gentleman without religion."

"Listen, then, sir. John Smith was an inventor, a husband, father, friend, citizen, and Christian. *John Smith, the inventor,* was a great man; in science he took a stand among the highest. All of his energies, mental and physical, were given to new machines. It was his one idea; he lived for nothing else. Had any one asked him to define the one object of life, he would have answered, New Machines. And he was faithful to his idea. But *John Smith the husband* was another man; his wife had for her sole counsellor and companion, her own thoughts; whatever she did, however well done, was never noticed or appreciated by her husband, because he had no mind for aught but new machines; and so the poor woman pined and labored, and pined and struggled, and pined and—died. That was the end of the first chapter in New Machines. *John Smith the father* was a miserable creature. Excepting in the fact that he was the sire of three fine boys, he had no right to that paternal name. He had plenty of mind for his new machines, but no mind at all for his sons, whom he left to take care of themselves. Poor lads! You know how children will wander, when left without a guide. One strayed among thieves, and became of their number; a second fell among gamblers, and became of their kind; the third associated with rowdies, became of their number, and was killed in a prize-fight. Thus ended the second chapter in New Machines. *John Smith the friend* was a misnomer; he was a friend to no one, not even to his wife, nor yet to the issue of his own loins; who assisted him with timely influence or capital, he never so much as thanked; friend after friend turned from him in indignation and disgust. By-and-bye, he had not a kindly wisher in the world. Thus ended the third chapter in New Machines. *John Smith the citizen* was a nonentity. He took no interest in public affairs. The country might have gone to pieces without his knowing it. He left the State to take care of itself. If a great moral movement came up, which, if carried, would relieve the people of a serious evil, and which, if lost, would work them vast ruin, John Smith knew nothing of it, cared nothing for it; or if a new measure was proposed by the agents of sin, which would endanger our liberties, and throw the country back twenty or fifty years, John Smith gave it no attention. At length a great reform measure was brought up; its passage would have saved thousands of men from drunkenness, idleness, and poverty, thousands of wives from penury and affliction, thousands of children from hunger and neglect, thousands of citizens from oppressive taxation, and the State from a burning shame; its defeat would have retained all this evil. John Smith knew nothing about it, John Smith cared nothing about it, and the measure failed for want of a single vote. This was the close of the fourth chapter. *John Smith the Christian* was a pitiful spectacle. He went to church from habit. While there, being naturally of a studious turn, he looked around to observe the peculiarities of the congregation in dress, physiognomy, and manner, and amused himself by ridiculing their weaknesses. When service was begun, he diverted himself by criticising the hymns, the choir, the literary merits of the prayer, the Bible chapter, and the sermon; the style of the preacher, his individualism in mind, form, feature, voice, dress, gesture; and in comparing, balancing, and measuring the relative nervous forces of his intellect and body. To the Message itself, he gave no attention. When he had finished his amusement, his mind returned to his one love—new machines, and continued upon that, to him, all-important subject, to the close of the service. Thus he spent his Sabbaths, thus he spent his life. At length he was summoned by the Last Messenger, to the presence of The Great JUDGE, to give an account for his neglect of his wife, for his abandonment of the children whom his Maker had committed to his care, for his ingratitude to his friends, for the ruin which had followed to thousands by his unfaithfulness in an important public measure, and for his sacrilegious amusement in the Temple of the Most High. Thus ended his last chapter. When he died, the unthinking said of him, 'What a great man the world has lost!' Ah! how much nearer to the truth would have been the remark: 'What a Great World hath this poor sinner lost!' If John Smith had only tempered his great mind with Religion—this institution which you so sneeringly deride—then how different had been the results of his career! Mr. Griscom," added the young Christian, impressively, "John Smith was one of many. He bent every attribute of his nature to a single idea. On that one altar, he sacrificed his wife, his children, his friends, his fealty to humanity, yea, even himself. Mr. Griscom, *your* new machine is Sarcasm—sarcasm against your fellow-creatures, who, believe me, stand more in need of your love than your scorn—sarcasm against the highest of all human institutions: The Institution of God! Oh, sir—this is not well, not generous, not noble!"

"You appear to be perfectly rabid upon the sarcasm question!" laughed the hardware dealer. "Most men are; but it generally arises from their inability to play even in the same line!"

Samuel made no reply.

17*

"One would think, to hear Mr. Leland," observed the idler, "that a fellow should never amuse himself."

"There are two kinds of amusement, sir," returned Samuel, "as there are two kinds of everything: the harmless and the harmful. I have no objection to the first, but every objection in the world to the second."

"You have such a funny way of answering a fellow!" observed the lounger. "Knocking religion into him with every word!"

"A little religion, my friend, would do you no harm!" said Charley Gibbs, coming up to Samuel's assistance. "I knew an individual like you, once, who was made quite a man by it."

"Ah! In what way?" asked the lounger, looking out from the bevy of blondes and brunettes by whom he was surrounded.

"It rendered him useful both to himself and to society!" replied Charley.

"My dear fellow," said the lounger, favoring him with a prolonged stare, "you are—"

"Didn't some one hear a bell?" interrupted Mr. Townsend, for the purpose of arresting the personality.

"No, sir," rejoined the witty editor, comprehending his host's idea, "it more resembled the noise of a beau in the midst of the belles!"

This hit was so palpable, that even the lounger himself condescended to join in the laugh which it evoked.

"Do you carry your Christianity so far," asked the retired banker, addressing Samuel, "as to expect a respectable congregation to mingle indiscriminately with the rag, tag, and bobtail of the lower classes?"

"Yes, sir: although I should not designate the poor by that appellation."

"A shocking doctrine!" observed the lounger. "Positively frightful! It wouldn't take in our church!"

"Nor in ours!" remarked the hardware dealer.

"Nor in ours!" said the brewer, with a grimace.

"Nor yet in ours!" said the banker. "We are very particular!"

"As for ours," said the little publisher, deeming this a good opportunity to reinstate himself in the good graces of the assembly, "the sexton has his orders; and would lose his situation if he should permit the riff-raff in. It's the only way. We have to be careful who we admit; or we should never be able to keep up our respectability."

"*Our* respectability!" repeated the cotton-broker, mimicking him. "Neighbor," he added, with a cutting sneer, "when your business fails to give you a living, bear in mind that I shall be in want of a *footman!*"

"You are too hard upon poor Mr. Sly!" observed the banker.

"Not half so hard as *you* were upon the dupes of your fraudulent banks!" replied the little wasp, quickly.

The banker was dumb.

"How *harmonious* are the ranks of the soldiers of Satan!" whispered Mr. Crittenden to Samuel.

"Their thoughts are evil, and their evil follows them!" returned the young Christian.

"Mr. Leland," said the hardware dealer, who fancied that he had at length found a way to throw his late opponent into a knot from which he could not easily extricate himself, "I should like to hear your reasons for opposing public opinion upon church exclusiveness. As for myself, I hold to the belief that respectable people should not associate with nobodies in the church any more than in society."

"My opinion also," said the lounger.

"And mine," observed the brewer.

"And mine!" ventured the little publisher, in hope, by following so popular a sentiment, to recover his former position.

"Now, look out," observed Mr. Townsend, in an under tone,

to his wife. "Samuel will not leave these rascals an inch of ground to stand upon."

"Come, Mr. Leland," said the hardware dealer, tauntingly, "face the music, like a man!"

The assemblage regarded the young Christian with interest.

"I have ever entertained the opinion," said Samuel, "that, of all places in the world, God's house is the very place where rich and poor *should* meet as on a common ground. Once within its sacred walls, we are no longer in the world—no longer in the midst of hollow pomps and little pride, of worrying poverty and sickening guile—but in the solemn temple of The Most High. When the rich man has crossed its threshold, he has left his wealth behind him; the poor man his struggles, his misery, and his cares. For both are then where wealth and poverty are as naught, where rich and poor stand upon the same level: IN DIVINE PRESENCE! Before them stands the sacred desk; behind it, the envoy of The Redeemer. The solemn silence awes them and subdues them; the solemn prayer stirs them, and reminds them that they are there, for all the wealth of the one, and for all the poverty of the other, mere journeyers to the Better Land. The song of praise, so arousing, so inspiring, they join in, and find comfort in their hearts, pleasure in their souls. Again the solemn silence awes them and subdues them; and then the voice of The Message, spoken by The Lord's chosen servant, falls—solemnly, warningly, cheeringly—on their ears, as never yet fell human voice, as never yet fell human word. At sound of that voice, the evil spirit within them stills its sinful whispers; the angel spirit within them holds its breath in awe and reverence: for One greater than them all—One whom all must hear—is speaking: GOD! Ah! where is society, THEN? Where wealth, with its glitter, its pomps, and its pride? Where poverty, with its rags, its stings, and its suffering? Where all are swallowed up and forgot—where the rich and the poor, the proud and the humble, are all alike inferior—in the presence of The *Only* Superior! Ah! who shall say which one of all that throng, whether he be rich or poor, has the best claim there? Who shall say to his neighbor: 'This is not the place for one like thee!' Who shall say to one beside him, before him, or behind him: 'This is *my* God's house; go thou to *thy* God's house: for *my* God's house is not *thy* God's house, nor is *thy* God's house for me!' Ah! no thought there, *then*, of that! For THAT Voice is speaking, to which cherubim and seraphim hearken as to their Highest Lord's, and it says: 'This is MY house—enter freely!' Ah! who shall gainsay The Omnipotent *then* and THERE! But The Voice ceases—The Message is spoken—and hosannas ascend from the contrite and humble throng. This over, all depart, with The Blessing in their ears, and incense burning in their hearts to The One Superior. Ah! happy, in that hour, the rich man who forgets his riches; and happy the poor man, if he think not of his poverty!"

As the young Christian concluded, his auditors expressed their opinion of his stand in the discussion by a general clapping of hands.

The hardware dealer bit his lip. He had laid a trap for his opponent, and had only succeeded in catching—himself.

"Mr. Griscom," asked Isabella, at the suggestion of her uncle, who desired to keep up the excitement, "what is your opinion of the pulpit?"

"If that fellow displays any more of his venom," whispered Mr. Crittenden, to his young friend, "you must finish him."

Samuel nodded, and bent his eyes upon the hardware dealer, who now fancied that he had got hold of a topic which would enable him to retrieve his fallen fortunes, and amaze the assemblage with his vast mental powers.

"The pulpit," said Mr. Griscom, ironically, "is a very good thing—in its way. It is a capital companion for society. They play into each other's hands very accommodatingly, on the plan of the two snow-ball factions—'you let us alone, and we'll let you alone.' You know the story, of course—everybody does. Men take to the pulpit with the same motive that other men take to the law, to medicine, or to dry goods—for a business!"

"What!" asked Mr. Crittenden, "simply to make money?"

"To make money—nothing more," said Mr. Griscom, with the air of a man who knew all about the matter, and could say some very cutting things concerning it, if he chose.

"But don't you think that a very harsh, wholesale, and ungenerous statement?" asked Samuel, indignantly.

"When a man takes *comprehensive* views," returned the sarcastic gentleman, "he is *somewhat* apt to get beyond the sympathy of circumscribed minds!"

"But it appears to me, sir," said Samuel, "that there is such a thing as taking views which are so *very* comprehensive that they never penetrate beneath the *surface*. I do not wish to insinuate that *your* views are of this nature; but I am tempted to believe that, when you hurl so unjust a reproach at the highest and noblest profession in the world, you really do not know how wrongfully you misjudge it."

"'Noblest?'" repeated Mr. Griscom, with a supercilious smile.

"Yes, sir. Perhaps you can name a nobler? I appeal to your candor as a man: What calling so high as that of the envoys of The Prince of Peace; what profession so noble as that which seeks to *save* men—to lead them, like little children, to the feet of their Redeemer?"

"One would suppose, to hear you talk," sneered the hardware dealer, "that you were born in some rural town where the inhabitants do nothing but cultivate greens!"

"Bravo!" exclaimed the witty editor, clapping his hands. "'A hit; a hit: a palpable hit!'"

"A great deal like your own, Mr. Chipp,," said Isabella; "and about as original!"

"Another hit, and far more palpable!" cried Mr. Brigham. "The Jolly Sneerer is declining in circulation!"

"Is it?" retorted the witty editor. "Fortunately, I have got an idea which will make it rally, commencing with the next number."

"Ah, indeed!" sneered Mr. Brigham. "Some fresh revamp from the venerable Joe Miller!"

"No, sir," cried the witty editor, trembling with rage; "the picture of a dry goods orang-outang, whose teeth form the principal part of his head!"

"Are there any painters here?" broke in Mr. Townsend. "I want a sign dashed off right away, with, in large letters, 'Mangling done here!'"

This sally restored good-humor, and Mr. Townsend added—

"Come, Mr. Griscom, to the point. You say that clergymen preach for money only, a position which Mr. Leland denies. Now favor us with the evidence."

"I fear," said Mr. Crittenden, "that our worthy friend will find himself a little behind time!"

"We'll see that," said Mr. Griscom. "I have a supreme contempt for the pulpit, because preacher and people are no better than they should be. They play into each other's hands—"

"You have already informed us upon that point, sir!" interrupted Isabella.

"I will now proceed to *prove* it!" said the satirical gentleman, in his dry way.

"Very kind in you, sir, indeed!" said Isabella.

"There are churches," said Mr. Griscom, not heeding her remark, "where the members, who call themselves *patrons* of the sanctuary, go, not to worship God, but, as to a play: to be seen, and—amused. This class—these *patrons* of the Lord! want in their preacher, not *piety*, but—ELOQUENCE. That edifies them, wakes up their dormant faculties, refreshes them. For this intellectual refreshment they will pay—liberally; while for piety they will give—nothing. These snobs want for their pastor one who will preserve them from mental imbecility, refresh them with ornate thoughts, and never disturb the tranquil calm of their self-complacency—that is to say, an *eloquent* preacher, and—nothing more. They do not *tell* him this; but they leave him to *infer* it, and to comport himself accordingly. If he fail to meet their wishes, they discard him; if he accommodate himself to their desire, they pay him a princely salary, and—despise him! Now," said the sarcastic gentleman, with a flourish, "I mean to say, with all due deference to the young gentleman from the rural district, that churches of this description experience no difficulty in obtaining pastors! Very 'noble' men, no doubt; but still *very willing* to adapt themselves to the wants of those who *employ* them!"

The satirical gentleman paused, with an air which implied that he was very well satisfied with himself, and that he was conscious that he had maintained his position like a veteran, *thus far*.

"There is some truth in this rascal's remarks, after all—eh?" observed Mr. Crittenden to his young friend.

Samuel made no reply.

"There are other congregations," continued Mr. Griscom, running his fingers through his hair, like one to whom triumphs of this sort were of daily occurrence, "or rather, other *patrons*, who, in patronizing the church, patronize—themselves. What *they* want in their pastors, is not piety, but—LEARNING. And so they look around for preachers who are capable of amazing them once a week with their rich treasuries of lore—preachers who will not disturb themselves with the consciences, but with the *brains* of their hearers—who will make it a point, every seventh day, to furbish up and put new life into their stupid, ignorant, and decaying noddles. Now, I respectfully submit, that churches of *this* sort find it *very* easy to obtain pastors who are willing—*very* willing—to humor them in these particulars!"

The satirical gentleman paused again, and while playing with his hair, looked down with modest triumph, like one who was perfectly aware that he had delivered himself of something very fine, and was quite certain of a great many rounds of enthusiastic applause.

"Have you got through, Mr. Griscom?" asked Mr. Crittenden.

"O, no, sir—only taking breath; that is all," answered Mr. Griscom. "Then there are churches who want pastors who understand the happy art of giving the Gospel as wide a berth as possible; who will sugar it over in so masterly a manner that it will hurt nobody, and yet be somewhat like the Gospel, after all; who will let them do just as they please, and not interfere with them; who will lull them into soft religious ease, and let them pass along, in their silken righteousness, without disturbing them. Well, churches of this stamp are not *often* compelled to do without preachers—not *very* often!"

"*Our* pastor is one of that sort," remarked the lounger, who thought that 'Miriam might suit him;' "and a capital fellow he is, too. Lets us all do just as we like. Never agitates us, nor himself."

"If he should make any attempt to arouse you, you would not let him succeed, I presume?" said Mr. Crittenden.

"Of course not," returned the idler. "We don't *desire* to be disturbed. What we want is to be let alone!"

"By all means, sir. Insist upon *that!* And in that hour when you stand before the JUDGE, tell *Him* how bravely and lordlily you compelled your pastor—one of His messengers!—to know and feel the littleness of his place! Tell *Him*, too, THEN, that you want HIM to let you alone!"

"*Sir!*" cried the lounger, starting from his chair, as if he had been stung.

"Sir," returned Mr. Crittenden, "if you have not power enough in *that* hour, and influence enough in *that* quarter, to crush and ride over HIM, where will you be? Will you say to *Him*, 'I don't desire to be disturbed? You let me alone, and *I'll* let YOU alone!'"

The idler's cheek became livid.

"Ha, ha!" he cried, laughing, to hide his agitation. "Very good—very good. But I don't like such jokes. They are positively shocking!"

"It is no joke, sir," returned Mr. Crittenden, calmly. "Making light either of Jehovah, of the Redeemer, or of the Redeemer's workmen—or throwing obstacles in the way of the latter, in their efforts to rescue men from the stream which is hurrying them onward to the Eternal Gulf, is no laughing matter, I assure you! If you think the contrary, laugh on—encourage yourself and your friends in neutralizing the honest labors of your pastor—insist upon his letting you alone—nay, *compel* him to do so; and by-and-bye, when you stand together at The BAR, he will say, 'This, Lord! is one of them who fought against Thee and me!'"

The lounger made no reply; but the lesson was not lost upon him. Ere many weeks, he was another and a better man.

"For my part," said Mr. Sly, "I agree with Mr. Griscom. The pulpit is an unmitigated humbug."

"Of course *you* do, Mr. Sly!" observed Mr. Crittenden. "We all understand *your* reason for thinking so. But one of these days, when your share of flooding the world with brothel and bar-room literature is finished, you will entertain views of a somewhat *different* color!"

"Sir!" cried the little publisher, boiling with rage.

"O, sir!" returned Mr. Crittenden, calmly, "reserve your airs for those whom they will impose upon. They are wholly lost upon *me!*"

"Perhaps," said the hardware dealer, coming up to the assistance of his ally, "perhaps Mr. Crittenden, who has never been *very* famous for his piety, may be wholly ignorant of the character of religious machinery. Many people are!'

"I admit the justness of your observation, sir," said Mr. Crittenden; "and I take shame for my delinquency hitherto in those duties which every man owes to his Maker and Redeemer. But I repent me of my error, and I call you all to witness that I am, from this hour, on the side of my Master!"

"Joy—joy!" murmured Miriam.

Charley Gibbs looked at his intended, and observed in a whisper, "Won't this be rare news for our next meeting in the packing-room? Won't there be great rejoicing!"

"All this is from the point," said Mr. Jessup. "The subject is not of the sudden conversion of Mr. Crittenden, but of the humbugs in the pulpit."

"One word, sir," said Samuel, stepping forward. "Language like this is unfair, unmanly, and ungenerous, unless you are prepared with something better than mere idle supposition, or unfounded conclusions, to sustain it. It is a common thing for worldly minds to inveigh against the sacred profession, and to mistake irony for wisdom. I hope, Mr. Jessup, that if you have any remarks to make upon the pulpit, you will make them in a spirit of manly frankness; that you will use particulars, not generalities, and employ facts, not sarcasms."

"Griscom," said Mr. Jessup, "give this young gentleman some facts. He wants facts—nothing but facts!"

And the cotton-broker roared with jolly laughter—at what, nobody else knew, for they could see nothing *very* funny either in Samuel's request, or in Mr. Jessup's remark.

"What sort of facts will you have, Mr. Leland?" inquired the hardware dealer, in a tone which implied that he had a very extensive assortment on hand, and could accommodade the gentleman with any desired kind, and in quantities to suit.

"Those which confirm your right to brand the clerical profession with opprobrium," answered Samuel.

"There'll be warm work presently!" whispered Mr. Brigham to Isabella. "Samuel is going to annihilate that fellow!"

"He is able to do it!" returned Isabella.

"Umph! y-es. Perhaps so!" returned the confidential clerk.

It was evident from the looks and whisperings of the company that they anticipated an engagement between Samuel and the sarcastic gentleman, in which they did not expect that the latter would come off conqueror.

Samuel himself was calm, earnest, and eager. He felt that he stood before the assembly as the champion of a profession which every worldling considers it a mark of sagacious cleverness to mock and say cutting things of; and he resolved, with his Maker's help, to do good battle for the messengers of his Prince.

"You want some facts, Mr. Leland?" said the hardware dealer, sneeringly.

"Yes, sir."

"You shall be accommodated. I always make it a point to gratify the whims of young men, because I was young myself once, and, like you, had an overweening desire to be considered wiser and sharper than I really was!"

"Ha, ha! ho, ho! he, he!" cried the cotton-broker, clapping his hands. "Very good. Hit him again, Griscom!"

"Not so very bad!" remarked the witty editor, with the air of a critic. "I've heard of cuts that were weaker!"

"The best of your own, for instance!" said Isabella.

And the laugh was against the editor.

"All this goes for nothing, Mr. Griscom," observed Samuel, quietly. "I asked you for facts, and not personalities. If, after so learned and oracular a flourish, you have no facts to give, confess it like a man, and retreat from your position. There is no shame in abandoning an untenable cause."

"Ah! you flatter yourself, Mr. Leland. My cause is both tenable and satisfactory, as you will discover to your dismay before I get done with you!"

"Facts, Mr. Griscom—not threats; facts!" said Samuel, calmly. "Don't beat about the bush with sarcasms, which are harmless, because unworthy; but come to the point at once. I am waiting for your facts, Mr. Griscom!"

The hardware dealer eyed the speaker for a few moments with a derisive air, and then said—

"You appear to be very *eager*, Mr. Leland. Be cool, sir; be cool. In discussion, there is nothing like preserving one's equanimity. When I see a youth of your years so very hot, I always feel a touch of pity for him. It's a weakness of mine to look with compassion upon the rashness of young blood; but I can't help it. Now, be cool, Mr. Leland—be cool. It will do you good—believe me!"

"These tricks do not impose upon me," said Samuel, quietly. "Now, sir, I am waiting for your facts!"

"You cannot throw Mr. Leland off his guard, Mr. Griscom," said Isabella, in a tone which provoked general laughter; "and therefore you might as well come to the point at once. Mr. Leland understands all your moves, and—so do we!"

"O, Miss Landon," sneered the satirical gentleman, "if I am expected to face two such terrible enemies. I shall most certainly retreat!"

"O, Mr. Griscom," interrupted Isabella, "be kind enough first to show yourself strong enough for *one!*"

"Come, come, Griscom," laughed the cotton-broker, "you might as well commence at once. Miss Landon will show you no quarter, else!"

"Well, then," smiled the hardware dealer, making the best of his position, "here goes. The pulpit is a humbug, because its members preach for their congregations instead of for their Master!"

"That is a *wholesale* charge, and therefore unworthy. It is made every day by superficial witlings, but has no foundation in fact. Wholesale denunciations never come from reflecting minds. Oblige me, Mr. Griscom, by descending to particulars. Name some one of our metropolitan clergymen whom you know to be a traitor to his Master."

The sarcastic gentleman's eyes sparkled with anticipative triumph.

"George," he said, addressing the lounger, "what is the name of your pastor?"

"Mr. Gadsden."

"There," said the hardware dealer, with a dry grin, "is one, to begin with!"

"How do you *know* that, sir?" asked Samuel.

"You heard what George said a while since, I presume, sir?" returned the hardware dealer. "That was *pretty* good evidence. It came from one of the gentleman's own parishioners!"

"Ha, ha! young man!" chuckled the cotton-broker, "Mr. Griscom rather had you there!"

"Stop, stop," said the lounger, who had been ruminating upon Mr. Crittenden's 'joke,' "I take back what I said of Mr. Gadsden. Upon further consideration, I don't think him a *very* bad minister. He preaches the Gospel as well as he knows how; and he *does* know how pretty well. And, now I think of it, he has been the instrument of leading a good many to repentance since he has been among us!"

The satirical gentleman turned pale.

The cotton-broker bit his lip.

The company indulged in a general titter, which glided off into a general roar.

"Pretty good!" observed the witty editor. "It will do for an article in my next number."

"Your second evidence, sir?" said Samuel, quietly.

"You know, as well as I do," said the hardware dealer, "what the general opinion is concerning ministerial unfaithfulness, and—"

"Evidence, sir—evidence!" interrupted Samuel.

"Well, then, if you will have it—your own pastor: Mr. Engold!"

"Mr. Townsend," said Samuel, turning to that gentleman, "you are a trustee in our church. You have known Mr. Engold for many years. Frankly, now, and as a man who is bearing solemn testimony: What do you think of his conduct as a pastor? Has he, till within the last fortnight, done his duty to the best of his ability? Has he been faithful, in season and out of season—making *all* times his season? Has he preached like one who appeared to feel the responsibility of his high office; like one who was in the service of his Prince: like one whose chief desire was to lead his hearers from sinful unto righteous ways? Answer, frankly—honestly; as if you were at JEHOVAH'S BAR!"

"Solemnly, then," answered the merchant, "I affirm it to be my belief that—bating a few suspicions, for which, after all, now that I reflect upon them, I can see no just reasons—Mr. Engold has been ever faithful."

"You hear, sir?" said Samuel, addressing the hardware dealer.

"I do," answered the latter. "But," he added with a sneering smile, "you forget the proviso in time: 'Till within the last fortnight!' What has happened since then? Has he proved traitor, at last?"

"Mrs. Townsend," said Samuel, "answer him."

"Mr. Engold has, within the last fortnight, been the instrument of spiritual happiness to over an hundred hearts," replied the latter.

Mr. Griscom colored, and ran his fingers through his hair, as if in quest of an idea.

The cotton-broker partook of his friend's confusion, and looked very much as if he wished himself somewhere else.

"Your evidence," said Samuel, to the hardware dealer.

"Now, where is the use in dragging up the incumbent of every pulpit in the city for examination?" demanded Mr. Griscom, impatiently. "It is unfair!"

"And yet, sir, you had no hesitancy in arraigning the *entire body!*" said Samuel, mournfully. "I put it to your candor, Mr. Griscom: Which is the most unjust?"

"And I had a perfect right to do so," returned the hardware dealer, in a fume. "Everybody knows the inefficiency of hundreds in the profession."

"The question is not of their inefficiency, but of their unfaithfulness, Mr. Griscom."

"Well, then, of their unfaithfulness!" answered the hardware dealer, fiercely. "Everybody is aware—"

"Evidence, Mr. Griscom! You are making a solemn charge, sir. Evidence!"

"My own pastor, then: Mr. Fenton!"

"Do you *know him* to be false?"

"I think that, for a minister of Jesus Christ, he takes things *rather* coolly!" was the half-laughing, half-sneering reply.

"How, coolly?"

"*Easy*, then; if that will suit you better!"

"How, easy?"

"Well," said the hardware dealer, showing more temper than was at all necessary, "he don't allow the souls of his congregation to disturb him *very* seriously. I presume you comprehend me, now?"

"I do not," replied Samuel, quietly.

"Then I'll be as plain as possible, sir, to accommodate the singular dulness of your mind!"

"I will overlook your uncalled-for personality, Mr. Griscom, providing you will be explicit."

"You are remarkably kind, sir!"

"To the point, Mr. Griscom."

"Well, then, sir," said the sarcastic gentleman, "I think that, for one who professes so deep an interest in the business of His Master, Mr. Fenton exhibits a remarkable lack of fire!"

"Energy, you mean?"

"Yes, sir."

"You forget, Mr. Griscom, that Mr. Fenton is not a man of a vigorous mould. He is, by nature, of a mild, tranquil temperament. His manner is easy, gentle, and subdued. It would, therefore, be unfair to look for the same flaming energy in him, that you would from a more robust man. Clergymen, although in the service of The Redeemer, are still human, and, for that reason, subject, like all other men, to physiological laws. One is not full of animal vigor, because he is suffering with a certain degree of palpitation of the heart; a second is comparatively tame, in physical display, owing to dyspepsia; a third, in consequence of a rupture; a fourth, from one of the many forms of consumption; a fifth, on account of a pleurisy; a sixth, because of some lung, liver, or other complaint, and so on; but nearly all in consequence of some internal disease, which an undue agitation of the nervous system might suddenly increase and render fatal. Inconsiderate persons would sneer at these; and, because they fail to exhibit the same muscular action which they evinced when in sound health, or because they do not come up to the strong, nervous, declamatory standard of other preachers of a sturdier and bolder build, they thoughtlessly brand them as easy, lukewarm, and indifferent, and charge them with want of faithfulness, enthusiasm, et cetera! Others are mild from constitutional causes. One has no taste for violent delivery, and therefore avoids it; another has no confidence in boisterous declamation, and hence steers clear of it; while a third is mild from temperament. Mr. Fenton is one of the latter. His organization is of a delicate, refined order. You would hardly expect him—a mere student, with a student's habitudes—him, a mild-feeling and mild-mannered gentleman by nature and education—to display the muscular powers of one cast in the rough, energetic form of an athlete. Mr. Fenton is of an entirely different make. In his formation, nature bestowed greater attention upon his mind than upon his body. He is, therefore, more remarkable for his mental than for his physical developments. But what he lacks in animal, he more than makes up in intellectual vigor. His style is calm, polished, and persuasive; his manner earnest and impressive. He has done, and is doing, good work for his Prince. However uncharitably you may judge him, he is yet a faithful and successful soldier of The Cross. Have confidence in him; for he is noble, worthy, and true. View him kindly, frankly—not as if he were a stranger, in whom you felt no interest—but as a man, a gentleman, an envoy from On High, and your pastor: and you will find him a man, with a warm and generous heart for you and all humanity; a gentleman, with all the delicate susceptibilities and refined instincts of a gentleman; an envoy, with a single eye to the service of his dear Lord; and a pastor, prompt, earnest, and watchful of his flock—yearning, striving, to lead and keep them in the heaven-path—and bending every energy of his fine, cultivated mind towards inspiring all with whom he comes in contact with the same oneness of purpose, the same gentleness of spirit, and the same Christian integrity which animate his own upright heart."

"You draw him with a flattering pencil!" sneered the hardware dealer. "But as I am not very *largely* gifted with faith in aught but humbug, you must excuse me from believing in the accuracy of the likeness!"

"Are there any others here," inquired Samuel, appealing to the assemblage, "who are acquainted with Mr. Fenton?"

There was no reply. After a brief pause, the young Christian resumed.

"Solemnly, then," he said, with an impressive gesture, "I aver, in the absence of all other witnesses, that I have known Mr. Fenton for two years and upward; that I have heard him preach many times, and always found him a faithful deliverer of The Message; that I have experienced much joy, comfort, and encouragement from his sermons; that I have conversed with him privately concerning the enterprises of our Prince, and always found him earnest, anxious, and affectionate; that I have seen him, when his best friends knew of it not, in the haunts of the poor, doing good as it were by stealth, giving advice with a liberal heart, money with a generous hand; that I have seen him, on many a pitiless night, and at hours when most men were partaking of refreshing rest, making his way, through stormy rain and sleet, to chambers in which you, sir, and most of this assembly, would unwillingly set foot, and pleading there, with all the might of his great mind, and greater heart, for mercy for departing outcasts; that I have known him to forgive and pray for men who have slandered and worked him injury; that I have known him to privately help many in their need, to give kind counsel to others, who wanted counsel only, and to sustain several while they were waiting for their little capitals—which were furnished by himself—to turn; that I have known of many whom he has persuaded from the path of crime; of many whom he has gently led from wretchedness to comfort, and from the darkness of sin to the irradiancy of Light. All this do I know, and to all this do I bear glad testimony: before Him, who knoweth it already—before you, who, not knowing it, have done one of the truest servants of my Prince a grievous and ungenerous wrong!"

A murmur of satisfaction rose from the assembly. Public opinion was setting in fast against the hardware dealer, who felt the ground gliding away from under him, and determined to make a last grand effort to sustain himself.

"Do you mean to say," he demanded, "that *all* of our clergymen are faithful?"

"As a BODY, *yes;* in every individual case, *no:* here and there a false one, like an occasional traitor in an army; but the instances are rare—rarer than you dream; and *so* rare, that even you, sir, upon a candid examination of the subject, would be amazed at the exceeding smallness of their number."

"If that be so, why don't they accomplish more good?"

"They *do* accomplish great good; more than you think."

"I'd like to see the evidence of it," sneered the hardware dealer.

"The evidence is all around us, sir. In the advancement of men in general uprightness; in the markedly improved tone of our country and the age; in the rapid march of morality in literature,—which has, of late years, turned a complete summerset, the better now taking the lead of harmful books, which formerly swept the field; in the public Press—which, with rare exceptions, are on the side of Truth and Right—few or no journals gaining ground in circulation save those whose columns bear witness of the progressive spirit of their conductors; in Legislation, which no longer laughs with impunity at the moral measures demanded by the moral voice of the people; in Politics, whose day for obtaining vast majorities, by pandering to the mere passions of the multitude, is over—those politicians only ascending high in the atmosphere of public sentiment and support who are enlisted, professedly, at least, under the elevating banner of reform; in Society, which is no longer openly arrayed on the side of vice—the card-table having disappeared from the drawing-room, the rum-bottle from the sideboard, slang, infidelity, impure song, and ribald music, from social gatherings—those only finding admission into refined circles who display at least an *appearance* of religiousness, those openly against religion being excluded, and confined to intercourse with their own kind. These are the *broad* results of the labors of that noble army of energetic, self-sacrificing men, whom you so ungenerously reproach!"

"Self-sacrificing!" repeated the hardware dealer, ironically. "Let me see: Mr. Engold obtains four thousand a year, and the perquisites; Mr. Gadsden four thousand a year, and the perquisites; Mr. Fenton, four thousand a year, and the perquisites. Very self-sacrificing—indeed!"

"A single word, sir," returned Samuel; "and let it be a frank one, as you are a gentleman! You are a merchant, that is to say, a business man, with a fair yearly income, which is derived wholly from your commercial knowledge and labors. *You* earn *over* four thousand per annum—do you not?"

"I should hope so, Mr. Leland!" laughed the hardware dealer, who, it was well known, had an establishment which netted him from twenty to thirty thousand a year.

"You will not deny that the clergymen just named are your equals in intelligence?"

"Of course not."

"You will admit that their respective chances in trade would be as favorable, at least, as your own?"

"Certainly."

"That, with their mental abilities, they could clear from ten to twelve thousand a year?"

"I admit that, too, sir."

"And yet you think there is no self-renunciation in these men when they voluntarily relinquish all hope of fortune, and take up a profession whose highest earthly reward is scarcely equal to one-third of what they might earn in commerce?"

The hardware dealer looked down, thoughtfully.

"More, sir. A merchant can garner up some portion of his income. But what can a clergyman save? You expect him to live in a style corresponding with his position as the pastor of a wealthy congregation. To have influence with them, he *must* live so. How far will his paltry income enable him to do that, and accumulate anything? What, then, remains to him, after five, ten, or twenty years of labor—his position not permitting him to husband aught while in service? *Poverty!*"

The hardware dealer was dumb.

"Let us not be so uncharitable," said Samuel. "Where one clergyman of high talents, learning, and piety, receives four thousand per annum, a thousand others, equally as devoted, learned, talented, and pious, do not obtain eight hundred. Nay, the average income of clergymen throughout the Union is but a fraction over *three hundred* dollars. Why, sir, our poorest laborers are paid better than they! And yet you brand them, in effect, as mere fortune-hunters! What would you say, if I should tell you that large numbers of clergymen are compelled to preach and earn their living, in other ways, into the bargain?"

"A rare case, I apprehend!"

"On the contrary, sir, it is the case with thousands! Look you, Mr. Griscom. While a small proportion of that noble profession receive a thousand dollars per year, the generality of them scarcely obtain a bare living. A clergyman's ability to pay for a new suit of clothes without feeling it for months afterwards, is the exception—the reverse the rule. After a long life of faithful service, that one is fortunate who can leave behind him enough of his own savings—let him have pinched ever so hard—to pay for his own funeral! And yet you impugn the motives of men who devote the best twenty, thirty, or forty years of their lives to the great cause of their Redeemer! Mr. Griscom, I blush for you!"

"Nay, Mr. Leland," said the hardware dealer, "you are too hasty. I was not aware of all this."

"And yet you—a business man!—have formed and expressed an unflattering opinion upon the highest of all human professions, without making the slightest examination of its details; have borne oracular testimony against it and its members; have vilified it and them, without knowing so much of either as the merest tyro in the world's affairs could tell you in half an hour! Mr. Griscom—Mr. Griscom!"

"I yield, I yield, Mr. Leland," said the hardware dealer, rising, "and thank you for the lesson which you have read me. There is my hand, sir; and," he added, with feeling, "I give you my word as a man and a gentleman, that I have uttered my last slander against the pulpit."

"O sir, you make me happy to hear that. For of all toilers along life's pathway, none *more* deserve our confidence, our respect, and our affection, than the workmen of The Cross: for they come to us as no others come—in our Redeemer's name; they labor as none others labor—fighting the battles of their Master as never fought soldiers in any lesser cause. Their work, to save men, not destroy them; to bring them happiness, not woe; content, whether carrying The Message to the civilized hordes of cities, to the untutored red men of the American forest, the savages of Patagonia, the bushmen of New Zealand, the mountaineers in the frosty Caucasus, the wild idolaters of Eastern Ind, or the dark sons of burning Africa, with the simplest pittance; struggling manfullyand bravely for men and their Redeemer, all the way—and when they come to lay them down at last, thanking God, with grateful hearts, for kindly having permitted them to do battle a few years for their dear Prince, and to die with their harness on in His service!"

"Enough, sir," said Mr. Griscom, frankly. "I see my error, and freely acknowledge it. Had I been aware of those facts before, I should have avoided many very silly blunders. In future, I'll do better. In the meanwhile, Mr. Leland, set down Tom Griscom among your friends!"

"O, sir, you make me very happy. All men who are friends to my Prince, are friends to me!"

"You are a MAN, sir," said the hardware dealer, pressing his hand with much warmth; "and as *men* are few, I am proud to make your acquaintance." Then turning to the company and presenting Samuel to them, he added: "Ladies and gentlemen, *my friend.* You would all do well to make him yours!"

Miriam's eyes sparkled with joy; those of the Townsends with pride; Mr. Crittenden's with enthusiasm; Isabella's with triumph; Charley Gibbs' and his intended's, with satisfaction; Mr. Brigham's with malignant envy.

Meanwhile the general assemblage, male and female, were crowding around the young Christian, shaking him by the hand, and vying with each other to attract his attention.

Half an hour later the party broke up, and the curtain dropped upon Mr. Crittenden's last exhibition of his gallery of living portraits.

CHAPTER XXV.

THE following day was a sad one at Enfield.

"I don't know what to make of Joe," observed Aunt Betsy to Mrs. Leland, as they were sewing in the kitchen. "The deai little creeter has got the dismals, the wust kind. Some'n is going to happen, sure as you live!"

"Why do you think so, Betsy?" asked her mistress.

"Because I'm sure on't. Aint Joe a reg'lar barometer whenever danger threatens any of his blood? He's such a sensitivo creeter, that if anybody says or meditates aught agin any of us, Joe feels it in an instant. Aint it allers bin so?"

Mrs. Leland made no reply. She was reflecting with an uneasy air.

"All families have got their barometers," continued the housekeeper, running her needle with amazing rapidity, and looking around to see if a speck of dirt was visible anywhere. "I never knowed one that hadn't. They aint all aware of it, though, because every one isn't pertic'lar in observing such things; but *I* know it to be true, 'cause I've noticed it. There's the Debevois family: don't they allers know when trouble's coming along to them, through their daughter Jane, the poor sensitive creeter, who, if she is an old maid, is one of the gentlest-hearted souls in town? Then there's Martha Brundage; don't she have a presentiment whenever anything's about to happen to any of *her* folks? And don't her presentiments invariably come true? My brother Tom—a poor, delikit, nervous lad—was the barometer of *our* family. For a week afore father died, Tom had a sing'lar idee that some'n was going to occur to one of his race, and so it turned out. Another time, afore I was a widder, Tom was troubled with the frights for three days, and then the fust thing we knew, news came tumbling along that my dead and gone husband, Frank Disosway, had been killed. And now here's Joe a-sighing and grieving through his pipe, with his warnings, for more'n a week. Some'n's going to happen, sure's we live!"

Mrs. Leland and her husband, ever alive to the least change in the pipe of their little one, had also observed the melancholy turn in the old familiar tune. But they had purposely refrained from referring to it in his hearing, as they knew by experience that such remarks always had the effect of intensifying the gloominess of the little minstrel's spirit, and consequently of his pipe.

"But to whom?" asked Mrs. Leland, anxiously. "Pa is at home, and well; *we* are all at home, and well; Samuel's letter of Saturday represented that everything was well as usual with him, and that he had every reason for believing that he was in good standing with Our Prince!"

"All that is very true," returned Aunt Betsy. "But still I have my fears, and I can't get rid on 'em!"

"Fears of what, Betsy?" asked the pastor, who had just entered the kitchen.

"That some'n's going to happen to the family," returned the housekeeper.

An air of mournfulness crept over the mild, tranquil features of the clergyman.

"Here's the old tune," continued Aunt Betsy, stitching away as if for dear life, "which, for a long time, has bin telling of nothing but roses, posies, sunny fields, bright clouds, and cheerful things gen'rally, is gone off all of a sudden into the most melancholy glooms and thickets, where the grass and moss are allers dark, and where the sun never shines; and what is wuss, it keeps growing sorrowfuller and sorrowfuller every day!"

"Don't speak so loud, dear Betsy," said the pastor, gently, "or the poor boy will overhear you!"

"I don't want to hurt your feelings," said the housekeeper, in a lower tone, "but some'n's going to happen, or the old tune would never go on so. Who knows but trouble's running up agin Samuel?"

"His usual weekly letter, which we received yesterday, tells us that all goes well with him," said the pastor.

"Yes, I know," said Aunt Betsy, uneasily. "But I can't get rid of the idee. Whenever the old tune goes off into the dismals, some'n allers *does* happen in the family. Don't you remember how mournful it was in July, for two days afore you run that big nail into your foot, out in the lot, which laid you up for three weeks?"

"True, Betsy," answered Mrs. Leland. "But what then?"

"Just this," answered the housekeeper. "Some'n wuss'n that is coming to some on us now, or Joe wouldn't a had such a long spell of the dismals. It's a warning of some'n—I feel it in my bones, and I couldn't get rid of it if I should struggle agin it ever so hard. Just hear," she continued, in a still lower voice, "how the poor child is going on now with his pipe, in the parlor. Isn't it *enough* to make one cry?" she added, by way of apologizing for the agitation of her voice and the humidness of her eyes.

Mrs. Leland rose up, in much distress, and quitted the kitchen.

"There she goes," said Aunt Betsy, "to soothe the dear little creeter. But it will be of no use. Joe will be as miserable as can be till the thing—whatever it may be—happens, and *then* he'll be sick. It's allers the way with him! Where are you going, sir?"

"To the post-office," answered the pastor.

"With a letter to *Samuel?*" asked the housekeeper, hopefully.

"To him," was the reply, in an uneven voice.

And the clergyman passed with a disturbed step from the parsonage.

"Gentle heart!" mused the housekeeper, following his retreating form with her eyes. "No woman's was ever more feeling and tender!" Then laying by her sewing, she followed her mistress, murmuring, "If anything has worked agin Samuel, we'll know all about it in a few days."

But neither the maternal tenderness of Mrs. Leland, the kindliness of the housekeeper, the gentle soothing of the pastor, nor the coaxing of Ada—the adopted one—had any influence upon the sad heart of the little minstrel. The pipe was still in trouble, still in sorrow—the tune was still a Foreboding, still a Fear, whose great terror increased with each succeeding hour, until the old entry clock struck three, when the tune suddenly shot up, into a loud, piercing wail, and then broke short off and was dumb—as if it were some poor human thing, whose heart-strings had snapped and parted, to unite again no more.

At the same moment, the little minstrel himself gasped out a single word, which resembled a moan more than a word, and fell from his chair in convulsions.

"SAMUEL!"

Ah! then there was woe in the parsonage.

They raised their blind boy up; they bathed him with cold water and hot; they rubbed him with oils, with towels and liniment; they called in the doctor, who powdered and bled him; and they restarted his blood, which had stood still for a time.

They put him to bed, softly and tenderly; they watched and sighed over him prayerfully, tearfully; and joy came back to them, for life had returned to him, on the fifth day.

Then, with grateful hearts, for they had done their parts, the parents laid them down to rest for the first time; but still beset with anxious fears, for one from whom they had not heard, and who was in some danger, out there, in the world.

They woke up in the morning, pale and unrefreshed.

The father looked into the mother's eyes; the mother looked into the father's eyes; and then both looked into the sightless eyes of their little one on the bed. In those blue blind orbs they read, plain as letters in a book, this one word:

"SAMUEL!"

On their eyes it fell, like the ringing of a midnight bell—warningly.

The minstrel's brow was pale; but on it, in imploring characters, which neither father nor mother could resist, was this sentence:

"*Go to him—to Samuel!*"

All night, they sighed and wept; all night, they moaned and prayed—the father and the mother, the housekeeper and the brother—the little adopted one sleeping the while.

But with the earliest dawn, there were hurrying and bustling, trembling and embracing, adieux spoken and repeated, and at length for the last time.

Then a wagon at the door.

Then a rattling of wheels—a dashing down the road—a word of hasty parting at the cars.

Then, in a poor preacher's heart, bubbled a thousand anxious hopes and fears—in his eyes and on his cheeks, rippled, in sad and silent streaks, the lava of a suffering mind, whose thoughts were gentle for all his kind—Dread's hot, unconscious tears.

Then, a whirling, roaring flight of cars, and of time.

Then, weary in heart and brain, and worn and heavy in limb, a stranger, of a noble air, sank on his knees in fervent prayer, in a chamber fresh and fair, as night was setting in.

CHAPTER XXVI.

The clergyman rose from his prayer, refreshed. Then making his toilet, and walking down his agitation, he descended from his room, and, supper having long been over, ordered a meal to be prepared with dispatch. The request was tardily, but at length complied with, and having recruited his exhausted frame, the anxious-hearted father set out, on foot, for Fifteenth street.

On reaching the Townsends', he observed a number of carriages drawn up in front of the house; the windows were a-blaze with light; music and dancing were going on within.

The clergyman rang the bell, which was immediately responded to by a porter in livery.

"I desire to see Mr. Leland," said the pastor, in an agitated voice.

"He isn't here any more," returned the porter; "he went away a fortnight ago."

"Stay, sir," said the clergyman with dignity, as the man was about to close the door.

"Well?" said the lackey, with an impudent leer.

"I wish to see Mr. Townsend."

"Then you must call some other time. We're busy now, with a wedding, and can't be disturbed!" answered the fellow, disappearing behind the portal.

A flush of indignation rose from the clergyman's breast, and swept up to his temples. He drove it back, however, and having completely mastered his temper, he again rang the bell.

"Hullo!" cried the porter, reopening the door just enough to allow his hand to protrude, "you here again, old gentleman? Be off, now, or we'll hand you over to a policeman!"

"Call your employer, sir," said the clergyman, "or I'll do it for you!"

"You will, will you, old gentleman? That's very good in you! But as we're very busy, you will have a nice time in seeing him—I *don't* think!"

"Have you no shame, sir?" said the clergyman, indignantly.

"There—there," said the flunkey, "run along, old gen'leman —run along. We can't be bothered with you all night!"

And the door was closed again.

And the bell was pulled again.

On this occasion, however, without any response from the porter.

After waiting a reasonable time, the clergyman repeated the ring; but meeting with no notice, he pulled it again, and with an energy which brought the porter out in an instant.

"Now, go away," he said, laying his hand roughly upon the visitor, "or I'll compel you!"

The clergyman made no verbal reply; but quietly disengaging himself from the flunkey's grasp, he brushed him aside, and passed through the open door with a calm dignity, which was the more impressive for the ease with which it was performed.

The porter could scarcely credit his senses; but by the time he had persuaded himself that the incident was not all a dream, the clergyman was in the presence of Mr. Townsend, who had been summoned from the drawing-room by one of the attendants in the hall.

"Be good enough to call to-morrow," said the merchant, blandly, on learning the clergyman's business, "and I will give you all the particulars of your son's sad affair. But just now, we are so busy, that, really—"

"I am a father, Mr. Townsend," said the clergyman, impressively, "and have a night of agony before me! Two words—but two; they will not detain you as many minutes."

"Well, Mr. Leland?" said the merchant, drawing himself up.

"What is the nature of this 'sad affair' of which you speak, Mr. Townsend? I judge, from your manner, that you deem my son culpable, in some way. You will please forgive my warmth, if I appear warm, which is far from my design. But I am a father, sir—and—and," he added, in a broken voice, "there are bleeding hearts at home, sir, and—and one in my breast, too. Of what—" he paused, tremblingly, and then continued, with an effort—"with what is my boy—my poor, dear boy, my Samuel!—charged?"

"With theft," answered the merchant. "The money was found upon his person. Now, sir—go!"

The clergyman stood as if transfixed. The light that fell upon his features from the gas-burners in the hall revealed a countenance of rare manly beauty, but clothed with so sickly a paleness that it might well have been taken for that of a corse.

"Come, come," said the merchant stiffly, "no scenes here. This is my eldest ward's wedding night, and I can't have any disturbance. Call some other time, and I'll give you any explanation you may desire. But at present, I cannot be annoyed."

"Stay, Mr. Townsend," gasped his visitor, with an effort, as the merchant was moving off; "one word. My son—my Samuel. Where is he?"

"I know nothing of him, sir. He has disappeared!"

And the merchant returned to the drawing-room.

The clergyman reeled from the house, and pursued his way, in a state of bewilderment, to his hotel, when, clambering to his chamber, he fell upon his bed—stunned.

How he spent the night—in what agony of heart and torture in mind, we shall not attempt to describe.

At ten o'clock, the following morning, he proceeded to the

store, in Liberty street. The clerks stared at him as he threaded his way, through the sinuous counter-passages, towards the platform. They fancied, for a few moments, so strange was his featural likeness to that of his son, that it was Samuel himself suddenly transformed into mature age.

The clergyman passed into the office, and beheld Mr. Townsend conversing with a gentleman whom he recognized at once as Mr. Crittenden.

Mr. Townsend colored as the visitor entered, and waved him, with formal politeness, to a chair.

"Mr. Leland, of Enfield, I presume?" said Mr. Crittenden, courteously extending his hand to the clergyman.

"Yes, sir," answered the latter, with an air of mournful dignity. "I have not called to take up your time, gentlemen; but to learn the cause of some ungenerous remarks which Mr. Townsend took the liberty, last night, of casting upon the character of my son."

That gentleman caught up his hat, and saying to his partner, "I'll take a run up to the bank," slipped out of the office, muttering, "A simple old fool! Does he think I feel any interest in *his* affairs?"

And yet Mr. Townsend was ashamed of his ungentlemanly conduct on both occasions; and, before he reached the street, would have given a few dollars if he had had sufficient manliness to say so. Had the visitor been a *dealer*, now, instead of a clergyman, he felt that he could have apologized for his low rudeness without any difficulty: "Because," thought the man of business, "a merchant experiences no mortification in making a thousand explanations, if necessary, to conciliate a—customer!"

Mr. Crittenden perceiving that the clergyman comprehended, in its true light, the character of the business which called the retiring member of the firm so suddenly to "the bank," observed, smilingly—

"I hope, Mr. Leland, you will excuse my friend's flight; but the fact is, he is so vexed at his shabby treatment of you at his house, that he has not courage to look you in the eye."

"No apology is asked for, Mr. Crittenden," said the clergyman. "I had forgiven him ere I reached my hotel."

"How is it you recognize me so readily?" asked the silent partner.

"From my son's letters. And now, sir, if you please, remember that I am the father of the man whom Mr. Townsend charges with—" he paused, with emotion, and then added, "with theft!"

Mr. Crittenden's brow became grave.

"Listen," he said.

"Go on, sir," returned the clergyman, whose voice, manner, and restlessness indicated that he was sitting upon thorns.

"Mr. Leland," began Mr. Crittenden, "I have a sad story to tell you; one which, as I perceive by your manner, you are utterly ignorant of!"

"A sad story concerning my son!" cried the clergyman, turning pale. "But I am interrupting you. Excuse me: I am a father, and have a father's feelings. Go on, sir."

But Mr. Crittenden had not the heart. The misery of the simple-hearted clergyman unmanned him. He rose, took a glass of water, and after pacing the office a few moments, he resumed his seat, and commenced again.

"For some weeks—indeed, I may say months—prior to the twenty-first of last month, when Samuel left us," he said, with an air of pain, "the money-drawer of Mr. Townsend, who, by mail remittances and customers coming in to settle up their accounts, receives, daily, large amounts of cash, had, from time to time, been rifled of numerous sums, varying from twenty to sixty dollars. The aggregate of these robberies was not very large, but, as you will readily comprehend, it was important to put a check to them at the earliest possible moment."

"And my boy—my Samuel," cried the clergyman, indignantly, "was suspected of this peculation!"

"Pray, pardon me," said Mr. Crittenden, "I said not that."

"But you *mean* it, Mr. Crittenden—you, who should have known my son better! I can overlook a suspicion of such a nature in an organization like that of Mr. Townsend. But with you, sir, it is another affair. You are a deep student in the book of human nature; you can read a man's character from a glance at his face, from the intonations of his voice, from his step, from his individual air, and from his utterance of a single sentence. With all this vast talent, you are an honorable man—not from policy alone, but from a higher motive: Principle. How, then, sir, could you—a man, with a man's heart, and a man's judgment—reconcile it with your conscience to heap so gross an injustice upon my pure, my high-minded boy!"

"You are condemning me unheard, Mr. Leland," said the silent partner.

"Nay, forgive me, Mr. Crittenden, if I have spoken unjustly," returned the clergyman. "I am a father—a man—an humble servant of my Prince, and—and my poor boy—my Samuel, whom I have known and loved from his earliest infancy—whose Christian deportment, all his days, has been to me a source of joy, and hope, and pride—who has taught me, his father, to love him more for his own sweetnees than for his relations to me as my son—is in affliction, and my heart is grieved."

"I feel for you, sir," said Mr. Crittenden, with emotion, "and I sympathize with you. Believe it!"

"I do," returned the clergyman. "But you must bear with me. I am an old man, sore beset with suffering in mind and body, and have known but little food or slumber for many days. Be brief, therefore, and let me know the worst."

"Listen, sir," said Mr. Crittenden. "The robberies of which I have spoken gave Mr. Townsend and myself so much uneasiness, that we concluded, after a consultation with our confidential clerk—but you are ill, sir!" he said, stopping abruptly.

"A shudder crept over me at the allusion to Mr. Brigham, such a feeling as I sometimes feel when in the presence of an enemy—that is all, sir," returned the clergyman.

"You appear to know Mr. Brigham?"

"I have had a weekly letter from my son ever since he left home," said the clergyman, explanatively.

"Ah! that accounts for it," remarked Mr. Crittenden. "But, as I was saying, we concluded, after a consultation with our confidential clerk, to lay a plan for detecting the guilty party. For this purpose, Mr. Townsend, for three or four weeks previous to the twenty-first, made a private mark upon all bills which came into his hands, and placing the money, as usual, in his drawer, quietly awaited the result. The first week passed away without any new theft. On Wednesday of the second, thirty dollars were missed; but without remark. Friday of the third, thirty-five dollars disappeared. Tuesday, of the fourth, twenty-eight dollars were taken. The money was counted at one o'clock; at two the abstraction was discovered. In half an hour, measures were taken to detect the culprit. Every clerk in the establishment was summoned into the office, the door of which was fastened, and the case laid before them. All demanded and acquiesced in the propriety of an immediate search—Mr. Brigham acting as searcher of the first half, Mr. Townsend of the second. You can imagine the interest and excitement of the examination. Mr. Brigham's part was unsuccessful; and then Mr. Townsend commenced. One after another of his eight were searched, but without alighting upon the culprit. Mr. Brigham and Samuel alone remained, both of whom requested to be examined, like their mates. Mr. Townsend declined—no suspicion being upon them; but Mr. Brigham insisting, he was thoroughly searched—but without result. The desk, together with every article in his office, was ransacked, his very coat upon the wall, his hat, chair, the cushion of which latter was ripped open and thoroughly dissected, but without avail. At length, Samuel's turn came; and—but I fear to pain you!"

"Go on, sir," said the clergyman, hoarsely. "I am trembling, you see; but not with fear of any guilt on the part of my pure, high-minded boy. I have had but little food or sleep for many days; and I am weak—weak, sir: that is all!" he added, in a voice that would have moved a stone.

Mr. Crittenden was himself agitated, and could articulate only with difficulty.

"In fine, Mr. Leland," he said, falteringly, "the missing twenty-eight dollars were found—"

"Not upon Samuel!" moaned the clergyman, blanching with mingled indignation and horror. "Not upon my son—not upon my bright hope—my poor, poor boy! O, no—not upon him—not upon Samuel!"

"In his vest pocket!" said Mr. Crittenden, in a broken voice. "It was in bills and gold—the former wrapped around the latter.

The clergyman, his face livid as death, surveyed the silent partner, with a proud, indignant eye.

"Nor was this all," said Mr. Crittenden, sorrowfully. "In the right corner of his coat, between the lining and the cloth, was found another roll of bills, with, as in the first instance, a ten-dollar gold piece in the centre, to make the whole sink down!"

The clergyman surveyed him as before, but without making any attempt to reply. He was pale and speechless. Had he been the marble thing he looked, he could not have been more dumb or motionless.

Mr. Crittenden pitied him; and would have refrained from

saying any more, but there was that in his auditor's eye which said—"Go on!" and he proceeded.

"The clerks were amazed. Had the money been found upon themselves, they could not have evinced more affright. Mr. Townsend and myself were paralyzed. As to Samuel, he staggered like a drunken man towards the partition, and would have fallen, but for Mr. Brigham. At that moment, the clock struck three. You are shuddering again, Mr. Leland!"

The clergyman was thinking of the wail of the old tune, and the convulsions of his poor blind boy, at that eventful hour in his first-born's career.

"Go on, sir!" he said, or rather moaned, in a feeble voice. "Let me know all."

"I have but little more to tell," replied Mr. Crittenden, with a sigh. "The money was found upon him—not all, nor yet the half of what had been stolen; but yet enough to brand him, among the unthinking, as the pilferer of the whole, and consequently—his religious pretensions considered—as a vile, deceitful man. The other clerks crept out of the office with an air of mingled loathing and surprise—hissing him as they left, and muttering, 'This accounts for his enlarged benevolence,' 'Splendid hypocrite,' 'Matchless rascal,' et cetera, to none of which did Samuel reply: but seating himself, pale and gasping, in a chair, he clasped his head with his hands, as if he feared that it would burst. Mr. Brigham, who was the last to remain, was the only one who regarded him with any show of compassion. He tendered the unhappy young man a glass of water, but it was declined. Then, with an aspect of real sorrow, he, too, retired, and Mr. Townsend, Samuel, and myself were the sole occupants of the office."

"And then, sir—" moaned the clergyman.

"Mr. Townsend looked at Samuel for a minute or so, as if undecided what to think, say, or do, and then snatching up his hat, he drew a long, fretful breath, and went home to dinner."

"And my boy—my poor victimized boy—"

"Remained in his chair, his hands pressing his temples, and his eyes staring at the floor like one mad, or stunned—or both. I spoke to him; but he answered not. I touched him gently on the shoulders; but he heeded it not. I then left him, and pretended to occupy myself with writing, in hope that he would eventually look up and notice me; but all to no purpose. At length, I went to dinner; and was gone an hour. On my return, I found him as I had left him—in the same attitude in the chair, his hands still pressing his wildly-throbbing temples, his eyes still staring at the floor; and his fellow-clerks standing around, and jeering him at the door. They fled at my approach, but still, from their departments, watched us both with eager gaze, pointing him out at times to their customers with all the scorn and indignation of honest men! I drew down the blind, to shut off their impertinent eyes, and spoke to him for a good long hour, but without eliciting a remark—nay, not so much as a word—in response. It was, for all the good it did, like talking to a block, a statue, or a stone. For he gave not a single sign that he either heard me, or was aware of my presence. Dusk came—the closing hour; yet still he sat there, motionless and tongueless as ever, in the chair, and staring, as before, at the same spot on the floor. At length I shook him. He awoke from his spell, surveyed me a while with a cold, half-absent eye, caught up his hat, and, still without a word, passed mechanically from the office and the store, and then home, where he arrived just in time for tea. The meal was dispatched in silence, and then all rose and proceeded to the drawing-room—Samuel following them more like a dead thing than a man. No one to spoke to him, he spoke to none; but his eyes wandered from one to another, to see if he had yet a single friend there, to read whether all believed him guilty. It was a nervous and an unpleasant hour. Mr. Brigham was announced. He bowed to all but Samuel, whom he regarded as a stranger. Miss Landon received the confidential clerk with unusual graciousness and favor; smiling upon him, coquetting with him, caressing him, and toying with him, as if she had never thought of any other man in the world. You will understand this the better, Mr. Leland, when I tell you that, almost from the first day of Samuel's arrival in the house, Miss Landon had exerted all the resources of her worldly mind to captivate him, without, however, so far as I know, making the slightest impression upon his heart."

"I inferred as much from my poor boy's letters," observed the clergyman.

"At length the clock struck eight," continued Mr. Crittenden. "Thus far, not a word had been addressed to Samuel—the Townsends not even deigning to notice him; (the clergyman's brow darkened mournfully,) Mr. Brigham glancing at him, now and then, with an air which said, 'Who is this fellow;' Miss Landon turning her back to him; Miss Selden, alone, evincing, by an occasional stolen look, that she was still friendly to him, still had confidence in him, and still believed him to be as noble, pure, and worthy as ever. (The shadow upon the preacher's forehead passed away, and was succeeded by a play of grateful light.) The poor girl would have told him so, and would have endeavored to chase away the agony of his heart, but was deterred by a secret fear that he might misjudge her motive, and deem her over bold."

"Therein," said the clergyman, with emotion, "do I recognize the modest, retiring spirit whom my boy has, in his letters, described to me so often."

"You but do my fair friend justice," remarked Mr. Crittenden. "Miss Selden is one in ten thousand; that is to say, in the form of a woman, she has all the attributes of an angel."

"I have long believed that," said the clergyman, "without ever having seen her."

Mr. Crittenden's eyes sparkled—why, the clergyman did not comprehend.

"At length," he repeated, "the clock struck eight. With its last stroke, Samuel rose to depart. The movement, although understood by all, was apparently heeded by none, save Miriam, who, not wishing that he should go away with an impression that he was wholly friendless, broke through all restraint, and springing towards him, exclaimed, in a tone which drew all eyes upon her—'Mr. Leland! though all the world believe you guilty, I do not—I will not! In my mind, you are still upright, still true, still loyal to Our Prince. And I shall pray to Him to-night, and to-morrow night, too, and ever more, to have you in His keeping, and to come up to your help in this great trouble!' Samuel pressed her hand convulsively, and with a light bow to all in the apartment, silently withdrew—for, as they intuitively felt, the last time. The Townsends suppressed, although not without difficulty, their emotion, as they beheld him retire. But what else could be looked for in persons who live mainly for the world! Should the time come, as I firmly believe it will, when this mystery shall be cleared up, my partner and his lady would be among the first to congratulate and take him by the hand."

"Doubtless," said the clergyman, charitably. "In any event, let us hope so. But Miss Landon?"

"Miss Landon," said Mr. Crittenden, "is a very different personage. She follows where the world leads. Whom society scouts, she scouts; whom society favors, she favors. From the moment that the cloud set over Samuel, she turned from him, as she would return *to* him, once the cloud should be succeeded by the sun. Her smiles and countenance are only for the Acknowledged; she has no sympathy for the *Un*acknowledged, let them be never so deserving. On that evening, Mr. Brigham's star was in the ascendant, and, seeing that Samuel's was apparently extinguished forever, she—more to evince that she had never really thought much of 'that young man,' than anything else—smilingly assented to the confidential clerk's vigorously pressed suit, and they were married yesterday. They had their wedding last evening, and this morning they started South, by way of Philadelphia, to spend their honeymoon, at the end of which time, or I do much mistake, they will detest each other like scorpions."

"But, my son?"

"On leaving the drawing-room, Samuel ascended to his chamber, from which he presently returned with his trunk, and passing out into the street, looked about him for a cab; but finding none, he shouldered the trunk, and, with agitated steps, moved off. Since then, we have heard nothing of him, nor have we been able to obtain the slightest knowledge of his whereabouts. I had myself, until this morning, supposed that he had returned to Enfield."

The clergyman bowed his head, for a minute or two, in mingled thought and sadness.

"*Your* motive in seeking him out, Mr. Crittenden?" he asked, at length.

The latter hesitated, but, after a few moments, replied—

"I am satisfied that Samuel is the victim of some artifice; and it occurred to me, a few days after his disappearance, that he might perhaps be able to give me some suggestion which would help me to the clue. I know not how he has represented me in his letters; but I do solemnly affirm that if, during the excitement of the twenty-first, I so far failed in my judgment as to then consider him guilty, I have from that day believed him as pure and high-minded as before."

"Samuel has always spoken very favorably of you, sir," said

the clergyman, rising; "and I rejoice to find that my impression harmonizes so happily with his."

And the two gentlemen shook hands warmly.

"I am very grateful to you, Mr. Crittenden, for your good opinion of my boy in the face of these appearances," continued the clergyman; "and rest assured your confidence in him will be sustained, when this wicked scheme shall be unfolded. But your partner, sir—Mr. Townsend?"

"You must not think unkindly of him, sir," answered Mr. Crittenden, gently. "He is a man of *facts;* that which he *sees,* he believes; that which he does *not* see, he has but little faith in!"

The clergyman's countenance became grave.

"The packing-room society?" he added.

"Are divided in their opinions," replied the silent partner: "although the majority are in his favor, and believe that the proofs of his innocence will yet be clearly established."

"His late fellow-clerks?"

"Are strongly inclined to hold him guiltless, and evince an eager desire to trace the matter out."

"Charley Gibbs?"

"O, Charley 'don't know what to think!' His mental capacity is somewhat circumscribed. He is a clever fellow, but not very deep. We must not, therefore, expect too much of Charley!"

A gloomy shade tinged the clergyman's forehead.

He pressed Mr. Crittenden's hand, and was about to depart, when the latter exclaimed—

"One word, Mr. Leland. I am somewhat anxious concerning Samuel, and shall spare no efforts to discover whither he has betaken himself. Let us both work in this matter, and see each other often. If you find him, be kind enough to let me know; should I be the first to obtain information of his abode, I will send you word without delay. Your address?"

"The Irving House," answered the clergyman, pressing the gentleman's hand gratefully. "Room No. Eighty-one. Adieu!"

"For a brief period only, I trust, Mr. Leland!" said Mr. Crittenden, with affectionate warmth. "Allow me to see you to the door."

The clerks stared at them as they passed through the store. "Gentlemen," said Mr. Crittenden, addressing them, after the clergyman's departure, "the individual whom you saw just now is Samuel's father, and *my* friend. In future, you will oblige me by bearing that fact in mind!"

The hint was too significant not to be understood. There was no impertinent staring at the clergyman after that!

Mr. Leland returned to his hotel with a bleeding heart, and indited two letters—one to his wife, the other to the chairman of the trustees of his church. To both, he gave a detailed statement of the result of his visit to New York; and from both he desired suggestions in reference to his own future course, together with the assistance of their prayers. The missives created the profoundest excitement and indignation at Enfield. The idea of Samuel's guilt was scouted at; and, at a meeting in the church, it was unanimously decided, first, to give their pastor a leave of absence for three months, in which to find his son; secondly, to send him a thousand dollars, with which to prosecute his search; thirdly, that the entire congregation should aid him with petitions to The Holy One; and fourthly, *that the thousand dollars should be forwarded to him* WITHOUT DELAY.

The third day brought back a letter from Mrs. Leland. Its contents were brief, but stirring:—

"DEARLY BELOVED—Come not back without tidings of our boy—of Samuel!"

A tear rushed to the poor clergyman's eye, as he murmured—"There spoke the heart of a true mother!"

On the fifth day, came the response of the trustees:

"DEAR PASTOR—We sympathize with you in your great affliction. But cheer up: Our King is merciful, Our Prince is kind—and THEY will be with you. Samuel is innocent, and HE will make it manifest. Find your boy, bring him back to us, and we will cherish both him and you. We are praying for you—our love, our affection, and our highest esteem are with you. Take three months—more, if necessary. We send you a draft for a thousand dollars to help you—should more be called for, our hearts are ready, our purses open. Find Samuel!"

CHAPTER XXVII.

LOSE a piece of money in a wood, and—look for it. Lose a boat on the broad Atlantic, and look for it. Lose a friend in a crowd, and look for him. Lose a son in the human sea of New York, and look for him!

Three months of weary walking, of weary inquiry, of weary advertising, and—no Samuel yet!

Alas! poor gentleman!

What a sad thing to write to her whose gentle heart is yet more gentle than thine own—to her whose eye is turned to thee so imploringly for a single cheering word—to her whose every letter back to thee has but a single line: *Find him, find my boy—my Samuel!*

What a sad thing to write to those dear friends whose sympathies are with thee, whose prayers are with thee, whose hearts are with thee and all of thine, and whose every weekly missive says to thee: *Find him; spend our money like water, if necessary, but find him*—find him!

What wonder, sir, if thy poor body grows thinner day by day; what wonder if thy voice is weaker than it was a few weeks agone; what wonder if thy step has lost a little of its firmness; what wonder if the bald ring on thy crown gets every week a little larger; that of the black and the white in thy hair, the white grows daily the thicker, the black, daily, the thinner; what wonder if thy cheeks are paling and wasting beneath the streaming pressure of those burning tears which well up, nightly, from thy great parental heart!

Alas! poor gentleman!

What a wild, fitful, surly knave is Winter! How he roars and howls, and screams and kicks, and fumes and yelps, and snows and blows, the nearer he approaches to the milder face of green and sunny Spring! And what a gallant, charming young fellow is April! How he smiles rude old Winter off; bowing his ugly, treacherous henchman, March, out of sight, with an air so full of irresistible assurance, that the grass comes laughing out of the ground, the timid buds laugh open their blossoms, the lambs frisk laughingly over the fields, the birds chirp laughingly on the limbs of the trees, the air brisks up into a jolly laugh, the sun laughs out from its nook in the sky, the earth laughs up and calls to the plough to join in the fun, the bees, and the ants, and the worms laugh out in their great, broad hum, sick men laugh into spirit and health, women laugh themselves out of their houses into the streets, business laughs itself into activity: and all nature looks jolly, and joins in the romp and the fun!

"Mirry, dear," said Mrs. Townsend, one morning, "let us go out and take a walk. You are growing so thin of late, that I begin to be alarmed for you. Come, put on your things. The bracing air will put new life into you. Come!"

A few minutes, and the ladies were moving down Broadway

with a lively step; for it was one of young April's most comical days, and he was so full of rollicking mischief, that everybody out caught a portion of his spirit, and felt like running, and jumping, and racing, and laughing, and cutting all kinds of hoydenish capers. Old men felt young again, and hopped about like gay urchins at tag; little boys, just escaped from the nursery, felt as big as full-grown men; old women felt as if they had gone back to childhood, and skipped, and laughed, and frollicked, as if they believed it: and little girls felt as if they were quite old enough to have company, and giggled away in great glee, like a young miss anticipating the first visit of her first beau.

Mrs. Townsend and her niece, carried away by the bracing, exhilarating atmosphere, walked down as far as the Park, and then turned back, with the intention of calling on Mrs. Brigham, on their way home.

As they passed Broome street, on their way up, Miriam started, and laying her hand upon her companion's arm, exclaimed, in a low, agonizing tone, "Aunt, dear aunt! who is that approaching us?"

Mrs. Townsend looked in the direction indicated, and then, with a countenance as livid as marble, seized her trembling niece by the hand, and hurried her up an adjoining stoop, whispering—

"Be firm, my dear; and let us see where he is going!"

Coming down the street was a poor, human thing, whose touching appearance arrested the attention of the passers-by, and filled them with commiseration.

Clad in a suit of plain, scrupulously clean, yet threadbare black, was a young man of some twenty-eight or twenty-nine years, whom an evidently long and fearful illness had reduced to a mere shadow. His pale, wan features, were mild, yet impressive. He carried over his left arm a carefully-folded overcoat, which the pleasant warmth of the atmosphere had doubtless influenced him to take off. He walked slowly, and with an air of fatigue, assisted by a rude, green stick, which he had perhaps picked up at the foot of some tree, on the wayside, and converted into a temporary cane. His boots, together with the extremities of his pantaloons, were dusty and soil-worn, giving evidence that he had been on foot for some hours, and that his journey had commenced in the suburbs: a fact which spoke eloquently of the feebleness of his purse. He passed along without noticing aught around him, and turned into Broome street, down which he moved, with the same feeble gait, in the direction of Laurens street.

It was the missing one—Samuel!

"He is going to Mrs. Farley's, I think," observed Mrs. Townsend to her niece, whose heart was throbbing violently. "But; let us follow him, and see!"

Miriam made no reply, and they walked on, with their eyes fixed upon the weary traveller.

Mrs. Townsend's conjecture proved to be correct. Samuel disappeared up the alley leading to the laundress's.

"Now, my dear," said Mrs. Townsend, "let us at once to Mr. Crittenden, and inform him of our discovery. Nay, love, cheer up. Samuel is not so bad as he looks. His innocence will yet be made clear, and—nay, don't tremble so; happiness is not always so distant as we think. Cheer up!"

Samuel paused, faint and weary, at the foot of the stairs which led to the apartments of his humble friend. While recovering his breath and strength, the following hymn fell on his ear, sung by a familiar voice, whose sad and occasionally quivering tones disturbed the gentle spirit of the listener, whose forehead became darkened with an air of sympathizing sorrow:—

"'One we loved has left our number
For the dark and silent tomb;

Closed his eyes in deathless slumber—
  Faded in his early bloom:
    Hear us, Saviour—
  Thou hast blessed the lonely tomb.

Through its dark and narrow portal
  Once they bore Thee to thy rest;
There a ray of light immortal,
  Like a sunbeam from the west,
    Burst the shadows—
  And the grave thenceforth was blest.

By the light that thus was given
  To the darkness of the tomb—
By the blessed light of heaven,
  Gilding scenes of earthly gloom—
    Star of gladness,
  All our night with joy illume.

From our circle, little brother,
  Early hast thou passed away;
But the angels say: Another
  Joins our holy song to-day!
    Weep no longer—
  Join with them the sacred lay!' "

"Poor heart, poor heart!" muttered Samuel, "I mourn with you, and rejoice with him!"

He brushed away a tear, and slowly ascending the stairs, tapped softly at the door. Mrs. Farley opened it, and started. She was pale, and in mourning.

The young Christian's pale, wan face was clothed with a cheering smile.

"How do you do, Mrs. Farley?" he said, extending his hand. "Do you not know me?"

His voice—ah! how unlike to its full, manly tones a few short months before!

"Why," cried the laundress, laughing and crying in the same moment, "it is Samuel! Dear, dear—I'm so glad to see you! Sit down in the rocking-chair—it's got a cushion. My dear, dear brother—where *have* you been? I've been so concerned about you! Dear, dear—how sad you look! Shake hands again—once more! Dear, dear—I'm so glad to see you!"

And the simple-hearted laundress wept and laughed by turns.

"I am very happy to see you, too, Mrs. Farley. Will you be kind enough to get me a drink? I am faint!"

"Shall I make you a cup of tea? It will revive you."

"Oh, no—some water will do. When did Robert go?" he asked, after a refreshing draught.

"Two months ago," faltered the widow. "He left a message for you."

"Ah?"

"Yes. 'Mother,' he said, 'tell Samuel that when I get Up There, I am going to ask God and Jesus to let him come up right away, too.'"

The young Christian shaded his face with his hand for a few moments, and then inquired—

"His departure—was it easy?"

"He closed his eyes with a smile, like an infant after its good-night, and fell asleep. A little while, and we held a feather over his lips, but it stirred not. He was gone!"

"Nay, sister—weep not. Rejoice rather; for blessed are they who are early called! Your little one is now where rudeness cannot harm, nor unkindness wound, him—in the bosom of Our Prince!"

The laundress dried her tears, and looking at her visitor gratefully, said—

"Here you are consoling me, when you want yourself to be consoled!"

"Nay—"

"O don't tell me, Samuel. I am a woman, and can see it. You are in need of nourishment. You are ill, fatigued, and fasting!"

"Oh, I'll be better soon," returned the young man, with modest diffidence. "I have walked a long way this morning; and as I am not very strong, it naturally shows itself upon me."

"How far have you come?"

"From the foot of Sixty-first Street. They brought me over in a boat from the Island, and as my means were very limited, I thought I would husband the little that I had, and walk down. Riding is expensive."

"What Island?" asked the laundress.

"Blackwell's."

"Why—you haven't been in the Penitentiary?" cried the laundress, indignantly. "Who dared to outrage you in that manner?"

"No one, Mrs. Farley. You know there are other institutions on the Island besides the one for criminals. The Asylum for the Insane, for instance."

"And you have been there, all this time?"

"Yes, Mrs. Farley. They discharged me this morning, at my own request, partly because I was cured, and partly because I desired to return at once to my friends."

"How much money have you got, Samuel?"

"A dollar, only. They gave it to me, to take care of myself with, until I should hear from my parents. And now," he added, with a timid smile, "I want to ask a favor of you, Mrs. Farley."

"You mustn't ask any *favors* of me at all, Samuel," cried the laundress. "You are my brother, my guest, and my friend. You have been good, a hundred times, to me, and I owe you more than I ever can repay. If you want anything of me, ask it freely—and not as a favor, but as a right."

"O, Mrs. Farley, you make me very happy. I knew, I felt, that *you* would not turn against me, because you were one of *us*;

and that was what emboldened me to come here, instead of going to the Mayor, who—so they told me at the Island—would let me have money enough to take me up to Enfield."

"To Enfield?" said the laundress, in surprise. "To Enfield, in your condition! Why, Samuel," she added, with equal frankness and feeling, "you would never reach it—I mean, alive!"

"That was what I thought, too, Mrs. Farley," returned the young man, with his usual diffidence; "and so I said to myself, 'If I see Mrs. Farley, and tell her how I am situated, both in regard to health and means, she will perhaps be kind enough to let me stay at her house for a few days, until I get sufficiently strong to be capable of enduring the journey home, and then I shall be in a position to reward her amply for all her goodness.'"

"Why, Samuel—how you talk! What are you running on so for?" said the laundress, sobbing.

"I hope, Mrs. Farley," said the young man, apologetically, "that you will not think any harm of me for what I have said. It was not my intention to wound you. I did not conceive for a moment, when proposing that course, that there would be any impropriety in your receiving a poor, sick man, for a few days. I might have thought so, but I didn't; the idea never occurred to me. But I see it now, and I entreat you to forgive me."

"O Samuel—how *could* you—"

"Nay, Mrs. Farley, don't cry; I didn't mean any harm. I really didn't. Now, don't cry—don't; and I'll get up and go away, right off!"

"Do sit still, Samuel," sobbed the laundress. "It wasn't that, at all!"

"You see, Mrs. Farley," continued her visitor, simply, "I am a doomed man. A few weeks, or months, at furthest, and I shall be with my Prince. I am ill; my body is wasting every day; I am dying—I know it, feel it, and desire to go home and see some hearts who are in suffering for me. But I am without means in pocket and in health, and before I can go home I must first have a little rest and nursing, to recruit my strength—a little would serve me, a very little; just enough to enable me to endure the jolting of the cars for eight hours, or so—the free country airs would do the rest: and then I could depart easy—for I should die among my kindred."

"And not a word against his enemies—not a word against those who have brought all this woe upon him!" mused the laundress, joyfully. "O, how true a disciple of his Lord!"

"What think you, Mrs. Farley?" asked the young man, earnestly. "Would it be improper in you—a lone woman—to receive a sick man for a few days? If so, be frank. I would not that you, or any one, should suffer in mind or name, for lending a helping hand to me."

"My dear friend," said the laundress, taking his hand and pressing it, "if I did not know the simplicity and uprightness of your heart, I should be inclined to think that you were mocking me. But enough. My home shall be yours, so long as you will favor it with your presence. And now, brother, no false delicacy. You are suffering, and stand in need of nourishment. Talk to me as you would to your mother or your sister. Go into my chamber and lie down upon my bed—I'll make up another for myself, to-night, in this room. Be frank with me: if you have any choice in food, say so; if you desire any particular kind of drink, speak freely, and fear not that either my patience, my purse, or my cheerfulness will weary. Now, then, lie down and repose yourself, while I make you some broth."

"I thank you, Mrs. Farley—I thank you!" faltered her guest, faintly. "Let me lean on you to the bed—I am so weak!" he added, with a wan, apologetic smile.

"Cheer up, Samuel—cheer up. You will thrive, yet!"

As the young Christian sunk upon the couch, exhaustion over came him, and he fell into a deep sleep.

"Dear—dear!" murmured the laundress, as she set about preparing a broth, "and that is the man whom they persecute and call evil names! Lord help them!"

She was interrupted in her thoughts by footsteps on the stairs. A few moments later, Mr. Crittenden, the clergyman, Mrs. Townsend, and Miriam, entered the apartment, crying—

"Samuel! Where is he?"

"Hush!" said the laundress. "He sleeps! This way—softly!"

Let us take advantage of the young Christian's restoration to his friends, to sum up the causes of his sudden disappearance.

Upon leaving the Townsends, Samuel staggered off, with his trunk, to a hotel, where he entered his name upon the register, and then sat down, in his room, to ponder upon the events of the day. But his mind was in a whirl. His thoughts were here, there, everywhere—settling nowhere. His brain was like a dark day when the sky is draped with vast masses of gloomy, solemn black, through which the lightning breaks and glides in small but frequent flashes. So came and went his thoughts; brokenly, hurriedly, pointlessly—the first being interrupted, broken up, and the fragments scattered by a second, which was, in its turn, suddenly invaded, shivered, and the splinters dispersed by a third, and so on, till that poor mind was like a foggy midnight, with only here and there a street lamp breaking through the gloom.

At a late hour, the watchman of the hotel, in making his round, through the lobbies, was startled, while passing the young man's door, with a smothered cry of

"Help, Lord—help—help!"

The watchman paused to listen, but hearing no further noise, he passed on, muttering—

"The poor fellow is having some dreadful dream!"

Samuel did not leave his room till late. He was pale, nervous, and still laboring under the pressure of a disturbed mind. A quarter of an hour in silent prayer somewhat comforted and tranquillized him; and he descended to breakfast: after partaking of which, he called at the office for pen, ink, and paper, for the purpose of communicating the events of the preceding day and night to his parents.

"Your name is Leland, is it not?" asked the proprietor

"Yes, sir."

"Samuel Leland?"

"Samuel Leland, sir."

"Late a clerk in the dry goods house of John P. Townsend?" continued the proprietor, referring to a newspaper which lay before him on the counter.

"Yes, sir," returned Samuel, with a slight blush.

"Well, Mr. Leland," said the hotel-keeper, blandly, "the Satanic Chuckle of this morning has a detailed account of your affair of yesterday; and as I am very particular about the reputation of my house, you will oblige me by settling up and taking yourself off!"

Samuel flushed to his very temples.

"Allow me to look at the article, sir," he said, in an agitated voice.

The proprietor handed him the paper, and his eye fell upon a paragraph commencing as follows:—

"*Another Pious Rascal brought up with a Round Turn—Startling Developments in the History of a Dry Goods Clerk—A rich Sample of Rural Piety—An accomplished Hypocrite nabbed at last.*—A rich scene came off yesterday at the great dry goods jobbing house of Mr. John P. Townsend, where a pious thief, rejoicing in the name of Samuel Leland, but better known under the expressive sobriquet of 'Rural Piety'—"

Samuel could read no more; a dizziness seized him, and he fell, senseless, to the floor. He was taken up and carried to his room, where the application of a few restoratives brought him, in the course of half an hour, to a faint sense of his situation.

"Now, sir," said the proprietor, "we can't be bothered with persons of your sort, and I will thank you to square up and clear out."

Samuel paid his bill, and, leaving his trunk behind him, went off, like one in a dream, in quest of other lodgings. He wandered, without being aware of it, into the suburbs, and thence to a small wood, where, seating himself upon a rock, he made a fruitless attempt to collect and arrange his thoughts. But in vain; his mental powers were already beyond his control, and his efforts to recover them were futile. The day passed away; night came: with the night a tempest, and with the tempest, rain.

A laborer, while passing through the wood, on the following morning, came unexpectedly upon the body of a young man, lying at the foot of a tree. He was drenched to the skin, and had evidently passed the night exposed to the cold and the rain.

The laborer surveyed the body for a few moments; then stooping down, he laid his hand gently upon the breast.

"It still beats," he muttered, "but feebly. There is life in him yet, with care and nursing."

Help was called, and the body conveyed to a neighboring house, where the respectability of the wanderer's appearance secured him immediate attention.

A few hours, however, sufficed to dampen the charitable ardor of the family, who, upon perceiving the mental weakness of their guest, at once lost all interest in him, and gave him in charge of the public authorities, who removed him, with many others, to the Insane Hospital, where it was discovered that, in addition to his lunacy, he was in the first stages of a serious pulmonic disease—the result of his night in the wood.

Mental darkness covered him for nearly three months, when the cloud passed away, and intelligence reasserted its empire. Then, he became conscious of his position, for the first time. His body had wasted, and was wasting, before the consuming tongue of his pitiless disease. He conversed with his physician, and having obtained from him a statement of his real condition, he firmly resolved upon making an effort to reach Enfield without delay. This determination the physician endeavored to shake, but in vain.

"Why don't you wait until you get better?" he asked.

"Because, sir," answered Samuel, with a sad but sweet smile, "if I wait till then, I shall never see my friends at all—at least on earth."

"Well, be it as you will," returned the physician. "I see there is no use in flattering you. I will attend to your certificate of discharge at once."

Samuel left the Hospital and the Island the next morning: we have seen with what result.

The feelings of the tender-hearted pastor upon beholding the sad change in the appearance of his beloved son may possibly be imagined, but not described.

Mr. Crittenden and Mrs. Townsend were visibly affected. Miriam wept not with her eyes; but in her heart were tears sadder far than those which were shed around her.

"I must get him to Enfield at once," said the pastor. "A mother's care alone will now avail him!"

"It will not do," ventured Mrs. Townsend, shaking her head. "He must first have time to gather strength for the journey."

"Wait," said Mr. Crittenden. And he ran for an eminent physician. The latter, on his arrival, remarked, after surveying the sleeper for a few minutes—

"He must remain where he is. To remove him, at present, would be fatal. A few weeks of medical attendance and careful nursing are indispensable."

"We put him into your hands, doctor," said Mr. Crittenden; "and remember that he is dear to us."

The physician bowed, and promising to call again in a few hours, when he hoped to find his patient awake, he took his departure.

"Mrs. Farley," said Mr. Crittenden, taking the laundress aside and putting a small roll of bills into her hand, "you must give up your business for a few weeks, and turn all your attention to our mutual friend. I will have some furniture sent to you, so as to enable you to make the place look cheerful and inviting. You know, Mrs. Farley, how these things affect sick minds? You will want a companion, and I think I can find you one with whom you will be pleased. Now, go in and talk a while with Miss Selden—I wish to exchange a few words here with our other friends."

The laundress moved into the chamber, and Mr. Crittenden called out the clergyman and Mrs. Townsend.

"My friends," he said, addressing them, "there is one nurse here whose presence at his bedside will do more for our dear boy, than all the doctors in the world. Fair lady," laying his hand upon Mrs. Townsend's arm, "you know to whom I refer, and you will bear me out in the assertion, that she will worthily, faithfully, and tenderly minister unto him."

"It is true," answered Mrs. Townsend, looking at him gratefully.

"Let me hope, sir," continued Mr. Crittenden, addressing the clergyman, "that you will consent to this, and take my word for the happiness which it will confer upon our Samuel, who, if he is your son by birth, is also mine from this hour by adoption."

"I am very grateful to you for the proposition," returned the pastor; "the more so, as I have long known the state of my boy's heart in regard to Miss Selden—although," he added, with a melancholy smile, "I scarcely think that he was himself aware of the depth of his attachment."

"Thank you, Mr. Leland—thank you!" cried Mr. Crittenden, heartily. "Now, let me say a word to the young lady herself." Then passing into the other room, he motioned the laundress to retire, and taking Miriam, who was pale and agitated, by the hand, he said—

"My Mirry—yours now the task of nursing our dear Samuel back to health, yourself back to happiness. His father and your aunt have consented—I need not ask if your own heart is willing!"

Miriam fell, sobbing, upon his breast.

"Cheer up, darling—cheer up," whispered the silent partner. "He has loved you long, if silently. Cheer up; the clouds are not always; look forward to the sun, which will yet shine for you both!"

The clergyman lost no time in communicating to his wife and friends the glad tidings of his son's reappearance. Three days afterwards, he received the following painful response:

"DEAR HUSBAND—Love to Samuel, to whom I send a thousand kisses; to Miriam, to whom I send a mother's affection; to Mrs. Farley, to whom I send a mother's gratitude; and to Mr. Crittenden, to whom I send the warmest thanks of a mother's heart. But for you and me, my husband, there is naught, at this time, but affliction. Our blind one is no more. From the hour of his brother's mysterious absence, his life has hung upon a thread. He but waited to hear that he had again been found, to take his departure. The intelligence came, a burst of joy escaped him, the thread snapped, and he was gone. Come up."

The pastor read this letter with a dry eye. He was in that stage of mind when the heart can no longer weep.

"Help, Lord—help!" he murmured. "Woe presses upon me

hard," he faltered, looking upward reverently; "but I do not murmur, Lord—no—I do not murmur!"

Alas! poor gentleman!

He handed the letter to Mr. Crittenden, who read it carefully, and then wrung the poor father's hand, in silence.

"My boy," said the pastor to his son, whose delicate heart comprehended, by intuition, the cause of the great grief which was written upon his father's face, "I must leave you for a brief season to the care of Miriam and Mrs. Farley. Mr. Crittenden will call and see you every day till my return. Adieu!"

"Adieu, my father!" returned Samuel, with a faint smile. "Bear my love to mother, to Aunt Betsy, and Ada; and place a flower for me upon *his* breast!"

"How, my boy—you know—"

"Father, I saw him last night in a dream. He was one of many who were clad in bright garments."

The pastor spoke not. He bent over his son, and they silently embraced.

"Kiss Miriam, my father," whispered the latter.

The clergyman did so, and then, pressing the hand of the laundress, tore himself away.

He returned in a few days, accompanied by his wife. The meeting between the mother and her boy was delicate and touching. Mrs. Leland embraced Miriam as she would a daughter; Mrs. Farley as a sister; Mr. Crittenden as a brother.

Surrounded by those who knew and loved him, and ministered to by three such gentle hearts as his mother, Miriam, and Mrs. Farley, it was no wonder if, in a few weeks, Samuel had so far recovered as to be able, with safety, to venture the journey to Enfield. At length the day was appointed. It came, and Samuel was sad, Miriam in tears.

The pastor and his wife exchanged glances; Mr. Crittenden and Mrs. Townsend looked at each other. All understood the cause of the emotions of those two young hearts, and sympathized with them. They would have spoken, but delicately refrained, out of consideration for Samuel himself, who was wrapped in contemplation.

At length he looked up, and calling to Miriam, who approached, he said, taking her hands in his—

"My Miriam, you see before you a poor invalid, who pines to look once more upon his native hills and on those old familiar fields whose memories mirror a childhood which was one lengthened holiday. And yet I would not go, and leave behind in sadness a heart which would, I know, rejoice to breathe with me dear Enfield's sylvan airs. I have known you long, my Miriam; and loved you—I may say it now without reproach—from the hour when I first heard, in the temple, the music of your voice singing of the goodness and the glories of Our Prince. It was on my first Sabbath in the city. I have not loved you less since then; and had my fortune been but a tithe in evenness with my affection, this confession would have found its way to your gentle ear long ago. And now, one word. Between us and our journey, but a single hour. Enfield is a pleasant place, and our home a pleasant one. It is not so gay as your uncle's mansion, but it is as cheerful, and as happy. Come, and share it with us. If I were a stronger man, I would say to you, knowing as I do the sweetness of your mind and the goodness of your heart, Come, and walk with me adown the pathway to the setting sun. But being of a frail and feeble mould—one whose summer will never behold an autumn, I can only say, Come, and partake of the love of one whose heart is stronger than his frame—his father shall be your father, his mother your mother, and his friends your friends."

Miriam bowed her head upon his breast.

"As my wife, my Miriam," he whispered.

A convulsive pressure told him that he was understood.

"My father," said Samuel, with emotion, "we await your blessing, as well as that of our friends here, upon our union."

"It is well," returned the clergyman. "Mr. Crittenden, are you content with this?

"Joyfully."

"And you, Mrs. Townsend?"

"Heartily."

"And you, my partner?"

"Truly."

"Then stand up, my children. You, Samuel Leland, do tender to this maiden your love, your sympathies, your affections, your confidence, your esteem, your protection, and all that you may have now, and all that shall come to you henceforth of worldly goods, in exchange for those of hers?"

"I do."

"Do you accept them, maiden?"

"I do."

"Shall ye be henceforth as one in love and in trial, in prosperity and adversity, in health and in sickness, in joy and in sorrow from this hour until death shall step in and sunder this solemn compact?"

"As one."

"Then, by virtue of my office as a delegate from On High, I do pronounce ye one; and what God hath joined together, let no man break asunder. Bless you, my children!"

CHAPTER XXVIII.

THE Brigham union was an unhappy one. Both were selfish, passionate, headstrong, and unscrupulous. With no innate governing principle to give a moral tone to their minds, and to discipline their hearts, their union was simply a Discord.

Their wedding tour was everything but a Happiness. On their return, they exhibited a cordial and hearty dislike for one another. They were mutually fretful, irritable, and disagreeable. Notwithstanding all this, they took a large house in Tenth street, and furnished it in a style which distanced the whole neighborhood. What they wanted with this big establishment, unless it was to have ample room for free fighting, would puzzle a wise head to determine. Once launched upon the sea of housekeeping, they appeared to be mutually resolved upon keeping it in a constant ferment. For a few months, they fared sumptuously upon elegant wretchedness. Their main desire seemed to be to render each other as miserable as possible. With this end in view, they contrived to get up a quarrel every morning at breakfast, every afternoon at dinner, and every evening at tea. Mrs. Brigham carried her complaints to the Townsends and other friends; Mr. Brigham took his to a neighboring saloon, where he buried them in old Otard brandy, which he sipped from time to time over a cigar, a lounging-chair, and The Satanic Chuckle.

This kind of life could not, of course, last forever. Daily irritation of proud, impatient blood, for any lengthened season, finds a period, sooner or later, in an explosion.

Mr. Brigham returned home generally as disagreeable as he could be. Mrs. Brigham, ditto: and *while* at home, they amused themselves by tantalizing each other to the last sufferable degree.

One afternoon, Mrs. Townsend dined with them, and was an unwilling witness of one of their daily strifes.

"'Bel," she asked, after Mr. Brigham had taken his departure in a huff, "why don't you, for your own sake, try to keep on good terms with your husband? It is better to give way, now and then, to his ill humors, than to be always quarrelling."

"I won't yield to him a single inch!" returned Mrs. Brigham, with a fierce curl of her proud nostril. "I know him better than you do, aunt. If I should submit to his imperious spirit once, it would be all over with me. I have no choice except to become his ruler or his slave—and *that* I will *never* be!"

"But, 'Bel, don't you see what all this dissension between you is doing—how fatally it is working?"

"What *is* it doing?"

"Mr. Brigham is idling away his valuable time, when it should be employed in business!"

"The trouble is, aunt, he won't do any business except for himself. His marriage with a lady of property has rendered him proud, insolent, and ambitious. He desires to go into business on his own account."

"Well, that is a laudable ambition, 'Bel."

"Very true, aunt; but he wants *my* money to do it with, and *that* he shall *never* have! My fortune is already large enough for both of us; and if he would only behave himself and remember his place, I should be perfectly willing to support him. But I will not peril my present secure position in wealth and society, by risking my money in the lottery of business, for forty thousand husbands!"

"Have you told Mr. Brigham this?"

"Have I? Yes—once a day at least, for the last four months."

"What impression does it make upon him?"

"None at all; or if any, it only increases his insolence to me, and his determination to compel me to let him have my money! Now, do you blame me, aunt?"

"You will, of course, do as you think best, 'Bel," returned the latter, who had no disposition to commit herself. "I have every confidence in your judgment," she added, with a significant smile, "and I believe that you know what you are doing!"

Mrs. Brigham laughed; the ladies embraced, and the visit terminated.

On returning home, Mrs. Townsend found a letter from Miriam. It was warm, affectionate, yet sad. It represented that Samuel was declining day by day; that he felt that the hour of his departure was at hand; and that he had but one regret, viz.: that he should be compelled to leave behind him a tainted name.

Mrs. Townsend showed the letter to her husband, who shook his head, exclaiming—

"What nonsense!"

"You still believe him guilty?" asked his wife.

"Certainly—why not? *The money was found upon him!*"

"But Mr. Crittenden thinks him the victim of some conspiracy, or of some one who was interested in his ruin."

"Mr. Crittenden is a clever fellow," laughed the merchant, "and, ever since he took up religion, a very charitable fellow—very charitable; but in this matter his charity carries him beyond common sense. Who *could* be interested in Samuel's ruin? He injured nobody; he stood in nobody's way. Why, then, should any one conspire against him? Fudge—fiddlesticks! There never was a rascal, there never was a criminal, who hadn't the same ridiculous story to tell. I went, some years ago, with a friend, to Blackwell's Island, and conversed, out of curiosity, with a number of the jail birds there—every one of whom was, according to his own statement, not a hardened reprobate, but—an 'innocent man,' and the 'victim of a black conspiracy!' Bah! When I am robbed of money, and lay a trap to detect the thief, the individual upon whom I find the money, were he my own brother, *is* the thief. That is a *plain* way of drawing correct conclusions. As to the fellow's antecedents, I care nothing. All I have to consider is, whether the money which I have lost is the same as that which I find in his pocket. If so, the case is settled, and my mind is made up. That is the way I look at matters, and I have always found it to be a pretty *safe* one!"

This was a clincher, and the topic was dismissed.

One afternoon, about a week subsequent to the foregoing conversation, Mr. Brigham returned home a little the worse for temper, which was somewhat spiced by a recent familiar acquaintance with French brandy.

"Well, woman!" he demanded, "have you made up your mind yet what you intend to do?"

"In reference to what, sir?" asked Mrs. Brigham, surveying him scornfully.

"To me, madam—to me! Do you design to let me go into business, or not?"

"You are at perfect liberty to go into business as soon as you please, Mr. Brigham; to cut as great a dash as you desire; and, as you have so often expressed it, to 'give the old house of John P. Townsend a stout tug:' but," she added, with a low, mocking courtesy, "not with *my* money!"

"Have a care, woman!" cried her husband, fiercely. "Have a care! You don't know me!"

"O, indeed! *Mysterious* man! I don't know you! O, dear, you almost alarm me!"

"Beware, madam—beware!"

"The very words the villains always make use of in the melodrama! Mr. Brigham—why *don't* you turn actor! You have no idea how you'd bring the house down with your grimaces and your *be-wares!*"

"Woman!" cried her husband, furiously.

"Well, sir. I *am* a woman; and what then?"

"Have a care—have a care, I warn you!"

"O dear! Is that all? What a disappointment! I really anticipated something rich; and it's only a 'have a care!' Why, sir, I *have* a care—the care of a silly husband, who innocently fancies that he is a person of sufficient consequence to be worth minding."

"Madam! you will yet mind me, be assured of that!"

"You think you will eventually break me in? How you flatter yourself!"

"I do not merely *think* so!"

"Poor dolt! Have you the assurance to suppose that you could ever disturb the serenity of a person of my intelligence—*you!*"

"I *have* that assurance, Mrs. Brigham!"

"You make me laugh!"

"Do I? See to it, then, that I do not make you weep!"

"You flatter yourself, sir. I do not weep at trifles, and least of all for trifles like you! Why don't you make use of language like that to one of your own sex? You would not dare. You are too much of a coward! A man would treat you, as I shall yet be compelled to call upon my black porter to serve you."

"How is that, madam?"

"To kick you out of my house, sir!"

The teeth flashed lightnings at her.

"Madam, be warned; be warned, in time. There is a devil in my breast, which, once aroused, is not easily subdued. He tamed a bolder spirit than yours once, as he will in time tame you, if you be not careful!"

"You always had a fine imagination, sir!"

"But the spirit to which I refer, madam, was not a mere creature of my imagination. You knew him well!"

"Some poor little boy whom you used to bully in your school-days, and before the approach of whose big brother, your own equal in size, you found it convenient to run!"

"I speak of a man, madam!"

"Out, dolt! You would not dare to trifle with a *man*. It is not in you!"

"A man, I say; a man, who annoyed me, threatened me, stood in my way!"

"And you overthrew him?"

"As certainly as I will you, madam!"

"Some poor wretch, who had neither friends, money, nor influence: a broken-down porter, worn out with rum and hard labor, for instance?"

"A man, madam; a man with friends and influence; one to whom money was as naught: a man of mind, also!"

Mrs. Brigham began to think she comprehended her husband's meaning. She was not certain of it, however; but she determined to satisfy herself.

"I'll draw him out," she muttered, musingly. "If it be as I fear, he'd better have hung himself than to have breathed aught of his villany to me!"

These thoughts darted through her mind like a flash of light, and without leaving any interregnum between her husband's last remark and her own reply.

"A poor man, doubtless, for all that," she retorted, "who, like yourself, was fonder of the bottle than of himself; and whom you, taking advantage of one of his drunken, helpless moments, approached and struck a mean, dastardly blow—from behind!"

"A man of mind, madam; a man who didn't drink!"

"And you destroyed him?"

"As I will you, madam, unless you alter your tone!"

"I'll believe that, when you give me the man's name, and not before; and that you dare not do!"

"I dare do more, madam, than you think!"

"There you go again, braggart! Give me the name of the party whom you uprooted so effectually, and then I'll reflect upon my own chances."

"Samuel Leland, madam!" hissed her husband, with an air of triumph.

Mrs. Brigham dreaded this name—expected it; and yet when it fell upon her ears, she experienced a sickness of heart which all the energies of her will could scarcely resist.

"Pooh!" she said, laughingly, for the purpose of drawing him on, "Mr. Leland destroyed himself. He stole his employer's money, concealing part in the lining of his coat, and part in the right pocket of his vest; at least, so guardy told us at dinner, on the day of his detection: and the money was found upon him. What did you do in the matter? You simply helped in the search. Any fool could have done that!"

"Nay, madam, I did more than *assist* in the search. I suggested it!"

"A *dreadful* mark of cunning, indeed; particularly when Mr. Townsend had previously determined upon a similar course!" laughed Mrs. Brigham. "Now," she added, for the purpose of sounding the villain's soul, and of testing the correctness of a suspicion which his words and manner had generated in her mind, "if you had had the daring genius to plan the whole affair, from beginning to end, yourself—to commit the robberies, yourself—to watch your opportunity, while conversing with the miserable young man, to drop one roll of bills in the torn lining of his coat, and the other in his vest pocket—both of which could, with some adroitness, be very easily done, why then—"

"Then, madam—" said her husband, with a satanic smile.

"Then, sir," returned Mrs. Brigham, looking at him with affected uneasiness, and purposely faltering in her tone, "I should say that you and I had better come to an understanding without delay."

"What kind of an understanding, madam?"

"First tell me how much money you need to go into business?" said his wife, somewhat deferentially.

"Ho, ho! I've brought you down a little, at length, have I?"

"Answer me, Brigham. Don't talk to me in that bitter way. You know very well that I don't like it. Why won't you be kind to me? I am a woman; and women, you know, love those who are good to them."

"Then set me an example," said Mr. Brigham, with a coarse laugh. "I am an apt scholar, and pick up rapidly."

"What do you wish me to do, Brigham? Be frank. I am a reasonable woman, if you will only employ reason with me."

"Furnish me with means to give the old house a stout tug, and we'll get along well enough."

"But how much do you want? Don't say too much, to frighten me, nor yet too little, to restrict yourself from operating with a free hand!"

"Thirty thousand dollars. Does that alarm you?"

"It is a large sum. Could you *insure* success with that amount?"

"Beyond the shadow of a doubt."

"Well, that is something, but not all."

"What more?"

"Will you promise to be good to me, if I let you have the money?"

"I give you my word for it! Is that security enough?"

"I am willing to take it. But one thing more. Will you give up swearing and drinking? They are horrid practices, you know!"

"I will swear—"

"No, don't do that!" interrupted Mrs. Brigham, laying her hand upon his arm, and looking up into his eyes with an assumed air of mingled confidence and generosity. "Your word, Brigham—your simple word!—ought to be enough for *me!*"

"My word, then!" said her husband.

"You give it to me, solemnly—as solemnly as when you affirm that it was you who planned and executed young Leland's ruin? I guessed aright the way in which you performed it, did I not?"

"Had you seen me put the gold pieces in the rolls to make them sink to the bottom, and beheld me drop one in the torn slit in the lining of his coat, and the other in his vest pocket, while we were talking together and looking each other in the eye, in my office, you could not have comprehended it better!" he said, patting her flatteringly on the cheek.

"Demon!" thought Mrs. Brigham, behind the confiding smile with which she had wormed the secret from the audacious wretch. "Thirty thousand—eh?"

"Thirty thousand, my dear."

"How soon do you want the money?"

"Right away, if possible."

"Then," said Mrs. Brigham, rising, "I must go up and give guardy notice. Let me see"—looking at her watch—"it is four o'clock; just the time to catch him at dinner. Wait here till I return."

"Shall I send John for a carriage?"

"O, no; it's not worth while. It is only a step."

"I say, 'Bel," cried her husband, rubbing his hands in great glee, "won't it be a rich joke to call on old Townsend, this week, for the money with which to flog him, in the way of trade, next week? Eh!"

"Capital! Ha, ha!" cried his wife, quitting the apartment.

"So *I* say. Ha, ha! ha!" ughed Mr. Brigham, throwing

himself upon the sofa. "There's nothing," he added, as he recovered from his sudden mirthfulness, "there's nothing like bringing a woman down a few pegs, especially when she is as fond, as 'Bel is, of showing too high a spirit. Spirit is all very well, in its way; but when a woman—and that woman my wife—attempts to make a display of it upon *me*, she must look out for the consequences! In future, we'll see who shall carry the whip-hand—*Mr.* or *Mrs.* Brigham!"

And ringing the bell for a match, the ex-confidential clerk lit a cigar, and concluded he would run out and "take a nip" to his success in "having broken Mrs. B. in," at last.

"The wretch—the demon!" mused Mrs. Brigham, indignantly, while on her way to the Townsends'. "To have cheated me out of so noble a husband as Samuel would have made me!"

The lady was evidently quite confident that she would have won that gentleman, in time.

"He would have been such a splendid fellow to enter a drawing-room, or a public assembly, with! So handsome, so elegant, so imposing! Why, with what a joy, what a pride, and what a satisfaction, one would have hung upon his arm! And he would have been mine—mine—all mine. But now—why, Brigham! what a mean, pitiful rascal—what a contemptible orang-outang—you are, in comparison! But you'll get your deserts for your villany—that's one comfort!" As she drew near Fifteenth street, she added, with a merry twinkle, "What a sensation the affair will make, when it gets out, down town!"

Upon reaching the Townsends', Mrs. Brigham laid before them all the particulars of the ex-confidential clerk's confession. The merchant was thunderstruck at the recital. Mrs. Townsend made no remark: she simply glanced at her husband with an expression which said, "What becomes of your positiveness, now?"

"I'll never believe in my eyes again!" exclaimed the merchant, springing from his chair, and ordering his carriage.

A few minutes later, the trio were whirling down to the store, to lay the startling intelligence before the silent partner. The latter listened to it in silence, and then remarking, "I had already suspected this!" he left the office, and calling the clerks, packers, and porters together, he announced the news to them, from the platform, and requested them to spread it far and wide. Then bidding his partner and lady friends a temporary adieu, he caught up his hat, and hurriedly proceeded to the various daily newspaper offices, and related the particulars to the editors. The following morning, Samuel's innocence, and the ex-confidential clerk's guilt, were known throughout the metropolis.

After seeing the editors, Mr. Crittenden bent his way to Fifteenth street, and informed the Townsends of his determination to start the following morning for Enfield.

"I'll go with you," cried Mrs. Brigham, clapping her hands. "I do so want to see Mirry!"

"And—Samuel!" thought her aunt, quietly.

"Very good," said the silent partner. "The train starts at seven. My carriage will be at your door at quarter past six."

"I'd like to go with you," observed Mr. Townsend; "but I don't see how I can get away. We have such a press of business!"

"Thanks to Samuel's happy system!" added Mr. Crittenden.

Mrs. Brigham returned home at nine o'clock, and congratulated herself upon finding that her husband's absence enabled her, with the assistance of her maid, to make the needful preparations for the morrow's journey. Then feeing the attendant with a half eagle, she bound the latter to secrecy, and ordering her to call her at five, she retired to rest.

The ex-confidential clerk let himself in, by the aid of a latchkey, about two hours after midnight. His step was unsteady, his manner maudlin, and his mind stupefied with brandy and cigars. He groped his way to bed, and was soon, to all appearance, as lifeless as a log.

He awoke, dull, heavy, and irritable, about noon.

"Where is your mistress?" he demanded of the maid.

"Gone out."

"Where?"

"I don't know, sir."

"Dull head! what *do* you know?"

The girl made no reply.

After dispatching his breakfast, the ex-confidential clerk went out for a walk; stepping in at a saloon for a morning "drink," to tranquillize his nerves, on the way.

While proceeding down town, he met and bowed to a commercial acquaintance, who passed on, however, without returning his salute.

"What's up now?" muttered Mr. Brigham, in surprise. "The fellow must have seen me!"

As he approached the Astor House, he encountered Charley Gibbs.

"How d'ye do, Charley?" he said, extending his hand to that young gentleman.

"Excuse me!" returned the latter, stepping aside. "I am particular in my acquaintance!" And he passed on.

The ex-confidential clerk was, for a few minutes, irresolute. He was half inclined to follow the young man and demand an explanation. But he thought better of it, and then continued his walk. A few minutes brought him to Liberty street, and muttering, "I'll step in and take a look at the old house," he suddenly found himself face to face with our old acquaintance, Bill Bradley, the packer, who was on his way to a restaurant.

"How d'ye do, Bill?" he said, extending his hand, patronizingly. "Excuse my glove!"

"Who are *you?*" demanded the packer, starting back a single step, and eyeing the ex-confidential clerk from head to foot, with insulting scorn.

"This rudeness is intentional!" thought Mr. Brigham, crimsoning to his temples. "What can it mean?" Then addressing himself to the packer, he said, haughtily, "You are impudent, fellow! Stand out of my way, or I'll cane you!"

"You'll do w-h-a-t?" cried the packer, rolling up his cuffs.

"Cane you!" repeated the ex-confidential clerk.

But he had scarcely uttered the threat, when a quick, heavy blow from the fist of the stalwart packer precipitated him into the mud. Wild with rage, he sprang to his feet, and advanced, with uplifted stick, upon his opponent, when the fist of the latter smote him, like a sledge-hammer, between the eyes, and sent him, whirling and staggering, back again into the slush.

"You'll try it agin, won't yer?" said the packer, tauntingly, as Mr. Brigham rose to his feet once more, and measured the huge proportions of his enemy. "I wish yer would. I *like* it, myself!"

The teeth of the ex-confidential clerk fairly screeched with rage; but their owner did not condescend to make any remark.

"I give yer notice," said the packer, shaking his brawny fist in the creature's face, "that yer must never appear in Liberty street any mo-ar, while I'm in it; 'cause if you do, I'll lam you. Now, mind! We're very pertickler about the safety of prorpertee down this way, and we don't like the smell of thieves! Come, *move!*"

Boiling with rage and humiliation, his face and linen covered with blood, his clothes begrimed with filth, Mr. Brigham hailed a passing cab, and muttering to the packer, "You'll hear from me again, sir!" he sprang into the vehicle, and was, the next minute, gnashing his teeth with madness, and on his way to Tenth street. On arriving at his own door, he threw the cabman a piece of gold, hurried into the house, renewed his toilet, and then, lighting a cigar, sat down to compose the wild tempest in his blood. He had scarcely seated himself, when he descried a small package upon his dressing-table. Upon opening it, he beheld a note addressed to himself, and a number of newspapers. The former read as follows:—

"MR. BRIGHAM:—I send you the city journals of this morning, trusting that you will find in them food for reflection.

"JOHN P. TOWNSEND."

"Short, and to the point!" muttered the ex-confidential clerk, with a trembling lip. "What does it all mean? Can that woman have betrayed me? If so—"

Tearing open The Satanic Chuckle, his eye fell upon a marked article with the following caption:—

"A PRECIOUS RASCAL—ASTOUNDING DEVELOPMENTS—THE TABLES TURNED—RURAL PIETY ALL RIGHT—EXCITEMENT IN LIBERTY STREET—A PROMISING CANDIDATE FOR SING SING."

Then followed a long detailed description of the ex-confidential clerk's plan for the destruction of the young Christian, the manner of its accomplishment, the results of that plan to the victim, the confession of the ex-confidential clerk himself, whose general character was delineated with a free pen, and a gentle recommendation to the press throughout the Union to copy the article, and "give the rascal all the notoriety he deserved."

Mr. Brigham dropped the paper, and sunk back in his chair perfectly livid.

"So," he muttered, "it's all out! The traitress has revealed all; the papers have got hold of it, and I am a ruined man! This accounts for my treatment in the streets to-day."

He rose, drew a long breath, and paced the apartment in feverish excitement. At length, he opened his trunk, and taking out a revolver, which was already charged and capped, he raised the threatening tube to his ear, and, with his finger on the trigger, paused for a few moments, irresolute. Then withdrawing the weapon, and muttering—

"No—not yet. Cowards only sink before the tempest. I'll brave it out!"

He laid the revolver upon the dressing-table, and paced the room again.

"Wait till the traitress returns," he exclaimed, with a meaning smile, "and then I'll give these newspapers food for *another* and a somewhat different article!"

But a week flew by, and the wish of the ex-confidential clerk was as yet ungratified: the traitress had not yet come back.

Brigham fumed and drank, fretted and drank, swore and drank; but neither fuming, fretting, swearing, nor Otard brandy had any effect. The lady still remained abroad.

He questioned the maid; but the half-eagle had been before him, and his interrogatories resulted in nothing.

"Can she have deserted me?" he muttered. "Perhaps, like many of her kind, she has gone off with somebody else!"

His brow darkened at the thought, and a green, ugly feeling commenced working in his breast.

The following evening he proceeded to the Townsends,' but did not find them at home.

"When will they return?" he asked of the girl, the porter being absent.

"I cannot say," was the reply.

"But you can guess," he said, sharply.

"Guessing is not one of my duties."

"You are impertinent! How long have they been gone?"

"Two days."

"Umph! Is Mrs. Brigham with them?"

"I don't know anything about Mrs. Brigham."

"When was she here last?"

"I can't say."

"You have been put up to this insolence, minx!" said Brigham, fiercely. "But it won't answer with me, I warn you! My wife!" he added, with a furiousness which made the girl tremble. "My wife, I say! where is she?"

"She is not here," was the answer, in a faltering tone. "She went away—to the country—some days ago."

"To the country! To what part? The place—name it. Quick, or I'll throttle you!"

"To—to—"

"Where—where?" shouted the man, reaching out his arm as if to carry his threat into effect.

The affrighted girl drew back, and stammered, or rather screamed—

"To Enfield!"

Brigham started as if he had been shot. His flushed cheek became livid. His eyes rolled in their sockets like the green glittering orbs of a serpent. His teeth gnashed as if each was instinct with human rage and power; the two rows appeared to the startled fancy of his auditor as if they were severally leaping from their cavities, and swearing, tearing, and rioting like enmaddened drunkards.

Brigham was no longer in the semblance of a man, but in that of a demon.

"Aye," he cried, or rather roared, "with that rascal, Leland. But I'll teach the brazen creature a lesson. As for him—"

He started, and rushed from the room and the house, without finishing the sentence.

He darted home; ordered a servant to go and procure him a bottle of wine; summoned her back, and bade her bring him "two, three—half a dozen, and not of wine, but—brandy!"

He wore away the night, and started, at daybreak, with a revolver in his breast, and a valise in his hand, for the railroad. He reached the depôt an hour too soon—breakfasted at a neighboring restaurant, and at length found himself rattling off, with lightning speed, to his destination.

The monotonousness of the ride, added to his broken night, lulled him in an hour into a nap. He awoke again, but unrefreshed; his nerves were on edge, his temper furious.

Fortunately, he was alone. Had another shared his seat, there might have been an altercation—a quarrel—a murder. For the ex-confidential clerk carried a revolver in his breast—each tube loaded to the muzzle—and was capable of everything.

As it was, the passengers viewed him with uneasiness. They had a suspicion that he was mad. "He acted so strangely, and had such a tiger-like mouth!"

It was, therefore, with a feeling of satisfaction that they at length beheld him catch up his valise and retire from the car.

CHAPTER XXIX.

IT was five o'clock in the afternoon when Brigham reached Enfield. He entered its solitary inn, registered his name, and then called for dinner, which was promised him in a few minutes. While the meal was in course of preparation, he stepped up to the bar, and uttered a single word, in a sharp, dry voice—

"Brandy!"

The host shook his head, with a smile.

"We don't keep articles of that nature in Enfield," he said.

Brigham bit his lip, and muttering a half-uttered curse, turned to the register, and ran his eye over the arrivals.

The list was small. It was plain that Enfield was not favored with very many travellers. But small as was the list, there were names in it which caused the reader to start.

The host eyed his new guest with mingled mistrust and dislike. The appearance of the latter was by no means in his favor. His eyes were bloodshot—his cheeks flushed with a sickly glow—his teeth were raving—his linen soiled—and his clothes dusty and crumpled. He had, as the reader is already aware, slept in them in the cars. But that was not all. He had rolled and slept in them throughout the preceding night.

"This fellow is a rascal!" thought the landlord. "I must watch him!"

The names which caused the new-comer so much concern were those of Mr. and Mrs. Townsend, Mr. Crittenden, and Mrs. Brigham.

"Are these people putting up here?" he demanded, somewhat fiercely, of the host.

"They are," answered the latter. "What then?"

Brigham did not reply. He was confused. He asked himself what *they* were doing in Enfield, and could not answer the question. He turned to the register again, and noticed that his wife and Mr. Crittenden had arrived three days in advance of the Townsends. What did that mean?

He was disturbed in his revery by the announcement that the meal which he had ordered was ready.

He followed the servant into the dining-room like one in a dream.

As he quitted the bar, the host ran to the register to discover the name of his ill-favored guest. As he glanced at the list, he, too, started. Then going to the door, he beckoned to three young men who were standing near the entrance of the village store, on the opposite side of the road. The latter approached, and entered the inn.

"What is it, Tom?" they asked.

"Look here. Read this name," replied the host in a low voice, as he pointed to the register.

It would appear as if no one could look upon the list without starting.

As each of the young men read the name of the new-comer, they fell back in surprise, and looked at one another indignantly. Their hands rolled up involuntarily into balls, so that they were no longer hands, but fists.

"Where is he?" one of them asked at length, with an eye that portended mischief.

"Taking dinner," replied the host. "But what then? I wouldn't disturb him."

"Wait!" said the other, turning to his companions. The trio whispered together a few moments. They appeared to be forming some plan.

The landlord suspected the tenor of their conversation, but did not permit it to appear. In fact, he was himself betraying signs of a pugnacious spirit; that is to say, his eyes were slowly firing up, his blood was mounting by degrees to his temples, and his knuckles were itching to hit somebody or something.

The young men having brought their conference to a close, the former speaker turned to the host, and said, in a low, cautious tone—

"Keep an eye on the fellow. We'll be back presently!"

The landlord said nothing; he did not even nod. But his eye and lip were eloquent.

The young men then retired—not openly and boldly, as when they entered, but lightly, carefully, as if fearful of being overheard. Once outside of the inn, they darted off—each taking a different direction, and all running, as if upon a mission in which their hearts had an equal interest with their heels.

In half an hour, the major part of Enfield was in motion. The roads were alive with indignant pedestrians, all running towards the village, and halting, as they reached it, in front of, and around, the inn.

When the ex-confidential clerk returned to the public room, he was somewhat surprised.

The apartment was thronged with young, vigorous men, whose threatening countenances were fixed upon himself.

Loud murmurs greeted his entrance, and as he looked around him for an explanation of what it all meant, a rude hand from behind suddenly forced his hat down over his eyes. Before he could recover himself, a stout grasp was upon his collar—three quick kicks were given him from behind—a shower of stunning blows fell upon his head, breast, and shoulders, and amid discordant cries of, "Give it to him,"—"Gibbet the rascal"—"Don't hurt him; march him out of town, but don't hurt him,"—"Cowskin the wretch,"—the ex-confidential clerk was dragged from the inn, despite his struggles, and thrown, like a bundle of wild carrion, upon a dung-heap, in the rear of the house.

"There!" cried a stalwart youth, "lie there! That is the only proper lodging-place for things of your breed. Lie there till morning; then get you gone, or we'll send you off on a rail, and with a coat of tar and feathers!"

Brigham looked up, glaring like a wild beast. For a moment, owing to the severe treatment which he had undergone, he could scarcely stir. Rage, however, speedily re-ennerved him, and, springing to his feet, he surveyed the fierce throng with a blazing eye. His teeth bristled like so many angry mastiffs making ready for a spring.

"Devils!" he exclaimed, in a thick, but unwavering voice, "if you want my life, you shall not have it without an effort. You took me by surprise, and have hurt, but not conquered me. Clowns! think you to subdue a MAN thus easily? Learn better."

As he spoke, he plunged his hand into his breast, and drawing forth a revolver, presented it at the crowd.

"Give me way!" he cried, "or your blood shall flow like water. Give me way!"

He took a step forward, to run down the dung-heap, when a

tall form closed in upon him from behind, and adroitly pressing in his arms, precipitated him to the earth. As he fell, his pistol went off, and the ball, owing to the sudden direction which had been given to his hand, lodged in his left arm, between the elbow and the wrist, shattering the bone, and splitting it.

"Let him up—let him up!" cried a hundred voices. "He hasn't hurt anybody but himself!"

Notwithstanding the excruciating agony of his wound, the ex-confidential clerk was upon his feet in an instant, and glaring like a wild boar at the crowd.

"There are five balls left!" he shouted. "Since you wish them, you shall have them!"

But again the same crushing form was upon him, and again he fell, overpowered, to the earth—retaining, with the tenacity of a drowning man, his weapon, which this time did not go off.

"Let him up—let him up! He is a brave fellow, after all. Let him up, and give him a chance," cried fifty voices in a breath.

Brigham wormed himself, like a snake, out of the grasp of his powerful antagonist, and then, with a fierce, sudden spring, broke through the throng, which, partly from terror of his ugly weapon, and partly from admiration of his high courage, opened before him, and away he sped, like a hunted boar, followed by the major part of the crowd.

Across the road—a leap—over the fence—across a field—a leap—across another field—a leap, and out upon the main road. A temporary halt—the fugitive looking up the road, down the road, across the road, everywhere, for shelter—finding it nowhere.

But little time for thought, or decision. His pursuers are behind, but hard upon him. Down the road, which stretches immeasurably away, with but now and then a house to break the monotony of its stretch—and with no friendly copse or wood into which one might plunge — down the road are fifty forms making with all speed for the village, to join their fellow-townsmen in punishing the demon who has wrought so much woe to hearts that never harmed him; up the road, thirty—forty it might be—who have sprung from the fields to head him off, and who are bearing down upon him like avengers; behind him, a hundred others, whose fleet limbs are bringing them nearer and closer each succeeding moment; before him, across the road, a farm-house, and on the other side of the fence five stalwart, fierce-browed men, each with a pitch-fork in his grasp, and daring the fugitive to advance.

The hunted man looks up the road, descries the inn, and boldly resolves to reach it, or perish in the effort.

In flight again—every nerve strained—his nostrils lapping up and down, with passion, ardor, and high resolve—his wild, expressive teeth launching lightnings at all in his path—his poised weapon warning them, as they love their lives, to beware how they impede him on his way.

Three hundred yards at best lie between him and the inn—three hundred yards: no more.

He'll get over them—yes—keep up, brave heart, and he'll soon get over them. What are twenty or even thirty men against a single one, like him, whose blood is up, whose high resolve is taken, and whose spirit is as resistless as that of proud, relentless death? Twenty or thirty men? Mere nothings—wooden things at best. Keep up, O heart! keep up, while we dash on and win.

These thoughts darted like flashes of light, through his brain, as the fugitive sped forward.

On—on—like a heroic Fury, he swept; onward, through the score who threw themselves in knots of threes and fives before him, but only to break, or fall like staggering drunkards, as the fugitive dashed through them, over them, and scattering them like sheep—reserving his fire, like a subtle, desperate man, to maintain himself when he once should reach the inn.

Keep up, O heart—keep up. Nerves be again as steel, for here are seven to dispute with us the road. Ha! well done, shoulders, well done, fist—for three of the dogs are rolling on the earth, spinning like schoolboys' tops at play, and the others are behind. Ha! ha! who'll try us next?

Ten more have leaped the fence, designing to head him off—but three of them are down, and two others falling over them. But five remain, and they—are now behind. Ha! ha!

"But fifty yards now between us and the inn. We'll soon be there. Ha! ha! Let who will, hunt down a determined man. But fifty yards—we have passed five of them already. Ha! ha! Brave sport—brave sport! Let come on, who will: for now not more than forty yards between us and the inn!"

But a cloud leaps over the fence and rises in the road: "The giant who dragged us from the bar, who hurled us on the barnyard heap, who pressed our arms and crushed us, causing us a mangled limb, as we set out to leave the heap. He alone, of all the crowd, our conqueror; but conquer us again, nor any other living creature, shall he—nor now, nor evermore!"

A pause—a snap—and a sharp, quick, loud report.

Is the giant down? No. But advancing with a laugh. The ball has missed its mark. Curses—curses!

Oh! to be so near, and yet not reach the inn.

Oh! to make so great, so glorious a head against full forty men, and be taken by a single one at last.

Oh! to be captured by him whose spirit we *feel* to be BRAVER than our own.

Oh! to be caught by him—him of all the crowd!

The stout heart fails at last. The legs, till now so dry, and brave, and wiry, grow moist and tremulous, as the giant comes up with outstretched arms—as if the physical part knew as well as the mental part, when bolder blood than its own draws nigh. The defiant eyes, erewhile so bright and flashing, have lost their strength, their vim, and wax confusedly weak, watery, and dim. The hidden will, even, falters like the rest. The invisible mind, before so clear, and sharp, and subtle, becomes misty, fleecy, and—

The laughing giant grasps him by the collar! The giant is his fate.

"Come!"

And he is dragged along, his legs trailing over the road, as a butcher might haul the skin of a calf, of a cow, or a bull; his wounded arm bleeding and hanging, nerveless, down, like a pendant, fluttering stick; back to the barn-yard in the rear of the inn, and with a "So, you will play your capers on men like our Samuel, hey?" thrown again, like a mean, pitiful thing, upon the smoking dung-hill, and left there.

To die? No! That was the first thought of young, indignant, and partially inconsiderate, blood. But now that the first impulsive outbreak of wrath was come and gone—now that the wretched game was quarried, reason came back, and with it better thoughts.

"Vengeance is mine! saith the Lord!" said a rebuking voice, which came from the lips of an old man—a sturdy veteran in righteousness.

Young blood bowed to the Scripture. Not a man attempted to justify his share in the transaction. The giant himself was mute with shame.

"Take him up," said the veteran, in the same stern tone; "take him up, and run one of you for the doctor."

"I'll do that; mine are the longest legs," said the giant, striding like a Colossus from the barn-yard, to the main road, down which he swept, despite of his immense size, with the speed of an antelope.

He returned ere long with the village doctor—a short, slender personage, with a mild, genial countenance—upon his shoulders, and set him down at the door of the inn as coolly as if he were a bag of wheat, and not a learned disciple of Galen. But as the action elicited no remark from the by-standers, not even provoking a solitary smile, it established one of two facts: either, that the doctor had no regard for his personal and professional dignity, or else that the incident was too familiar a one to create surprise. Whichever it was, the worthy doctor did not stop to say, nor even to make the observation that it was one of Long Bill's funny ways, which everybody in Enfield knew; but, assisted by the giant himself, pushed his way, with his usual good-nature, through the throng in the public room, into a broad entry which separated the latter from the dining-room, and, preceded by the host himself, ascended to a small neatly furnished chamber on the second floor, where, on a bed, lay his patient, groaning with agony from his wound.

It was a long and tedious affair for the worthy doctor—who also, like most of country physicians, combined with his art the practice of surgery—to extract the ball and set the injured bone, but it was done at length, and if not as well as before, at least as well as could be expected; and then the ex-confidential clerk was left to a reviving cup of tea, a plate of toast, and—his own dark, bitter thoughts.

It was late when he slept, late when he awoke. He summoned a servant, and ordered breakfast. While swallowing an egg, the doctor made his appearance. Brigham nodded to him, and continued his meal in surly silence.

Meanwhile, the physician quietly inspected the features of his patient.

"A bold, bad man," he murmured to himself. "If the Creator ever branded a human creature with the outward impress of innate wickedness, this must be that creature. What eyes, what nostrils, what teeth!" he added, with a shudder. "That such a being should have it in his power to destroy so pure a flower as

Samuel! Yes, our pastor is right: 'There are men who know no god but Satan; they are his agents, and serve him with the same zeal that the good do their King and Prince. They have power upon God's children to-day, as Satan himself had power upon Job.' This man is one of them."

Brigham continued his meal; his features squirming every now and then, as a careless movement disturbed his wounded arm, and caused it to shoot a thrill of agony throughout his nervous system.

The worthy doctor surveyed him with his calm, intelligent eye.

"That men can be found to work for so stern a master," he said, musingly, "and for such wages, too! For his labor in worrying Samuel, this bad man has received a long tissue of malignant thoughts, domestic misery, the detestation of all who know him, and last, though not least, a broken arm, which will always remind of his shame. What wages! And then, in The Hereafter—well! well!" he added, checking himself, "it is not for me to say what his wages will be there!"

"Now, doctor," said his patient, wiping his mouth with a napkin, "I am ready for you. Handle me delicately, for I am in torture!"

The physician rose and dressed his arm, with his usual carefulness and skill.

When the operation was finished, the patient took a portmonnaie from his pocket, and opening it, drew out a bill, which he silently tendered to the doctor.

The latter mildly but firmly declined it, and then, with an air at once courteous and dignified, moved from the apartment.

"As you like!" returned the other, haughtily.

"Money from a being like him!" murmured the phsician, as he descended the stair-case; "it would burn me!"

Thus far the ex-confidential clerk had preserved his own

thoughts, his own counsel. Excepting his brief conversation with his host upon his arrival, the few words which had escaped him during his exciting and humiliating adventure, and his curt observations to the doctor, he had not exchanged a syllable with any one in Enfield. He was, therefore, wholly ignorant of the real state of affairs at the parsonage. He only knew that while his wife detested himself, she as warmly loved Samuel. He was also aware that she was not one to let either pride or principle stand in her way, when once she had an idea to carry out, or a whim to gratify. These facts, when united, formed, in the ex-confidential clerk's opinion, a key to the coming of Mrs. Brigham. But the presence of Mr. Crittenden and the Townsends mystified him. Unless they were there as aiders and abettors in his wife's proposed infamy, why were they there at all? It was true, they had a reputation for piety and respectability, which ought to shield them from so ungenerous a suspicion; but Brigham knew the flimsy character of the Townsends' piety too well to believe that *that* would have any influence upon *their* conduct. Mr. Crittenden's religion he judged to be of the same plastic nature.

"The Townsends' piety!" muttered Brigham, with a sardonic smile. "Show them a glittering bait, and they would do the work of devils. Their piety, indeed! They worship but one god — Money. If there be any real vitality in religion, the Townsends in the Church are enough to strangle it!"

With these thoughts, the ex-confidential clerk ran his eyes around the room in search of his revolver, but the latter had disappeared.

Brigham smiled, darkly. Then taking up the knife which had accompanied his breakfast, he carefully examined its edge; and muttering, "This will do as well!" he cleaned the blade by drawing it over the crumpled napkin, and then concealed it beneath his vest.

"Now for a solution of this enigma!" he muttered. "If it be as I suspect, let the traitress look to herself. As for *him*—"

He paused, drew out the knife, and again examined its edge.

"Yes," he murmured, returning the weapon to its hiding-place, "it will do!"

And he descended, with a moderately firm step, to the public room, where he found the landlord leaning over the counter, and quietly drumming a tune with his fingers.

"Good-morning!" said the latter, surveying his guest carefully.

Brigham returned the salutation with surly haughtiness, and was passing towards the door, when the host added—

"Two words, stranger!"

Brigham paused, and drawing himself up, demanded—

"What are they, sir?"

"The first is, that you are wanted at the parsonage, as soon as you can make it convenient."

"Who sent that message?"

"Mr. Leland. You know him, I presume!"

His guest colored, but made no answer to the latter remark.

"Your second word?" he said, sternly.

"That you will, from this moment, relieve me of the favor of your patronage!" returned the host, with a satirical bow. "I am very particular about the character of my guests, and yours don't come up to my mark!"

The eyes of the ex-confidential clerk glittered, his cheeks paled, his nostrils swelled, and his teeth darkened, as if shadowed by a passing cloud.

"Your bill!" he cried, striding fiercely up to the counter.

"Excuse me!" returned the host, with a cool, mocking bow. "I have none made out." A second bow. "I shall make none out." A third bow. "I have no desire to make one out." A fourth bow. "But," with a fifth bow, more mocking than either of its predecessors, "I should be happy—*very* happy—to see you march out!"

"Your bill—your bill!" cried Brigham, in a tone which bore a strong resemblance to a shriek.

As for his countenance, at this instant, it was really a picture. His eyes glared like those of a beast of prey when meditating a spring; his nostrils did not merely swell, they flapped; his cheeks and lips were absolutely livid; his teeth were so many screaming vultures. In fact, an imaginative mind would have fancied Brigham's features, at this moment, to be so many angry bullies who accompanied him to "do his fighting."

Most men would have quailed before that frightful face; but Tom Lowndes, the landlord, not being of a very timorous nature—that is to say, having Revolutionary blood in his veins—he didn't quail, a bit. On the contrary, he was as cool as a November breeze; and that is generally very cool—in Enfield. Therefore, he looked at the ex-confidential clerk's gratuitous exhibition of ferocity as tranquilly as he would if surveying a painting or a statue of some ridiculous hobgoblin, and wondering whether it was designed to frighten children to sleep, or to make them laugh, or what.

"And so," he said, thrusting his hands into his trowsers' pockets, and then raising himself on his toes, and then returning to his heels, and then up on his toes again, as Quakers are supposed to do every time they say "Hum!" and leave the presence of a lady, "and so, you funny man with your left arm in a sling, and your eyes, and lips, and teeth making such comical faces—you would like me to make out a bill? Well—pray be cool, now, be cool, bubby—don't shake yourself to pieces, it might hurt you!—well, all I've got to say is, that I don't like to do such a thing, at present; at least, not in your case. How do I know what you might want to do with my signature after the 'received payment?' Keep cool, bubby—keep cool. Don't try to climb over that counter; it's against the rules: and besides, you might scratch off the paint. Why, how you roar! You remind me of Deacon Disosway's bull when it had the colic. But, as I was saying: there's no telling what you might want to do with my signature. As for your board and lodging, you are perfectly welcome. Pray, young man! is there anything the matter with you, that you throw yourself around in that manner? Aint you afraid—"

"Afraid?"

"Yes—of breaking your suspenders, or something of that sort! But perhaps I am mistaken. You can't be a circus-actor—a clown, or anything of that kind—can you? You look—"

"Well, sir!" thundered Brigham, "how do I look?"

"Mean enough to be a pickpocket—a house-thief—or to steal spoons!" said the host, with a quiet bow. "Mean enough to be a watch-stuffer, a thimble-rigger, or a blackleg!" A second bow. "Yes, mean enough to steal your employer's money, and drop it in the vest pocket and between the cloth and lining of a fellow-clerk's coat!" A third bow—very low—head almost touching the floor.

The enraged ex-confidential clerk could stand no more. He reeled from the inn to the road like a drunken man; gritting his teeth like a savage. He, paused an instant or two, in the middle of the highway; drew a long breath, as if to throw off the overwhelming insults which had been heaped so pitilessly upon him; sighed for his revolver, and then, with a broken curse, staggered across the road to a dwelling, which his instinct told him was the parsonage.

On reaching the fence, he leaned against it for a few moments to recover himself, breathing hard the while. Then passing through the little gate, he knocked at the door, which was opened by our old acquaintance, Aunt Betsy.

The latter recoiled, a step or two, at sight of the visitor, and surveyed him as she would a serpent.

The worthy housekeeper had heard so much of the individual who stood before her, that she recognized him at a glance; and although she knew, as the poor soul afterwards expressed it, "that it was both uncivil and improper to show her scornful feelins, and the horror with which she regarded him, she could no more help it than fly—not a bit more."

Brigham smiled, darkly.

"Mr. Leland and my wife!" he said, or rather hissed. "Where are they?"

"Come in," said the housekeeper, in a tone of mingled loathing and terror.

The ex-confidential clerk followed her up to the front room on the second floor—his hand buried in his vest, and grasping the handle of his knife.

Aunt Betsy knocked softly at the door. The ex-confidential stationed himself at her side.

A gentle step was heard—Brigham, unseen, drew out his knife.

The door opened; a single glance, and Brigham started back in amazement.

The knife fell from his hand. It was picked up by Aunt Betsy, who looked at him as if she had more than half a will to sheathe it in his heart.

"It was very wrong of her," she admitted subsequently, "but she couldn't help it!"

Where is that bold, bad man's haughty spirit now? Where the tiger fury which was consuming him but a little moment ago? Where the jealous demon that possessed and drove him to the very verge of green, raving madness?

Gone—like a breath, like a flash, like a sudden waking from a wild, insane dream.

On a bed, thin, and wan, and pale, and wasted, his dark eyes looking calmly out from underneath his lofty brow, the edge sharpened, like his nose and chin, by disease, lay, in the closing stages of dissolution, the innocent victim of this bad man's wiles.

On a chair beside the bed, her head bowed upon the pillow, sobbing lowly, as if her pure, warm heart were bursting, her small, slender form thinned by the stern pressure of long watching and her first great grief, sat Miriam.

Around this couch, on chairs, their heads bowed in sadness and in silence, were the Townsends, Mr. Crittenden, the bold, bad man's wife, a little girl, and the parents of the pale, wasted form on the bed.

"Room for Mr. Brigham," said Samuel, in a clear but feeble voice.

The parties moved their chairs aside, and Brigham, recalled to his presence of mind by a touch from Aunt Betsy, entered the chamber—his step shuffling, and his countenance flushed with shame.

He approached the bedside like a guilty thing—with the air of a thief detected in the act.

The young Christian extended his hand to his enemy, with a look so full of magnanimity, forgiveness, and love, that it compelled the latter to avert his head.

In his long commercial and other calculations, Brigham had never made provision for a look like that, nor a scene like this.

"I have sent for you, Mr. Brigham," said Samuel, gently, "to show you how calmly a Christian can die!"

Brigham groaned. "Would the earth but swallow me!" he muttered.

"I am going to my Master, to my Saviour," continued Samuel, "and on learning that you were in Enfield, I had a strong desire to see you. I wanted to assure you, on the faith of a dying man, that neither now nor at any other time have I harbored a single unkind thought against you, and that I fully, freely pardon you for all that you may have said or done to me. And I feel very grateful to you for coming here, at my request, and allowing me so kindly to say to you these words!"

He dropped his hand, and Brigham, pale, and gasping hard for breath, reeled from the bedside to a chair in the furthest corner, where he sat, staring at the floor, with his eyes as hard and dry as stones, and with a wild sensation, as if his brain had been transmuted into wood, and was all on fire.

A long silence followed, which was broken only by low sighs.

Samuel lay calm and tranquil; with an occasional long-drawn breath. At length, he made a sign. He was about to speak.

"Mrs. Brigham," he said.

The latter approached, and took his hand.

Samuel looked at her with a fraternal air.

"If you would only be reconciled to Mr. Brigham," he said, tenderly.

Brigham himself pricked up his ears, and listened.

"The marriage-vow," continued Samuel, "is a holy one. It is made before man and God, and should not be broken. You have vowed to cling together unto death, and it is your duty to do so. The voice of duty is imperious, because upon it depends our happiness here, and hereafter."

"Oh, Samuel," cried the lady, "do not ask me to do that. I do not love him."

"But you are his wife," returned Samuel, gently, "and it is your duty to love him; and you would find it a pleasant duty, too, if you would only consent to try. Mr. Brigham, my friend, be kind enough to step here a moment."

Brigham complied, looking very much like a man who was about to be hanged.

"Mr. Brigham," said Samuel, kindly, "look your wife in the face. Mrs. Brigham, turn your eye upon your husband." The speaker then added, solemnly, "You two, who are looking upon each other, have registered an oath on the tablets of the recording angel, that you would love one another, cherish one another, abide with one another. Why do you not remember it? If evil counsels have stepped in between you, is that a reason why you should forget your compact? Should you yield to evil counsels your honor, your oath, your duty? If evil thoughts have come in upon you, suggesting your estrangement, is that a reason why you should mutually forget your oath? Or is an oath nothing, God nothing, duty nothing, and your own whims everything? Say you do not love each other. Is that a reason why you should not try to do so? Is not duty worth, at least, an honest trial? If you *do* not love, how know you that you *cannot?* Duty is worth an effort. Think—your oath!"

He paused. There was no answer. He resumed—

"It may be you think hard of one another; that you entertain opinions adverse to each other's personal worth. This for your encouragement: There came never yet from the Creator's hand a heart that had not its good corner. Who looks for it, in a kindly spirit, will find it; but who looks for it with an ungenerous key, will never find its lock. The human heart is a simple thing to him who'll try to understand it. Would you see its rudeness, touch it rudely, and its rudeness will spring out. Would you taste its sweetness, touch its better part, and its sweetness will gush forth. Who would receive kindness, must themselves be kind. You two, who are looking at each other now, have each your better corners, and room, too, in your hearts for tender affections, although you may suspect it not. Hitherto you have only played upon each other's evil; make a noble effort now to reach each other's goodness. The fountain of love is vast, and will increase day by day, excluding in time all the bitterness, so we but feed it daily. Mr. Brigham! have you not in your heart a kindly feeling for this lady, who loves you, though she thinks it not?"

"I confess it," said Brigham, glancing stealthily at his wife.

"And you, Mrs. Brigham, have you not in your heart a kindly feeling for this gentleman, who loves you, though you think it not?"

The lady was silent. But brave Samuel did not despair.

"Listen," he said. "The heart that truly loves is slow to admit it, lest its love should be too lightly esteemed. But it need not be so in your case: your husband will appreciate your love, value it, and teach you, by his own ardor, how it may grow and deepen for him, as his will grow and deepen for you. Let him once see *your* goodness, and his will run out to meet it."

He paused again; but the lady was still silent.

Mr. Townsend glanced at his wife, and silently inquired—

"What do you think? Will she consent?"

His lady answered with another glance—

"No. Or, if she does, she will not adhere to it."

"What Mrs. Brigham means," said Samuel, addressing the lady's husband, "is, that she may not love you enough at first, perhaps, and that you will yourself grow discouraged; that she has certain little fixed whims which she may not be able to get rid of all at once, and that you will not kindly make allowance for them while they are passing off; so that her love, which is now away down in her heart, may gradually work its way to the top, and look out and meet the sunshine of *your* love. She fears that you will not give it time to reach the surface, but chill it back ere it shall get up very far! Is not that it, dear lady?"

"Yes!" faltered the latter, glancing stealthily at her husband.

"But her fears are groundless—are they not, Mr. Brigham?" said Samuel. "You will pledge her your word as a gentleman, that you will give her affection ample time to thrive and reach the sun?"

"I will—I do!" said the latter, with every intention of keeping his pledge.

"Then I will meet you half way, Brigham," said his wife, generously extending her hand. "I will be good if you will, kind if you will. I give you my word, as a lady!"

Brigham took her hand and pressed it. The pressure was returned.

A flush of pleasure spread, like a play of light, over the brow of the young Christian.

"Be again as one," he said, solemnly. "Think kindly of one another; have consideration for each other's weaknesses; bid the evil depart, and let the good rise, and expand, and deepen. So shall you find peace, and love, and joy. Go," he added, touchingly, "go and be happy!"

The reunited couple passed away from the bedside.

"'Blessed are the peace-makers,'" murmured Mr. Crittenden. "O, Jesus! what great hearts thou placest in the breasts of Thy people!"

"Hand me a drink," said Samuel.

It was done by her who loved him as she loved none other on earth.

Samuel rewarded her with a grateful smile.

"Miriam," he said, taking and pressing her hand, "Miriam, my sweet one! yours has been an unhappy love."

"No, no, Samuel! no, of joy, rather; of great, *great* joy!" cried the young girl, through her tears.

"We were wed in my affliction," continued her husband, gently; "when death had already marked me for his own. From that hour until now, your tender eye has been upon your mate, but it has only been to see him move day by day nearer and nearer to his tomb. This is not the sight for a young wife's heart. Surely an unhappy bridal!"

"Not for me, Samuel! Not for me. Oh, no. Do not think it!"

"Pardon me," said Samuel, shaking his head, "but I must think it. The honeymoon may bring tears to a young wife's eyes, but they should be tears of joy, not sadness. It should tell of present bliss, not misery, and promise a bright, not a gloomy, future. I mention this, sweet one! to assure you that if I have been a silent witness of your devotion, I have appreciated it as well. I have sympathized with your fond feelings, and mourned for you over your unfortunate lot in having fixed your woman's affections upon one who could only reward them with a smile; in having, out of your great goodness, allied yourself to one who could be with you but a little time, and that time only in sorrow. But take comfort, sweet one! we shall have another union, in a land where sorrow comes not, nor parting hours: THERE!"

He pressed her hand, and she sunk upon a chair, like one heart-broken.

"Mr. Crittenden," said Samuel.

That gentleman stepped up and took the young Christian's extended hand.

"Dear friend," he said, falteringly.

"Dear brother," continued Samuel, "I wish to congratulate you upon your coming to our Prince, and to ask you if you have not found joy in believing?"

"Great joy, my friend—joy unspeakable."

"Ah! you make me very happy. You will, I know, adhere faithfully to the standard of our Prince, because you are a brave and upright man. We are about to part, dear brother; but only for a brief season. I shall see you again, and *when* I see you, you will be clothed in the bright garments of the Redeemed."

"God grant it!"

"He *has* granted it, already, dear brother," said the young man, affectionately. "I can almost see the raiment and the mansion which have been marked out for you There, even now. Oh, could the world but be persuaded of the noble heart of our dear Prince! How full it is of love, of hope, of kindness, of gentleness, and of generous magnanimity—they would rise up in myriads, and strive with each other for precedence in His acquaintance and affection! Believe it!"

"I do—firmly."

"I am sure of that; for you, dear brother, are one of the few who, when once convinced, act resolutely and at once upon the line prescribed by your conviction. Ah! you cannot conceive what joy there is in heaven when a great mind like yours takes up arms for Christ; for the angels know that great minds will not be content with making offering to Him of *themselves alone!*"

The merchant bowed his gratitude for these obliging words.

"There's not a being on Life's pathway," continued Samuel, glancing at the Townsends meaningly, "whose steps are not watched from Heaven—joyfully, if he walk in the light of the Right; mournfully, if he continue in the darkness of the Left!" Then pressing the hand of his friend, he said, "Dear brother! my society will want looking after. Its members are leal men in Christ, but they would, I know, feel additionally strengthened and encouraged, if you would but make one of their number. Your ripe, comprehensive mind, rich in suggestiveness and experience, would be to them like a vast granary, to which they could resort, in time of need, for nutritious food, in the way of counsel and direction. If you would only make one of them," he added, pressing Mr. Crittenden's hand tenderly, "it would make you and them so happy!"

"I will do so, joyfully!"

"Thank you—thank you! O what a world of light, and love, and pleasure, it will open unto you! And now, one word."

"Say it, dear friend."

"I have made out a list of my poor, which Miriam will hand you when I am gone. Many of them, I have reason to believe, are His children. You will find a figure 1 mark before *their* names. Some are conning the subject over, but have not yet found Him; these want encouragement: their names are marked by a figure 2. The others, whose names are prefixed by a figure 3, are warped in mind by views bordering upon infidelity, and can only be led to Jesus by slow and patient stages. If only one of them can be saved, it will be matter for rejoicing. But they are all more or less friendless and helpless, all deserving. Three of them are paralyzed, four bedridden, one blind, one a struggling widow with four small children, one a noble-hearted wife with three helpless little ones, and a husband chained to his bed with consumption; two are helpless with rheumatism, and one a noble orphan girl, of eighteen, struggling to keep her two little orphan sisters from the alms-house. They are all honest, virtuous, deserving people; and I should rejoice in the knowledge that their little wants will not be forgotten when I shall be no more."

"I will take charge of them," said Mr. Crittenden, with emotion.

"And you will encourage those who are laboring in mind with hope, and be kind and patient with the others, and lead them, if possible, to the Right?"

"Yes. I promise it."

"Oh! thank you—thank you. You make me very happy!" cried Samuel, with a parting pressure.

Mr. Crittenden returned to his seat, sobbing like a little child.

Samuel paused a while to gather a small degree of strength, and then called up Mr. and Mrs. Townsend. He surveyed them alternately for a few moments in silence, and with an air of mournful sadness. He knew, by that peculiar intuition which enables the children of God to single out those who are really of Him, from those who are only seemingly so, that the piety of this pair was simply a pretence; and he felt it a duty which he owed to his Maker, and to the couple themselves, to warn them of their danger.

"My friends," he said, in a tone which they alone would be likely to understand, "you have often seen a city missionary. He goes, like a messenger from heaven, with his little pack of Gospel messages, from house to house—leaving a tract here, a Bible there, a kind word everywhere. One door opens to him freely, and receives his tract or book with the same kind spirit with which it is tendered; a second, coldly; a third, sometimes from pride, sometimes from policy, and sometimes from both, opens to him with affected pleasure and politeness, and receives his heavenly messages with a show of genial gladness, which deceives no one but themselves—the humble missionary, never; while a fourth bars itself against him, and though he knock or ring ever so long and loud, neither mistress nor servant will come—that door remains closed against him. On his second round, his reception is the same; the third, like the first and second; and the fourth, as the third—the fourth door is ever closed against him. On his fifth, he *may* try the fourth door for the fifth time, but if he find it impenetrable still, he puts it down in future as a door at which there is no use in knocking, and ever after passes it by without attempting to enter. The Holy Spirit, in its tours among men, is like that humble missionary. As the latter knocks from door to door, the Spirit knocks from heart to heart. One receives it kindly, gratefully; a second, coldly; a third, to serve some worldly policy, receives it with a show of great gladness and rejoicing, which sometimes deceives the world, themselves not at all, the Spirit itself, never; while a fourth fastens its door against it, as if with locks and bolts, and will not let it in. The Spirit calls again, but with the same ill success; and again, and yet again, but with no better result than before. It is grieved at the stubbornness of that heart which will not accept of goodness for its own sake, if not for His, and it departs in sadness. When again it comes that way, it sets the door of that heart down as one at which there is no use in knocking, and mournfully passes it by. If it never, in mercy, knock at its door again—as sometimes it *does* not—WHAT THEN? Let it bolt and bar itself in, though never so strongly, there comes at last a second spirit which it can *not* shut out: Death! That spirit is God's constable. It holds out its warrant, and laying its cold hand upon the trembling, unrepentant heart, says: 'I arrest you in The King's name. Your time's up. *Come!*' Dear friends," added the young Christian, impressively, "if either of you are acquainted with any heart that has closed its door upon the Holy Spirit, warn it, for its own sake, to do so no more: for its time is not always, and the constable is at hand!"

The Townsends returned to their seats with misty eyes and troubled minds: as thankful for the solemn admonition, as for the delicate manner in which it had been given.

"Great heart—great heart!" murmured Mr. Crittenden, who understood and comprehended it all. "O, would they but remember it, and take heed!"

"Ada," said Samuel.

"My protector!" said the child, approaching him.

"Ada," he said, laying his hand gently upon her head, "I promised your mother to educate, watch over, and bring you up in the light of the Divine Eye. I cannot keep that promise in my own person; but, thanks to my Redeemer! I have friends who will do it for me, when I am gone. And you, Ada, darling, are one of these friends. You will help me a little, will you not?"

"How?" asked the child, innocently.

"By being good; by loving God and Jesus, and your teachers and your friends, and everybody in the world?"

"I'll do that. I'll be good—always," said the child.

"Ah! thank you, darling—thank you; you make me very happy! Now, look at me—look at me well, and remember my face. One of these days, if you will only be good, you will go up to heaven, and then you will know me, and then you will see God and His Son, Jesus—The Prince. Oh, Ada, darling, don't forget to be good—don't. I shall look for you so anxiously. You won't forget?"

"No," said the child. "I will be good!"

"Ah! thank you—thank you. Miriam, sweet one! unto you I intrust the keeping of this child. Take her, love her—rear her, as if she were born of your love and mine, as a pearl for Our Prince's crown."

"I will!" said Miriam, pressing the sobbing child to her breast. "I will!"

"Ah! thanks—thanks! You make me very happy! Kiss me, Miriam—and you, too, Ada!"

"And this is the man against whom I raised my hand!" murmured Mr. Brigham. "God help me!"

A pause followed. The young Christian was recovering his strength. At length he glanced invitingly at his parents. They approached.

Samuel, with his eye upon the pillow, surveyed them for a few moments with an air of touching tenderness.

"Your hand, dear father—dear mother, yours!" he said, in a tone which showed how deeply he was stirred. Affection, sympathy, respect, pity, were in his air and voice. "I feel for you," he added, pressing their hands. "The rod of affliction is laid upon you hard—you, whose delicate hearts feel affliction's slightest touch so keenly! But a few months, and you were called upon to surrender up"—his voice faltered—"brother Joe—your little one. The grass is scarcely yet formed which covers his little form!"

He paused; emotion shook him: a tear fell from his eyelid to his cheek. He recovered again, and continued:

"And now you are commanded to relinquish your first-born

—your only one. I sympathize with you in your great sorrow. Pardon—pardon!" he added, in a voice which struggled in vain to be firm. "I wanted to console, to strengthen you; but I find—I find I am not so strong as I thought. I—I—my heart is breaking. I—I—father—mother!"

And unable longer to restrain his agony at parting, even for a time, from those whom he so tenderly loved, the affectionate youth gave way, and his great heart melted away in tears.

His parents bent over him, and their sobs mingled together.

Samuel himself was the first to master his emotion. He glanced alternately at the two dear beings whom he understood so well, and whom he now beheld bowed down by the sternest of human sorrows. He knew that their delicate natures could not bear to see even an humble insect suffer; and he comprehended what then must be their agony in parting with their son, whom they had known and loved so long, whom they had seen pass from infancy to childhood, from childhood into youth, and from youth into manhood—loving him fondly all the way.

They were upon their knees, their foreheads bowed in mingled prayer and agony, upon the coverlet.

Samuel laid his hands affectionately upon their heads.

"Take comfort, dear hearts," he faltered, "your loved one is on his way to Our Prince—The Prince of the Happy Land. There, ere many years, you will re-meet him, to part no more forever—rejoice, dear hearts, rejoice in that!"

The parental pair looked up, and thanked him with their eyes.

"Take comfort," he repeated, tenderly. "For the two whom He has taken from you, He has given you two in return: Miriam and Ada. Love them—cherish them: Ada as Joseph, Miriam as Samuel."

"We will, dear boy! We will!" said the pastor, pressing Miriam to his breast.

"They shall be as ours!" said Mrs. Leland, embracing Ada.

The brow of the young Christian became radiant with happiness.

"I thank you!" he faltered. "I thank you!"

Emotion overcame him, and he was silent for a time. At length he grew calmer.

"Father—mother," he said, "let me testify my gratitude for your great kindness and affection to me from my infancy until now; for your noble precepts and examples; for your careful training of my mind and heart; and for your parental goodness and Christian lovingness in having led me early in the way to God. I love and revere you both—I cannot say how deeply. But if it were permitted to men to be born again as children, and to have their choice of parents, I would select you, sir, for my father—you, madam, for my mother, out of all the world: so profoundly do I honor and esteem you!"

His parents bowed their heads upon his hands in thankfulness, and to evince to him their appreciation of this generous compliment.

"Kiss me, my father—and you, my mother!"

And these three pure, sympathizing natures embraced each other for the last time.

The agitated parents then tore themselves away.

The young Christian sighed, and breathed faintly.

"Shame upon me—shame upon me!" murmured Mr. Brigham. "Oh, that the earth would open and swallow me! My mother—my mother! upon you rests the blame for this!"

At length Samuel turned a glance over at Aunt Betsy, who was sitting modestly, and sobbing mournfully, by the door. She rose, and moved, with a tottering step, towards the bed. Samuel held out his hand to the good old creature, who, he knew, loved him with a tenderness scarcely second to that of his mother.

"Betsy," he said, "your laughing boy, who used to give you so much anxiety when he was a child—whom you have tossed and dandled in your arms as if he were your own—whom you so humored and caressed, but never spoiled, wishes to thank you for the many kind things which you have said and done for him throughout his brief but happy life."

"Don't mention 'em, Samuel—don't!" cried the faithful old creature. "I'm sure you were always a very good boy, and it did my heart good to be as kind to you as I could. But pray don't mention 'em—don't!"

And yet the dear soul knew that it almost made her burst with mingled joy and pride to think that Samuel not only remembered, but spoke of them, too.

Samuel smilingly shook his head. He understood her fond, simple heart.

"Do you recollect the old time, Betsy," he asked, "when you, and mother, and I used to romp among the hills, while father was composing in his study?"

"Oh! dear—yes!" cried the housekeeper, smiling through her tears.

"And how you and mother used to drag me in the little wagon which pa gave me on my birthday; how I used to hold the reins which mamma made for me, and flourish the little whip which you gave to me on *your* birthday, and how I used to cry 'Gee up, my horsey-wows?' "

"Oh! my dear boy!"

"How we used to go off in the woods, and play hide-and-go-seek among the tall trees—father going sometimes with us, and joining in the sport; and after play was over, telling us, you, and mother, and me, as we listened to him, of all the beautiful handiworks of God; how each had their individual duties to perform, and their missions to fulfil—the tall trees, the fallen leaves, the birds, the insects, the flowers, yea, the very loam itself, and all—as if they were human beings like ourselves; and how we used to sit and hang upon his sweet words, so full of truthfulness and beauty!"

"Oh! Samuel—Samuel!" sobbed the housekeeper. "I'll cry if you go on so. Yes, I will. Why, you were a little, teeny, weeny fellow then—the brightest and lovingest in all Enfield!"

Samuel smiled.

"Then our gambols through the bright, green fields, chasing the butterflies and the grasshoppers. Don't you remember how you used to let me beat you, and how you pretended that it was with my own little legs? And then in kite-time, how you used to show me how to raise mine, and how to pay out the string, until the old kite was away up almost as high as the clouds? Ah! those were happy days, Betsy. What rompers we were then! The dear old hills, with their green slopes, and their sunny tops, methinks I see them now, as then; and the green fields, too, with their rich earthen odor, which I scent even now!"

He paused; he was growing feebler and paler with each succeeding moment.

"Be kind to father, and mother, and Miriam, and Ada," he said, after a few moments. "And now, kiss me!"

Mr. Townsend looked at his wife with a glance which said, "The end is approaching of our young friend."

Mrs. Townsend was pale. Her husband regarded her for a few moments in silence, and then whispered—

"Is anything the matter?"

Mrs. Townsend shook her head—without, however, withdrawing her eyes from the great Christian light which was slowly waning on the couch.

"She is affected—poor thing!" muttered the merchant.

"Miriam—a drink!" said Samuel.

It was given him, and he breathed easier.

"My time is approaching," he said, with a serene smile. "If there are any here to whom I have ever brought a single tear, or a solitary pang, forgive me. If there are any here who have ever done me wrong, in word, or thought, or deed, I forgive them. Peace on earth—good-will to man!"

"Friends," said the pastor, in a shaken voice, "let us pray!"

All knelt, and the clergyman sent up a touching petition to the Most High. At its close, the pastor rose and approached the bedside; but Miriam was there before him, her arm around the young Christian's neck.

The tender-hearted father sighed.

"Yes," he murmured, "she has the best right. Poor girl—poor girl!"

Mrs. Leland fell upon his breast.

A pause followed; a pause, not of silence, but of sobs, of heart-stirring sighs, of glittering tears.

The face of the dying Christian grew paler and paler. His large, dark eyes, bright with joy, appeared to be fixed upon some object invisible to all but himself. His attent ears quivered, as if struggling to catch the slightest vibrations of sweet harmonies upon the air.

"Music!" he murmured, softly. "Do you not hear it? Music! Oh, how melodious! Spirit forms, preceded by seraph bands, are coming up to meet me, and—Our Prince is at their head! He dazzles me with His brightness!

"Hark! they sing. Their voices mingle with the harps, the pipes, the timbrels. Oh, how sweet, how glorious—how stirring!

"I see faces that I have known—forms that I have loved; Joseph, too—among the seraphs. He is blind no more. And little Robert, too—his sorrow all gone—his eyes radiant. O, how beautiful!

"Behold!" he cried, rising with the last spark of expiring

energy, and supporting himself with his left hand, while he pointed upward with the other, "behold that dazzling host! They are coming for me—rejoicing as they advance. Come, let us join in their glad song—'Glory, glory to Thee, O my Redeemer! Hosanna! hosanna to the Highest!'"

His arm fell from under him, and he dropped back upon his pillow, motionless—his face beaming, shadowingly, with angelic sweetness, and his eyes radiant with joy.

But all knew, as they looked upon that pale, sweet countenance, that it was as one of marble, and that those radiant eyes were as eyes of glass.

The spirit had shaken hands with its old companion of clay, and gone up to its God.

"The Lord gave, and the Lord hath taken away," said the pastor, in a stirring, but quivering voice. "Blessed be His Holy name!"

CHAPTER LAST.

The reunion of the Brighams was only for a brief season. Without an innate moral tie to bind them, a few months saw their solemn promises broken, and themselves apart. The ex-confidential clerk strongly desired to open a jobbing house, and, as he expressed it, give the Townsends a tug. His lady was perfectly willing that he should do both, but not at *her* expense. "Her money," she said, "was settled upon herself, and she was determined that it should remain so. Mr. Brigham married her because she was rich, and she was not disposed to place it in his power to render her poor. She held the whip in her own hand, and she intended to keep it there!"

Language like this could end only in one way—rupture and separation. So the rupture came, and with it separation—the lady returning to the Townsends, who were very glad of her society, and—the use of her money; and the gentleman retiring in disgust to the South, where he turned gambler, an occupation which charmed him by its excitement. Three years rolled away; at the end of which time, the newspapers announced that Mr. Brigham had fallen by the bowie-knife of an indignant planter, whom he had defrauded at play.

Mrs. Brigham, on hearing of his death, went at once into an interesting suit of mourning, which induced an English gentleman, who saw her at a soirée, to make some inquiries concerning her "means;" and on learning that she was set down at eighty thousand dollars, he at once decided that he could spend that sum easily, and hastened, therefore, to make an impression upon the lady's heart. How far he succeeded in the latter, we have no method of ascertaining; but of one thing we are satisfied: he led the lady, eventually, to the altar. The honeymoon passed away very pleasantly; but at the end of that period the gentleman found that he had committed a mistake in supposing that he could have the handling of his wife's funds. She quietly, but firmly, notified him that *that* could never be the case, and the English gentleman went off in a huff—naturally expecting that the lady would call him back and give him what he wanted, upon condition that he would kiss and make up. But the ruse did not succeed; and then the gentleman returned of his own accord. But Isabella, or rather, Mrs. Bulkhead, found, after a while, that her new lord "wasn't much." In a note to her old friend, Mrs. Townsend, she stated that "the fellow was fond of getting tipsy; that he spent three hours a day in dressing and surveying himself in the glass; and that he did not appear to live for anybody but his tailor." A few years, however, released the gentleman from his "dear, delightful torment," as he was wont to term his better half, leaving her, as he laughingly remarked in his closing moments, "equally as well off in funds as he had found her, for which, he thought, she ought to be sufficiently grateful to give him a tip-top funeral." Mrs. Bulkhead again returned to the Townsends, who, now that they were getting into years, felt the want of some one to amuse them. Mrs. Bulkhead pleased them satisfactorily in this respect; that lady being as fretful and whimsical as a life without an aim, or a heart that was wholly selfish, could reasonably be expected to make her. One evening, attended by her maid, she ascended to her apartment to dress for a party. When she had completed her toilet, she dismissed the girl, and was preparing to go down to the drawing-room, when she was startled by a pain in her breast. She rang the bell for her servant to return, and then seated herself on her bed. The maid came in, but it was to find her mistress speechless and staring. She hurriedly called the Townsends, who as hurriedly summoned a physician, who dwelt next door. But before the arrival of the latter, Mrs. Townsend had made the discovery that her friend was beyond human aid. "Disease of the heart!" muttered the doctor.

With the Townsends matters moved along as usual. They waxed neither better nor worse; they increased in riches and in years, and with but one ambition—to be amused. Meanwhile, the old house went on, as Mr. Townsend expressed it, with the "honest dodge," extending year after year in customers and wealth. "The thing paid" so well, that other houses took it up, and with more or less success, according to the energy of their conductors; but as the majority of the latter were previously notorious for everything but honesty or truthfulness, dealers were shy of them. "The fact is," said Mr. Townsend, in discussing the matter with his wife, "the country trade are picking up in sharpness. They are cautious whom they buy of. The house that gouges them once, will not do it a second time. And this brings me to my great point, viz.: It is always important to success to preserve an *appearance* of honesty. Lose *that,* and you are gone." His wife smiled. "So," continued the sagacious worldling, "in the Church it is always well to preserve an *appearance* of piety. It helps one wonderfully. It assists you in getting people's confidence and—money. Besides, it secures one a respectable position in the best society. Well—well, after all, Jane, there's nothing like a judicious mixture of honesty and humbug, of worldliness and religion. It *pays!*"

"All the world appears to think so, at any rate!" returned his wife; "and it does seem as if all the world could not be wrong!"

"Oh, it's all right, my dear—all right, depend upon it. Whatever pays *is* right—it *must* be; and when a man doubts it, let him put his hand in his pocket and feel the *evidence.* If the *stuff* is there, his suspicions are wrong; if the stuff is *not* there, then he is incompetent to form an opinion. It is only those who *haven't got* the raw material, and *can't get* it, who rail out against our doctrine."

Mrs. Townsend made no reply. In fact, she entertained herself similar views; but, in moments of honest reflection—and these *would* come sometimes—she thought differently, and so did her husband: but neither considered it *convenient*, JUST THEN, to encourage them, and so they glided on into old age and its infirmities, gracefully and respectably.

One day, the old lady was unusually meditative.

"Any new idea?" asked her husband, who was now a hale, hearty, handsome gentleman of sixty-five, with small, white, fat hands, a sleek, rosy face, and a bald, polished head, with a small silky fringe on each side.

"I'm thinking, my dear," returned his wife, "whether we *are* right in our views, after all?"

The merchant looked at her with his pleasant eyes.

"You didn't sleep well last night!" he said, in his calm, practical way.

Mrs. Townsend confessed that she had not.

"Ah!" laughed her husband, "*that's* it. I notice that people are apt to be very thoughtful on such subjects, after a broken night. You are weak, my dear. That's all. Lay down and take a little rest, and you will feel better. With returning strength, will come back your confidence. We are all right, depend upon it!"

"Perhaps you are right, John. At all events, I'll lay down."

"I am going to take a run over to Trenton," said the merchant, "to see one of our customers who has failed and made an assignment, doing us out of some thirty-three hundred. I'll be back about six, when I shall look to find you more cheerful. So, good-bye, my dear, and make yourself comfortable. Next week, if you say so, we'll take a jaunt to Virginia, where you will rejuvenate and get rid of all this nonsense."

"Well, take care of yourself," said his wife, tenderly, "and I'll be as cheerful as I can on your return."

The old gentleman kissed her, and went his way, disturbed, in spite of himself, at what he termed the lowness of her spirits.

Mrs. Townsend laid down, as she had promised, but without finding any relief. In fact, her thoughts took a severer range than before. They were no longer mere misgivings—they were so many accusing witnesses.

"Yes," she murmured, uneasily, "the system *is* false; I know it—feel it. But I must not think so now, or I shall go mad. I'll think of it when I get stronger; yes, when I am stronger. To-morrow, perhaps. Yes, to-morrow: for things like this ought not to be delayed. Yes, to-morrow!"

Ah! poor lady, how long have you been saying this? For how many times, and how many years? To-morrow—ever to-morrow!

The old lady called her attendant, and said to her, in a feeble voice—

"Get a stupid book, Susan—the most stupid one you can find—and come and read me to sleep. Make haste. I am suffering!"

The attendant took up a dull, heavily written history of the early races of mankind, and seating herself beside her mistress, commenced reading.

The history of the early races was not long in answering the object of its reader. It had all the essential qualities of a soporific. Long ere the attendant had reached the close of the first chapter, her mistress slept, with every intellectual faculty wrapped in calm, dreamless repose.

The girl then descended to the library, and selected a French novel, to reward herself for her arduous labor upon the history of the early races.

An hour glided by, and then another, and yet another. The French novel was very interesting, and the attendant forgot all about time. At length, however, she put down her book and approached her mistress. The latter was still asleep; calm, pale, and motionless—but *too* calm, and too pale, not to disturb the girl, who remembered that she was of late restless and uneasy in her slumbers. She therefore approached the old lady, and laid her hand softly upon her forehead. *It was cold!*

The spirit had passed away from that old, feeble form, while she slept, as a dream glides away from the mind.

But the thing that was to have been looked into ON THE MORROW!

The merchant was shocked at the discovery, on his return: shocked, as a man naturally would be under the circumstances. A few days, however, brought him all right again—because he was a man of a *practical* mind.

"After all," he would say, in his practical way, "what is all this humbug about death? Stuff—mere stuff! When a man's body is worn out, he must go—that's all. Life won't stay in an exhausted body—it *can't;* the animal vigor isn't there to sustain it; the wheels won't work, and the man must travel—that's all. He'd stay, if he could; but when his body won't let him, how can he help himself? No, he must start then, by the first train. To be sure, clergymen and writers make a great fuss about the matter, and succeed in frightening some weak-headed people, because it pays them to do so. But what do *they* know about it, more than any one else? They are imaginative fellows—nothing more; and we all know what paltry stuff imagination is. Practical minds laugh at such rubbish. Death? Humbug—all humbug! Why, only look at it once. Face it, manfully, in a sound, practical way; grapple with it, as you would with any one of the every-day realities of life! And what does it amount to, with all their pother? Simply to this: a mere dissolution of the body. Nothing more. That's what it is, when faced down by a plain, common-sense mind, and I don't pretend to any more. The body breaks up and dissolves into gases, which strengthen and enrich the earth —that's all. If the dead man has a soul, as they call it, it goes somewhere; if he has no soul, it *don't* go anywhere. There's the whole story in a nutshell, as examined by the light of common sense. To be sure, certain persons will tell you of the comfort which they find in religion. I had a very fine young man with me once, by the name of Samuel Leland, who used to talk very eloquently upon it, and who succeeded in persuading a great many over to the same opinion—but, after all, what does that argue? The human heart is so happily constituted that it can find comfort in *any* thing. Some find it in a large business, some in a small one, others in dress, others in pleasure, and others, again, in religion. But after all, sir, the only solid comfort is in that which enables you to feel the ground under you, to buy what you please, go where you please, do as you please, and whack whom you please, *because you have got the raw material in your pocket to pay for it*—MONEY! *That*, sir, is the *legitimate* article. Who has *it* in plenty, is solid, sir—*solid*. Rocks can't move him! Show me an imaginative man, and I'll show you, in him, a fellow who can't pay his notes. Why, sir, one good practical man could buy up a thousand such, any day, and not feel that he had done much, either. No—the only substantial comfort is in *Money*—THAT is what I call *practical* comfort. Ha! ha! Something in *that* —hey, sir?"

Sixty-five — sixty-six! How steadily, how mercilessly, the pendulum of human life ticks on! If some smart mind would but devise a plan by which the clock of man's day could be put back from sixty-six to thirty, now! What millions would flow in to him! Or, if some sharp Yankee would but invent a machine which would enable a sixty-six man to always *remain* at sixty-six. *That* would do!

How much more honestly a man will think at sixty-six than at sixty-five! The idea smites him then—steals in upon him, as it were, and hits him, suddenly, like a fierce, rude blow from the hand of some sneaking, cowardly bruiser—that he is one year *nearer* to his jumping-off place, and—he don't like it! Well, the thought *isn't* pleasant—is it? Particularly if one is by no means satisfied of *where* he will land *when* he takes his leap! If a man has such a thing as a soul, as our old friend, John P. Townsend, used to say, it goes *somewhere*—THEN. Eh? And he is likely—*very* likely—to find it out. Eh? But if he only discovers the fact of his soul's existence *after* he has taken his jump! *Eh?*

What an insidious serpent Rheumatism is! How gently, quietly, and stealthily it creeps in upon a man, and snugly ensconces itself in some inconvenient corner of his body—never making its presence known until it is so firmly rooted that it can laugh at all efforts of its victim to dislodge it. Then, old boy, look out! Don't move your arm *too* freely; if you *do*, you will feel something in your shoulder. Pull on your glove gently; if you *don't*, you will feel something in your fingers. Be careful how you draw on that stocking, or you will—ah—ugh! Holloa! what are you about? My leg—my toes. Agh! Some liniment—quick, rascal! Now bathe it—flannel it—soothe it down, gently. There—that's better. Now, rascal, remember what you are doing in future. There's a dollar for you, you dog. But if you ever serve me in that careless way again, I'll break every bone in your body. Ah-ugh—there it is again. Oh! this is terrible. Ah! it's easing off a little. There—it's better. Get me a glass of wine—I'm exhausted!

Sixty-six—sixty-seven!

Old gentleman not *quite* so hearty. Begins to think tnat his system is undergoing a change, *not* for the better. Has a suspicion that if he withdrew from the cares and excitements of business, it would be "better for him." Don't like to do so, however—feels that he has a fond affection for the old house and its interests; enjoys the pride of being the head of so vast an establishment. But *health*—that is to say—*life!*

Ah! life *before* business. Sells out to old partner, and—retires.

Finds, however, that retirement don't suit him. Feels the *need* of excitement, but thinks the feverish excitement of business would be *too* exciting. Joins a riding-school; but discovers that that won't do: his system can't stand it. Is told that a certain gymnasium does wonders for old men—rejuvenates them, reanimates, re-endows them with amazing animal vigor. Bravely determines to give it a trial for one year. Pays a twelvemonth's fees, has a gymnast's suit made, and—breaks down, despairingly, in the first lesson. Discovers that his system is knocked up, and concludes that rest would be the best thing for him. Determines on rest.

Finds that his housekeeper is not a companion. Misses his wife; thinks she might have done better than to die and leave him—misses her *very* much. Got along, miserably enough, after her death, even with the assistance of business excitement to divert him; but now, now that he is confined to the house, *feels* her absence.

Realizes the want of a companion; of one who will understand him, nurse him, and—*take care of him.* Watches housekeeper, to see if she would answer—notices her carefully; observes that she is a mere block—cold, selfish, and—occasionally impertinent. Concludes that *she* won't do.

Reflects. Converses with his friends, who suggest to him the propriety of his marrying some young woman. Old gentleman shakes his head—thinks no young woman would like to marry an old man like him. Friends reply that it is quite common for young women to marry worn-out old men, on condition that the latter pay them well, and leave them a stipulated proportion of their property in their wills. Retired merchant ponders the matter over, and thinks he won't do anything of the kind. And yet he perceives that he must have some one to take care of him. Notices that housekeeper is throwing out lures to entrap him; but pretends not to perceive them. Is privately of the opinion that he *hates* THAT woman.

Housekeeper changes her tactics, and does all she can to make old gentleman miserable. Removes his little comforts—gradually brings the servants round to pay little or no attention to any one but herself. Makes old gentleman feel the want of some one to look after him. Puts on airs—imperious ones, as if she were the mistress of the mansion and of its owner's destiny. Old gentleman apparently submits—meanwhile thinks, and—lays his plans.

One day housekeeper is surprised by the appearance of three young blacks; brave, oily, crafty fellows, whose special business is to guard the interests and protect the comforts of old gentleman. One is to attend the door in the place of the old porter, who is kicked out; to faithfully deliver all letters, and see that none are—intercepted. (Housekeeper winces, and turns pale; perceives that she has made a—mistake!) Second is to take up the letters and visitors' cards, deliver them to the third, and perform all the errands which the latter may order. Third is to wait upon old gentleman himself; watch him, nurse him, take care of him.

Neither John — number one, William — number two, nor Robert—number three, are to pay any attention to housekeeper, whatever; but the latter and all hands shall give implicit obedience to Robert—number three. Housekeeper indignant, but cool; knows she is well paid, and thinks that *that* is worth remembering. Concludes to play the amiable.

Old gentleman chuckles at the result; and thinks he has at length got everything fixed to his mind. Finds out, however, in a few weeks, that Robert is somewhat disposed to regard himself as an individual of great consequence. In fact, the new régime is simply a change in bullies. Old gentleman gets excited, and privately concludes that of the two, he would rather be under petticoat rule; but is so well broken in by both parties, that he does not deem it advisable to make his opinion known. Meanwhile, he thinks, and is at length struck with an idea, which fills him with joy. Hurrah! he sees his way at last! a beautiful idea. Why did it not occur to him before? He writes—

"MY DEAR MIRIAM—I want a housekeeper; one who will take charge of my house, and of its owner; one who understands me, and who will be to me at once a daughter and a friend. Come, my dear niece, come and be my heir. Think—a million for simply taking care, a few years, of YOUR OLD UNCLE."

A few days, and he receives an affectionate letter, stating that the writer would come cheerfully, not for his money's sake, but for his own, and in acknowledgment of the many years of kindness which she had experienced while under his guardianship and the shelter of his roof; but that, owing to the age and infirmities of her parents, whose delicate health requires her constant attention, and to the necessity of watching over the education of Ada, her daughter, she was unable to do so. In case, however, he should ever be taken with illness, she would then consider it a duty to fly to his assistance.

Old gentleman very much disturbed by this letter, which upsets all his hopes. Becomes despondent. Wonders what money is good for, since even a million won't tempt the only being that he loves in the world to come and take care of him. If she only *would* come, how comfortably, how *very* comfortably, he would get along!

The days roll by gloomily. Black man gradually tightens the rein. Old gentleman becomes restive, and thinks of rebelling; but black man's eye is on him—menacingly: old gentleman apparently gives in, and—*thinks*. Sends for Mr. Crittenden, talks with him in a low tone, which black man don't like. Mr. Crittenden retires, and black man looks sulky. In an hour Mr. Crittenden returns, accompanied by a young Englishman who has been strongly recommended to him for honesty, truthfulness, and capacity: young man was brought over from London by an English family, in whose service he had been for many years, and who were grieved to part with him, but were compelled to do so by their pecuniary inability to keep him. Black man kicked out, Englishman installed; housekeeper still amiable. Everything moves smoothly—old gentleman apparently comfortable.

Housekeeper gradually makes up to John, the new man, who is young, but "knows on which side his bread is buttered," and is therefore rather shy. Housekeeper, however, is artful, and works upon him step by step—entrapping him at length. Housekeeper and new man concoct a plan to inveigle old gentleman into marrying the former, who will then "send old gentleman off" right speedily, and marry John, who will *then* be rich. Meanwhile, both harmoniously agree that, as the best devised schemes are frequently thwarted by simple and unlooked-for incidents, that they might as well provide against all contingencies by each making it a special business to do all in their power to prevent the old gentleman from *leaving too much*.

Old gentleman very much disturbed by his rheumatism, as well as at the changes which are going on in his system. Wonders if there is such a thing as punishment in the future, after all?

Hopes not, any how. Makes an heroic effort to consider that sort of thing mere bosh, which preachers deal out for so much per annum. Thinks the Universalist doctrine, that all men will be saved because Christ died for all, a very reasonable and comforting one. But then SAMUEL had a different opinion; and Miriam holds to Samuel's view, and Mr. Crittenden also, viz.,—that heaven is only to be attained through repentance *and* faith in the atoning blood of Christ, and that *without* these, there is but one destination for the soul—HELL!

Old gentleman very much distressed. Don't like to believe in *that* doctrine. It isn't pleasant. According to *it*, man's principal business on earth would be, not to make money, but to—prepare for heaven. "Fudge—ridiculous—tell that to children!"

Housekeeper comes in, and is very amiable.

"Mrs. Rodgers, what do you think of the future?"

Housekeeper knows old gentleman's sentiments very well, and answers accordingly. She thinks all men will be saved.

Old gentleman agrees with her, and wonders how he ever disliked a woman who held such *liberal* views!

Housekeeper talks with him a little while, and then retires, leaving a good impression behind.

Old gentleman's system grows no better; rheumatism adds its torments, and old gentleman thinks he will be compelled ere long to take to his bed, and—stay there. Meanwhile grows irritable, and finds some small relief in calling John a rascal, and the housekeeper a vixen, both of whom wonder whether he suspects anything.

Sunny morning. Old gentleman cheerful. For a week housekeeper has been exceedingly amiable, which has left an impression upon the mind of old gentleman, who remarks to John, that she is very good to him of late. John laughs, and winkingly replies that he thinks he comprehends the reason. Old gentleman would like to know it. John is under the impression that housekeeper is troubled in the heart about some one—she is all the time sighing. Old gentleman is smilingly incredulous; but John knows it—yes, sir, *knows* it.

Old gentleman looks in the glass, and begins to spruce up; thinks that he has been giving himself a great deal of useless anxiety, and that he isn't so very old, after all.

New man thinks so too—yes, *sir*, he has been thinking so h'all h'along!

Old gentleman laughs, throws him a dollar, tells him to go away with his nonsense, and attempts to cut a caper, but is immediately brought down to a realizing sense of his actual situation by a fierce, sharp shock of his old enemy—rheumatism. Screams with pain; housekeeper runs in, very much concerned; learns his trouble, and orders John to bathe him gently with the liniment, and departs, with an air of anguish, audibly regretting that she is not in a position to take care of the poor dear sufferer herself. Old gentleman looks after her, thinks her an angel of mercy, and—sighs. John turns his head, and—laughs.

Old gentleman persists, however, in sprucing up. But gloomy November days come along, and his spirits decline. Wonders if the soul *has* any existence at all, after death. Hopes it hasn't, that is, in case the Universalist idea that all men will be saved should *not* be true.

"John, what is your candid opinion about the future? Does a man dissolve into gases, and so become extinct, or what?"

"I have never given the subject much consideration, sir. But I think he *does!*"

"Does what, rascal?"

"Vanish into gases, sir!" returns John, on a venture.

"But his soul, rascal—his soul?"

"Ah! sir, I have never given myself any trouble about that!"

"Why not?"

"Because—because—yes, sir, because!"

"Because what, rascal?"

"Because nobody does, sir; or if they pretend to, it's only for show, sir. Why, only look at it, sir. The minister preaches a sermon on charity, which is so very affecting that it makes the congregation weep like little children. Well, sir, the very next day a poor woman or child knocks at that very minister's door, and says—'A shilling, or a piece of bread, sir; I'm starving.' And what does the minister say, sir—he who preached so eloquently the day before on charity? Just this, sir—'Go away, good woman, and don't come here any more; if you do, I'll call the police.' The same way with the congregation, sir; only instead of saying they'll call the police, they tell the poor thing, rudely, to 'clear out!' The same way in everything else, sir. 'We ought to be humble and pious,' says the minister. 'Yes, we must be humble and pious,' say his hearers, and they go home—the minister to congratulate himself upon his eloquence and sumptuous living, the congregation to prepare for another week of knavery, and routes, and show, and pride."

"Too true, John—too true. They are humble and pious only one day in the week."

"That's it, sir—only one day in the week. Now, if the minister believed what he preaches, sir, he'd act up to it—wouldn't he, sir? And if his congregation believed it, they'd act up to it, too. But neither of 'em does, sir; which goes to prove that if neither of them believe in it, I needn't believe in it, either!"

"Right, rascal—right. It is so, it must be so; or all the world wouldn't act so."

"That's it, sir—that's just what I say, too. And therefore, sir, the idea that what nobody believes in or acts up to can be true, is all gammon, sir."

"I almost agree with you, rascal. It does look so, indeed!"

"And, sir," said the new man, "that brings us back to where we started from."

"Where was that, John?"

"To the gases, sir. We do all dissolve into gases, sir, and that's the end of us!"

"You are a very sensible man, John," said the old gentleman, rejoicing to find his uneasy doubts so triumphantly removed, "and there's a dollar for you!"

John smiles, and old gentleman thinks he will lay down and take a nap. Servant enters with a letter, and gives it to new man, who hands it to his master, who, notwithstanding his conversation with John, feels the very reverse of comfortable. Breaks the seal, and glancing over the letter, mumbles—

"So, from Enfield. Ha! from Miriam. Dear girl; I was afraid she had forgotten me! Let me see. Mum—mum—Ada well, and rich in spiritual promise—mum—mum—Mr. Leland confined to his bed, but cheerful, resigned, happy—mum—mum. Mrs. Leland cheerful, fond, happy—mum—both waiting for the blissful hour when they shall rejoin their and our dear Samuel—mum—mum—Aunt Betsy—ripe old age—cheerful—tranquil—happy—mum—mum—mum—I am myself happy—mum—rejoice to learn that our dear friend, Mr. Crittenden, is well, and doing so much good for the cause of Our Prince—mum—it is a blessing to be rich, it enables us to do so much good—mum—mum—dear uncle, how is it with you—all well within? Do tell me—father, mother, Aunt Betsy, Ada, and I pray for you every night—mum—your loving Miriam!"

"Anything the matter, sir?"

"Eh?"

"Bad news, sir?"

"What?"

"I was fearful something had happened, sir, seeing your lids were wet!"

"Are they—*are* they, John?"

"Yes, sir—very wet—very! Shall I help you to some drink, sir?"

"Ye-yes—a little wine—just a drop. A man's memories will come up, and his feelings work up, sometimes, John! Take care of me—take good care of me, John—and you will find your name and a nice little sugar-plum, in a certain document, one of these days."

"You are very good, sir; and I am very much obliged to you, I am sure. Cheer up, sir! you are worth fifty common men yet!"

"Do you think so, John—you jolly dog!—do you really think so? Really?"

"Really, sir. I *know* it!"

"*Do* you, though! There's an eagle for you, rascal. Now go away; I want to sleep."

Dusk—night—dawn. Invalid pale, feeble, and covered with cold moisture.

"How do I look this morning, John?"

"Like a top, sir. Eyes bright, skin clear—at least ten years younger, sir."

"But it appears to me I've been sweating, John?"

"All right, sir; showing that you've had a desperate struggle with your rheumatism, and come off conqueror."

"I don't know about that! I've a singular sensation."

"What sort of a sensation, sir?"

"As if my system was breaking up."

"Take a glass of wine, sir."

"No; put it back, and send for the doctor."

Doctor comes, prescribes a powder, which patient takes, and thinks he feels much better. Housekeeper very amiable, and so wears away a week: when the sun bursts out, and the atmosphere clears up, and becomes milder. Old gentleman much stronger, and inclined to believe that he will come out all right, yet.

But the gloomy days come again, and the poor old gentleman's uneasiness returns. Thinks that there *may* be a heaven and a hell, and that the ministers may not be so far out of the way, after all. Turns again to John, who reassures him that the soul business is all gammon, and that when a man dissolves into gases, that's the end of him. Old gentleman gives him a dollar for the consolation, for which new man thanks him very much.

Meanwhile, housekeeper grows killingly amiable. Old gentleman grows more and more convinced that she is a very excellent, affectionate, and, as she entertains the same views with himself in reference to the gases, right-minded woman. Finds himself, at least once a day, tempted to make her an offer of his hand.

"I want some one to look after me," he thinks, and justly; "some one who understands me. John is very good in his way, and does all he can to make me comfortable; but then he hasn't the quick eye, the noiseless, quiet tread, nor the ready hand of a woman. Women understand these matters better than men. There are a thousand little things in managing an old, sick man, which a man would never think of, but which come to women intuitively. Men are but clumsy things in these matters. I must have a nurse—yes, sooner or later, it must come to that. Mrs. Rodgers, now, appears to take a deep interest in me; and if I could only persuade myself that she would not desert me, tyrannize over me, or neglect me, after marriage, I'd settle the matter at once. But—"

He broke off here. He could not bring himself to a belief in the genuineness of the housekeeper's goodness. He made an effort to do so, for several days, but could not succeed. He remembered her conduct before the arrival of the blacks, and shuddered.

"After all," he murmured, "there is no principle except that which is based upon religion."

And he thought of the principle which governed Samuel and Miriam, and sighed.

In contrast with these two pure beings, loomed up before him the two hollow creatures who pandered, daily, to his own unfounded and delusive thoughts.

"May I come in?" said, near him, at this juncture, a low voice, which was intended to be very sweet and alluring.

The old gentleman started, as if he had heard the hiss of a serpent. He surveyed the housekeeper for a moment or two with an air of measureless loathing, and then said—

"Begone, and never set foot in my presence again till I send for you. Go!" he added, with an imperious gesture.

Mrs. Rogers turned pale, bit her lip, and hurling at him a threatening glance, retired, without closing the door behind her.

"So," mused the old gentleman, noticing her glance, "she has hoisted her true colors. But let her beware—I am not wholly powerless, yet!" He paced his chamber in deep thought, utterly unconscious of the agitated state of his frame. From the abstractedness of his air, it was evident that he was pursuing an idea. At length he reached that point where thought terminates in decision. "Well," he muttered, audibly, and with an energy which had of late been a stranger to him, "there shall be no more of this. I'll end it at once!"

He passed, with a step which might have been considered firm, but for a certain slight quivering in his joints, from the apartment, and descended to the drawing-room. As he drew near the door, he overheard the words—

"The old fool shall pay for this. I—I'll strangle him in his sleep!"

It was the voice of the housekeeper.

"No you won't, madam," said her master, gliding into the apartment. "You will have time to think *better* of it!"

The guilty woman started, and turned pale.

"Is it you, sir?" she said, recovering herself quickly, and assuming a fawning tone. "Why, how well you look! You are quite recovered."

"John!" said her master, sternly.

"Yes, sir!" returned that worthy, with the air of a thief caught in the act.

"Show that woman to the door!"

"Sir!" stammered John, scarcely knowing how to act. "If I obey him, she will blab, and I'm ruined; if I do *not* obey, he will kick me out, and then I'm equally done for!" he muttered.

Mrs. Rodgers saw that her game was up, and eyeing the old gentleman with an air of mingled hatred and defiance, she said—

"Miserable, cowardly dotard! take back that order, or—"

"John!" interrupted the retired merchant, "take that woman and throw her into the street!"

"Fool! he will not dare—"

But Mrs. Rodgers was mistaken. John *did* dare. Of the two dangers, he wisely chose the least. "The master to the woman!" he muttered, taking the astounded housekeeper by the shoulder with one hand, and, to prevent her from using her tongue, suddenly and rudely covering her mouth with the other. Then, with a quick, energetic movement, he forced her first into the hall, and from thence into the street.

"Now, traitress!" he said, with a mocking laugh, as he reclosed the door, "yell away, and I hope it will do you good!"

"Throw her things after her!" said his master, sternly.

John called one of the servants, and hurried up to the housekeeper's room, from which he presently returned with a large trunk, followed by his companion with a large swagging bundle of frocks, shawls, and hats, all of which were flung out after their owner, who was standing upon the walk and glaring up at the door like an infuriated tigress.

"Pen, ink, and paper!" said Mr. Townsend, when John returned.

They were brought, and placed upon the centre-table.

The retired merchant sat down and wrote a single line.

"DEAR MIRIAM—Come to me, as you promised. I am ill."

It was as he had foreseen. The excitement of the last half hour upon his feeble frame terminated in prostration.

In forty-eight hours, Miriam stood at the bedside of her uncle, who was in a raging fever.

Miriam was changed from a slender, delicate girl of twenty, to a handsome, matronly woman of thirty-three. Her form was more developed than when in youth, but so charmingly rounded as to intensify its beauty. Her face was full, but of a fair, polished smoothness, which rendered it at once impressive and majestic. Her dark hair, parted over her mild but earnest forehead, unblemished by spot or wrinkle, fell in a smooth, modest mass down either cheek, from whence it curved off to, and over, her small, symmetrical ears. A straight, flat collar, confined by a ribbon, revealed a faint glimpse of a throat and neck white as ivory, and of exquisite chiselling. She wore a black velvet basque, or jacket, of black velvet, which developed a bust of rare gracefulness, modesty, and symmetry, and which closed over a flowing skirt of plain silk of the same ebon hue. Her small hands, with their plump but tapering fingers, were in keeping with her complexion, which was of a dazzling, yet transparent whiteness. Over her features still lingered that mingled tone of calm serenity and thoughtful earnestness which rendered her so winning in her earlier days. Her general air was that of one whose pious mind never descended to an unworthy thought.

Miriam's presence was electrical. A few days worked wonders in the disorganized household. Chaos vanished — order came back; and quiet reigned, and comfort. The old gentleman smiled gratefully upon his niece.

"Dear Miriam," he said, pressing her hand, affectionately, "how I recognize the hallowing influence of your gentle spirit!"

"Don't flatter your poor Mirry, uncle, for a merit not her own!"

"Not her own!" repeated the invalid, feebly. "Whose, then?"

"*His!*" answered his niece, with a reverent gesture.

The old gentleman sighed. Miriam descended to the drawing-room to receive some visitors who desired to learn the state of the invalid's health, while the invalid himself dropped off into a revery, at the close of which he sent for his attorney and Mr. Crittenden. The trio were closeted for upward of two hours, carrying on their conversation in low tones, much to the annoyance of the new man John, who, although he listened very carefully at the key-hole, could only make out three facts, viz.: that the old gentleman was making his will, that he was leaving over a million, and that he was constituting his niece as his sole heir.

A few days passed on, and the invalid was apparently better, although by no means in a condition to leave his bed. Nevertheless, he felt comfortable. A sense of security stole over him as he looked at Miriam. He felt that in her he had one who would "be good to him," from a nobler motive than interest. He flattered himself that if there *was* such a thing as spiritual danger, the purity of that simple heart would do something in *his* favor.

They conversed together daily upon general topics, but—how could it be otherwise with Miriam?—mainly upon religion; the old gentleman—partly from habit, partly from a desire to conceal his life-long hypocrisy from his niece, and partly from an unwillingness to take a stand against statements which *might* be true, after all—always siding with Miriam, with a calm, matter-of-course air, as if he fully shared in her sentiments; and always carefully omitting the most distant reference to the gases. And yet the old gentleman was sensible that he was doing himself a great wrong by this course; but—habit—habit!

"Never mind," he would mutter, by way of consoling himself, "I will pluck up one of these days, and face the subject like a man. I am mending now in health, and when I get perfectly well—as I certainly shall do under Miriam's kind treatment—I'll make a calm, honest examination of the matter, and abide by the result. Yes—one of these days!"

In the meanwhile he had his fears, and found it necessary to resort to John for consolation; which the latter was always ready to administer.

"John," the invalid would say, whenever his niece was called away by her other duties from his bedside, "you heard what Mrs. Leland said in the course of her remarks?"

"Yes, sir—every word."

"Well, what have you got to say now?"

John understood his master very well, and considered it his policy to be consistent.

"The same as before, sir."

"I am amazed at you, rascal!"

"Can't help that, sir. I stick to my own views, because they are founded upon common sense."

"Yes, John," said the old gentleman, waveringly; "but it appears to me that my niece's views are based upon common sense, also!"

"Not a bit of it, sir," returned John, who saw how his master *desired* to be answered, and shaped his reply accordingly. "They are founded only upon Scripture, and that, as all the world knows, is all gammon. I don't pretend to be any wiser than the world, sir!"

"Well, but John—don't you see how happy my niece is in her belief? Don't you see *that*, rascal?"

"Lord love you, sir, we can be happy in *any* belief, if we only *do* believe in it. That's all that is required, sir, depend upon it!"

"Perhaps you are right, John—perhaps you are right!" returned his master, persuading himself, but very faintly, that *he* believed, very firmly, in *his* doctrine; and yet wondering how it was that *he* didn't feel so very, *very* happy.

Sixty-seven—sixty-eight.

How merciless is Time! Never pausing, not even for an old man, but rolling on, driving on, *hurrying* on, as if bent upon forcing him, whether he be ready or no, into the yawning loam.

"When one gets old," mused the invalid, attempting to enliven himself with a small, sad joke, "he don't like to be hurried! What he then wants is rest! Here I am pushed on to sixty-eight. Why, it was only yesterday that I was fifty. By the same rule, I shall be sixty-nine in less than half an hour! Well—well; that rascal, Time, is without a conscience, or he would never press a poor old fellow in this manner. Sixty-eight? I could never have believed it. And yet I feel very well this morning, too! But sixty-eight! If some one would but push me back again to fifty, or so! Fifty! What a prime age—so full of mental ripeness and physical nerve! Dear me—what a man *I* was at fifty! So strong in mind, and body, and business, and—money! And *now!* Well, well! I'm older, a *little* older; that's all. I shall see ninety, yet—yes, ninety. What a prime old codger I'll be at *that* age! Wonder if I shall have any teeth left then, or hair! *Some* of the nineties *don't!*"

The sun was shining (the old gentleman was fond of the sun), the air was bright, clear, and invigorating, and the old gentleman was very happy, and—sixty-eight!

But the next day was cold and cloudy, and the old gentleman was silent, meditative, and gloomy.

"John!"

"Yes, sir."

"Are you quite, *quite* sure about the gases?"

"Quite sure, sir! I'm confident of everything that's got good sense to back it!"

Old gentleman shakes his head in doubt.

"But here comes Mrs. Leland, sir!"

"Then, John, go you away. Go down stairs, John. I shall not want you again till noon; for Mrs. Leland will stay with me till then. Go down stairs, John."

"Yes, sir." John vanishes, as Miriam enters.

"Good-morning, uncle. How did you rest during the night?"

"Quite well, my dear. But I don't feel very bright this morning. Sit down here, and talk to me."

Miriam seats herself by the bedside, and surveys the old gentleman with an air of mingled tenderness and solicitude.

"How do you feel at heart, uncle? Is all well, within?"

Old gentleman don't like to expose himself, and pretends not to have heard her. Is suddenly touched with an idea.

"Miriam, my dear, what was that strange conceit of Aunt Betsy's, of which you were telling me?"

"That every family has its appointed year or period, beyond which its members rarely or never go."

"A singular notion. Have you any faith in it yourself, my dear?"

"I presume it to be true in the main, uncle. Aunt Betsy keeps a private record of the ages of our Enfield families, and it certainly bears out her theory."

"Indeed? Be kind enough to get our old family Bible, and let us see how the Townsends run!" said her uncle, with a faint smile.

Miriam took the volume, and turning to the family record, commenced reading:—

"'John Townsend, son of William, died January 12 1750, aged 37 years.'"

"Ah! yes," remarked her uncle, "he was killed by the Indians. But never mind the young fellows, who perished by accident, or disease. Read only of those who 'held out,' as Aunt Betsy expresses it, 'to the regular time.' Run through the record with your pencil, and then read them off, omitting everything but the names and ages. Now," he said, when his request had been followed, "now go on."

"'William Townsend,'" began Miriam, "'aged sixty-eight years and ninety days. Francis, second son of William, sixty-eight years and twenty days. Rachel, daughter of William, sixty-five years and forty-seven days. Joseph, son of Francis, sixty-eight years and twelve days. Charles, son of Francis—'"

"My father," mused the listener, pricking up his ears.

"'Sixty-eight years and seven days'" (old gentleman starts). "'Edward, son of Charles, sixty-eight years and three days.'" (Old gentleman white as a sheet.) "'Joseph, son of Charles, sixty-eight years and nine days. Elizabeth, daughter of Charles, sixty-seven years and fifty days.'"

Old gentleman pale and speechless—his eyes glaring with terror.

Miriam agitated, but calm. Rings bell for assistance and the doctor. The latter comes, surveys patient, prescribes a powder, and retires, shaking his head while descending the stairs. Old gentleman comes to, and feels better towards evening. Miriam is fearful, and sends for Mr. Crittenden, both of whom spend the night with the old gentleman; praying for him while he is yet awake, and praying for him while he sleeps.

Morn comes, and finds the Christian watchers at their posts. Invalid wakes up much better. Watchers survey and talk with him a little while, and then finding him apparently mending, retire for a few hours' sleep—John and female servant taking their places.

The sun is shining, and old gentleman feels somewhat stronger.

Thinks, however, that a change is taking place in his system, but is not quite sure. Has an idea that a torpor is settling around his feet; but is not certain. Tells John of it, who, assisted by his fellow-servant, rubs the affected part with liniment, after which invalid thinks he is fresher and more comfortable than for many days. Becomes meditative, and is disturbed ere long by serious thoughts. Begins to think the gases all fudge, and the Scriptures solemnly true. Is startled at length by an admonishing voice within him :

"Old man, old man—what *art* thou doing? Be up, be up, and stirring: for this is thy last year. It is thy *soul*, thy SOUL that's speaking. Be up, sir—be up and stirring. If thou hast any thinking to do—think it at once, and quickly. If thou hast any resolve to make—make it at once, and bravely. If thou hast any words to say, say them at once and firmly. Wake up, old man—wake up. For thou hast reached thy family's closing year. Wake up, old man—wake up!"

Old gentleman *very* much disturbed. "Yes," he mutters, firmly, and in alarm, "I will—I will. I'll think of it, and face it, bravely, like a man, the first thing to-morrow!"

To-morrow? Ah—habit, habit!

"John—"

"Yes, sir."

"Rub my feet and legs again with the liniment, and then bolster me up comfortably. My head aches with lying down so much."

"Yes, sir." In a few minutes: "All right now, sir?"

"Yes. Now go over there by the window, and don't talk, John. I want to think. When I want you, I'll call for you."

John takes up paper and reads—fellow-servant takes up a book, and in ten minutes old gentleman is forgotten.

Old gentleman is thinking. Memory has come back in all its freshness. He sees himself in the old school-room beneath the church once more, with his mates around him, and the old teacher behind the desk; anon rollicking over the green, climbing the neighboring hills, gunning in the woods, listening on the Sabbath morning to the summons of the old church bell. The dear old days of innocence, truthfulness, and—happiness.

Young manhood. He has reached the city, and commenced his man's career. His brow grows cloudy—at what? The memory of *his first business lie!* He feels again the guilty blush which came up with it, and the hot glow which darted like a low fire through his veins.

Middle manhood. In business on his own account. Plans—bad ones—laid down, and followed out. Marries—joins the Church, affects piety for lucre, and—a long train of years, made up of an equally long train of lies, hypocrisies, and little mean frauds. Old gentleman horrified. But he will repent—yes, he will repent—he will. When? To-morrow.

Torpor coming back to his feet again. Makes a sign. John and the woman approach; the liniment does its work, and old gentleman feels a little better, once more. But not long. The torpor is returning, and this time in a cold, crampy way, which fills the invalid with affright. A cold sweat starts out from his brow and cheeks. His eyes enlarge staringly with a wild, fixed air of dread—of horror.

"John—" in a tone, sharp and shrieking, and yet half broken and half smothered—"call Mrs. Leland, Mr. Crittenden—the doctor—quick. Don't you see—something is the matter. Quick!"

John flies with a "Yes, sir—keep up your heart—be back in a moment, sir!"

The woman would follow, but cannot. She is fascinated—appalled by that tone and that countenance, so full of maniacal terror.

"What!" cries the voice again, in a piteous moan. "It *can't* be—CAN it? I am not prepared for it. Oh, no—don't. One day more—but one, and I'll get ready!"

Mr. Crittenden enters, deeply agitated. One glance at his old partner, and he is down upon his knees.

"Lord, Lord! have mercy upon him! O, Jesus, Prince of Righteousness! come Thou to his rescue!"

Enter Miriam, pale and trembling.

Old gentleman struggling, confusedly, every feature alive with terror.

Miriam and Mr. Crittenden—

"Lord! Lord! have mercy upon him! Jesus, Prince of Goodness! befriend this trembling soul in its parting agony. If it be not already one of Thine, stretch out Thine arm kindly—"

Old gentleman, shrieking—

"Death! No—no. I am not ready. Go away. I haven't thought of it. Away—away. It won't do—it mustn't. I—I can't afford it—I mustn't. Give me time—a day—an hour. Let me go, I say. I can't give in—I dare not—I will not. Ah! help—help. There's a devil here—he's strangling me. Take him off. He's got me by the throat. Help—mercy—help. Fire—fire. Help—help, somebody. Take him off—help—hel—"

A fierce struggle with some invisible enemy—eyes staring in terror—voice choking in horror—the bed-clothes rumpled and torn, and—*the* IMPENITENT *has taken his leap!*

Charley Gibbs had a stern legal tussle with his guardian; but he came off conqueror in the end. With the money, he purchased a sixteenth interest in the great house of John P. Townsend: a judicious investment, and one which he has never yet repented. With his triumph in the lawsuit, came a union with his little Fan. A rural cottage in a suburban village completed his felicity. He occupies it still; and is regarded by those around him as a good neighbor, and a mild, pleasant, even-tempered gentleman.

We should like to say more of him, if we could; but we have no more to tell.

Bill Bradley's adopted mother has joined her Prince. She was called away on a pleasant autumn evening, and set out on her journey with a smile. She departed with the joyful knowledge that her affectionate son was in the ark of safety; and with the equally pleasing consciousness that he was mated with one who was worthy of him, and that he was the father of a gallant boy who would yet do good battle for his Prince, and who gave evidence that he had in him the brave, earnest spirit of him whose name he bore—Samuel. They are a happy Christian family—the manly packer, his gentle consort, and their noble boy—in the serene features of whose mother, we recognize those of our old friend the laundress. Pleasant is their noon; and as pleasant will be their even: for they are of His people.

Mr. Crittenden still lives: a brave and loyal soldier to his Prince. His heart fails not, his scrip wants not, his hand faints not. The great house of John P. Townsend is now the great house of R. Crittenden. It grows stronger year by year, and it remains true to the noble principle which led to its present gigantic trade. Notwithstanding his vast business cares, Mr. Crittenden finds ample time for other matters, as many, whom want and suffering have stricken down, will gladly testify. He is somewhat in years now; but Time deals gently with him. His tall, slender form is neither bent, nor weakened. His hair is somewhat silvered, but it is so delicately mingled with the black, that it ennobles and intensifies the impressiveness of his air. The deforming sneer has long vanished from his lip; in its place reigns an expression of rare sweetness. His general aspect is that of a mild, earnest-minded gentleman, whom every one would instinctively respect, but whom any one might approach. He is known and loved. Abounding in wealth, he scatters it freely among the various religious, benevolent, and educational institutions of the day. Young strugglers in business, whose moral character is without stain, find in him a ready and unwavering friend; and many who were young strugglers once, but who are now staunch and prosperous, regard him with an eye of affection, as one who, in their early days, helped them kindly on their way. Young men studying for the ministry partake continually of his means; and many of the energetic preachers of to-day are living monuments of his timely aid in helping them through college. Missionaries at home, and in distant lands, speak of him with gratitude and affection. Embarrassed churches or educational institutions never appeal to him in vain. Whenever and wherever good can be done with money, his heart is ever eager, his hand ever free. His friends sometimes chide him for what they term his too great liberality; but he answers, gently—

"Why, what would you have? I am simply an humble cashier of my Lord's treasury; and when His people present their demands, they must be paid. My Master's workmen must live, as well as the world's. Be content: if you should yourselves come to want, apply to me. In the meanwhile, the operations of my Lord and Prince must go on."

And thus, loving and loved, he glides down the shore of Time; scattering his benefactions kindly, freely, yet judiciously, on the way; and drawing nearer, day by day, to his inheritance in The Bright Beyond.

CONCLUSION.

Man along The Pathway! who, absorbed in life's daily business, hast inadvertently forgotten the comforting lessons of thine early youth, and art wandering, uneasily, thou knowest not whither—halt, and shake off, for a moment, thy dream of money and of little greatness, thy little hatreds and corroding cares, thy surface piety and little pride, and call up memories of Childhood's nobler, happier time.

Then thy lip was honest, thy smile genial, thy mind easy, and thy heart at rest and without guile.

It was thy holy time.

Then thou wert a spring-bud which had not yet wholly blossomed, nor opened all thy petals to the world.

There were hours then, when God spake to thee—when thou didst hear His voice, when thou didst feel the impress of His finger on thy heart.

It was through thy father's voice in prayer, thy mother's in the hymn at even, thy teacher's in the Sabbath School, and in thy pastor's, when he told thee and all of Him who said—"*I* am the Way and the Life."

Through the seraphs who whispered thee in thy dreams, and bade thee, throughout life's many struggles, to make thy *greatest* struggle for a bright home Up There.

It was a season when thou wert happy—when thou wert but a little way from an angel; when, hadst thou gone, like many of thy mates, to a couch in the Silent Lodge, the immortal part of thee might have taken wing for a place among the cherubs.

And thou *wert* happy, THEN—happier than ever since—than now!

Thou hadst not then, O flower in earth's garden! thrown open all thy petals to the world. Thou hadst not then, O heart! wandered away, little by little, from the Right to the Left. Thou hadst not then, O soul! set up an altar to thyself, and burned incense daily to thine own little pride, thine own selfishness, and thine own little greatness. Thou hadst not then set out for money and fame, and picked up, with your dollars, little mean weaknesses, little mean hatreds, little mean jealousies, and little mean desires to be thought a little smarter, a little better, a little richer, a little greater, or a little braver than your fellow-men.

You were fair and artless, then—with no fretting ambition to neutralize your thoughts of goodness, your occasional glimpse of heaven.

Happy when you rose from your couch in the morning; happy through the day, which was like a long sunny noon; happy when you laid down at night to rest and to dream—with angels for your watchers, and God for your security, till the dawn.

Ah! *how* happy, how guileless, and how good! And therefore a *holy* time. Bless it, then, as the one lone season in your journey along The Pathway, to which you can look back without regret's inner pain. Bless it as the hallowed and the hallowing time when all things wore an air of loveliness, because your pure eye saw them as they *appeared*, and without a lurking suspicion of the danger or the evil that they veiled; and when your mind, in the simplicity of its goodness, judged all men and all things by the honest standard of Right and Wrong, and not by the cold gauge of worldly Policy.

Happy? Yes, thrice happy. For then, *in* thee, was the sweet balm of mingled innocence and simplicity; *around* thee, the refreshing odors of parental love, of pure thoughts, of truthful utterances, and trusting confidence in God.

Why not be as happy, once again—as guileless, loving, gentle, and confiding?

It is easy.

Turn again to the simple artlessness and honest truthfulness of childhood—turn again to the happier time. Become again a little child, in heart; turn again, as *when* a little child, to Him, innocently, confidingly, on thy knees.

And again will come back to thee comfort; again, purity, simplicity, sweetness; again, bright pictures in hallowing dreams; and again, seraph whispers, telling thee of dear ones whom thou hast known and loved, who are awaiting thy coming in THE LAND BEYOND THE STARS.

THE END.

www.ingramcontent.com/pod-product-compliance
Lightning Source LLC
LaVergne TN
LVHW090544110826
845146LV00001B/12

9781425559762